AMERICA STRIKES BACK!

A salvo passed close overhead, sounding like a locomotive in the sky. My stomach squeezed tight as the pitch whispered into that half-second of silence before the watery explosion.

But that was only the beginning . . .

The barrage began in earnest, sounding like a rumbling chorus of mighty kettledrums. The muzzle flashes were like so many flashbulbs, etching the shoreline in half-second bursts of yellow light.

Another thousand yards would put us inside the northernmost cove of Subic Bay. And nestled there to a makeshift pier would be two Jap destroyers.

The PT moved through the darkness and I kept my eyes on the compass. We were really going to do it. We — the nobodies of the fleet, lousy little Motor Torpedo Boat Squadron Two — were going to strike America's first blow against the Japanese Imperial Navy. My limbs felt like high voltage lines, humming and crackling.

I raised my voice to carry over the the boat. "All right, guys, lock and load! We're going in!"

ASHES
by William W. Johnstone

OUT OF THE ASHES (1137, $3.50)
Ben Raines hadn't looked forward to the War, but he knew it was coming. After the balloons went up, Ben was one of the survivors, fighting his way across the country, searching for his family, and leading a band of new pioneers attempting to bring America OUT OF THE ASHES.

FIRE IN THE ASHES (1310, $3.50)
It's 1999 and the world as we know it no longer exists. Ben Raines, leader of the Resistance, must regroup his rebels and prep them for bloody guerilla war. But are they ready to face an even fiercer foe—the human mutants threatening to overpower the world!

ANARCHY IN THE ASHES (1387, $3.50)
Out of the smoldering nuclear wreckage of World War III, Ben Raines has emerged as the strong leader the Resistance needs. When Sam Hartline, the mercenary, joins forces with an invading army of Russians, Ben and his people raise a bloody banner of defiance to defend earth's last bastion of freedom.

BLOOD IN THE ASHES (1537, $3.50)
As Raines and his ragged band of followers search for land that has escaped radiation, the insidious group known as The Ninth Order rises up to destroy them. In a savage battle to the death, it is the fate of America itself that hangs in the balance!

P.T. COMMANDER

ERIC HIGGS

ZEBRA BOOKS
KENSINGTON PUBLISHING CORP.

ZEBRA BOOKS

are published by

Kensington Publishing Corp.
475 Park Avenue South
New York, NY 10016

First printing: September 1985

Printed in the United States of America

To Special Boat Unit Thirteen

Chapter One

Tracers ripped close overhead, turning the night into a canopy of bright orange ribbons. Searchlight beams crisscrossed the waters, groping for us tirelessly. The hair on the back of my neck prickled as a powerful beam slithered toward us . . . then angled safely astern. Shore-based howitzers let go with a sudden barrage, the sharp explosions echoing off the mountains which ringed the bay. My hands tightened on the boat's wheel as the whistling of a high-flying shell deepened to a low, throaty purr. It smacked close aboard to starboard, sending sheets of cold salt water cascading into the PT's cockpit.

"Jesus!" It was the voice of Ensign Oakey, standing next to me in the darkness. He shivered as water poured off his helmet. *"They know where we are, skipper! Christ o' fuckin Mickey they got us zeroed in—"*

"Steady, boy," I said crisply, as if I weren't completely terrorized myself. The staccato flashing of the shore batteries let me see that Oakey's eyes were wide and sweat was running down his face. His fear made it easy to keep my own knee-knocking private.

"They're shooting blind, don't you see? They don't know where the hell we are." I had to shout above the pounding of the three Packard V-12s. "Look, this bay's eight miles along and four wide, right?"

"R-right!"

A shell landed well to our port quarter, sending up a white geyser. "That's thirty-two square miles they've got to hoe. We ain't gonna be here that long, right?"

"Yessir!" It came out like a high, excited squeak.

Two geysers blossomed better than a mile astern. Their aim was getting worse, and now I had some breathing space. I pulled the throttles back slowly and evenly, and the eighty-foot boat slowed to bare steerageway. The Packards rumbled uneasily, making the plywood deck vibrate and hum.

The Japs might be way off base, but they weren't the only ones.

"Here," I said, shoving a pair of heavy binoculars in the ensign's gut, "Now we've got to start figuring out where the hell we are."

"What?"

"We're lost, or didn't you know? C'mon, let's get to work on a fix."

Oakey snapped the glasses up and peered into the black void, but his hands were shaking so hard he couldn't have spotted the Empire State Building at one hundred yards. I put my own binoculars up and stared into the velvet curtain.

Navigation had been fine right up until Nash—Lieut. John Nash, my second in command, driving the only other PT for this op—and I split up. That was at the mouth of the bay, and according to plan. The monkeywrench had been some joker on the beach flashing a dot-dash challenge, asking us who we were. As we were "foe" we both increased speed and zig-zagged away.

It was then that I lost sight of the nav picture, as it had to take a back seat to dodging a very intent machine gun nest. Then other nests opened up as word spread down the line. And searchlights! I hadn't thought there'd be so many. My only hope was to pour on the coals and drive like a crazy man, praying that our dark, forest-green paint might do some good should a beam chance upon us. And then the god-damn 75mm shore batteries had opened up — as Oakey had so eloquently put it, *Christ!*

God, it was black. I couldn't even make out a horizon.

A salvo passed close overhead, sounding like a locomotive in the sky. My stomach squeezed tight as the pitch whispered into that half-second of silence before the watery explosion.

But that was only the beginning . . .

The barrage began in earnest, sounding like a rumbling chorus of mighty kettledrums. The muzzle flashes were like so many flashbulbs, etching the shore-line in half-second bursts of yellow light . . .

Etching the shoreline.

I closed my eyes and kept the image in my brain, quickly hunkering down and calling for Oakey to pull out the chart and a flashlight. Well off to starboard waterspouts began to erupt in a jagged column. Oakey knelt and put his fingers over the lens so that a weak, reddish light played over the water-spotted chart.

One quick look was all I needed, and it made me

9

want to weep with relief.

We were almost there.

I stood and tenderly nudged the throttles forward, held them steady when the breeze freshened. Ten knots.

"You got it, Mr. Leander? You know where we are?"

I nodded, too excited to speak, spinning the wheel to the new course. I knew where we were, all right, and where we had to go. Another thousand yards would put us inside the northernmost cove of Subic Bay. And nestled therein, tied to a makeshift pier, would be two Jap destroyers.

The PT moved through the darkness, and I kept my eyes on the compass, the digits barely legible with the rheostat turned so low. The compass card swiveled as I came to the new heading, and for some reason it began to remind me of a roulette wheel. I could even see a croupier's hand reach down and snap the white ball into the bowl, and I imagined it circling round and round to finally jump and clack against the numbered slots.

And the chips, boy, the chips were Mark Eight torpedoes, all four of them angled over the side, armed for a close shot, and ready to go.

We're really going to do it, I realized, and it was an entirely different thing from planning it and talking about it and imagining it. That had been like some kind of pipedream. This had more of a weighty texture to it, like the feel and heft of a fifty-pound sledgehammer. The thing was actually going to happen. Nothing could stop it. We were going to shove these Mark Eights right up those Japs' hineys. We—the nobodies of the fleet, lousy little Motor Torpedo Boat Squadron Two—were going to strike America's first blow against the Japanese Imperial Navy. My limbs felt like high voltage lines, humming and crackling.

I raised my voice to carry over the boat. "All right, guys, lock and load! We're going in!"

The man in the port turret—I think it was Simpson—charged his twin .50-caliber machine guns. Then I heard another double-clack as the starboard gunner armed his set. From back aft came the sound of the bolt being pulled on the 20mm antiaircraft gun. Chief Torpedoman Turner scampered from one tube to another, checking his fish like a worried mother hen.

Tracers howled low enough to make us duck. A piece of the mast snapped off and thunked in the water. The orange streaks marched ahead, the Jap gunner unaware of how lucky he'd nearly been. I peered through the windscreen, then unbuckled my six-three of shaking meat.

There she was.

It was hard to make out her silhouette against the mountains, but the burst of an artillery shell had given me what I needed. I closed my eyes and the afterimage was clear. A smokestack.

We were bang on the money.

"Skipper?" The voice of the man in the port gun tub. I knew what he was calling my attention to.

"I got it," I called. I twirled the wheel to port and the bow moved sluggishly. I held her steady when I judged us to be aiming at the stack.

Another flash etched the outline of a cargo boom. She was there all right, but it looked like I'd steadied too far to the left. Now we were angling in on her starboard quarter. Well, so be it. This was good enough for the business at hand.

Ensign Oakey swallowed hard. "I-I'd say the range is five hundred yards, sir."

"Sounds about right."

Oakey stared at me, licking his lips. He didn't dare say it, but I knew what he wanted to scream: *Why don't we fire and get the hell out of here?*

Because the only way to be sure is to go as close as you dare and leave nothing to chance. We had come too far and had been through too much to do anything but make sure these four sweet potatoes were going right into their wardrooms, served up piping hot.

No lights on the pier, none on the ship. Four hundred yards. The gunners' thumbs hovered over butterfly firing bars. Chief Turner fitted a gangster-style barrel magazine into the Thompson .45 he'd brought along. The inside of my chest was icy cold.

I heard the splashing of her overboard discharges. Diesel exhaust from her generators hung in the air, acrid and close. I clicked the engine-room buzzer three times and the PT's mufflers were disengaged. The throaty, burbling sound grew louder. We were ready.

We were going in a shade too fast. I eased on the throttles, stopping when I felt them click into the slot for forward idle. The tachometer needles buzzed at the five-hundred rpm mark, the screws pushing us along at that reduced speed. I shifted uncomfortably; the deck was vibrating, humming with ready power. She felt like a live thing, a wild Brahma bull pushing its horns against a stall, splintering the wood, ready to charge into a rodeo's pandemonium.

Two hundred yards. And we still had the drop. I

grinned and whispered, *Here it comes, Mr. Jap.*

Voices drifted across the water, excited voices, high-pitched and chattering, clearly heard even against the background of cannon fire. A light switched on from her signal bridge and the narrow beam swung right to us. Dot-dash. Challenge.

I couldn't believe it. What did she think we were? Lost fishermen? Japs were plenty smart most times, but now and then you caught them dumb as Arkansas.

I chuckled softly as I moved my hands to the waist-high firing panel. I had a reply that'd be exactly right. I felt for the buttons which would ignite the charges in the forward tubes. I held my breath and pressed the studs . . .

Nothing.

I dropped my thumbs to the buttons for the after torpedoes and jammed hard.

There was a flat *bang* and a flash of white light. The Mark Eights sailed through the air, tiny propellers spinning in a scream of escaping compressed air. They smacked the water and immediately burrowed in for their run.

I shoved the throttles forward and the screws grabbed the water hungrily, making the bow surge up and ahead with reassuring suddenness. The Packards' roar was so loud my chest hummed with a steady vibration. I spun the wheel to starboard and the PT banked like an airplane nosing over for a hard turn.

Our port side came to bear and Simpson turned his fifties loose. Chief Turner grabbed the cockpit's after bulkhead, held himself upright, and yelled *"Two fish running hot, straight, and true!"*

"Fine!" I yelled, not knowing what else to say. Turner had spent most of his time on the pig boats, and I think they had some kind of elaborate ritual associated with firing torpedoes. Me, I just read the instruction manuals that came with the equipment.

The Jap opened up with small arms fire and the water around us came alive with miniature geysers. There was a string of hollow explosions as lead ripped across the plywood day cabin. Chief Turner collapsed, cursing. A bullet starred my windscreen, and I heard the metallic *ta-wang* of a ricochet off the armor plating which protected my back.

I held her in the turn. The starboard fifties and after twenty opened as soon as they had a clear shot. My stern came to bear and I wheeled hard to port. Zig. I spun the wheel in the opposite direction. Zag. We weaved through the water, grabbing distance, the PT banking sharply with each turn.

"Chief Turner's hit!" Oakey screamed, *"He's hit! He's hit!"*

Abruptly, it was bright as noon; my shadow ran from the cockpit to the tip of the bow. There was a piercing thunderclap and the shock wave snatched the helmet from my head and sent it spinning ahead. The coolness of the night was gone in one hot breath, and the sound of colliding freight trains rocked and reverberated across the bay.

I looked over my shoulder. A column of fire boiled hundreds of feet into the sky, turning and twisting like a huge, tormented demon. At its base was the blackened hulk of what had once been a ship, its giant propellers angled skyward, its entire forward section askew upon a smashed pier. Explosions sent hull plating sailing through the night like cardboard, and I saw the insect shapes of terrified men scattering in all directions.

The man on the PT's fantail was sharply defined against the flames. He had stopped firing his 20mm and was swinging his helmet back and forth, his head thrown back in a cheer of victory.

Night dropped its black cloak over us again.

"Cease fire!" I called, "Cease fire!"

Phase Two of the plan was now in effect: find some way to get out alive. We needed to fade into the background. The open ocean lay eight miles ahead; at forty knots that would give me a running time of twelve minutes.

The machine gun fire from the surrounding hills was sporadic and uncoordinated, as if the heart had gone out of it. The searchlight beams were frozen and motionless. The 75mm shore batteries were silent, as if in stupefied reverence for the holocaust in our wake. And why shouldn't they be? They had screwed up royally. I laughed aloud. *We had done it! We had done it!*

But how much longer before they collected their wits?

I turned my head sideways. "How's Turner?"

The chief answered. "Winged, skipper." He was sitting on the deck with his back against the day cabin. His eyes were tightly closed and his lips were compressed in a thin line. One hand pressed against his thigh and scarlet oozed between his fingers. Ensign Oakey was next to the chief, kneeling, his hands trembling as he rummaged through a first-aid kit.

I raised my voice. "Everybody else okay?" There were grunts in the affirmative.

15

The burning ship was well astern now. The night was so black I was sure no one ashore could spot our long wake. I heard the crack of a seventy-five, then eerie whistling as the shell spun through the sky. It exploded far away. More machine gun nests opened up, and the searchlights moved in lethargic sweeps. They were waking up.

But we were going to make it, I felt sure of that. The freshly-tuned Packards were running like hotcakes. We had more than enough fuel to make it back to home-plate. My only casualty had a minor wound in the leg. We had been lucky, and I told myself the luck was going to hold.

Then why did I feel there was a problem some-where? It lay in the back of my mind, too nimble to catch, running up to smack me between the eyes and quickly scamper away.

What had I overlooked?

Chapter Two

The call for the mission had come in the form of a handwritten note from Rear Admiral Whitefield, commandant of what was left of the 16th Naval District. He operated, as befitted his command, out of a dank, poorly-lit tunnel on the Isle of Corregidor.

It was Ensign Oakey who'd taken the 44 boat to the island earlier this morning. It's a straight shot of five miles from the PT base at Sisiman—an abandoned native village at the southern tip of Bataan—to Corregidor, and I sent someone there every day to pick up any messages or gossip. Oakey returned shortly before noon and handed me an envelope marked "C.O. Motor Torpedo Boat Squadron Two." I ripped it open.

Army reports two warships lying off Subic Bay. Have two boats attack between dusk and dawn. Whitefield.

I couldn't believe it. I had nagged the admiral long and hard about the right way to use this PT squadron, but up until now he'd acted like we were some kind of garbage scows built for running messages and other second-string errands. Sure, he gave us the occasional go-ahead to attack Japanese landing barges trying to land troops behind our lines, but this was still a waste of what we'd been built for. Old Whitefield just couldn't get it out of his head that we were toys in comparison with the cruisers and destroyers and submarines that had once been the U.S. Asiatic Fleet. But the big ships had bugged out shortly after the Japs established control of the skies, and the three-star who owned the fleet left Whitey behind to hold the bag with some minesweepers and auxiliary craft and a little backwater outfit called M.T.B. Squadron Two.

Now he was telling us to go get some cans. Things must be getting pretty damn desperate. I asked Oakey to round up my exec, Lieutenant Nash.

I walked over to the Operations Department, a tiny nipa shack which doubled as my sleeping quarters. Its stilts creaked as I stepped inside. A sluggish breeze slunk through the holes in the thatched wall. Ventilation courtesy of a couple of recently-visiting Zeroes.

There was a lopsided table in the middle of the room. A battered field telephone held down the chart which showed the U.S. minefield bottling up Manila Bay. I sat down heavily, making the shack quiver.

Two months ago I had a nice little office at Cavite, the U.S. naval base next door to Manila. Two months! Way back then life had been different, and I was quite content to have my fun with the PTs and not be bothered by anyone. Nobody cared about M.T.B. Squadron Two—we were less than dirt. Half the staff officers weren't even aware we were homeported in Manila! But that was okay. It suited me fine. I was *glad* not to have anyone on my back. Then one fine Sunday morning I'm nursing a hangover at the officer's club and word comes down that the Japs have handed us the biggest defeat in the history of the United States Navy.

"Air raid on Pearl Harbor," the messages say, "This is not a drill." A surprise attack, we tell each other at the club, and we wonder how our friends at Pearl could've been caught so totally unaware. It wasn't long before we had our answer. Less than eight hours after the raid on Pearl the major U.S. airfield in the Philippines was attacked, and after five more days of "surprise attacks" we're suddenly down to maybe one or two scout planes we can call our own.

So everyone went to red-alert in the way only a bureaucracy can. Memorandums were written and given emergency priority. File cabinets slid open like the gears of a well-oiled clock. The mimeograph was put on round-the-clock duty, and not one typewriter was given a moment's rest. Tight-lipped commanders trotted through busy corridors, carrying letters for urgent signature. Bulletins were given appropriate classification, routed, and quickly initialed. Cool and seasoned hands kept the office running with quiet, grim purpose.

The Navy's office building at Cavite became a busy place indeed. I kept trying to find someone to report to, to find out what they wanted done with the PTs. I got a lot of strange looks. You're in charge of M.T.B. Squadron what? Sit tight, I'll get back to you later. I got excited once, when this commander sought me out. He said we need your help, lieutenant. Chief Greenborough over there has been doing a great job as the senior yeoman; why don't you take these notes and see if you can rough out a letter of commendation for him, eh?

But I kept coming, if for nothing more than a look at the huge wall chart of the Philippines. At first there were a lot of blue pins in the north, against a few pockets of reds. Looked good. Then I noticed that the blue pins were taken out and some but not all were put back in positions that were further south. And when this became a daily ritual I began to notice a change in the operations staff. They were running around as busy as ever, but they had this funny, stiff-legged walk, and their eyes seemed wide and glazed over, and whenever you tried talking to one you got this ghastly little grin.

When the air raids finally came to Cavite itself I got my boats out in Manila Bay where we twisted and dodged the bombers trying their luck against us. I saw the office building go up through my binoculars, and the contents of a thousand filing cabinets made it a bright fire indeed.

One month after Pearl we were hiding in the bushes, Japanese flags fluttering over Manila. Operations moved to Corregidor, the fortified island twenty miles across the bay. Admiral Hart, Commander-in-Chief Asiatic Fleet, took his destroyers and submarines and moved out, citing the lack of air cover as the reason for the withdrawal. Rear Admiral Whitefield got to stay behind and supervise the leftovers.

The field telephone buzzed. I picked it up. It was a Major Southworth. Had I received orders to attack enemy ships?

"Yeah."

"Thank God, Lieutenant. Just wanted to confirm that someone's doing something about getting those bastards off our backs."

He gave me some background. One of his companies had been on the offensive, pressing along the western coast of Bataan, when two "goddamn big" Japanese warships sailed into the neighborhood, right off Mayagao Point. They cruised leisurely up and down the coast, banging away at the troops. The ships took their time. There was no opposition. They did a good job. What was left of the company had been forced back into the foothills of Mt. Silanganan.

"Can you describe these ships in detail?" I asked.

The Army man wasn't sure, but he described them as best he could. Sounded like destroyers all right; in my mind I narrowed it down to one of two classes: *Kagero* or *Kamikaze*.

The major's scouts had seen the ships moored in Subic, a medium-sized bay at the northwestern edge of the Bataan peninsula. I knew that bay well. It had once, after all, been ours.

"We'll be underway shortly, Major. Nobody wants those ships more than I."

I rang off and sat back to think. Moored at Subic . . . the only decent-sized warships that prowled these waters were based out of Formosa, five hundred miles to the north. If these cans had set up housekeeping in Subic it meant the local naval picture was getting ready to change, and change drastically. But for the presence of my PTs, the Japs could put landing craft behind our lines at will. With destroyers running interference . . .

John Nash came in without knocking. His only clothing was a pair of baggy shorts and rotting jungle boots. Rice and spam had thinned him down, and his eyes had that funny glint people get when they're constantly hungry. His black beard was coming along nicely—a lot of them had been sprouting since we'd gotten down to a squadron supply of one blade for officers, one for enlisted. My own sand-colored beard looked nothing at all like the sea-wolf whiskers I thought I'd end up with.

"Afternoon, John."

"What's cooking, Buck?"

I pointed to a chair. There was a pewter hip flask on the table and I unscrewed the cap. Nash's eyes widened. He knew it contained the last bit of sippin' whiskey within a radius of several hundred miles.

"Serious, eh?" He leaned forward, grinning. I pushed the chipped glass to his elbow.

"Yeah," I said, "Looks like tonight we go a-hunting."

Nash raised his glass. "Well, then. For something bigger than a landing barge."

We laughed. The Hardy Boys on their latest escapade.

I unfolded a greasy chart and outlined the situation. I pointed out the area where the Jap cans had shelled our troops, and the place where the major's scouts had seen them moored—Apalit Point. I showed him the admiral's terse note.

Nash studied the chart intently, and I could see the wheels turning inside his head. His eyeballs slid up and down the coast, then settled on Subic Bay. There was a big fly crawling across the chart. Looked to be a quarter of an inch long. On a chart with a scale like this, that'd make the insect cruiser-size.

I sat back and lit a butt, giving Nash time to think it over. Nash had been the exec of M.T.B. Squadron Two when I first assumed command, and the guy I relieved told me that Nash was just about the most pitiful exec I could have. Nash himself readily confirmed this accusation. "Go ahead and give me lousy fitness reports," he told me on the occasion of our first interview, "See if I give a shit." Over many evenings, visiting one bar and another, I slowly got him to tell me his story. And it was truly awful. Nash had been chief engineer on a destroyer. They were on a port call in Canada when he got a telegram saying his wife had been in an accident. He requested emergency leave. His captain, incredibly, refused. Said the telegram didn't say anything about her being near death, and besides there was an important engineering inspection coming up. Nash said he was leaving anyway. The captain said try it and see. Nash went to the gangway and was stopped by the quarterdeck watch. He punched out the petty officer, tossed the OOD overboard, got a taxi to the nearest airport. Made it home in time to hold his wife's hand as she succumbed to the complications of a miscarriage. Then he turned himself in. Told his story to a thunderstruck board of officers at his court-martial. His captain was hauled in and there was another little court-martial. Captain was relieved, reprimanded, ruined. But Nash couldn't get off scot-free, of course. The quarterdeck fracas was "an exercise in poor judgment," as was duly noted in his service jacket. Thus had he come to a dead end like the PTs, and so would stay until he was passed over for lieutenant com-

23

mander and kicked the hell out. Kept a shabby apartment in Manila where he entertained prostitutes, some of whom were actually quite pretty. Wasn't the least hesitant about telling his skipper to go fuck himself. Found some satisfaction in roaring around under sunny skies in these crazy boats.

But December 7th changed all that. Nash loved the war right from the start. First he gave up his off-base pleasure shack and lived, breathed, and ate aboard the PTs. When we were forced from Cavite to this abandoned village he seemed to like it even more. The lousy food, the constant backbreaking work of keeping the boats up and running—it all seemed to be honing him down to his true purpose in life. He was the best exec any man could have. I sent the burnt match sailing across the shack.

Nash was lightning-fast. He had the fly in his hand before I knew what was going on. He looked at me and smiled, then opened his hand. There was a greasy smear.

I exhaled smoke. "Nice, going, Poseidon."

Nash slowly wiped his paw. "Think those cans are here on a permanent basis?"

"If not now, then later. The Japs have air superiority. Their army is advancing every day. The only place where they don't have the upper hand is on the seas. The Jap Navy is moving in sooner or later, and we've got to make it later. We've got to buy time. The reinforcements—"

"It's a good thing you're so tall, Buck," Nash interrupted, "Otherwise you'd drown in it."

"What's the matter, John? Doubts?"

"Doubts?" Nash grinned wolfishly. He waved his

hand at the bullet holes in the thatched wall. "Doubts?"

"Yeah. Well, be that as it may, any suggestions for tonight?"

Nash put his elbows on the table and spelled it out. Underway at dusk for a thirty-knot run up to Subic. Split up, proceed to the destroyers' pier with Nash hugging one coast and me the other. Slip 'em the fish on a first-come first-served basis. Rendezvous outside the bay and proceed home.

I was disappointed; it was the same plan I'd thought of. Well, if crude, then maybe effective.

"Weapon status?" I asked.

"All tubes loaded and ready. Plenty of .50 for everybody, but we're getting low on 20mm."

"Engineering?"

"Don't know. Last time I checked, Strip had the heads off the 41's engines."

"Would you kindly ask the engineering department head to step in here?"

Nash turned his head toward the door. "Hey! Strip!"

There was an answering call.

"Get in here!" Nash shouted, "Skipper wants to see you!"

I refilled the exec's glass. We heard the approach of the motormac, slow and deliberate, and presently there was a polite knock at the bamboo doorframe. "Permission to enter, sir." Strip said "sir" the way most people describe a gooey place on the sidewalk.

"Come in," I barked in my officer-voice. I loved to needle him, and the fact that I couldn't have gotten away with it without the protection of my rank added to the fun.

Motor Machinist Mate First Class "Strip" Cunningham was an imposing package of prime Texan beef. He was covered in grease, the whiteness of skin betrayed by the rivulets of sweat oozing down his chest. The tattoos on his arms rippled as he worked his hands with an oily rag. "Watcha want, skipper?"

"Boat status."

He turned, spat out the door. "Everything's down 'cept them new Elcos."

"No kidding?"

"No shit, sir." His eyes had locked onto the flask. "And maybe even the 41 won't be up for a while."

"We got a mission tonight."

Strip worked the rag harder. "Underway at sundown, right?"

I nodded. "Pull up a chair, Strip. Let's talk."

He stuck the rag in his back pocket and sat. I poured him a couple fingers' worth and he took the shot glass reverently, cocking one eye as he moved the glass to the light. He might have been born hundreds of miles from the ocean, but he looked like he'd spent all of creation being reincarnated from one sailor to the next. It didn't take too much imagination to see him in the rigging of a brigantine, laughing as a helpless merchant begged for quarter.

He showed us his uneven teeth. "Now ain't this nice? Having a little drink with my own C.O. and exec—all civilized, like."

Strip put the glass to his lips and snapped his head back. He sighed. "Thanks, sir."

So we got down to our civilized chat. Strip began with the main problem. Fuel. Not only was it scarce, a good deal of it had been sabotaged with wax. It clogged fuel lines, carburetors, everything. Even the most junior motormac could now disassemble, clean, and reassemble one of the finicky Packard carbs blind-folded.

We'd once captured a Jap landing barge loaded with drums of gasoline, but the stuff was useless. The PTs require 100 octane, same as for fighter planes.

"I'll get a crew running fuel through the last of our chamois strainers," Strip said, "So you'll have enough sweet gas for the mission tonight."

Nash absently ran his fingers through his beard. "So no breaking down when it's . . . inopportune?" His boat had conked out a few days before. A Zero had been after them, but Nash's 20mm gunner had gotten off enough of a lucky shot to send it wobbling away.

Strip shook his head. "No breaking down 'cause of fuel."

There were six PTs to choose from. Two Elco eighty-footers, brand new, two of the older seventy-seven-footers, and two Higgins seventy-eights. When I'd assumed command of the squadron there'd been two more—one got boxed up in an inlet and became the victim of a dive bomb attack, the other was out of the water for hull cleaning when the Japs rolled in Manila. We torched her before we left.

Strip recommended we take the new Elcos. Their bottoms were still clean. He'd have the 41 ready in time.

"Okay," I said, "Underway before sundown. The 41 and the 44 are the lucky dogs."

Nash and Strip left to spread the word. The other boat crews drifted to the Elcos, helped with the check-ing and rechecking of the weapons, loaded extra ammo, tested the engines. I watched the activity with

27

excitement building in my gut. Tonight was the big night. The first *real* mission. I had trained all my adult life for this sort of thing, and like a worried concert pianist stepping up to my instrument at Carnegie Hall, wondered if I'd be up to it. Stage fright? Maybe. One thing was for sure—if I fucked up I'd get a lot worse than bad reviews.

We chugged from the base just as the sky was turning red. We threaded through the minefield and made a sharp turn when Cochinos Point was dead abeam. The new course, 288° magnetic, took us for a ten-mile run along the southern coast of Bataan. We turned to 333° when Luzon Point was just a tad abaft the starboard beam, then doused our running lights. This final leg, an eighteen-mile shot, would take us along Bataan's western coast and square into the mouth of Subic Bay.

The trip was uneventful. The day had been hot enough for shorts, but once the sun dipped below the horizon I was glad of the sweater I'd brought along. Everybody was dead quiet, alone with their thoughts. I was scared and excited at the same time. Wondering how it'd come out. Wondering how I'd do. The swells came on our port bow at two to three feet. Just enough to make the boat pound and rattle a little; nothing serious, though Oakey did blow chow. Salt water sprayed over the bow occasionally, dampening the cockpit. Someone had the foresight to pack along a thermos of coffee. We heard gunfire coming from Bataan as the night patrols mixed it up. It was overcast and moonless, truly a black night.

We arrived off Subic a little after midnight. We split up, proceeded in. The firing from the beach started right off the bat, steadily increasing until I made the attack . . .

And there it was. The thing that had bothered me. I replayed the image of the burning ship. What was so obvious now must've escaped me during the excitement of the kill.

The stern of that ship was as rounded as a canoe's, not a straight transom like a destroyer's was supposed to be. And then the other details began to sink in. The high freeboard. The cargo booms. The nature of the explosion itself.

I smacked my hand against the console. We hadn't sunk a destroyer! It was an oiler of some kind, a lousy support ship.

"Mr. Leander?" It was the voice of Ensign Oakey.

"What?" I replied, irritated.

Oakey ran his hand over the firing panel, brows knitting together. "I can't understand why the forward tubes didn't work. Chief Turner and I tested the firing circuits twice . . ."

"You and the chief, huh?" My mind was still on the burning ship.

"Yes, sir." He grinned, making him look all of fourteen. "I graduated at the top of my class at the torpedo familiarization course."

This was news, but then everyone's service record was so much Japanese toilet paper. Maybe the kid actually had some useful dope. Oakey began unscrewing the panel. "Mind?"

"Help yourself." The ensign got the panel loose and peered at the wiring.

I turned to port a little. Another couple of miles and we'd be out of the bay. The machine gunners on the beach still had no idea where we were. The roar of the Packards was loud and at a constant pitch; there was none of the wavering or sputter which heralded clogged fuel lines.

Everything was in various shades of black. The mountains which ringed the bay were coal, the waters dark gray, the sky pitch. Dead ahead I could barely make out where the mountains curved down to the entrance of the bay. The tiny islet known as Grande had just passed astern, and ahead was a black lump which . . .

Hard to port, boy! The turn was sharp enough to get the gunwale awash. The boat I'd nearly rammed erupted with machine gun fire, slamming the lead at us point-blank. Bits of wood flew through the air as slugs ripped across our hull.

The gunners needed no order to commence fire. The man on the starboard turret looked like he was holding onto two jackhammers, spent shells cascading from the breech like brass confetti.

What in god's name was it? A Japanese torpedo boat? A landing barge fitted with machine guns? I knew it couldn't be Nash—the sound of its guns was too high-pitched for .50-cal.

"Oak!" I shouted, "Get them fish ready!" I held the boat in its turn, intending to come full circle and meet the Jap head-on, then show him the wrong end of two Mark Eights.

Bullets smacked into the bow and marched to the cockpit. *"Down! Down!"* The ensign and I knelt as lead rang off the armor plating. A leg of the mast splintered in two. I peered over the steel and saw the circle was almost complete.

I looked at Oak. "You ready?"

He bobbed his head, his shaking hands ready to bring the naked wires together. I stood and wheeled the boat to starboard; the bow swung rapidly and when it was pointed at the black shape I yelled *"Now!"*

The bang was immediate. The starboard Mark Eight shot ahead and splashed, but the port torpedo only lurched halfway from its tube before it jammed. And she started making a hot run right where she was, propellers spinning inside the firing tube. Escaping compressed air screeched like a thousand broken radiators.

I spun the wheel, turning from the Jap. Maybe the poor bastards saw what was coming; there was a moment of silence just before the fish smacked home. The flash of the explosion revealed nothing more than a landing barge—enraged, I pounded my fist against the console; we could've outrun her and saved the torpedoes for something better!

Things heated up.

The flames of the barge gave new purpose to the shore gunners' firing. A searchlight's beam came dangerously close. The seventy-fives came back to life.

That damn torpedo! Its hissing was driving me nuts! I looked at it angrily, trying to think of what to do.

Then, incredibly, I saw Oakey crawling right along the top of that firing tube. Gutsy little guy, but a dead duck if he didn't know exactly what to do; that torpedo's casing would soon go white-hot and disintegrate.

My ears still rang when the hissing abruptly stopped. Oakey had found the right valve, the one which closed the air line to the combustion pot.

The sounds of the sea came back slowly. It was getting choppy as we neared the ocean, and the boat made loud smacking noises as we pounded through the waves.

I looked at Oakey and sucked in my breath. His skinny body was still on top of that fish — and he was crawling to the warhead! Then I realized what had to be done.

There's a little propeller at the tip of the torpedo which spins as the fish runs through the water — and it was turning as the waves broke over the bow. After a set number, all that warhead needs is one sweet kiss.

The Mark Eight was hanging more than halfway out over the side. Oakey had his legs wrapped around it, lying full length, looking like a child crawling along a drainage pipe — a pipe with enough TNT to write the end in an eyeblink.

The tips of his shoes touched the deck, but underneath his body cold water rushed by. I wondered when the torpedo would jar free.

Oakey got to the warhead, carefully reached into his back pocket, and withdrew a handkerchief. He jammed it into the propeller's vanes . . . and that did it.

He backed down the tube. A sailor appeared from nowhere, grabbed the ensign's belt, and hauled him aboard.

We shot into the open ocean. I was surprised to find I hadn't taken a breath recently. Oakey was balled up, shivering, soaking wet. The sailor put a blanket over him, muttering something I couldn't hear.

I put a little more distance between us and the coast, making a conscious effort to slow down the beating of my heart. I began a long, wide turn to port, eyes straining as I looked for the 41.

Nothing. Not a damn thing.

But only half my mind was on Nash. I wanted to know where those destroyers were. Had they quit Subic, returning to the main body of their fleet? Or were they on patrol in Philippine waters, not intending to return to Subic until later?

It might even be they were right here, just licking their chops.

Chapter Three

I throttled down to twenty knots.

The hammering of the Packards was soothing, each piston-stroke lulling me into a feeling that all was well and under control. False security, perhaps, but there was no denying the comfort of three high-powered engines running sweet and true, of a hull that was as strong and flexible as prestressed steel, of fuel tanks that were two-thirds full.

There weren't any mountains to echo against now, so the engines' thrumming lost a certain flatness. The seas were coming from the northwest at three to five feet, the wind brisk at twelve knots. I glanced at my wristwatch. Almost 0100.

Everyone was on a sharp lookout for the 41. Binoculars dangled from my neck, and whenever we'd crest a swell I'd quickly put them to my eyes.

Nash wasn't anywhere to be seen.

Ensign Oakey had shed his wet khakis, and his improvised garb consisted of tattered dungarees and a huge oilcloth parka. He had put himself to use, checking damage above and below decks. That boy was proving to be right handy. I shook my head slowly, thinking of him dangling on top of that torpedo — Lordy! When he first came to the squadron he was just another goofball ensign. Now I was glad to have him aboard.

I cupped a hand around a cigarette and spun the wheel on my Zippo. It wasn't going to be easy to find Nash. These seas and this darkness were tailor-made for a PT to go a-stalking. Its low silhouette and forest green paint enabled it to slither through troughs like these unseen. Even when we'd crest a swell and hang there big and bold, we couldn't have been spotted by an Apache.

Anything could've happened to Nash. He could be drifting helplessly, carburetors goozed with wax. A 75mm shell could've lucked into his fuel tanks. Perhaps he'd tangled with one of those barge-cum-gunboat affairs. Or he could be within five hundred yards, searching for us as desperately as we were for him.

The narrow door to the tiny charthouse opened and Oakey stepped out. "Checked everything, Mr. Leander."

"What's the deal?"

"Couple holes below the waterline, but the bilge pumps are way ahead. Miscellaneous holes through the berthing compartment and day cabin. And Chief Turner's not the only one who's been hit — the guy on the twenty took a slug in the foot."

"Philpot?"

"Yes, sir. Seems like he'll be okay."

"How about the forward port torpedo? Should we let it be?"

The ensign straightened, pleased I had asked him for a recommendation.

"I say leave her as she is. With these seas she'll eventually jiggle loose and drop over the side. I think that'd be safest."

Sounded good. "How long do you think we should look for the 41?"

"I was thinking . . . maybe we could turn on our running lights. That way, if he's out there, he'd—"

"No way. I have to assume those destroyers are out and about in the neighborhood."

Oakey bowed his head and sighed. "I thought the draft of the ship we got looked awful deep for a destroyer. It was nothing but an oiler, wasn't it? A lousy, goddamn oiler."

I had to smile. "Everybody earned their pay."

He looked up. "Chance calling him?"

The radio's handset was set in clips next to the charthouse door, tantalizingly handy. I shook my head. "There must be a thousand yellow bastards drooling over their receivers right now. They'd get a fix on us in no time."

"Then there's not much point in circling out here, is there?"

He had me there. I eased the throttles forward, the stern sinking low as the screws dug in deep. I squinted at the magnetic compass, watching the points tick by. I steadied to the southeast, holding 153°, the reciprocal of the course we'd taken up.

The swells were now coming in on the starboard quarter. It was fun when one of them would catch us just right and shoot us along like an eighty-foot surfboard, the boat pitching forward so that it seemed we were racing downhill. This was going to be a fast run; figure homeplate by sunrise.

I told myself Nash was a big boy. The signal for the end of the mission had certainly been obvious enough. And how the hell were we to find each other anyway? That little point hadn't been covered in my plan. Chalk one up to experience.

If he wasn't out here, he wasn't out here. Two boats operating together hadn't been the point of the operation, anyway—Nash's presence was only to increase the odds of mission success. If he didn't come chugging home in the morning, well . . . we could come back tomorrow, cruising close inshore keeping a weather eye for those cans. Maybe land some guys near Subic—they could beat their way inland and take a look-see.

Hell, why worry about it now? He might be beating me to the pier right now.

Oakey's inspection yielded an unexpected dividend: an extra thermos of coffee, steaming hot. The joe was passed around, starting with the guy on the fantail. The starboard gunner finally poured his cup and tossed the aluminum cylinder over. I caught it and unscrewed the cap. I poured a cup and sipped it slowly, savoring the bitter warmth. This was going to be a jolly little boat ride, all things considered.

I began to look on the sinking of the Jap oiler in a new light. So it hadn't been a destroyer—it was still a ship of the Japanese Imperial Navy, wasn't it? I smiled grimly, thinking of what the admiral might say when I made my report. First kill of the war. I'd just let it hang in the air that the job hadn't been done by any destroyer or cruiser. God, I felt good!

I took another sip of coffee. Just another midnight

37

cruise and not a care in the world. I let my mind relax and take it easy, using one hand to keep the PT to its heading. I whistled softly, the muscles in my back loosening.

But my senses were still on the job. Suddenly the skin on the back of my neck grew tight and an icicle slid down my spine. Something was wrong, dead wrong . . . and the alarm bells clanged on, screaming for me to wake up and punch back in. I threw the coffee over the side and strained to unravel the message — Smell. Touch. Sight. Hearing . . .

The pitch of the engines. It had subtly changed. There was a hollowness to it, a ringing flatness, as if it were echoing off something close aboard to port.

I turned to the left. Looming against the moonless sky were two jet-black smokestacks. Great sweet Jesus K. It was a Jap destroyer, and not more than a quarter mile off my beam. She was churning northwest, the opposite course from mine, and unaware of our presence. My engines were reverberating off her long steel hull.

My confidence was gone in one quick heartbeat. I felt as naked and vulnerable as a baby bird on a city sidewalk. I couldn't take my eyes off her, not any more than could a cornered rabbit stop staring at the drool on a coyote's fangs. The other guys spotted it. I heard Simpson utter words of awe and reverence. Ensign Oakey sucked in his breath. There was a distant *whee-ee-ee* sound, and I recognized it as the turbines of a destroyer's forced draft blowers, sucking in air for her boilers. It was like Jack hearing the Giant thunder a fe-fi-fo-fum.

No doubt about it this time. This was the real

McCoy, a bona fide DD, chock-a-block with heavy guns, torpedoes, depth charges . . . everything they needed to squash us like a gnat. Fast, maneuverable, and deadly, a modern destroyer can handle many jobs, but when they were first built, decades ago, only one task had been on their designers' minds. Then they had been called *Torpedo Boat Destroyers*.

Could we slip by, unseen? I was turning for forty knots and the Jap looked to be doing thirty. We were on opposite courses, so our relative speed was seventy knots. Why was it taking so long? I whispered a quick, fervent prayer. Let her after lookout be struck blind!

The Jap finally slipped to our port quarter; the echoing abruptly ceased. My shoulders slumped in relief . . .

But God decided I had welshed on too many other deals.

The world lit up with the incandescence of a 10,000-candlepower searchlight. I was blinded by the sudden brilliance, and instinctively spun the wheel to starboard.

"The Jap's turning!" Oakey yelled, "She's coming hard to port!"

The chase was on.

The fifties opened up and I shouted for them to aim at the searchlight. I jammed the wheel left, then right. Weave! Weave! The boat pitched steeply, snaking through the waves, flying over crests, the searchlight wavering and slipping but holding us as tight as a prison spotlight on an escaping con.

The Jap gun crews were on the ball; there was the crack of a 4.7-inch battery. Her shells roared directly overhead and exploded off the starboard bow. We roared through the falling spray; mist was still wet against my face when the next salvo snapped off. The shots were as loud as the splitting of a giant tree, but through it all I heard the lesser music of her small arms fire — 13mm, 7.7mm, a constant racketing buzz. Bits of splintered plywood spun violently through the air, slugs bounced and sang off the small pieces of protective armor.

A shot landed dead astern, close enough to make the boat yaw uncontrollably. I spun the wheel furiously and regained control. The man in the starboard turret screamed as his lifejacket erupted with jagged holes, his arms moving spastically as the Jap hammerblows ate him up.

I steered like a madman, crouched over the wheel, taking quick, furtive glances over the console. The Jap was still making her turn, coming about for a flat-out pursuit when the combination of my zigzags and her turning did it — the world fell into blessed darkness.

"Cease fire!" I called, "Don't fire unless we're caught in the searchlight again!"

The Jap's main batteries fell silent as soon as the searchlight lost us — Japs aren't big on wasting ammo, though her small arms fire let us know the chase was far from over. I continued the wild course alterations, one eye to the searchlight frantically sniffing the seas. I thought about the yellow trigger fingers itching to slam the firing circuits home. Tracers came in low, fanning wide, alternately kicking into the water or arcing into the blackness ahead.

Distance. I needed more distance. I steadied up, sacrificing the zigzags in order to grab yardage. I was on my original southeasterly course, spinning along at the boat's top end. Some Jap cans make thirty-five knots or better, but our bottom was clean and the engines freshly overhauled; I knew it must've been a long time since the Jap had seen the inside of a drydock, so figure her flank speed at thirty or so. We could put ten miles between us with each passing hour. Home free, if I could keep from the searchlight.

The starboard gunner was slumped over his smoking fifties, limp arms thumping against turret as we crashed through the waves. Ensign Oakey scrambled to him, put his hands under his armpits, lifted him out. Another man helped lay the gunner down. Oakey climbed in the turret and grabbed the handles of the fifties.

I glanced back. The Jap looked to be three thousand yards on my starboard quarter and on the same course as I. The searchlight was just aft of her pilothouse, the beam fanning to the right, then left, over and over. I could see the muzzle flashes of her small arms — from the fo'c'sle, from amidships, from the signal bridge. Black smoke poured from her stacks as the engine-room opened the throttles wide.

Chief Turner lay prone across the top of the day cabin, his Thompson .45 aimed at the searchlight. The port fifties were trained on the same target, the two muzzles wavering as Simpson held a steady bead. Oakey jacked in fresh rounds.

The seas were getting rougher — call them at six feet now. Good. They were pushing us right along, hiding us pretty well. Occasionally we'd take a swell just right and PT 44 would sail through the air like a flying fish, then slam the water with a bone-jarring smack. I was glad of every knot I could find.

Suddenly the Jap's small arms fire stopped. I looked over my shoulder. Her searchlight was still raking the water, but she wasn't firing so much as a pistol. Conserving ammo? Why?

We bore on, pounding through the seas, snaking between the waves, outdistancing the Jap yard by precious yard. Then, from the horizon dead ahead, a searchlight switched on, swiveled to the right and left.

Jap DD number two!

The squeeze play. I thought of the last baseball game I'd seen, of two basemen casually tossing the ball to each other as they closed in on the dodging runner.

To starboard lay the South China Sea. Two Jap cans after a PT across that pond would be like a pack of hounds chasing a fox across an open field. With no place to hide it'd only be a matter of time before the 44 became splintered plywood, her hardy crew so much stinking hamburger.

To port lay the coast of Bataan. Shallow water would shake the DDs loose, but the coast was totally unknown to me. I'd be driving blindfolded. How far would they pursue? Enough to let a jagged reef do the job instead?

The handholds on the wheel blurred as I hove to port.

The Japs coordinated their search as they closed one another, their searchlights swinging in opposite directions. It was a triangle with the DDs at the base, heading toward each other, and PT 44 at the top, barreling for the beach. What does a guy do with an angry destroyer on each quarter?

I took a quick look around. All that could be done was done. Ensign Oakey had his mount trained on the newcomer. Simpson was keeping his bead on the first. Two .50-cal gun mounts—one for each destroyer! Maybe I should ask the Japs to strike colors.

The thought of what was going on within the bridges of those cans angered me. The yellow runts must be having a grand old time. I could see them now, patting each other on the back and grinning so hard their little eyes squeezed shut. One Yankee PT boat for breakfast—a fine bit of sport!

"Oakey," I called.

"Sir?"

"If she finds us again, aim for their pilothouse."

"Pilothouse, aye."

If he could just get one burst through the pilothouse windshields the lead would ricochet inside until the bulkheads were covered with Japanese mincemeat. That might create enough confusion to make good our escape.

There was a sound like a garbage can being rolled across the deck, then a splash. It was the forward port torpedo, over the side at last. Oh, but that I had not wasted my last good torpedo on that stinking barge!

The seas were coming dead abeam now that I'd made the turn to the east. We lifted on a big swell, and it seemed like we hung there for minutes. A PT's silhouette could be no prouder.

That's when the searchlight caught us again.

I closed my eyes against the sudden brightness. There was an immediate explosion of a full salvo. The shells swooped over our heads like the long scythe of a monstrous Grim Reaper. They landed dead ahead, a wall of neatly-spaced geysers one hundred feet wide and a million years deep. We roared through as the sea fell back on itself.

Simpson and Oakey commenced fire. They kept their thumbs on the firing bars, not giving their weapons a break, knowing each piece of lead they sent could be their last. Chief Turner emptied his magazine at the target Oakey'd taken under fire, the brass casings of spent shells snapping out of his Thompson like ticker tape.

I looked at the destroyer that was coming from the south. She was turning toward us now, her long searchlight beam swinging through the night and settling right on us. All her 4.7-inchers erupted simultaneously, four brilliant flashes blossoming orange and red in the darkness. The crack of her salvo was so loud I could feel it vibrating in my chest. *Dear sweet God!*

My knees pressed together as I awaited the accuracy of their shot. The sea erupted, rising high into the night; the nearest round landed not more than fifty yards to starboard. Salt water rained on us so densely I couldn't make out the bow. When the spray finally cleared I saw Oakey slumped and motionless over his silent fifties.

Full salvos—what in hell was this manner of firing? A boyhood memory flashed before my eyes: toss a cherry bomb into a creek and watch the tiny fish float to the surface, belly up . . .

The beam lost us, then quickly found us again. A huge swell caught us broadside and heeled us over seventy degrees, damn near enough to capsize the boat. Suddenly I found us inside a wave, riding the base, the crest actually breaking just over my head. A big swell started to rise before us, and we tore over it like an eighty-foot bullet.

"Smoke!" I yelled, "Get the smoke screen generator going!"

The generator was set on the aftermost part of the boat. I saw a sailor kneel over it, then heard the *pocketa* of its small engine. Black smoke billowed astern and fanned upward.

The air was berserk with hostile lead; it looked like the inside of a storeroom gone crazy with burning fireworks. My little windscreen was pocked with holes, and slugs whined off the armor plating. Two of the four stanchions on the bow had snapped off, the lifelines they had once supported now curled on the deck like macaroni.

At least the seas were working to my advantage. Destroyers are only a little less susceptible than PTs to seas like these, and I knew their rolling and pitching wasn't making an easy job of their fire-control.

The roar of my engines lessened — part of it suddenly whined down, then off. I could feel the boat slow. The needle in the centerline tachometer bounced down to zero. So one engine had gone down. Now I had . . . thirty knots?

I looked back and decided I definitely wasn't going to slow as I neared the coast. I could still make their outlines through the smoke, and that was enough to cancel out the years of training that told me to slow down as I thundered ever-nearer the treacherous coast. Let there be a beach, I prayed, a nice, long, wide beach! It would be too much to hope for an inlet in which I could hide from the DDs. What I wanted was to run up on some nice, smooth sand. Otherwise it would be a sheer cliff, or rocks . . . and we would end up like a watermelon dropped off a skyscraper.

The searchlight beams were sharply defined but their intensity was decreasing as the smoke expanded and grew. They were three thousand yards astern, no more than five hundred yards from each others' beam, and bearing down on us goddamn fast. They were slavering wolves snapping at the runners on my sleigh. I wish I had a child to throw 'em.

And suddenly I realized I had.

"Depth charges!" I yelled, "Set both for the surface!"

We had them secured in rollover racks on the fantail. Men bent over them, cursed, spun the arming screws. Depth charges on a PT—how perfectly asinine! With no underwater sound gear they were as useless as an admiral's staff. Now I wanted to get on my knees and offer heartfelt thanks on this momentous occasion: inadvertently, they had come to use!

The sailors signaled that the charges were ready.

"Roll 'em!"

They hit the water at the same instant. Three seconds. Five seconds. Eight sec-

The explosions came so close together they could've been one and the same. The Japs' main batteries fell silent and the searchlights finally lost their hold. I looked astern, hoping desperately . . . No, they were still there, but they'd opened the distance between themselves, maneuvering from the still-falling geysers, momentarily distracted. Now the bastards knew this PT had a price tag.

The Japs' searchlights fanned from side to side through the expanding smoke screen. It seemed they had slowed—wariness born of the depth charges? or of the realization that they too were in danger of running aground? They still knew our approximate location—

as evidenced by the lead zinging by—but maybe, just maybe, I could confuse them long enough to turn from the beach. I still didn't want to run blind into this unfamiliar shoreline, not if there was something else I could do.

I had an idea. Yank the throttles back. Let the boat abruptly slow. While there was still way on, maybe ten knots' worth, jam the starboard engine ahead, put the wheel over hard, yank port into reverse. Come about in the tightest turn in the history of power boating. Run through my smoke cloud and right between the destroyers, heading seaward. The Packards would never be the same, but it—

A gigantic sledgehammer smashed against the keel and the boat jerked and shivered like a con in the electric chair. Pain was a hot poker jammed in my right armpit; I was dimly aware of being in the air, my hand tightly clenched on the wheel which was somehow far below . . . Below! I let go and felt weightlessness, total disorientation. Cold water suddenly engulfed me and I thrashed wildly. I broke free and gulped air.

I had racked up the 44 but good. Her remains were twenty yards away, the bow out of the water and angled skyward, the underside clearly visible. There was a large gash running from the forward part of the hull to a point just behind the cockpit—here the boat rested atop a big, jagged rock. The hull was all but broken in two upon the reef, the after section angling down into the water and ready to snap free. Smoke still churned from back aft, but as I watched the fantail slid further into the water and the generator hissed off.

I began swimming. My right arm hurt so much I

had to kick and grab in a sort of half-assed crawl. I wanted to slip my heavy boondockers off, then thought no, coral.

The fantail groaned and eased further into the water. I came alongside and saw Simpson, still in the port gun tub, firing his fifties. Only his shoulders were above water, and the guns made a weird, burbling noise as he squeezed off the last rounds.

"Cease firing, goddamnit! We've got to get everybody off!"

He ignored me, grimacing as he held down the butterfly firing bar. The salt water finally kissed them off, and only then did Simpson take notice of me. He seemed surprised, as if he were trying to figure out how he'd suddenly come to be chest-high in water. He struggled out of the gun tub, reached over, and pulled me on deck. We crawled forward on our hands and knees, grabbing anything that would make a handhold, then stopped at the point where the deck was cleaved in two.

A PT's hull is made of two layers of mahogany planking, airplane fabric set in between. It seemed that this fabric, ripped as it was, was the only thing holding the boat together. The bow still pointed skyward, but as we watched it groaned and dropped a few feet to starboard, settling on the rock. This PT's book was just about closed.

The Japs' main batteries were still quiet but tracers from 13mm and 7.7mm machine guns passed close overhead. Judging from their accuracy they were unsure of exactly where we were and what had happened. The smoke generator was underwater but a good deal of the screen still hung in the air.

PT 44 could be a question mark for the Japs, or . . . they knew exactly what had to be done: lay off and take enough time to get the PT right in the crosshairs, then fire at will. Maybe they were doing this already; if the Japs still had way on they'd already be on top of us.

The charthouse's door kicked open and Strip Cunningham struggled on deck. He carried the only other motormac aboard, a boyish Oklahoman who was limp and unconscious. Strip looked at me, disgusted. "I thought it was you who was driving."

"Get the fuck off the boat!" I jerked a thumb over my shoulder. "Japs!"

He took a quick look at the searchlights sniffing through the last of the smoke. Strip dragged his shipmate to the bow and laid him next to the PT's small life-raft. He started unlashing it.

Chief Turner lay behind the cockpit, unconscious. Oakey hung from the starboard gun tub and I was relieved to see his back moving up and down with short, labored breaths. The man he replaced lay at the turret's base, and this guy was definitely a goner. Two young boatswain's mates sloshed from the fantail, the limp figure of the 20mm gunner between them.

The smoke was dissipating rapidly, and I could just make out the dim outlines of the DDs. Orange balls of flame appeared on one's fo'c'sle, and an instant later I heard the report. Everybody ducked—as if that would do anything!—and the salvo landed close enough to make the fantail kick out of the water and slap back down.

The muscles in my back shivered involuntarily as falling water drenched us afresh. Next pot-shot would have our birth certificates, and I fought to contain the insane panic rising in my guts. The destroyers surely knew all about our predicament now, and were maneuvering to hold their position, lying off for shooting that would be leisurely and accurate. We were meat on the table.

So this was it. The end to end all ends. This would be the last conscious thing I knew, two Japanese destroyers swinging their main batteries right to my belt buckle, my command a helpless cockleshell cowering before the new Masters of the Pacific.

There was a holster on my right hip. I reached down and grabbed the .45. As soon as I had my hand around its cold steel my fear was gone, replaced with a terrible and unreasoning rage.

"Come and get it!" I yelled, leveling the Colt, *"You slant-eyed sons of bitches!"*

There was another flash of orange, but this time it came from astern of one of the DDs. I narrowed my eyes, puzzled, and when the rumbling explosion reached my ears I knew it wasn't the bark of any 4.7-incher. I looked at Simpson. He was looking at me.

"Torpedo," we told each other.

There was another explosion on the Jap's fantail. Her searchlight faded from bright white to a dirty brown, then out.

The unharmed DD immediately surged forward and began a turn to starboard. We caught a glimpse of her silhouette broadside, then she was heading seaward.

"It was Mr. Nash," Simpson whispered, "The 41 boat done slipped it to 'em." The gunner's mate squinted at the burning DD, marveling. "May he live long enough for me to kiss his sweet behind."

That's what it had to be — John Nash had been out

there all along. He must've been fairly close when the DDs began their pursuit and then followed, lying well off from the chase, waiting until he could maneuver for a shot.

Nice timing!

The wounded can had a good-sized bonfire on her fantail. I could see the shapes of her damage control parties silhouetted against the flames. The other destroyer was churning seaward in pursuit of the 41.

Time. Nash had bought us time. This was the whole war in miniature. We had enough time to make our escape and come back to fight another day. But it wouldn't be long before the damaged DD realized that fire-fighting and firing on grounded PTs were functions that could be handled simultaneously.

"Pick up what you can," I told Simpson, "Then we'll get everyone on the beach."

The boatswain's mates dragged their man forward. Strip eased the life-raft into the water.

Simpson and I made a quick trip belowdecks. The gaping hole along the port side of the berthing compartment was enormous. Water surged in with each wave. We waded through a flotsam of bedrolls, lifejackets, broken laminated frames. I grabbed three .45s, as many magazines as I could slip in my pocket, and a first-aid kit. Simpson filled a small canvas sack and threw it over his shoulder. We went back above.

The sound of 4.7-inch gunfire was distant. There was the faint, rhythmic crashing of waves on the nearby beach. A hundred-yard swim?

Simpson and I were alone. Everyone else was gathered on the bow, and Chief Turner and Oakey were already bobbing in the raft.

The corpse of the man who'd been in the starboard turret was at our feet. We knelt to examine him and saw he was one of the new kids, only eighteen or nineteen. His thin chest was ripped apart, exposing the ruptured organs. I couldn't tear my eyes from the glistening lungs, stomach, liver . . . his face was smooth and unlined, as peaceful as a cherub sculpted by Botticelli.

"Got enough time to take him with us?" Simpson asked, "I'd like to see the kid buried decent."

"Just make it snappy."

Simpson started to pick him up, then stopped. The Thompson submachine gun lay nearby. Simpson grabbed the gun, slung it over his shoulder, and adjusted his canvas bag. He took the boy by his armpits, dragged him to the side, and dropped him over. Simpson followed, hitting the water feet first.

I made one last circuit of the boat, found some more useful things, wedged them in my belt. I looked over the side and saw the life-raft bearing the unconscious forms of Oakey, Chief Turner, and the 20mm gunner. The stiff lay on top. The boatswain's mates were kicking, pushing the raft, and Simpson was out front, pulling. Strip was swimming back to the boat, probably to check on me.

I walked aft cautiously. The fantail bobbed with the waves, grinding at the last shreds which held it to the bow. The engine-room hatch was open, and I looked at the three Packards below. The space was flooded half-full and stank with gasoline. I thought about the three engines—come morning, the Japs would have no trouble salvaging them. The thought of the Imperial Navy having an extra 1,350 horsepower was unbearable.

I had two grenades. One would have to do the job. I took one out and slipped my finger through the ring.

"Watcha doing, skipper?" It was Strip.

"What does it look like?" I replied angrily. Snipes give me a pain. They get crazy about their machinery, worrying about them beyond all reason. I knew Strip was particularly fond of the 44's sets, and I wasn't in the mood to hear any cockamamie plans about coming back in the distant future to salvage them.

"That ain't gonna do nothing," he said.

"Yeah? Watch."

"You gotta do it like *this*!" The grenade was snatched from my hands.

Strip grimaced as he yanked at the stubborn pin. He leaned over the hatch and aimed the grenade at some part of the engines he deemed most vital, then neatly tossed the pineapple down. We turned and ran forward, the boat groaning and shifting under our feet.

We dove off the bow head first. We'd gotten about three good strokes toward the raft when I heard the short, hollow explosion. I treaded water, watching the shattered fantail clunk noisily into the waves. Then the bow crashed down. I waited for it to slide into the sea, but it held fast to the rock.

Strip and I swam to the raft. The pain in my armpit, momentarily forgotten, returned vengefully. I grabbed the side of the raft and began kicking.

The sound of crashing surf grew louder. The waves broke over our heads at increasing intervals, pushing us nearer the beach. Salt water suddenly found its way into my gullet, and one of the boatswain's mates had to hold me while I hacked and coughed.

Chapter Four

I lay on my back a long time. The overhanging jungle was so thick I couldn't detect where it left off and night began. I closed my eyes and dreamt about the pain in my arm, and when I opened them again I could see violet through the chinks of jungle canopy. The color slowly changed to gray. Dawn was on the way. I rolled over and stood up.

We were only thirty yards from the beach, but the climb was so steep it took us a full hour to get this far. Due to the darkness, and our collective exhaustion, this was as much as we could hack. Gigantic trees were all around, their buttress-like roots intertwined with the yellowish trunks of climbing palms.

A standard PT crew consists of three officers and fourteen men. What a laugh. That figure had come from someone's easy chair in Washington, and had as much relevance here as orders from Mars. The 44 had been carrying seven, myself included.

Simpson, the gunner's mate, was propped against a tree. He had rescued a quart can of gun oil and was cleaning the weapons with the rags of his skivvy shirt. A straight twig served as ramrod. Our armory consisted of the Thompson submachine gun and four Colt .45 service issues. The Thompson's gangster-style magazine had fifty rounds, and Simpson had popped out enough cartridges to fatten the handful of spare magazines. Simpson was one of the career men, old and tough though something of a wise guy. He looked up and spoke quietly, like we were in a church. "How you doin', skipper?"

I picked up one of the pistols and wedged it in my belt. "Fine. You know anything about jungle survival?"

"You kiddin'?" He looked at the pistol in his hand. It glistened in the dim light. "All I know is my rate, Mr. Leander. And goddamn little of that, now that it's finally come down to it." He was a second class. I had seen little of him prior to the war. He had always neglected to address me as mister or sir or anything which I might construe as respect. Up until now.

"Simpson, you did good on the fifties."

"Misfired enough."

"I didn't notice any lack of firing when it was needed."

He looked up. "I'm glad you were on the helm last night."

I was totally surprised. "I racked up the boat!"

"We're alive, ain't we?"

For better or worse, that was true. I nodded and walked on.

Chief Turner was on his side, sleeping. Dried blood caked the right leg of his khaki trousers. He was one of the reasons we took so long to get this far. He was in his late thirties, by far the oldest guy in the squadron.

Ensign Oakey lay nearby. His eyes were at half-mast, and his parched lips opened and closed as if he were quietly talking to himself. One hand covered the wound in his left shoulder. The slug had gone clean through, which was some kind of blessing. I knelt, fished out my last cig, and stuck it in his mouth. His eyes kept that faraway look, but his lips closed around the butt readily enough. I lit it and he inhaled deeply. Tough guy. You never would've known it from the way he acted when he first reported to the squadron. He was a regular university graduate, had taken some reserve officer courses and was to serve out his two-year obligation in my unit. He was your standard happy goofoff, typical product of a life in which everything is served up on a silver platter. Now this. Downed by a Jap slug, lying on the jungle floor in the Philippines. Enjoying his smoke. I gave him a pat and stood.

Philpot, the 20mm gunner, had died shortly after we made the clearing. He'd taken two more slugs after the initial wound in the foot. A foul weather jacket had been thrown over his head; we would bury him come morning's full light. One of the boatswain's mates who dragged him off the boat was just sitting there, staring at the corpse. He was a young kid, one of those lanky farmboys they grow in Minnesota. He was staring at Philpot like he was in a trance, lips slack. I went over and shook him out of it, then told him to go lie down and get some sleep.

Strip Cunningham lay nearby, snoring like an innocent babe. There wasn't a scratch on him.

A little beyond the clearing was the spot where we

buried the kid who died in the starboard gun tub. We could've dug a deeper hole but we didn't. We could've said more words but we were too tired. One of his dogtags was in my pocket. Departed this vale of tears in the first blush of 1942.

At the far end of the clearing, facing seaward, was the boatswain's mate keeping watch. I went over and relieved him, and he went looking for a spot to sleep. I lay down where he'd been, rolling and squirming a bit to favor my arm. It didn't hurt so much anymore — just felt like a sack of grinding, jagged glass. I crawled forward, pushing aside the leaves and ferns which obstructed my view.

Before me was a steep hill which ran down to the thin strip of mud that was the beach. The hill was covered with plants that looked something like cattails and were almost as high as a man. Looking at it now I marveled that it'd taken only an hour to get where we were. Our clearing was on level ground, like a plateau, and the jungle behind us marched up an even steeper hill and into the tractless wilds of Mt. Silanganan.

The remains of PT 44 were one hundred yards out, a recognizable bit of bow still hanging on the rock which killed her. Bits of plywood bobbed nearby. The after section was no more.

The wounded Jap DD was one thousand yards further. She wasn't sunk, but she was in trouble. She lay very low in the water, the sea coming almost to her main deck, her stern looking like the petals of a flower sculpted in steel.

The other destroyer was a little further seaward. She'd returned after giving Nash a five-hour chase. I had a gut feeling Nash was okay. For some reason I felt sure if this destroyer had been victorious she would've come back with PT 41 strapped across her fo'c'sle, like a successful hunter.

Both cans were riding at anchor. The current ran from north to south, so the ships were broadside to my view. Their silhouettes were black, and the sea a purplish gray. It was calm as a lake out there; sea state zero.

Now and then a hatch would open on the further of the two destroyers and I saw the white lights of her interior. No such lights on the nearer DD, which meant she couldn't even get it up for electrical power. Small boats were running between the ships as busily as the ferries in Hong Kong. Carrying damage-control equipment, probably.

I wondered how many times the skippers of those cans had run around the problem, trying to figure out what to do. There was only one solution though, and I knew it'd be the last thing they wanted. Rig the wounded destroyer with enough pumps to keep ahead of the flooding. Throw a tow line and haul her to the drydock she was obviously going to need. That meant Takao, the Jap naval base in Formosa.

I chuckled quietly. This was almost as good as sinking her — hell, maybe even better. One destroyer out of commission for months, and the other would be slowly towing her back home, a trip that would take a long, long time.

We had done it. The Japs had been slowed down. Time had been bought, maybe enough to hold out until reinforcements came for the States. It had been a Pyrrhic victory, perhaps, but . . . mission accomplished. A warm glow crept over me, as if I were freshly showered and shaved and settling down to the Sunday paper with ham and eggs tucked in my belly. The discomforts of the jungle were no more, the pain in my arm forgotten. We had really done it. We had gone toe-to-toe with the big boys and thrown a nice big monkeywrench into their steamroller.

Dawn was minutes away, and more details became visible on the destroyers. I studied their outlines intently.

Two stacks. Length . . . let's call it something under three-fifty. A 4.7-inch mount forward, another amidships, two back aft. Two very big torpedo launchers. The lines of the ships were unusual. In between the pilothouse and the fo'c'sle the deck seemed to dip down into a kind of well. That design . . . ah, yes. Now I recognized them. That well had been experimental on this class of destroyer, a design to help break the force of long Pacific swells.

Kamikaze Class destroyers, both of 'em. I knew a lot about this particular class. There would be six torpedo tubes, to be exact. Lots of small arms. Four Kanpon boilers, two shafts. Design speed thirty-seven knots. Full load displacement at seventeen hundred tons. I wish I'd brought the damn binoculars.

The water was now a flat gray. I could make out the meatballs on their battle ensigns. I squinted at the hull numbers. The damaged one was "twelve." The other was "seventeen."

I froze for a moment, startled. I rubbed my hand against my eyes and looked again. It was "seventeen" all right. I couldn't believe it. DD 17 was a ship I knew! She was called the *Matsukaze*. Her captain was someone I knew, someone I had met before the war, a *buddy*. Jesus! I whispered his name, unused for so long.

Ohiro Kagemaru . . .

I shook my head in astonishment. In the service you're always meeting up with people you haven't seen for years. But this!

I tried to remember the last time I'd seen him. Was it in San Francisco? Yes, that seemed right. At the Top o' the Mark, to be exact. For cocktails . . .

We had met in 1935. That was in California, while I was attached to the Long Beach Naval Shipyard. Long Beach was a dump, which suited my inner mood perfectly at that time. I'd just completed my first tour at sea, and as a freshly-minted lieutenant (junior grade) was morosely awaiting the arrival of my new ship.

I hadn't had much fun on my first tour, and knew the next wouldn't be any better. The shipdriving part was okay, but everything else sucked. The captain was one of those guys who screamed a lot. Everyone in the wardroom hated each other's guts. Most of the chiefs were expert shirkers, their prime topic of conversation being why something couldn't be done, or how soon their twenty'd be up.

So it was a bad ship. Very few can be considered "good," but hell, that's been true since the time of the Phoenicians. But I thought I might eventually get used to the contentious life of a seafaring man if it wasn't for one thing—it turned out I hated worse than anything taking orders from other men. Not a good trait to have in a career military officer, to be sure; but there you have it. I could always think of better ways to get things done, and was forever impatient with going by the book. I ached to have my own shop and call my own shots.

And it'd be a long, long time before I was in that position. First I would have to finish out my division officer tour—which the ship coming to pick me up in Long Beach represented—and then, perhaps after some shore duty, a couple of department head tours. Then one or two executive officer tours. Then finally, when I'm humped-over and burnt out, a commanding officer's tour. It was a long haul. I was filled with despair.

Temporary duty at Long Beach meant drinking a lot of coffee and reading the paper till quittin' time. My many bosses would occasionally throw me some flunky chore, and on the day I met Ohiro it was to check on the needs of a visiting Japanese naval officer, one of my own rank.

There was a Jap admiral and his aides, plus two officers who'd completed postgraduate study in the States and were in Long Beach to rendezvous with their brass for the trip back home. The youngest officer was Ohiro, and my job was to touch base with him and make sure he knew where to buy toothpaste and so on.

I took my time finding him. I had done this sort of courtesy-visit thing before with British and South American officers. They seemed to be made from the same cookie cutter, telling me how great their country was, then how great their navy was, then an allusion or two to their great sexual prowess and how soon could I get them a date? This guy was going to be my first Jap, and I wondered if he was yet another dumbbell.

I spotted him on a quay wall standing by himself, admiring the view of the shipyard. A brisk wind was kicking up whitecaps out in the Pacific, and Catalina Island lay on the horizon, crystal clear for a change. I walked up and introduced myself. We were both in dark blue uniforms, his being a single-breasted rig with a high stiff collar. He inclined his head as we shook hands, and I saw his eyes flicker over the gold stripes on my sleeve. I duly noted the two silver cherry blossoms on his collar tabs—three would've meant full lieutenant, so we were of the same rank. Later I would find we were also the same age.

He was built like a tough featherweight, his face broad and rugged for a Jap. But smart, I could tell that right off. Those black eyes shone with a quick intelligence.

He regarded me in a skeptical but not unfriendly way. He waited for me to say something further, and when I didn't he turned back to his comtemplation of the shipyard. I followed his gaze.

There were a lot of ships, a forest of gray masts, radio lines, flags snapping in the stiff wind . . . all of them foothills to the mountain of steel that was the U.S.S. *Arizona*. She had a red signal flag up, which meant she was taking on fuel.

"A beautiful sight, is she not?" He was politely starting off the small talk.

"Too big for me. I'd go nuts on one of those."

His eyes sparked with interest. "Isn't duty on a battleship something everyone strives for? In Japan, only officers of the second rank gain assignment to a battleship."

"Yeah? What do officers of the first rank get?"

"Staff."

I laughed. "Then put me way down the list. I don't think I can even hack it on a destroyer. I know I'd go crazy on a battleship."

"Really?"

I pointed at the *Arizona*. "Friend of mine's an ensign on that tub. Know what his job is? He's in charge of the passageway that runs from the admiral's cabin to the flag barge's davit. Has a division of fifteen men working around the clock keeping it spic n' span. And it is no joke when I tell you that it is truly a high-pressure job."

"A great responsibility," he replied. He seemed serious, but his black eyes showed amusement. "I understand the great *Arizona* is based out of Hawaii . . . what is she doing here?"

"Don't know," I lied, then, "You speak English very well."

"Thank you. I've spent the last year in New York, taking an advanced course in hydrodynamics. I have had much opportunity to practice English."

"Yeah? Like New York?"

This time his smile wasn't hidden. "Oh, very, very much. What a fabulous city! I am trying to convince my admiral to let me stay another year so that I may attend lectures in Los Angeles."

"Think you'd like L.A. too?"

"I like what I've seen so far."

I sent my cig sailing into the harbor. I liked this guy. He was the first foreigner I'd met who had a kind word for the United States. And he seemed wide open for new experiences. "Well, shit. I've got the loan of a jalopy. What say we go toodlin' up to Hollywood this afternoon?"

His eyes widened. "May I . . . get into something more comfortable?"

We walked back to the Bachelor Officers' Quarters to peel off the monkey suits. What started out to be another lousy day now had the promise of some fun. Best of all this gave me a legitimate excuse to take the rest of the day off. I hummed as I changed, wondering what adventures the day would bring.

Chapter Five

The car was a '32 Dodge roadster with a ragtop that wouldn't come up. We screeched from the naval station shortly before noon, heading toward San Pedro. It was bright and sunny with just a hint of cool, a typical California winter day. Perfect for driving fast.

Ohiro's clothes were casual but beautifully tailored, worn with the unstudied ease of one who has grown up around big bucks. He was a good companion; kept his mouth shut, chain-smoked, asked me to drive faster. We took the scenic route along Palos Verdes, letting the sun and air cascade into the two-seater, enjoying the view of the Pacific. We hit Santa Monica and stopped for chow, then pressed on.

Hollywood was, as always, no big deal. We saw some sights, cruised the Strip. Dusk was on the way but I didn't want to go back to Long Beach.

"Say," I began, "I know an actress hereabouts. Feel like visiting?"

"Ah. Actresses."

"Or should I say sluts?"

He laughed. "My father has given me careful instructions about this. He says dating actresses is a boys' pastime, not something for men."

"I can't help myself, Ohiro. What do you say?"

"Does she have a friend?"

I gave her a call and she said no sweat. Somehow the four of us managed to wedge ourselves in the Dodge, and we got underway for an evening of laughs.

We had a big dinner at a lavish joint, thus laying the base for the alcohol to come. Then came the night-clubs, so many, in fact, that we could only stay at each long enough to finish the quota of one champagne bottle per. Ohiro took the checks with unobtrusive good manners, waving away my attempts to pick up the tab.

Things got dizzy and spinny as the night wore on, but if you took care to dance hard enough it sort of bled the booze from the system. So we did a lot of that, and a lot of laughing, and Ohiro's date cried on his shoulder, sobbing and cursing, wondering what the hell had gone wrong with her career.

I don't know what time we wound it up, but the girls said it was too late to for us to drive back to Long Beach. So . . . well, they asked us, didn't they? My last sober act was to get on the horn and tell the duty officer not to expect us back until late Saturday. There was some more booze, some kind of dancing to a radio, then Ohiro's date took him off to a bedroom and I followed mine into hers and therein followed a drunken session of the old humpety-bump.

I awoke in the middle of the night half sober. Stella lay next to me, smoking a cigarette. Or was it Robin? I replayed some fuzzy images, began to suspect this was not the girl who had led me into the bedroom. I asked her as much.

She was matter of fact. "Why, no."

"What're you two doing? Taking turns?"

"Ohiro's nice, Buck. He's a real high roller, and you meet precious few in this town. It's been a long time since me and Stella have been taken to such swell joints."

"Yeah, but . . . "

"But what?"

"Well, he's a Jap. That doesn't bother me, but—" I had honestly thought they might find an Oriental repulsive. But Stella only laughed, told me I didn't know anything about how to get a job in Hollywood. She ground out the cigarette and we began the wrestling match afresh.

Next day was a treat. We drove the girls down to M.G.M. for their walk-ons in some western. The producer let us hang around. Ohiro was fascinated with the lights and camera equipment, and asked so many questions the producer finally told him there weren't any jobs available. Ohiro told him he already had a steady job. The producer considered this, then asked if he wouldn't mind doing a bit. Ohiro laughed. The producer said there was a sawbuck in it. My new friend went down to makeup.

The bit entailed Ohiro—now an Indian brave—to ride into camp, shake his rifle in the air, and let out a war whoop. This would galvanize the other redskins into preparing for the cavalry's surprise attack.

Lieutenant Kagemaru turned out to be an excellent horseman. He did everything just right, had the pony under perfect control, whooped to curdle the blood.

The cameraman said there was a few more feet in his film magazine, so the director called for another take.

When everyone broke for chow Ohiro and I headed back to Long Beach. Over the next few days, before my ship came in, we spent our free time at the pool or on the tennis courts. My Long Beach sojurn was no longer depressing.

We drank together often, talking about the sea, ships, women, bestsellers. Now and then we talked about ourselves. I told Ohiro about my hometown of Savannah, Georgia. My father had been a surgeon, and wanted the same thing for me. But an uncle of mine — master of a big cargo vessel — planted the bug to see faraway places. Ohiro told me about his home in Kyoto, but it was a travelogue, and he never said anything about his family. Sometimes I sensed he wanted to talk about something more personal. It was apparent — as I came to know him better — that something was eating him. But I never pried.

He wrangled his extra year of postgraduate study. When we parted there were polite promises to keep in touch. If we saw each other again, fine; if not, that was okay too. One really gets used to this sort of thing in the service.

My new ship was everything I feared. She came into Long Beach for fuel, picked me up, and we went back out for a huge fleet exercise. Two hours after reporting aboard that can I was on the bridge, listening to the captain scream at the chief engineer. The boilers had suddenly lost the load, we were slipping from formation . . .

The only good thing about her was her homeport, which was San Francisco. Two other officers and I rented an apartment, and that was our base whenever we were in port. It was a strange time. Weeks at sea on one exercise or another, like some kind of bad movie you have to watch again and again. Then a day or two in port, when I could get drunk just watching the way the sun played over the bright, clean city, the way people walked around without a care in the world. I grabbed all the good times that I could.

It was in this environment I met Linda O'Donnely, a girl who had everything but everything going for her. Face straight out of *Vogue*. A body that made you want to get on your knees and chew up deckplates. A big, rich daddycakes. An equal capacity for the good times I was running after. She became the center of my world, and whenever I was at sea all I could think of were those beautiful legs and the way she laughed as she took her Jag to its upper limits . . .

I took the big plunge and asked her to marry me. She had to think about it. Her father went berserk when he found out who she was considering. He already had some lawyers and bankers lined up for princess . . . Linda promptly made up her mind.

I called all my friends to spread the good news, and Ohiro was on that list. He was at U.C.L.A. I invited him to the wedding and he showed and for this I was grateful. We didn't get a chance to really visit, but then the whole world was mere background to my lithsome new wife.

The last time I saw Ohiro was before he left for Japan, almost two years to the day after we'd first met. He was in San Fran for the night, awaiting the ship that would take him home. We met at the Top o' the Mark for a farewell drink.

I had just made full lieutenant. So had Ohiro, although in his navy it was called senior lieutenant. This called for several toasts. Ohiro soon waxed maudlin, the thing that had always been on the verge of our Long Beach drinking bouts.

"I'm going to miss America," he sighed, "I'm going to miss it so much I wish I never came."

"So quit the Navy and sign citizenship papers." I was uneasy. I wasn't in the mood to watch Ohiro bare his soul. All I wanted was a jolly evening. I had other things on my mind.

"Resign from the Navy?" He raised his highball, keeping his eyes on mine. They were black as obsidian, fathomless. "Impossible."

"C'mon. You're not exactly manacled."

He looked down, a thin smile working itself across his lips. "You do not understand, Buck. My family raised me to be a warrior, to give myself to the military as would a priest to god."

"And?"

"My family has done their duty." He gulped his drink, signaled for another.

"America is so amazing," he continued, "A young man can do anything he wants, put his hand to whatever he desires. There are so many ways to make money."

"Your family has lots of dough."

"That is not the point. My family's property comes from being strong, from taking from the weak. Everywhere in the world wealth is a matter of taking things by force, but here in America you actually *make* money." The booze arrived and Ohiro took a long pull. His face was flushed, excited. "Remember that day we spent together in Hollywood? The things I saw there, it was so stupid, so disorganized. With just a little sense you could turn that place upside-down and make millions. Think of it, Buck. It'd be so easy, so much fun. That is just one example of what you can do in this country."

I shrugged. Hollywood was the least of my worries, as was the desire to make money. My beautiful wife had so much dough I was thinking about having my working khakis tailor-made. The marriage itself was having the first rumblings of discontent, and I thought about telling Ohiro all about it. But stopped. Why burden him? Like he was burdening me? I wanted to escape from my troubles for a while, instead of compounding them.

Ohiro looked into his half-empty glass. "That day in Hollywood . . . driving around as we please, visiting the movie set . . . those actresses. Me thinking and planning of all the ways that film could've been made cheaper and better . . . " He looked at me, and for a moment seemed like a terribly shy schoolboy. "It was a very happy day for me, Buck. Maybe the happiest of my life."

The words trailed off and I looked away, embarrassed. His happiest day? Now that was truly pitiful. What kind of upbringing could he have had to look back on that idle day with so much affection? I shuddered.

Ohiro composed himself, slipping on a mask. The heart-to-heart bit was over. "I've already received my new orders, Buck."

"Staff, I'll bet."

He nodded as he drank. "I always knew it would be,

despite my standing at Ita Jima, our Naval Academy. My family is extremely well-connected." He worked up something that looked like a grin. "But I've decided to use those connections to my own end, if need be."

"Yeah? How so?"

"I don't want to go back to Tokyo. I want to go back to sea. You understand, don't you?"

"It's not going to be lonesome on a battleship, Ohiro. You're not going to be your own man there any more than you would on staff."

"Truly. That's why I've decided on destroyers. The crews are much smaller, and succession to command is swift."

"You get to be skipper of a can and you'll still take plenty of orders."

"True. But not as many as in your Navy. The Japanese Navy is interested in only one thing, and that is winning a great naval victory with battleships. Destroyers are only escorts. I'll have plenty of leeway, Buck. Count on it."

"Why not go whole hog, Ohiro? What is there in your Navy more unimportant than destroyers?"

He shrugged. "Officers of the fourth rank are assigned to cargo ships and other vessels of that nature. That does not interest me. Officers of the last rank, the fifth, are assigned to aviation. I've flown before, and I don't like it."

He looked at his watch and the evening came to a close. We went downstairs, shook hands wordlessly, and then he was gone. I felt sorry for the guy. I hoped he'd get what he wanted, but I just couldn't see him getting the freedom he craved on a destroyer. I pulled the collar of my bridge coat to my ears and started walking home. I had all sorts of bad thoughts about destroyers. The one I was on now was driving me nuts. And I was just about due for my first shore duty, a fact which I kept telling my wife in our ever-increasing arguments.

Shore duty turned out to be the New York Navy Yard. Things started out nice. My wife got us an apartment overlooking Central Park. For the first time since I was seventeen I began to have days that had some similarity to each other. There were thousands of things to see and do in New York, and I went at it ravenously.

Maybe it was too much of a good thing. It was like I was on a merry-go-round going so fast parts of it were flying off. I had the feeling the whole thing would soon come apart, and it did, brother. It did. The arguments, dormant for awhile, started anew. The shore duty itself was terrible — the building where I worked was in a constant state of turmoil similar to that of a destroyer's bridge during a complicated fleet exercise. Female yeomen insisted on calling the floors "decks," something which irritated me to no end. I drank a lot. My wife and I had a knock-down drag-out that finally did it. She called old daddycakes, who was only too glad to wheel in a couple of expensive lawyers to oversee the speedy divorce. I got a call from Washington telling me that my shore tour was nearly up and it was time to start thinking about what kind of ship I wanted next.

It was in this environment I received a communication from Ohiro. It was an engraved invitation to a ceremony in which Senior Lieutenant Kagemaru would assume command of the destroyer *Matsukaze*. I couldn't believe it. Captain of a destroyer! He had really done it. The walls of my office seemed to close in, like something in a horror movie. My desk was piled high with meaningless paper. I pushed the stacks to the floor, like an angry boy, then began writing Ohiro a letter of congrats. How had the son of a bitch done it? In the U.S. Navy only lieutenant commanders get to be destroyer skippers, and senior ones at that.

And, as I wrote, I looked out my grimy window at the experimental PT squadron at the main pier. Thick exhaust hung at the PTs' sterns, and even at this distance I could hear their rumbling engines. It was a beautifully sunny day, and they were fixing to take a little spin out in the Hudson.

I had seen the PTs before but hadn't given them much thought. They were controversial items, the story being that Roosevelt himself had ordered their development. The Navy brass had not taken to such detailed guidance kindly. They told the president that torpedo boats were useless, and, more important, they didn't care to be instructed by an amateur in matters of naval warfare. Roosevelt countered that, as Assistant Secretary of the Navy in World War I, he'd been impressed by torpedo boat actions. Hadn't two Italian boats sunk a battleship in 1917? The admirals said we understand, Mr. President, that your yacht-building buddies are pressuring you to start this crazy program so they can get the contracts . . . but, if you insist, maybe we can get something going in a few years. Roosevelt, impatient, went ahead and purchased test boats from the British, and ordered an experimental squadron to be set up. This did not add to the admirals' love of PTs.

The more I thought about it the better I liked it. I watched the squadron outside my window get underway. They wheeled in a turn to starboard, their wakes clean and white against the garbage dump that was Upper Bay. I saw that they weren't going up the Hudson after all; they were heading out for a little romp in the Atlantic.

All of a sudden I longed to be with those guys.

I went downstairs, mailed the letter to Ohiro, and began the process of attaching myself to the PTs.

It was harder than I thought. Everybody but everybody told me it was a lousy idea, throwing myself away on a career deadend like torpedo boats. Time and again, as I ushered the transfer through my chain of command, other officers' eyes would gloss over as they spake the Holy Gospel—the U.S. Navy is a big-ship navy, son. PTs are for bums. Where do PTs fit in with the sacred progression of division officer-department head-executive officer-captain? You'll never make commander, boy. On and on it went, even to an interview with an admiral.

The admiral was my last hurdle. He listened to my request and then, without comment, picked up the phone and called a buddy in Washington. Pull Lieutenant Leander's service jacket and read me a few fitness reports, he says. He kept his eyes on me while he listened for a few minutes, then covered the mouthpiece and said Buck, you're throwing away a mighty promising career, you know that? I said nothing. The admiral asked his buddy a couple more questions, then said he's got some hot and juicy billets for the likes of me. How about assistant gunnery officer on a battleship, what lieutenant wouldn't jump at that? I said give me those PTs, admiral. He hung up the phone and asked if thirty days' leave might restore sweet reason. No, sir. He sighed as he signed the transfer. When he handed it over he looked at me as if I were a piece of machinery that wasn't working right. And was now consigned to the trash heap.

There were only three squadrons. Twelve boats at Pearl, eleven in the New York Navy Yard, and six boats recently moved to the Asiatic Fleet, based in Manila. I was to get the Manila slot.

But first I had to undergo a familiarization course in New York. I loved it from the start. Nobody gave a damn whether I came in or not. My usual day began early; a nice little run up the Hudson, maybe a little spin out into the Atlantic. Some of those bastards could go forty-five knots, and when you got behind five-foot swells it was the most heart-pounding roller coaster ride on earth. Then a leisurely, gentlemanly luncheon. Then maybe a nap, maybe another boat ride. It was the best deal I ever had in the Navy. Sure, I'd paid a price. My career was effectively over. I might make lieutenant commander, but certainly no higher. But I didn't care. It seemed a small price. I was doing exactly what I wanted. If the Navy thought these boats were useless . . . well, fuck 'em.

Manila was fine. It was unbelieveable, but Motor Torpedo Boat Squadron Two wasn't even listed in the Asiatic Fleet's assets! The guy I relieved was vague about who we had to report to. Since we were a commissioned unit, all our supply needs were drawn out of our own account. Administratively . . . hell, I figured on not reporting to anybody, just to see what would happen. Nothing did. It was great. The Asiatic

Fleet was totally uninterested in our doings.

And now . . . now I was commanding officer of the only naval unit in the big-ship Navy facing the enemy. Or, more accurately, I was watching the enemy from my hiding place in the bushes. I looked at Ohiro's ship riding peacefully at anchor. He was probably in his cabin, tanking up on some hot chow. Maybe a little sake to start the day off right. I wondered if he saw the war for what it was—a career officer's jackpot—or if he still pined for an entrepreneur's life in America. I still felt sorry for him and hoped that he'd found some happiness in his destroyer. But these strings of friendship would have to take a back seat to the issue at hand. Dreamy as Ohiro was, I knew he was thoroughly professional and there'd be no mercy in any combat action. Assuming, of course, that I could get out of this goddamn jungle first so there would *be* some future action.

Strip crawled next to me and peered through the foliage. The damaged DD had several hoses over the side, each vibrating with a torrent of oily water. He chuckled softly, then asked me what we were going to do.

Good question. I took a quick look at the landward side of the clearing. The jungle seemed as solid as the Great Wall of China, and ten times as high. We'd need food, machetes, stretchers, a guide . . .

"We wait here," I said, "Lieutenant Nash knows approximately where we went aground. He'll be back with a rescue party after these guys leave."

"Yeah, if that can didn't get him last night."

"We're behind our own lines, Strip. There's lots of patrols about. Don't sweat it."

"Whatever you say, sir." He was disgusted.

The early morning light was harsh. The destroyers were planes of flat gray and sharply-defined purple shadows. On the fo'c'sle of the wounded can I could see a working party preparing for tow. On the fantail of Ohiro's ship I could see his men rigging a towing cable. They'd be leaving soon.

One boat departed the *Matsukaze* and headed for the remants of PT 44. Only the coxswain wore sailors' whites, the rest were in khaki. Marine khaki, Japanese-style. There were twelve, sitting with rifle butts on the deck, muzzles straight up. Long bayonets glittered like polished mirrors.

But the boat didn't stop at the 44. It headed straight for the beach, exactly for the point where we'd come ashore. Ohiro was having his men take care of one final errand.

"Uh oh," Strip whispered. Simpson had walked up unnoticed; his eyes flickered from me to the Japs and back again. "What we gonna do, skipper?"

I cursed myself. We should've gone further into the jungle. We should've chosen a better hiding place. Ohiro wasn't the type to leave any loose ends dangling. Stupid! Stupid!

But no use crying over spilt milk. I decided what to do and there wasn't any need to waste words. I sat up and took the .45 from my belt. I pulled the slide back and saw that it was empty. I took a magazine from my pocket and it slid home with an oily click. I thumbed down the release lever and the slide snapped forward.

The two men stood and went back to the clearing. Soon I heard the clicks and snaps of the weapons being loaded. I rolled back on my stomach and moved the fronds from my view.

The gig was fifty yards from the beach. The noise of their engines carried over the breeze, a busy little *pock-pock-pock*.

I looked at the *Matsukaze*. Officers were on her bridge wing, each with binoculars trained on the landing party. I wondered which one was Ohiro.

Two of the Marines hopped out of the boat as it beached. They dragged it up on the mud. Their officer unsheathed his sword and pointed it to the right, then left. His men deployed. They began moving forward, loudly crashing through the brush.

Thirty yards up the hill to where we were. Twelve of them—every shot would have to count. I looked to my right; four men were prone, three with .45s, Simpson with the Thompson.

"Don't fire until I do," I whispered. Each nodded, then carefully aimed their weapons downhill, pushing leaves aside.

The officer was in the forefront, heading right toward me. He grunted as he chopped the shrubbery aside, his long sword swinging through thick vines effortlessly. He had a beard, making him look like one of those oriental demons. Twenty yards now. There were lines on his face, an older guy, but I saw that his rank was junior lieutenant. Wartime promotion from the ranks? I began squeezing on the trigger. The head would be best, but I'm not that good a shot. I leveled the sights on the middle of his chest.

The gun bucked and a shell snapped from the chamber. The Jap caught it where I aimed, and it lifted him off his feet. He tumbled downhill backwards.

My guys immediately let go and the stillness of the tropical morning was gone in the sound of firecrackers and the smell of cordite. The Thompson submachine gun was like a buzzsaw, tearing through the vegetation, planting bright red blossoms on the Japs' dirty khakis.

Our barrage was sudden and deafening, and if I'd been on the wrong end of it I'd have turned and run like hell. But the Japs didn't. They responded without hesitation, as if they'd been expecting it all along. They charged forward, bellowing with rage, their banzai screams louder than our weapons, the sun flashing off the razor-sharp edges of their leveled bayonets.

I emptied my .45, hitting no one else. Simpson's machine gun cut through the jungle like a scythe, taking three Japs down. I rolled on my back to slip in a fresh magazine, but a Marine broke through just to my left. I threw the pistol at his face but it bounced off his shoulder. He raised his bayonet on high.

The side of his face fell apart and he dropped like a sack of loose bones. I saw several men rush into the clearing—Filipinos, clad in U.S. Army hand-me-downs.

They came from the far end of the clearing, tommy guns blazing into the Japs now cresting the ridge. A slug whizzed close to my ear and I rolled over and buried my face in my hands, thinking let the landlubbers have it out, I'm nothing but a goddamn sailor.

Chapter Six

"You awake, bub?"

I opened my eyes. The concrete ceiling was a rounded arch, like the interior of a railway tunnel. A naked light bulb hung directly overhead, showing all the dirt.

The voice belonged to a guy whose chest was wrapped in bandages. Big bastard he was, too. He was in bed, as were the men extending beyond him down the length of the . . . cave?

"Wanna smoke?" he asked. I nodded. A deck of Camels landed on my chest. I got one out, the effort making me feel tired and old. The guy leaned over, a pack of matches in his hand. I reached, but my arm seemed too stiff to raise. My benefactor thumbed out a match and fired it off.

"Welcome to the Rock," he grinned. So that was it. I was on Corregidor, the island fortress laced with underground tunnels. Ever since the Japs established air superiority all operations, including medical, had moved below.

"Thanks," I said, "Where's the doc?"

"Beats me." The guy had a strong Texas accent. He smiled in a friendly way, like he was settling down for a nice long visit. I blew a smoke ring. It floated lazily, evaporated at the light bulb. I had a tremendous headache and my limbs felt as delicate and brittle as a year-old newspaper. The air was so stale it stank. I rubbed my hand against my eyes, feeling like I'd just waked up from a three-day drunk in the Tijuana hoosegow.

"Name's John Flexner," he said. "What's yorn?"

"Leander. Call me Buck. Army?"

"Yep. Army Air Corps. Captain."

"Navy. Lieutenant."

He chuckled, an unusually high-pitched sound for such a big man. "Swabbo, eh? Thought all you guys shilly-shallied out of here when the going got rough."

Nice manners, this guy.

"Not everybody." I stared to tell him about my boats but stopped. I was tired. The cigarette wasn't too much of a treat anymore, either. I ground it out on the rickety nightstand. Sleep was what I needed, but Tex had other ideas. He launched into his sad sack tale about how his plane was shot up just as he was taking off.

"Fucking lil' bassards. Bushwhacked us, what they did." He clenched his huge fists, staring at the ceiling angrily. "No damn declaration of war, neither. Just like the president said, a Day of Infamy."

"More like a Week of Infamy," I replied sarcastically. There was a time there when it seemed the Japs were starting off every day with a surprise attack.

"Say that again." His tone was full of menace. "I

hope for your sake you didn't mean what I think you did."

"You heard me, Tex. Why don't you just hop out of those bandages and slap me full of respect?"

I closed my eyes and got ready for some shouting. Maybe he would even crawl out of his rack and uphold the honor of the Army. I didn't care. I wanted to go back to sleep.

But Tex kept his mouth shut. Curious, I opened my eyes. And saw the reason why.

Standing at the foot of my bed was a nurse, and this wasn't your usual lantern-jawed dyke. This was the kind they use on calendars.

She was dressed in army khakis about eight sizes too big; still, it did not hide her figure. The baggy shirt was loose about her wide shoulders, tight where it strained at the full and heavy breasts. Lord Almighty, a man could lose himself in those. A belt was cinched tight around her narrow waist, the beige cotton curving down to the flare of wide and lovely hips. Dark hair was gathered underneath an oversized baseball cap, loose strands hanging about a long and elegant neck. She was studying the clipboard at my feet, her lips tightened in a thoughtful pout. I wasn't tired anymore.

"What, may I ask, is a gal like you doing in a place like this?"

She didn't raise her eyes. "Gosh, I never heard that one before." Her voice was listless. She let the clipboard cover snap shut and brought up her eyes. And I got me a shocker. Those eyes were as dead and empty as I'd ever care to see. She sighed wearily. "How you feeling, sport?"

"Sister, maybe I should be asking you instead. Things rough around here?"

She rubbed her hands across her forehead, shaking her head slowly. "I don't wanna hear it. I don't wanna hear it. I've heard every goddamn pitch ever made, so please let's not get personal. Save both of us some time and just tell me how you're feeling."

"Well . . . shouldn't I be talking to a doctor?"

"He's got plenty better things to do, bud." She looked at me like I was a slab of beef. "All right, you look okay to me." She lifted the clipboard and started to write something, then stopped. She weaved back and forth, eyes fluttering, then stepped to the side of my bed and sat heavily. "Okay," she said quietly, to herself. She breathed deeply. "Okay. Okay."

"You all right?"

She turned her eyes to me. Sweat beaded her upper lip. She brought her breathing under control, then lifted the clipboard's cover. She grunted. "So you're a Navy guy. I've never met a Navy guy before."

"Call me Buck. What's your name?"

"I thought all the Navy guys left."

"Not all of them."

"You gotta get out of here today, you know."

"Whoa! I wanna see the doc."

"Your arm's sprained, hero. You're going back out on the road gang."

"Sprained arm? C'mon! I feel like I'm half-dead."

"Says here you got a touch of dehydration, so drink that glass of water on the nightstand. As for this exhaustion part, well, you've been racked out for three solid days so you should be plenty rested."

"Wait a damn minute! I want to see a doctor!"

She flipped another page on the clipboard. "Note says some admiral guy wants to talk with you as soon as you wake up. I'll go get him now. When you two've had your little chat, I get the bed back." She hefted herself off the bed, grunting like an old woman. "So long."

"Hey!"

She walked down the corridor slowly. The roll of hips was strangely accentuated by the loose G.I. rig, the tent-like trousers hanging free and pulling tight over and over.

Tex was having a good look too, eyes bright and wide, two rows of teeth clearly visible.

"Hey . . . Flexner."

He didn't take his eyes off her. "What?"

"Know her name?"

He laughed. "Go fish, loo-tenant."

I eased my head back into the pillow. That nurse was getting ready to fall off some kind of tightrope. I wondered what it must be like for her here. In this place, in this time, men came in one of two varieties: wounded or desperately horny. That was too bad. A dame like that deserved to be wrapped in luxurious furs and told how beautiful she was. I closed my eyes and replayed our brief interview, letting it wash over me afresh. This is a knack developed from standing countless watches on a destroyer's bridge, filling the endless days at sea with memories of brief port visits. I savored each detail, the way the khaki strained at her ripe loveliness, the way the tip of her pink tongue had flicked over her lips. I felt something warm uncoil in my belly and travel down to my crotch. I was getting a hardon. Then I remembered the admiral'd be here shortly. Not wanting him to mistake my intentions, I returned to the here and now.

So I would be back on the job this afternoon. I felt weak as a kitten. And thirsty. Dehydration? What had happened after the Filipinos had saved us? I took the glass of water and drained it. It made me thirstier.

Rear Admiral Whitefield came walking down the corridor. I was surprised to see him decked out in his khaki jacket — usually he stuck to shirtsleeves and an open collar. But then this outfit was more impressive, and perhaps it comforted him to gather up his ornaments of rank as his command shrank bit by inexorable bit.

He pulled up a chair and sat, smiling an actor's smile. His shoulderboards were gold, embroidered with anchors and two stars. Two rows of ribbons were sewn into his jacket, foremost of which was a Navy Cross. His face was as lean as a boy's, his regulation haircut gray flecked with iron. He looked like someone's handsome grandfather. Not a kindly one, though. Having made flag rank meant he was mean as a rattlesnake and had a bag of ice for a heart.

"Good morning, lieutenant. Feeling better?"

"Feel like I'm dead, admiral."

"Fine," he nodded. He wasn't listening. "First off, I'd like to confirm that destroyer you sank in Subic."

"We didn't."

He raised an eyebrow, thunderclouds gathering. "I beg your pardon?"

"It was an oiler, admiral. An auxiliary ship. The destroyers weren't in the bay; they were out on patrol. Did Lieutenant Nash give you the details about our little clambake?"

He nodded. "He saw the . . . ship burning in Subic Bay. Said he inflicted heavy damage to one of the destroyers, one that was evidently pursuing you."

"I'll confirm that, admiral. I saw her being rigged for tow next morning. Both those cans are going to be out of this area for some time."

I waited for the pat on the back. Instead he looked down, shuffling through some papers. He looked politely embarrassed, as if I committed some *faux pas*. "I'm afraid that's not the case, Mr. Leander. One of our patrols has spotted them again, in Subic."

My heart skipped a beat. "Sir?"

"The damaged ship was towed only as far as Subic."

"But that can's going to need a drydock!"

"And she's in one, lieutenant. It's that floating drydock we had up there prior to hostilities." His lips curled back in a humorless grin. "A U.S. Navy drydock."

"I thought our guys put it out of commission before they left."

He sighed testily. "Then I suppose the Japs have *fixed* it, eh?"

I felt my fist clenching up. Painfully. Mission unaccomplished. In a few days both DDs would again be out on the rampage. The admiral cleared his throat. "Lieutenant, why don't you give me a rundown on the op?"

I began with the beginning, the words coming out clipped and short. It took ten minutes to tell. The admiral looked at me frostily while I spoke. He hadn't made up his mind whether I was worth something to him or was some kind of hopeless fuckup. I was, after all, on PTs. Strike one. And now I had dashed his hopes of reporting to fleet that a destroyer had been sunk. Strike two.

I had only met him once in pre-war days, and that was when he and his bootlickers had come down for a demonstration of PT operations. We put on a good show for the admiral, running the boats around Manila Bay in tight formations, wheeling into attacks, the whole bit. My guys performed perfectly too, busting their guts to impress the Mighty One. And when we pulled back to the piers he bestowed upon us but a meager half-smile. "Fine, fine," he said absently, glancing at his wristwatch. "These PTs are certainly peppy." Then his black sedan pulled up and he climbed aboard. He paused halfway in and smiled back. "Of course, I prefer something bigger." Slam.

It didn't look like he'd changed his mind in the interim. When I finished my report he gave me a half-hearted well done, as if asking himself what can you expect when you send a toy after a real ship's job?

There were some blank spots in my story. The admiral filled them out. Nash made it back okay—one crewman wounded—and used the field telephone to tell the Army approximately where I'd gone aground. A patrol of Filipino scouts searched for us, found us, saved us.

"Admiral, may I ask a question?"

"Certainly."

"How long before reinforcements arrive?"

He smiled enigmatically. "The specifics on that are top secret, lieutenant. But I can tell you the situation is a lot better now."

"You think the Army can hold out?"

"Definitely. Although they've been pushed into the

Bataan peninsula, at least they're in the best defensive position possible."

"Has the line changed since I've been unconscious?"

His eyes remained blank. "The line now runs from Bagac to Orion."

I kept silent. While I had slumbered so peacefully the Army had pulled back another six miles. This new line was but eleven miles from the southern tip of Bataan. Bad news!

"Anyway, it doesn't all hinge on Bataan," the admiral continued, "Corregidor's so well fortified it's impossible to take. Then there's the units we have on Cebu, Pannay, and Mindanao. Believe me, it'll take *years* for the Japs to drive us out."

"Any word on our aircraft coming back?"

"Any day now. A year ago secret fuel dumps were set up for emergency refueling of aircraft. This has turned out to be most provident, for these will become the bases for the return of the Air Corps."

My ears pricked up. "Admiral, if that's one hundred octane fuel I'd like to know where those dumps are, just in case."

He considered this a moment, then leaned close, dropping his voice. "I guess you do have a legitimate need to know. One cache is on Panay, near the provincial capital."

"Ilo-ilo?"

He nodded. "Another is at Laparan."

I didn't know that one. I repeated it.

"Sibutu," he continued, "Bangka. And Calusa."

I whispered them back until I had it down. "Thanks, sir. I hope that's information I don't have to use."

He straightened up. "You shouldn't. Everything is going more or less according to plan. War Plan Orange, drawn up back in 1921. It foresaw withdrawing into Bataan until reinforcements could arrive from the States."

I sighed, perhaps a little too loudly. "That's certainly comforting, sir."

His eyes bore down like a battleship's main battery. "Do I detect a note of sarcasm, lieutenant?"

"Sir?"

"Listen, mister." He smiled sweetly. "I don't have to take any crap from you."

"I wasn't giving you any, Admiral."

Those eyes held me down like a bug in a display case. "Who exactly do you think you are?"

"C.O. of M.T.B. Ron Two. Sir."

He snorted. "PTs. Strictly coastal craft. I don't see why the Coast Guard doesn't have this program. I didn't even know you people existed until after the war started."

"Then cut me loose, admiral."

"Cut you loose how?"

"My main job, as I see it, is to assist the Army. We've intercepted Jap landing barges trying to sidestep the front. We've . . . harassed destroyers which were performing shore bombardment against our troops."

"So?"

"So let me perform those ops without prior authorization from you. Due to the current tactical situation, I think you'll agree flexibility is at a premium."

He examined his fingernails. "You're correct in your assessment that PT boats are more properly the concern of the Army rather than the Navy. But you belong to me."

"I'll keep you advised, admiral. But it just seems we could both save each other a great deal of time—"

The admiral stood, looking as if I'd been nagging him for an advance on my allowance. "All right, all right. I'm willing to give this idea of yours a try. But I want to be kept well advised, understand?"

"Yes, sir!"

He turned his back and walked away. Had he given me free rein for the reasons I stated? Or because he thought we were entirely useless? I didn't care. All these years in the Navy and at last I'd gotten exactly what I wanted. Freedom. No bosses. A command unfettered by the paper monster. All success and failure would be my own doing. I felt like Michaelangelo contemplating the blank ceiling of the Sistine Chapel.

I threw back the covers and rolled my feet to the deck. Suddenly I didn't feel so hot anymore. But I didn't want to get back in bed. I wanted to get back to the boats in the worst way. There were a thousand things to do.

An orderly came and handed me my freshly washed but unpressed khakis. I put them on as fast as grandma plays bridge. I began walking down the arched corridor. It spun this way and that, like a tunnel in a fun house. Then, somehow, a nurse was at my side . . . the same one who'd given me the brushoff. She grunted as I leaned against her.

"C'mon, exit's this way," she said. "God, you're heavy."

"Sure you can do this?" I remember how exhausted she was.

She nodded. We continued through the corridors, and my legs began to think about coming back on the line.

She guided me through the extensive network of tunnels. At one point she became friendly enough to tell me her name was Ginger. Wounded men moaned softly, their cots lined up like so much cordwood. Fat-assed corporals banged away at Remingtons on wobbly desks. We passed Ensign Oakey and Chief Turner, both of them unconscious. I made Ginger take me by Oak, and when I put my hand on his shoulder his eyes opened a quarter-inch. I squeezed his shoulder hard and looked into his eyes and he smiled thinly before he punched back out.

Finally we got outside. It was a beautiful day, the cumulus floating across the sky like big lazy sheep. Their shadows dappled the island pleasantly, reminding me of Honolulu.

"Whew," Ginger slipped from under my shoulder. She leaned against the concrete wall that was the tunnel's entrance. "You walk all right now?"

I nodded as I moved into the sun's warm rays. It felt like a hot washcloth against my skin.

"Listen," she said. "I'm sorry I gave you such a hard time back in the ward."

I looked at her. She had a pack of smokes in her hand, one of the butts extended. I took it. She lit it with a battered lighter. She looked at me speculatively. "You said you were a Navy guy, right?"

"Yeah."

She nodded as if that had some significance. "Can we talk for a while? Private like?"

My belly glowed warmly. "Sure."

"Let's go for a walk."

We started walking up the grassy hill that the tunnel's entrance was set into. I let Ginger get a tad ahead of me. Those baggy pants may have been way too big, but her wide hips filled them with a maddening loveliness. How on earth had such a beautiful doll become an Army nurse?

"How many nurses are stationed here?"

"Fourteen," she said over her shoulder. "Just fourteen. And four thousand men in the garrison."

"I know some dames who wouldn't think that was such a bad deal."

She laughed shortly. We reached the top of the hill. From here I could see Corregidor's North Dock, downhill. No PT. The dense jungle of Bataan was straight ahead, separated by the four miles of water that was North Pass. All of a sudden my knees began to wobble. I sat down fast and heavy.

Ginger sat too. "Sure you're okay?"

"Just a little unsteady. I'll be all right."

She took off her cap and shook her head, her lustrous brown hair melting and flowing like so much silk. She leaned back on her arms and turned her face to the sun. Her face was lean with a wide, angular jaw, cheekbones pronounced but cushioned with smooth and flawless skin. Beyond her, twenty miles to the east, was the outline of Manila, a low silhouette of shops, houses, government buildings. If I had binoculars I could've seen Japanese flags fluttering in the breeze.

"How did you come to be an Army nurse?"

She turned violet eyes to me. "I've always wanted to be a nurse."

"Yeah, but why the Army?"

She looked over at Bataan. "The way it works, you join a hospital and start building up seniority. If you switch to another hospital you lose that seniority. I wanted to be a nurse, but I wanted to travel too. So . . ."

"I get it. That makes sense. How have you liked it so far, Ginger?"

She ignored me, continuing to look across the water. She was lost in her thoughts.

I sat back on my elbows. She'd get around to it when she was ready. The wind picked up and the clouds passed swiftly overhead, their shadows racing up to us and then on to the south.

Boy, this was nice, however you wanted to cut it. A sunny afternoon with a beautiful woman at my side . . .

"I thought I'd have fun in the Army." The quiet words drifted to my ears. It was the voice of a little girl. "I never thought we'd actually end up in a war. Never in a million years. It isn't anything like I'd thought it'd be. The men they bring in with their legs blown off and shrapnel in their eyes. Working on some poor joker when the electrical power goes out . . . " Her words caught in sobs.

I sat up. Her shoulders heaved as she wept. Now I had the size of it. And felt sorry for her. But shouldn't she be spilling this to the head nurse? Tentatively, I put my hand on her shoulder. She immediately thrust herself into my arms, burying her face against my shoulder. "Hey, hey," I said softly. "Everybody feels this way. But you'll make it, Ginger. Believe me, you'll make it. I know you've got enough tough inside to make it through this."

"No, I don't," she cried bitterly. "I can't take it. I just can't take it anymore."

"You'll make it."

"You're so wrong." She turned up her face, showing me the tears spilling from her frightened eyes. "I've been into the morphine. I've been injecting myself with dope. I'm a goddamn dope addict. What do you think of that?"

I looked at her, speechless. No wonder she couldn't unload this on her boss. She twisted from my arm, wiping away the tears.

"You won't tell anybody, will you?"

"No."

"I mean, you're in the Navy and you don't have anything to do with the Army. You won't tell, will you?"

"I told you I wouldn't."

"Good, because—"

Her eyes grew wide; she was looking at something behind me. Something that scared the hell out of her. I turned.

They were coming in from the west. Chunky bombers. Small fighters. They were banking into a turn, preparing for their run over Corregidor. The meatballs on their wingtips were clearly visible. The sound of their engines came and went, carried uncertainly by the wind.

Ginger was on her feet and suddenly I didn't feel so tired anymore. We ran downhill as the growl of air raid sirens quickly built to a scream.

The fighters came in first and they came in low. The bombers were right behind, methodically dropping their eggs. A fighter headed right for us, machine gun fire blossoming on the leading edge of his wings. Twin rows of dirt popped up on the ground and tore at us with incredible speed. Ginger and I dove into the tunnel entrance, bits of concrete exploding around our heads. I looked at the fighter as he screamed by. The Zero was so close I could see a white headband tied around the pilot's helmet. He was looking at me, grinning and waving.

We got up and ran inside the tunnel. A blast slapped our ears and a sudden wave of hot air pushed us down. The floor shivered like a derailed passenger train and the light bulbs danced on their cords. Concrete dust covered us like flour. We got up and ran deeper into the tunnel. Another explosion sent us sprawling and the lights went out. Ginger was underneath me and I instinctively wrapped my arms around her.

"Get your mitts off me!" She wriggled away and ran into the darkness. I followed, then tripped over some blubbering guy balled up on the floor.

Chapter Seven

"Attack in broad daylight? Are you crazy, Buck?"

"By dawn's early light. We're going to give the Japs a big surprise, and this time we're going to have enough light to see what the hell we're doing."

The lantern was too weak to light the walls of my nipa shack, but it threw lurid shadows across Nash's face. He was so surprised by my plan he couldn't keep his mouth from hanging open. "You just got out of the hospital this afternoon, Buck. Are you sure they didn't pump you with some funny juice?"

"Now's the best time for an attack. This is when they'll least expect it."

"I'll say!" He looked at me with unmasked contempt. "Going through Subic in daylight is the last thing they'll expect because we'd be fish in a barrel!"

"That's where you're wrong. Look." The chart of Subic was on the table between us. I placed my finger on the bay's northernmost end, Apalit Point. "That's where the oiler was docked, right?" Nash nodded. I slid my finger down to a cove on the southeastern edge of the bay—it was just inside the bay's mouth. "Binanga. That's where the drydock is. All we have to do is come around Ilinin Point, let 'em have it and get the hell out."

He looked at me, eyes wide, shaking his head. "Just come pounding around Ilinin at forty knots, huh?"

"The faster the better."

"What the hell about shore batteries?"

"Like I said, the faster the better."

"So one can will be in drydock; what about the other?"

"I'm banking she'll be alongside. All the Japs have in the way of repair facilities is that drydock they captured. Maybe that oiler we sank had repair shops, but now those services are going to have to be provided by the undamaged can: electrical power, men, welding—"

"What about aircraft?" Nash interrupted, "We'd be sitting ducks."

"That's not true and you know it. Look at what happened in Manila Bay—as long as we have maneuvering room we can twist out of the way."

"Yeah," he sneered, "Just like the good old thirty-two."

"The thirty-two boat got boxed in an inlet and that's the only reason those bombers got her."

Nash leveled his forefinger. "This is nothing but a stupid idea, Buck. Men are going to die on a crazy mission like this."

I smacked my fist against the table. "What the hell do you want to do?" My lips curled back in a sneer. "*Withdraw* with the rest of the fleet? Those destroyers have got to be put out of commission and by Christ I'll keep going after them until they're on the fucking bottom!"

Nash bolted to his feet so fast his chair tipped over. "Don't you *dare* raise your voice at me, you cocksucker!"

I stood, bringing my eyes to his level. I remembered all the bad things about Nash, the hard times he had given me back in peacetime. "Maybe I've got you figured wrong," I said evenly, "Maybe you haven't got the belly for it."

We stared at each other for a long four-count. Then Nash wheeled and stormed out of the shack. I sighed, letting out more pent-up air than I thought I'd taken in. I lit a cigarette as I went to the door, and stood there watching Nash clomp down to the pier. I could hear his harsh voice calling out all hands. Men rolled from the spots where they were sleeping topside, guys climbed out of the berthing compartments belowdecks. I watched the chiefs and senior petty officers cluster around Nash, black silhouettes under a starry sky. He gave them their instructions, pointing to the boats which would be making the run. I looked at my watch. It was almost midnight.

Three boats, twelve torpedoes. That's what I figured would do the job. It was a crazy plan, but I had a gut feeling it would work. Surprise would be the most important element. Hell, the Japs had taught us that, hadn't they? They would be expecting us at night, concealed by darkness and rolling seas. A daylight attack would be the last thing they'd be looking for.

Back when Roosevelt foisted the torpedo boat program on an unenthusiatic Navy only one tactic had been considered. Send buckets of torpedo boats after a battleship and the odds are maybe one or two will get through. Over those long luncheons in the New York Navy Yard the other PT officers and I talked about that a lot. We developed a tactic of our own, which was basically nighttime ambush. Tomorrow's plan would be a combination of both.

We left the base well before sunrise, taking our time to thread through the minefield, then picked up time making a flat-out forty-knot run along the southern tip of the Bataan peninsula. We hooked it around Luzon Point, but instead of heading for the mouth of Subic Bay we angled for Napo, a point seven miles down from Subic.

We hit Napo and slowed it down to fifteen knots. From here on out we would be hugging the coast as close as we dared.

Timing was perfect. Overhead the last stars were winking out. There was just enough red sky to make out such details as rocks poking up out of the cobalt water.

I was in the lead boat, a PT which belonged to Lieutenant j.g. Herring. He was driving; I stood next to the cockpit, the radiotelephone dangling from my hand. Nash was one hundred yards astern in his PT, and tail-end charlie kept station one hundred yards astern of Nash.

I told Herring to angle it in further, further . . . then had him hold steady, parallel to the coast at a distance of three hundred yards. I looked astern. The other PTs followed our lead, keeping to a textbook column formation. Things looked so good I told Herring to bump it up to thirty knots. I pressed the transmit button on the radiotelephone and informed the other boats of the speed change.

I knelt and fired up a cig. Nash's arguments continued to haunt me. Down deep, if truth be told, wasn't this mission a little vainglorious? Was I really just trying to prove something? For Admiral Whitefield? Or Ohiro Kagemaru? I stood, letting the wind press against my face and whip the cigarette smoke from my lungs.

I had been scared during the attack in Subic, more scared than I'd ever been in my life. But the thrill which surged through my gut when my torpedoes smacked into that oiler! God help me, but I had loved it! There was nothing on earth I would rather be doing than riding this PT, getting ready to round a bend and fight. I felt supremely happy, and in a strange way, fortunate.

Herring spun the wheel to starboard, following the line of the coast. Now we were heading due north; Binanga was only three miles distant. The sky had lightened to a flat blue; the coast was an impermeable green. I put on my helmet and cinched the chinstrap tight. I heard the clacks of the first rounds being jacked into the twin fifties. Nervously I untied and then retied the straps of my gray kapok, making sure they were extra tight. My heart began to pound with a dreadful excitement.

I told Herring to put a little more distance between us and the coast. He eased the wheel to port and I watched the other boats keep to our wake. I lifted the radiotelephone and pressed the button.

"Attack formation."

Nash's boat heaved out of the column and angled for

a position two hundred yards off my port quarter. The other boat increased speed and maneuvered to a point two hundred yards off my starboard quarter. Three boats arranged as an arrowhead.

"Battle speed."

I watched Herring ease the throttles to full rpms. Forty knots. The other boats kept pace. We were almost into the mouth of Subic Bay. I looked at the fantail and saw a sailor kneeling over the smoke screen generator; he was looking at me. I nodded.

Black, oily smoke billowed astern, and the PTs on my quarters were just outside my screen. They started their own generators and soon out little formation was trailing a voluminous cloud. I brought the radiotelephone up.

"Standby to commence fire."

The PT banked to starboard as Herring hove around Ilinin Point. I watched the other PTs keep to the strict formation.

Then Binanga lay before us—a rectangular cove one mile long and one-half mile wide, situated on an east-west axis. We had rounded the cove's southwestern edge. Midway down the cove, on the northern side, was the drydock. Its forward end was nosed into the bank, a Jap destroyer nestled high and dry inside. Just on the other side I could see the masts of Ohiro's ship. There wasn't a sign of life on either of them—their flags hadn't even been raised for the new day. If this had only been a Sunday, the irony would've been perfect.

Herring performed minor course corrections, keeping the bow pointing at the drydock. I watched the other PTs hold to the formation. When I looked back at Herring his hands were holding the wheel steady and his eyes were on mine. The range was eight hundred yards. I had no qualms about firing at this distance. Not only did we have enough light to see what we were shooting, the target was totally incapable of maneuvering. I bobbed my head.

Herring hit the buttons for the forward torpedoes and the fish exploded from their tubes. They hit the water just as he pressed the studs for the after Mark Eights. The other PTs were on the ball; there were four more flat bangs, then four more. Twelve torpedoes in the water, running straight and true. The .50-cal gunners started banging away, angling their barrels high in order to bring the lead onto the destroyers.

We continued at forty knots, our own torpedoes already falling well astern. A Mark Eight travels at only twenty-seven knots; they were of World War I vintage, originally designed to be launched from aircraft.

So far it had been a simple plan — now came the dicey part. It was impossible to turn around at this point, not with our own torpedoes behind us. We had to angle for the far side of the cove, let the Mark Eights continue on their course, then turn around and get the hell out, hopefully as the fish smacked home. I had briefed the skippers that at this stage they were to break formation; it was every man for himself until rendezvous back outside.

The drydocked destroyer was the first to wake up. Two machine guns opened up from a point just aft of her pilothouse and little geysers began to kick up around us. Herring put the PT into a steep bank to starboard and I held on tight. I could see men running on the Japs' decks and hear the clang-clang-clang of the call to battle stations. On Ohiro's destroyer—its stern was sticking out—I saw half-naked men clamber onto the after 4.7-incher.

I looked astern and all I saw was smoke; no sign of the other PTs at all. I looked to port and saw the wakes of eight torepedoes, still churning straight for their target. There was a crack from the 4.7-incher and a geyser exploded dead ahead.

Herring yanked the throttles to all stop and the PT immediately slowed. He pulled the throttles back and the boat shuddered fearfully, then the fantail pitched as our wake caught up. Suddenly we were engulfed in our own smoke screen, which suited me fine. I couldn't even make out the tip of our bow. The gunners kept their thumbs down on the firing bars, shooting blind. Herring spun the wheel hard to port, then drove all three throttles to the console. The PT shuddered again, then surged from the water and nosed around to port. This would be a fine time to meet up with another PT!

We roared along, shrouded in dense smoke, trusting to nothing. I wondered if the bullets flying over our heads were Jap or American. Herring had the boat pointing toward the mouth of the cove—or so I thought. We suddenly cleared the smoke screen and saw that Ohiro's destroyer was five hundred yards dead ahead. The Japs on the after battery spun elevating wheels furiously, ratcheting the muzzle of the 4.7-incher toward us. Herring began a frantic turn, intending to head back to the safety of the smoke screen.

I raised my binoculars and saw what I had prayed to see—Ohiro, shirtless and shoeless, standing on the bridge wing and screaming orders to his men. He saw us and raised his binoculars. Without thinking, I immediately tore the helmet from my head and raised my arms and waved.

"Here I am!" I screamed, *"Here I am, Ohiro!"*

I laughed as we roared back into the smoke. Herring looked at me as if I'd lost my mind.

There was a racketing detonation—the first torpedoes smacking home. Then more, close together; painfully loud blasts which stung my ears like the slap of a hand. The first bits of debris began cascading from the sky, chunks of steel and rubber and wood spinning through the gray smoke screen and landing all around. Something whizzed by my face—a bullet? shrapnel?—and I hunkered down, balling myself up. Stupidly but instinctively I locked my fingers over the top of my helmet. Suddenly my fingers felt wet and gooey and, feeling sick, I whipped them down and looked. They were splattered with blood.

There was no pain, but they say it takes a little time for that to catch up. I looked up at Herring and realized that the blood wasn't mine. It was his.

He was lying over the console, his cheek a mashed jumble of red where the bullet had gone in. His eyes were wide with the shock of sudden death, his mouth open for a scream that never came. I got up, grabbed his shoulder, shoved his body to the deck. I grabbed the wheel and—trusting to luck—hove to starboard. All around was thick, gray smoke.

We cleared the screen and I saw we were nearly out of the cove. I turned the bow to the southwestern edge of the cove's mouth and held the wheel steady. This course would take us through the smoke screen again.

I noted the course on the magnetic compass, then looked over my shoulder.

The drydock was on its side, the forward part resting in the shallow mud, the after part angling down into deeper water. The destroyer which had been inside was slipping out stern first, steel scraping against steel as she slowly slid along the interior. Both her smoke stacks had already snapped off, and black smoke churned and billowed skyward. I could just get a glimpse of Ohiro's ship—she looked to be sinking at her stern, the ship canted at a funny angle.

Then the smoke screen enveloped us again. I kept my eyes on the compass, holding the course that would take me out of the cove. There was the crack of a cannon—deeper-pitched than a 4.7; it had to be one of the shore-based 75mms, on the line at last.

The PT began pitching and slapping against the waves; that meant we were out of the calm waters of the cove. I held the course, and then we were in the dissipating screen we'd laid down when we first entered the cove.

The screen cleared and we were in the light of a beautifully sunny morning. I looked around and saw that close aboard to port—not by more than ten yards—was another PT, pounding along on the same course as mine. It was Nash's boat and I could see him at the helm, looking at me with as much surprise as I.

We immediately opened the distance between ourselves, then began an easy turn to port, heading along the reciprocal of the course we had taken up. Five hundred yards ahead was the other PT. To starboard I could see the other side of Subic Bay—and the puffs of smoke from the shore batteries that were trying their luck. The place had come alive like a nest of hornets, but too late, too late.

Keeping one hand on the wheel I picked up the radiotelephone and called for a status report. A shot landed dead ahead and I dropped the phone in order to heave away from the geyser. By the time I picked up the phone again the boats were coming in with their reports. Two dead, three wounded, altogether. We had gotten off light.

There was a noise behind me. It was the starboard gunner, out of his gun tub, throwing a blanket over the body of Lieutentant j.g. Herring. In the background I could see black smoke pouring from Binanga. I pressed the transmit button again.

"Make best speed back to homeplate. No formation, just keep in sight of one another." The PTs rogered and I cradled the handset.

Time for a smoke. My hands shook as I brought the flame to the cig. Jesus, we had really done it. We had gone into the lion's den and snatched away his meat. A hundred things could've gone wrong—one of the boats could've had engine trouble, some of the torpedoes could've misfired, we could've rammed each other in the dense smoke . . . but everything had gone all right. Somehow. As if my fervent desire for success had made it so.

I looked over my shoulder. Two sailors were bent over Herring. They had him snugged against the day cabin; there was a bloody smear on the deck where he'd been dragged. Herring had been a relatively new officer, reporting to the squadron last November. He had talked about his new wife . . .

"Norris," I called.

One of the sailors looked up. "Sir?"

"Get back on those fifties."

"We still at G.Q.?"

"Goddamn straight."

There was muffled chattering on the handset. I grabbed it and pressed it to my ear. Nash. *"Zeroes starboard quarter! Zeroes starboard quarter!"*

My knuckles whitened as I gripped the handset hard. The cigarette fell from my lips, forgotten. I turned.

Two of them, flying wingtip to wingtip, range eight thousand yards. They were low, skirting the water at one hundred feet. I pressed the transmit button. "Get away from the coast and start evasive maneuvers."

I didn't take time to recradle the handset; before it clanked to the deck I was spinning the wheel. The PT banked into a hard turn to starboard. Before me lay the South China Sea and all the elbow room I needed.

All three PTs were heading straight out from land; the Zeroes were coming in on our starboard beams, perpendicular to our course. The Zeroes broke at five thousand yards, one of them banking over to take me. He steadied on a point a little ahead of me, giving me enough lead so that I'd be in his sights when he pressed the button.

The PT pitched as I put her in another hard turn. For a moment we were pointing at each other nose to nose; that's when we both opened fire. I kept the boat in its turn, steadying when I was pointing back at the coast; too late for Zero to make a correction in his strafing run. His guns were silent as he screamed by, but my fifties and 20mm kept a constant stream of lead hammering at the silver blur.

The pilot yanked the Zero into a steep climb, the bright morning sun flashing off unpainted metal. I put the PT in another turn, my eyes on the sky. He rolled to the right and nosed into a power dive. I steadied the bow in his direction, waiting for him to commit himself to a stafing run. Down, down . . . then he began pulling out of the drive, deciding to take me on toe-to-toe. He leveled out a scant fifty feet from the deck and I saw machine gun fire blossom on his wings. I spun the wheel hard, making a tight forty-knot turn to port, getting the hell out of his line of fire. As soon as he saw my bow nose over he rolled the aircraft over, desperately trying to alter course. His wings were vertical as he screamed by, giving my guys a bigger target.

Over the sound of the Packards I heard my guys let go with a cheer. Smoke trailed from the Zero as he made another climb, a thick, greasy plum streaming from his engine cowling. He grabbed altitude, the smoke growing blacker and thicker. The Jap had a serious problem on his hands. Was he going to call it quits, or . . .

Up and up he climbed, far higher than he had gone before. What the hell was he doing? A column of smoke trailed up to a tiny, silvery speck directly overhead. Then he snapped over and pointed his nose straight down, heading right for us. He was going to have us, and it was quite literally the last thing he was going to do.

This was going to be tricky. I kept the wheel steady, heading in a straight line, my head thrown back as I kept my eyes glued to the Jap. Which way was he going to commit himself? His nose was aimed a little ahead of the PT, giving us enough lead for a perfect intercept. I pitched the boat over to starboard. He immediately rolled his wings, steadying on our new direction. I spun the wheel again. He corrected. His altitude was five hundred feet.

If I kept in a circle he'd have us for sure. I steadied up. He performed his last course correction, aiming for a point just ahead of us. Three hundred feet. I jammed the throttles to all stop, then pulled them back for full speed astern. The PT pitched forward steeply, every piece of the boat shuddering and vibrating. I crouched behind the console, my mind burning with the after-image of a blur of silver dead ahead.

There was an explosion and the PT pitched to port. Water rained down as I stood and yanked the throttles to neutral. There was so much spray I couldn't see. I eased the throttles up for ten knots. By the time rain turned to mist I saw that we had drawn up even with the Jap — the tail was sticking up out of the water, twenty yards off the starboard beam.

My guys took time for a savage cheer. I looked around, spotted the other PTs safe and sound. Zero number two was distant, his wings wobbling this way and that, engine sputtering and smoke trailing. He was heading back to the coast for an emergency landing. I picked up the radiotelephone.

Nash was the first to tie up to the pier. There was a crowd of sailors, waiting anxiously. I was working my PT alongside when I saw Nash leap off his boat and onto the dock. "Scratch two cans!" he shouted to the waiting sailors, "Scratch two Zeroes!" A thunderous chorus erupted.

As soon as I cut the engines Ensign Capillo scampered aboard. He was the officer we'd left behind to hold down the fort. "The admiral wants to see you, Mr. Leander."

"Fine. I'll get cleaned up."

The ensign's eyes were wide with fear. "Nossir! You can't ! He said right away, as soon as you got back. He sounded pissed off."

"Did he call on the radio?"

The ensign nodded, looking worried. "I've got a boat all ready to go. I told him you'd be on the way as soon as you got back."

I sighed. An admiral's tantrum is a distressing thing, especially to an ensign. Well, at least I had some good news. "Let's go. You driving?"

He nodded. We walked over to the 31, whose engines were already idling. The lines were cast off as soon as I stepped aboard. I watched Capillo work the boat away from the pier, then he shoveled on the coals.

I went to the bow and grabbed the lifeline, keeping my knees flexed as the PT pounded through the chop. I couldn't wipe the smile from my face. This had to be the most delicious moment of my life, and I was savoring every drop.

So PTs were nothing, eh? Putt-putt toys that weren't worth a shit. So who gets the first kill of the war while the big ships are off somewhere shaking in their boots?

My grin spread from ear to ear. I turned my face to the sun, loose khaki shirt snapping in the wind. My insides thrummed in fierce exultation. I felt an urge to dance, to cavort in a wild paroxysm of celebration, like a victory-crazed Zulu.

A battered jeep was waiting for me at Corregidor's North Dock. We bounced uphill and screeched to a halt near the entrance of the main tunnel. I walked into the gloom, went right, then left, got lost, and finally came to the rickety desk which was the admiral's office. It was piled high with stacks of paper, and I wondered what on earth could be in them. He looked at me with Olympian disdain as I eased my weary carcass into the supplicant's chair.

"Reporting as ordered, admiral."

He put his elbows on the desk and laced fingers under his chin. "Couldn't take time to get in a clean uniform?"

I looked down at my shirt. It was specked with Herring's blood. "They said you wanted to see me right away, sir."

"That's correct. The army's decided to transfer some personnel between here and Bataan, and they needed your boats." He raised an eyebrow. "Imagine my embarrassment when my aide informed me most of your squadron was off on a mission. I got on the radio myself and spoke with your Command Duty Officer, and he managed to confirm this little escapade."

"He had two boats at his disposal, admiral. He could've started that transfer right then."

"I doubt it, Mr. Leander. Your C.D.O. was so tongue-tied and balled-up I doubt if he could order himself to go to the little officer's bathroom. Was he even qualified to be a C.D.O? Did you hold a Qualification Board? I'll wager there's not even a letter of qualification in his service jacket."

What the hell can you say? And would a court-martial be worth it?

"Lieutenant, I thought I made it clear you were only to assist the Army. I didn't say anything about charging around as you please."

"I thought you said I was on my own."

He looked at me with blank astonishment. "What are you talking about? I didn't give you a blank check, Mr. Leander. I just wanted you to have enough flexibility to assist the Army without having to confirm those operations with me. But no. You have to bend my orders to the point of out-and-out disobedience. I assume you know what that means."

I spread my hands and sighed. "Admiral, would you like a briefing on what we did?"

The chair squeaked as he leaned back. He looked at me with regal disgust. "This had better be good, mister." He gripped the arms of his chair. "And I mean *very* good."

So I gave it to him, bit by bit. The ice in his eyes slowly melted, then widened with surprise and interest. He hiked himself forward to hear all the better. Then, in ultimate blessing, he began taking notes. When he asked me questions, it was an old friend helping me along. "So you shot down one Zero and disabled the other, eh? Interesting. That's contrary to doctrine — aircraft are supposed to have an easy time of PTs."

"That simply hasn't been the case, Admiral."

He nodded and scribbled. He had me go over the story again in detail. "This will all be in my post-op report, Admiral."

"Just make one for your squadron files, Buck. I want to make this report back to fleet as soon as possible."

We finished. The admiral walked with me through the tunnels, beaming at me with fatherly pride. "I'll run down with you to the piers, Buck."

"What about this personnel transfer, Admiral?"

He waved his hand, as if in dismissal of such a trifling concern. "Since you were coming here this afternoon anyway, I told the liaison officer to have one load ready. They should be there already. You can take care of the rest tomorrow. There's plenty of time, anyway — there's been an unexpected lull on the line."

"How so?"

"No engagements along the line for the past forty-eight hours. None at all."

We stepped into the sunlight and walked toward the admiral's jeep. A driver was already behind the wheel. We climbed aboard.

"Yes," the admiral continued, "We're finally in a really defensible position. The Japs have been slowed down."

"That's good to hear, sir."

"Lots of good news all of a sudden." He showed me all his pearly whites. "Lots of good news."

We bounced down the hill and pulled to a halt in front of the pier. A truck was alongside the PT, transferring medical supplies and . . . nurses.

The admiral walked with me to the boat. "The army's taking advantage of the lull to bring wounded back from Bataan. Some medical personnel are going over there to work in the field hospitals."

I nodded. My eyes were searching for Ginger.

The admiral was looking at the PT, smiling and nodding. " 'Give me a fast ship,' " he said, quoting John Paul Jones, " 'For I intend to go in harm's way.'

Right, Buck?"

"Right. By the way, sir. About my orders—"

"What orders?" His was a merry laugh. The admiral slapped me on the back. "For a hard-charger like you? You're on your own free and clear, Buck! Go get 'em!"

"Thank you, Admiral." I thought about asking him to put that in writing, but why spoil the magic moment?

The Packards suddenly coughed to life; the nurses and supplies were aboard. The admiral looked at the PT again, smiling beneficently. "You know, these scrappy little boats are really proving their worth here. I'll hammer that point home in my report. We need more PTs. They'll be useful in this war."

"Yes, sir. We need lots of PTs."

I saluted smartly. He snapped his off, grinning. I hopped aboard and the lines were loosened.

Ginger was on the bow, standing by herself. Her smile grew bigger as I approached, as did mine.

"Hello, Buck. Nice to see you again." The wind blew hair into her face; she shook her head, clearing it away.

"You look great, Ginger. You are really something."

"You flatter me, sir." She was wearing the formal army nurse rig, a skirt and blouse. Military clothes are always poorly tailored, but some kind soul in the War Department had specified that female outfits should be exceedingly tight.

Ginger looked at the coast of Bataan, one hand shading her eyes from the intense afternoon sun. "Last time I was over there was before the war."

"You make it sound like a million years ago."

She turned to me, brows knitted as if I'd just told her two and two made five thousand. "That's right.

115

The war started only last December. God," she laughed, shaking her head, "Seems like it's been going on forever, hasn't it? At first I couldn't believe it when it started. Then when the Japanese landed it seemed like I was in the middle of some kind of movie, like *Gone With the Wind*. It was exciting. Then all the wounded started coming in, and . . . "

She let the words die as her eyes glazed over. Then she turned those violet eyes on mine. "I talked with you about the morphine thing, right?"

"Yes."

She looked back at Bataan. "That's right. You were the one. I haven't had any since I talked with you on that hill. I feel a lot better."

"Nervous about going to Bataan?"

"The fighting's supposed to have stopped, hasn't it? We won't be there long, anyway."

"You don't . . . have any of that stuff with you?"

"No, no . . . I've really given it up. I'm going to make it without it."

I was standing close enough to get a whiff of her freshly-scrubbed aroma. It was intoxicating. That nurse's outfit clung to her curves like it was sprayed on. "When you're not too busy, how about dropping by the PT base for a visit?"

"I'd like that." The violet eyes looked into mine, then traveled down to my toes. Suddenly she put her hand to her mouth and laughed deeply, turning away.

I was puzzled, then . . . my face flushed hot and red as I realized that my pants bulged with an erection.

Chapter Eight

"I agree," Nash said. "gasoline's getting as precious as gold nuggets. But do you suggest we give up routine patrols entirely?"

We were sitting in my nipa shack, sweat dripping onto the conference table. It was hot as a lead skillet. "We've got plenty of diesel, right?"

Nash nodded.

"Then we'll use one of the LCMs for night patrols in Manila Bay. Fit her out with a couple fifties for protection, tell the crew to fire off a red flare if anything comes up."

"At that signal we'll send a PT out for assistance?"

"Right. One PT ready around the clock. Two more on a half-hour standby for heavy duty jobs. We've got five PTs altogether, so this gives us a margin of two extra."

Nash thought it over, then beamed and smiled. "Great, fine. I'll get to work on those watchbills for the patrol barges."

"What's the matter, John? No arguments? No whining and moaning? You feeling okay?"

He leaned back in his chair, acting like he'd eaten ten canaries. The heated words we exchanged prior to the drydock raid were now ancient history. "Things just seem to be going good all of a sudden." He spread his arms, looking as innocent as a bearded boy scout. "Can't we just sit back and bask in the PT's new-found glory?"

"As soon as we win the war."

He laughed. "The front's been quiet for three days now. That Jap General Homma is stymied up good. And I'm starting to believe that reinforcement story. And—" He leaned forward, putting his elbows on the table, "We took us down two good hunks of the Imperial Japanese Navy, didn't we? All by our little selves."

"*One*, John. Just one's confirmed. Nobody saw that can which wasn't in drydock go down."

"Confirm, consmerm. We cleared the seas in this neighborhood. That's what counts."

"You're getting cocky, John. We were goddamn lucky."

"Yeah," he said, standing, "Lucky. Anything else, Buck?"

I shook my head and he turned and left. Everyone was still enjoying the sweet smell of victory. Everyone . . . except me. And I couldn't figure out why. One minute I'm grinning ear to ear, the next I'm feeling let down. Why?

I got up and went to the window. The PTs were snugged against the pier, their forest green paint several shades lighter than when we'd first slapped it on. Everything I'd wanted for these boats had come true. They had proved themselves in combat. Had gone against destroyers and come out on top. They weren't toys.

And as for myself . . .

Let's face it. I wanted the whole Navy to know about Buckley Leander, the guy who threw away his career and found glory. It was a story to enthrall midshipmen. The troublemaker who all along was a hero.

Then why was I feeling so peculiar? So itchy?

I went back to my desk and sat, fished the dogtags from my pockets. I had to catch up on a lot of correspondence. Mail was still going out, thanks to an occasional visit to the Rock by a U.S. submarine. They brought in medical supplies, took out mail and the severely wounded. Both Ensign Oakey and Chief Turner were on that waiting list.

"Dear Mrs. Herring," I began writing, "By now the Navy Department has notified you that your husband Brian has been killed in action. As your husband's commanding officer, allow me to extend my most sincere condolences. Brian was a fine man, and—"

I stopped writing. I kept seeing Herring's smashed face splattered over a PT's console. I had dreamt about it last night and woken up in a cold sweat. Couldn't get back to sleep.

The field telephone jangled.

"M.T.B. Squadron Two," I said. It was my old pal Major Southworth.

"There's a landing going on behind our lines right now," he said, "We need you guys right away."

"How big a landing?"

"Seventy-five to one-hundred troops. They came in one of those landing craft."

119

"Any big ships protecting them?"

"None that I can see," he replied, "And it doesn't look like they've got any air cover, either. I think this was supposed to be more a commando raid than anything else."

"I take it they're not far inland, then?"

"We've still got them pinned down on the beach."

"Where?"

"Got your map handy?"

"Shoot."

"Right near Canas Point," he said, "About five hundred yards north, and dug in nice and tight. Know it?"

"Not that well, major. That's . . . " I paused to look at the chart. "That's not even really a beach, is it? More like a cliff."

"That's the problem. They're dug in on the side facing the sea. Seems like some of them are holed up in caves and the rest are on the ridge. I've got two companies pinning them down, but there's no way I can shake them loose. Savvy?"

"Got it. We're underway right now."

"See you in a while, lieutenant."

I hung up, grabbed a shirt, buttoned it as I ran out the shack. It was midday, and work had stopped for the men's repose. I trotted down to the pier. The boat at the end, PT 38, was ready-boat. Halfway down I circled my index finger over my head—the "wind her up" signal. The drowsing men on the other boats got to their elbows as I ran past. I hopped aboard the 38 just as the Packards coughed and sputtered.

The boat's skipper, Lieutenant j.g. Hokulani, came out of the charthouse rubbing sleep from his eyes.

"What's up, Mr. Leander?"

I grabbed his shoulder. "I need marksmen. Go to the weapons shack and bring me some gunner's mate. Find Lieutenant Nash."

He jumped off the boat and hit the pier running. He didn't have to look far for Nash; he was already barreling down the pier. Hokulani continued toward the weapons shack.

It took me five seconds to give Nash the wheres and whys. PT 38 would be underway shortly, and I wanted another PT following as soon as she was manned up. He gave me a thumbs-up and skipped over to his boat, the 41.

I turned to a huge gunner's mate, a grizzled career man who'd once been fleet boxing champion. We conferred on weapons status, ammo. All was as it should be. He threw his cigar over the side and bellowed for his men to take the canvas covers off the fifties.

I went to the cockpit. The tachometers showed the engines had smoothed out and were idling at the proper rpms. Temperatures looked good. Oil pressure fine. I looked back down the pier.

Hokulani was running back. In each meaty fist three Springfields dangled from their slings. Behind him were two sailors with six Springfields per. One of the sailors stopped at another boat, shouted something to its crew: marksmen.

I found I'd unconsciously put my hands on the throttles. I took them off, wiped the sweat on my shorts. The boat bobbed as Hokulani jumped aboard.

Guys from other boats crowded near the 38. Every one of them started coming aboard, but Hokulani restored order. He pointed to the men he wanted. Springfields were thrown from the pier and grabbed by sailors aboard the 38. Hokulani came forward.

"We're ready skipper," he said breathlessly. A minute had passed since I'd first come aboard. I nodded and again put my hands on the throttles. Hokulani's face fell. This was his boat, but I was commanding officer and therefore had the right to all the fun. But I'm a tender-hearted kind of guy, so I squeezed by and stood outside the cockpit, gesturing toward the wheel. He smiled as he slapped his mitts on the controls.

Hokulani looked forward, then aft. "Cast off!" he roared. The lines came aboard. One of the sailors on the pier sat down, put his feet against the bow, and shoved his legs forward. The boat moved from the pier as delicately as a butterfly. Hokulani pushed the port throttle slightly ahead, leaving starboard and centerline in neutral. The boat shuddered a little, then began nosing forward. We cleared the pier and Hokulani brought up the other two engines. Ten knots.

He turned to me with a grin. "Where to, boss?"

"Up the western coast of Bataan to Canas Point."

"What's the deal?"

"Fill you in after we get through the minefield."

He nodded and turned his attention to the waters ahead. I reached in my back pocket and withdrew the small harbor chart which showed the placement of our mines. I unfolded it and put it on the console.

Hokulani's eyes flickered from the chart to the waters ahead, looking for the landmarks and bearings he needed. Hokulani was a unique kind of guy, being the only native-born Hawaiian naval officer I'd ever met or even heard of. He was absolutely huge, and looked every bit the typical happy-go-lucky pineapple knocker you see roaming Waikiki. But he came from a family with plenty of money and pull, and when university time came his rich daddy said take your pick. He selected the Naval Academy.

Now one would think a brown-skinned guy would have more than his share of trouble in a joint like Annapolis, but he told me his only problem had been with academics. I once asked him about hazing. He said he'd had a little talk with the first upperclassman that had given him a hard time, and that had been the end of it. A talk? Hokulani had shrugged and said well, not exactly a *talk*.

Guardia Shoal was now dead abeam; we were out of the minefield. Hokulani looked at me questioningly.

"Come right," I said, "Hug the coast until we get to our turn."

"At Luzon Point, right?"

I nodded. "Then angle northwesterly. I want to come on Canas with at least two thousand yards between us and the beach. We're going to provide a little support for the Army. Japs are dug in there on the seaward side."

"Thirty knots okay, skipper?"

"Fine."

Hokulani shoved the throttles forward and the boat pitched upwards. It would be ten miles to the turn at Luzon Point, then another three until we arrived off Canas. A little less than a half-hour run.

It was a middling day. There was fifty per cent cloud cover—stratus—and far out into the South China Sea I could see a squall line marching across the horizon. Maybe it would reach us before the day was over.

Maybe not. I unrolled my shirtsleeves and buttoned them at the wrist.

The PT slammed through the waves, shuddering as it smacked the water, smoothing out until we flew up and over the next swell. One thing about PTs; they aren't pleasure craft. Half the damn boat is engine room. And they are designed from the keel up to take punishment, the hull heavily braced for the stress of high speed.

Salt water sprayed across the bow and stung my face like a swarm of hornets. Hokulani didn't bother to wipe the drops from his face. I could hear his laughter over the roar of the engines. "I love it!" he shouted, "Love it! Give me more!" he told the sea, "Pour it on!"

Morale had been high indeed of late. Surely, everyone thought, the next submarine would bring reporters from *Life* magazine and we'd get the fame we deserved. The young guys held their backs straighter, following Lieutenant Nash's cocksure lead. The old guys knew what they had on their hands — and couldn't wait for the fleet to return so they could meet in the bars of Manila and make sure the big-ship sailors knew who held down the fort while they were gone.

I looked aft. The other PT had just rounded Cochinos Point. Water churned so thickly around her bow I knew she was pushing better than our thirty.

Water fanned over my head, crashed onto the day cabin and sprayed the sailors gathered on the fantail. I could hear their laughter. Quite a difference from the dead quiet that had preceded our other missions. A festive mood was in the air. It was a grand day, and we were going to grease some Japs. What more could a man ask for?

But I couldn't join in on the fun. I felt no excitement, nor did I feel any fear. It was crazy, but I felt now that the PTs had been proven . . . somehow my job was over. I felt strangely out of place, like an imposter.

I knelt behind the cockpit. It took five spins on the Zippo to get my Lucky going. Then I noticed something which I had only heard about. Hokulani had indeed removed the cockpit's armor plating. He wanted no more protection than had any other man on the boat. His was a tight crew, maybe the tightest in the whole squadron. And jolly. Back when we had lots of food it was not unknown to see Hokulani and his men having a cookout topside. And drinking a little illicit booze, to which I had looked the other way. Now that I thought on it I could use a drink myself. I couldn't shake the feeling that the party was over.

Picture the White Cliffs of Dover in quarter-scale. Add some caves. That's what Canas Point looked like.

Hokulani put us right where I wanted to be, two thousand yards off the beach, broadside-to. I told him to go dead in the water. He pulled the throttles back slowly and the Packards whined down to an uneven burbling. Hokulani handed me his spare binoculars. We scanned the bluffs.

The Jap landing craft was beached between rocks and was unmanned. It was the Type A, a flimsy rig forty-nine feet long with an eleven-foot beam. It looked somewhat like an American LCVP, though bigger and cheaper. It had an oriental touch: the hull line curved up fore and aft, like the corners of a roof on a Japanese building. Choked to the gills it could carry up to 120 men. Its two .25-caliber machine guns had been taken from their mounts and were probably being employed in the action topside. Nobody was on the beach except for a half-dozen stiffs.

I moved my binoculars up. The climb from the beach to the top of the cliffs was fifty feet. The cliff wasn't all that steep. A string of Japs were lined along the top of the ridge, prone, firing into the jungle. And they had reserves aplenty, couched on the ledges below, sitting at the mouths of the shallow caves. The caves seemed to be bare indentations in the cliffs, certainly not deep enough to offer protection from our guns. The major's estimate of one hundred troops seemed to be right on the nose.

The Japs were dug in nice and tight. It was going to cost the major plenty to take them as is. His call for our help had been the right thing to do. As I watched a Jap threw up his arms and went tumbling down the cliff. A guy from the ledge below immediately climbed up and took his place.

I turned around just in time to see PT 41 slowing down. Her engines cut to neutral and she coasted alongside. Lieutenant Nash hopped aboard. The 41 continued on ahead.

Nash joined us in the cockpit. He asked if there was any particular way I wanted to do the job. It seemed pretty damn obvious: work the Japs over with the fifties, then close in to pick off the survivors with Springfields. Duck soup, right? Right. Nash went portside and waved his arms. The 41 put on a little power, came about, and Nash jumped back aboard.

We maneuvered to within fifteen-hundred yards of

the beach. You have to angle your fifties high at that range, but you can blanket the lead with reasonable accuracy.

Hokulani had the 38 at five knots, parallel to the beach, starboard side to. Six hundred yards ahead of our bow was the 41 boat, driving slowly at us, portside to the beach.

We commenced fire.

The first cracks of the fifties were as loud as a yacht race's starting cannon. Then it seemed like my ears slammed tight, the sharp highs eliminated as the world became a pounding, deafening roar. The deck hummed and vibrated as the fifties jackhammered against their mounts. I brought my binoculars up and watched the tracers—visible even in the daylight—arc to the beach, then begin swaying up the bluff. As if the gunners were using a garden hose to bring water to a particular spot. Dirt exploded in powdery geysers around the shallow caves, puffing so thickly I could barely see the Japs double over in their death throes.

I looked around the boat. A man lay prone on the fo'c'sle, a Browning automatic rifle kicking against his shoulder. The starboard gunner had found his range and was walking the lead back and forth across the ridge. The port gunner had also found his sweet spot and was working the caves one by one. The 20mm gunner back aft was having a little trouble putting them right where he wanted it, but the sheer volume of his fire was enough to cancel out inaccuracies, as evidenced by the splintered remains of the Jap landing barge. A couple guys were atop the day cabin taking pot-shots with their Springfields. A wiry boy was next to me, leaning his rifle over the charthouse. His weapon had a scope — of the twenty Springfields in our weapons locker four had telescopic sights.

I watched the sharpshooter take careful aim. Adams was his name, a North Carolinian who never made it past the sixth grade. His cowlick wavered in the breeze; his forehead lined in concentration. The shot came suddenly, sounding like a cap gun. Adams kept the same posture, continuing to sight down the scope. Finally he eased back, snapping the bolt. "Got him," he said mildly.

Hokulani called a cease-fire as the 41 passed in front of our field of fire. I noticed that someone on the 41 had brought a field machine gun, a .50, from God knows where and had set it up on her bow. Adams took time to wipe his forehead. The 41's stern finally slipped by, then it was back to the chuck wagon for seconds.

It was a fine old time, a turkey shoot; sailors not occupied in the firing walked about the boat casually, cigarettes dangling from their mouths, making idle comments to the gunners. Some of the Japs were actually firing at us, but at this range their rifles were pitifully inaccurate. We could've been on a firing range, killing time with an afternoon's practice shoot.

I scanned the ridge. I thought I'd laugh when I finally had the Japs where I wanted them, but the laughter caught in my throat and the food in my stomach went sour. This was about as much fun as watching the inner workings of a slaughterhouse.

I could see no cover big enough to entirely protect a man. The U.S. and Filipino troops in the jungle were carefully advancing, laying down continuous fire, more than keeping the pressure on from the landward side. Jap bodies bounced down the bluff, arms and legs splayed wide. The heap at the bottom was growing bigger.

But I'll say this. Even in the midst of this massacre the Japs kept fighting as if they could somehow turn the tide. None of them bunched up in little balls to try and hide. None looked desperately for an escape. They looked like they were getting ready to charge.

We eased nearer the beach, held steady at eight hundred yards. Springfield range.

The spectacle was sickening. Maybe it was the letter I'd been writing to Herring's widow, but some door in my mind opened up and my mind began to flood with raw, butcher-house images of death. The pulp of a face mashed by a bullet. A kid wheezing out his last bloody breaths as he tries to hold in his slimy intestines. A body jerking and bouncing against the sides of a gun tub as slugs drill through the lifeless torso.

I rubbed my hands against my eyes. What was coming over me? All of a sudden I wanted to be anywhere but here.

I pressed the binoculars to my eyes. Down to a dozen. Good. It would soon be over. My binocs locked onto their officer, a young guy with a sword. His jacket was in shreds and he was covered with dirt and blood. I felt sorry for the bastard. The last thing he'd ever know would be the utter destruction of his first command. He looked to the right and left, desperately trying to figure out what to do. His men were dropping like flies, staggering on bloody legs, slipping in their own gore. One guy grabbed the officer's arm and held on, saying something, then dropped and rolled downhill. The young officer watched his comrade hit bottom, his eyes wide and mouth hanging open in disbelief. What was he going to do? Summon his men for one last glorious *banzai*? Beg for quarter? Talk about raw drama, this was bare-bones as you could get. The officer pressed his pistol against his temple and closed his eyes tight. I sucked in my breath. His head snapped sideways with sudden force.

That did it. I took two steps to the far side of the boat, got on my knees, heaved breakfast over the side.

By the time I'd finished Hokulani had called a cease fire. The popping of small arms drifted from the beach; our troops would be coming over the ridge now, eager to adminsiter the *coup de grace*. I brought up the back of my hand and wiped away the slop. All I could think of was Ohiro Kagemaru. Had he gone into the army it might have been *him* on that ridge . . .

I looked seaward, toward the horizon, feeling dizzy and sweaty. The squall line had moved closer, now no more than three miles distant. It was dark and purple underneath the neat row of clouds, and—

My whole body tensed as I made out, within the rain, the shadowy outlines of vessels.

I was on my feet instantly. I called to Hokulani and pointed at the shapes. His eyes grew wide.

"C'mon! I yelled, "Let's go!"

He used one massive hand to push the throttles forward, the other to spin the wheel. We were pointing at the vessels by the time the stern had dug in deep. I rushed to Hokulani's side. My guts thrummed with excitement. Fighting ships, now this was different! This was more like it! The other men had turned to see what was happening, the older ones already staring at the ships in the squall line.

I looked over at the 41 boat. As soon as we roared off they knew something was up, and presently white foam churned from her bow as she put on speed. Nash was the sort to figure out things on his own.

The ships came out of the rain; more barges, and a small escort ship of some sort. They were the calvalry . . . but too late to help their buds. I brought up the binoculars.

Three landing craft, same type as before, and every one choked with troops. Their escort was . . . destroyer-shaped but much smaller, single stacked . . . a minesweeper. Two 4.7-inchers, one forward, one aft. The minesweeper was in the lead, the landing craft trailing aft but not directly astern.

We were coming in on her starboard bow and Nash was coming in on her port. The .50-caliber gunners hammered away at her bridge and I could see sparks fly where lead ricocheted off the fo'c'sle.

We were two thousand yards away when she opened up, and she went for PT 41. Smoke erupted from her 4.7-incher and an instant later I heard its report. The shot landed well astern of Nash. A machine gunner on top of the minesweeper's pilothouse aimed right at us.

I crouched as the lead punched into the charthouse. I yelled at Hokulani, telling him that when I said to fire, I wanted two torpedoes only, not all four. He nodded. Hokulani reached up and grabbed a cable near the console and yanked hard—it was a jerry-rig he'd made, a cable which energized the smoke-screen generator from the cockpit. Nice idea.

The Jap gunner lost his range. Hokulani and I stood.

Another shell splashed near PT 41, this right in

131

front of her and much nearer than before. Nash was eight hundred yards from the minesweeper when both of his forward torpedoes shot from their tubes. He veered away as the fish splashed.

Then the 4.7-inch round caught the 41 right along her port side, stopping the PT in a disintegrating mass of plywood, armor plating, and meat.

We closed to five hundred yards and the target angle looked good. Hokulani had his eyes on mine. I bobbed my head. He pressed the firing studs.

The deck shook as the torpedoes lurched from their tubes. Hokulani spun the wheel hard to port and the boat banked into the turn. We roared down the minesweeper's side, the fifties pouring lead into the superstructure, the smoke generator billowing a thick black cloud astern.

Hokulani kept the wheel to the stops, bringing the circle short of the landing craft. They fired at us as we screamed by. We laid a smoke screen between them and the beach.

I had my eyes on the minesweeper when she went up. Two torpedoes — who knows whether they were ours or the 41's? — smacked somewhere amidships. The bow lifted out of the water and the stack vaporized in a geyser of flame. The bow was about to crash back down when another explosion sent it up again. The fantail suddenly lifted; the ship had been neatly snapped in two amidships.

We continued the wide circle, heading to the spot where bits of PT 41 were scattered on the water. The landing craft were now hidden in the smoke, so the gunners gave their weapons a break. Smoke from the minesweeper's explosion rose skyward and fanned wide. The whole area became hazy.

We slowed as we neared the wreckage. There were survivors, but the number was far less than had mustered on that boat. I went to the side. This was going to be a hurry-up rescue.

It turned out there were only four. Nash was in the water, cursing me, cursing the Japs, cursing God. I hoisted him aboard. " 'bout time," he sputtered.

The wind had blown the smoke in our direction, wrapping us up in a dense fog. I couldn't see the remains of the minesweeper, but I heard the last of her magazine going off. Small arms fire came from all directions; the troops in the barges were shooting blind. Gentle rain began to fall; the squall was almost upon us.

"Okay," I yelled to Hokulani, "That's everybody. Let's go."

He slowly pushed the throttles forward. We began picking up speed, driving through the curtain of thick gray smoke. I knelt next to Nash and offered him a cigarette. He took the butt and angrily ripped it in two.

There was a loud, flat *boom* and I sprawled forward. I looked to the bow and saw the landing barge we'd run into — *brother! What a time for a collison!* The landing craft bounced and scraped against the bow, and while we had our half-second of total surprise the Japs took the initiative. The soldiers let out hoarse banzais as they clambered aboard.

Maybe a dozen of them made it before Hokulani yanked the throttles and backed down with full power. Jap Johnny-come-latelys fell into the ever-widening gap, some of them making desperate leaps at our retreating boat. I got to my knees and reached for the .45 in my holster. I had it halfway out when the biggest bastard in the history of Japan slammed into me and pinned me to the deck.

The guy must've been a goddamn sumo wrestler! The fingers around my throat felt like a steel vise. My left hand was clasped around his other wrist, fighting a losing battle with the Nambu pistol whose muzzle was inching to my skull. His face was so close I could smell fish on his stinking breath and count the hairs on his week-old beard. He grunted as he forced the pistol ever nearer, intending to blow out my brains if he didn't first yank off my head.

My right hand was wedged between us, jammed under the awesome weight of the Jap. The world began to swim with black dots and the enormous bore of the cheap pistol moved ever nearer. I wormed the .45 all the way from its holster and nudged it into the Jap's fat belly. *Christ—was there a round in the chamber?* My thumb found the hammer and pulled it back. I jerked the trigger.

The weight was suddenly gone. The Jap flew backwards, a stream of blood pouring from the black hole in his stomach. He landed upright, sitting on his butt, bellowing like a wounded bull. I sat up fast, brought the sights to his screaming face, and the pistol jacked in my hand. His head exploded into bits of flying brains and bone, and his body cartwheeled overboard.

I stood, laboring to suck air down my throat. The PT was still going full astern; the landing barge had slipped back into the smoke and was no longer visible. Hokulani was too busy to drive; he had a Jap laid over the console, his two giant hands squeezing tight on the yellow throat, his victims's eyes bulging from his head.

I looked around. The North Carolinian was backed up against the day cabin, and his scream was high-pitched and terrible as a bayonet slid in his guts. I aimed for his attacker's head and my shot bounced off his helmet. The Jap staggered away, his rifle's bayonet dripping with Adams' blood. I popped off another round and the force of it took the Jap off his feet and over the side.

Another Jap came running at me, bayonet leveled, and I instinctively fired at the long blade. The broken rifle snapped from his hands and he stopped short. He looked at me with disbelief, mouth hanging open, utterly surprised. I aimed at his chest and squeezed the trigger. He doubled up and rolled overboard in a backward somersault.

Hokulani lifted his Jap on high and tossed him in the water. He grabbed the throttles and jerked them to neutral.

Then it was suddenly over. I rushed to Hokulani's side and told him to get us clear of the smoke. He shoved the throttles forward.

Nash came up, his eyes round and his mouth hanging open, a Jap army knife clenched in his hand. He started to speak but I impatiently waved for silence. My blood was running high and hot, hammering through my veins like a racehorse. I was ready now to go to work on those landing craft, ready to laugh while the Japs begged for mercy, ready to watch hot lead rip and tear into their stinking yellow flesh.

I looked around the boat. Some men were dead. Some were wounded. The ones standing had tight lips and narrow eyes, and they were searching the waters for Japs. I thought it was a goddamn shame we didn't have cutlasses to pass around; they were a lot more personal than bullets.

We cleared the smoke and soon found the barge that had run into us. Its top speed was ten knots and its armament consisted of two light machine guns — a joke in the face of what we had to offer. We circled her, eating her up with the fifties and 20mm. They might as well have been using pea shooters against us. This time my tum-tum wasn't so queasy about the job. My heart was as hard and cruel as a cobra's, and my only joy was to see more and more Japanese floating face down in an ever-widening pool of blood and intestines.

The barge took a full five minutes to dispose of. Then we went looking for the other two, making a wide circle around the debris of the minesweeper.

It didn't take long to find them, and when we did the sailors let go with a savage cheer and hurried to lock and load. The Japs used their machine guns and rifles to fend us off, an attempt as sad as a wagon train of tenderfoots fighting the entire Indian nation.

But these landing craft were tougher nuts to crack. Their sides were armored. So I discovered another use for the depth charges: make a high speed run past your target, let the charge roll over the side as you pass, then turn away.

The results were most satisfactory.

Chapter Nine

As soon as we tied up I wobbled over to my nipa shack and slammed myself into the rack. I felt drained, more tired than if I'd been wrestling a grizzly bare-handed. My blood-lust had completely subsided on the trip back, drying up my emotions with such finality I thought I'd never laugh nor cry again; indeed, the loss of the men who'd gone down with the 41 was something that affected me not at all. My nostrils filled with the sweet smell of the cot's rotting canvas. Sleep swallowed me up like a hungry cyclops.

But I was not to enjoy the sleep of tender innocence. My dreams put me right back on the boats, into a dreamscape of silvery water and blinding sun. I was listening to the men laugh and joke and horse around as we sailed to some unknown assignment. Morale was high and the men invited me to join in on the fun and good times. There was more laughing and hearty back slapping, but whenever they looked me in the eyes I saw suspicion and distrust, as if they wanted to say *who shall die today, lieutenant? Which ones have you selected?* And the flesh melted from their faces and their grins were the grins of skulls.

Then I was all alone, standing in a PT's cockpit, gliding through a hundred bodies floating face down. Japs. Americans. Guts spreading in an ever-increasing stain. I spun the wheel and yanked the throttles but the PT had a mind of its own. Bodies bumped against the hull, then were ground into bloody hamburger by the hungry screws.

Two wet hands suddenly slapped onto the gunwales, and I watched a grinning corpse heave itself aboard. It was the Jap I'd shot point-blank. There was a big hole in his belly, and his face . . . his face . . .

I tossed and moaned until finally, covered with sweat and shivering, I bolted awake. I rubbed my eyes as I swung my feet to the deck. The last part about the Jap . . . everything about it was so clear and vivid. I could even remember what his collar tabs looked like. Red with yellow horizontal lines. Two stars. The guy had been a sergeant.

There were distant rumbles of thunder.

My watch and a deck of smokes were on the desk. I picked them up, noting that it was a little past 0300. The rain beat the roof with a comforting staccato, and when I listened hard enough I could pick up the broken drumming of small arms fire. The front line was close indeed. Patrols on both sides were mixing it up—small stuff—but the Jap's main thrust was still mired. I fired up a Lucky.

When we sank those last landing craft I had been glad. But that was temporary emotion, brought on by the heat of the moment. Now I realized my tum-tum *had* been queasy about the job. And it was queasy now.

138

I thought about how I felt when I was leading that raid into Binanga, and it seemed like that Buck Leander was another man, a stranger. A lunatic, when you got down to it. A fool who gambled some very high stakes indeed just to prove that he and his PTs were some-bodies.

Well, the point had been made. Two Japanese destroyers were disabled. The admiral had given me an offical slap on the back. So what did I want to do now?

Get the hell out of this crazy bughouse, that's what. This kid didn't have it in him for the long haul, not for the workaday killing the rest of this war would surely entail. I wasn't such a tough guy after all.

I got up and went to the window. The black shape of Corregidor lay across the water, barely visible. One day soon a flotilla of American troops would sail through these waters and the Philippines would be saved. Help from the good old U.S.A.

Wish it was happening now.

The rain softened to a drizzle and the thunder grew more distant. The machine gun fire continued un-abated. I wondered how Lieutenant Kagemaru was making out. Had he been wounded during that raid? Killed, even? I took one last drag on the butt and snapped it into the rain. Maybe there would be a day when we'd meet again, the war over, and discuss who'd gotten the better of whom. Maybe. I hoped so. I smiled, recalling that day in Hollywood we'd spent together. Over in Corregidor there's a print of the movie he was an extra in. *War Cry of the Prairie* it's called, a typically boring western. His bit lasts two seconds. I'd never told anyone who that extra was, and

I don't think I ever will. Who'd believe it?

The rain stopped. I put on my clodhoppers and walked outside. The air smelled sweet and fresh and felt good against my bare chest. I clomped over to the pier. Four boats were tied up, all that were left. PT 38 had a nice gash where the Jap landing craft had run into her, but it was well above the waterline—the problem was purely cosmetic.

There was a big empty spot where the 41 used to park. Back in the makeshift barracks there were six empty racks.

Nash was taking it hard. By the time we got back home he was a different man. He had drawn into himself, and whenever I tried to talk to him he'd shake his head and look away. He shivered but tried to hide it. I saw what he would look like when he was an old man, all fire and juice gone.

I walked to the boat at the end. It was PT 22, a Higgins seventy-eight. She was ready-boat. Two sailors were sitting topside, watching for the flare which would signal trouble.

"Morning," I said.

They greeted me warmly, asked if I wanted coffee. Did I ever. I stepped aboard and took the steaming cup. The sailors and I chatted for a while. They were nice kids, draftees. A completely different breed than the career guys. A little sloppy in the military department, but they turned-to readily enough.

They wanted to know what was on deck come morning. I said I planned on taking two boats a little way up the coast to see if any more landing craft were about. One guy said his boss—Strip Cunningham, the motormac—had been wondering when a boat could be spared to run over to the *Canopus*, the repair ship, to pick up an overhauled Packard. No reason why it couldn't be done first thing come daylight. I made a mental addition to things I wanted to do today.

I left the boat just as the eastern clouds were turning iron. The base would soon be coming alive. I felt much better than when I'd woken up. Yes, much better. Take the day as it comes, I told myself. That's the way to get through this war.

The field telephone rang as I was opening a tin of dry salmon. My stomach suddenly shriveled to nothing. Another mission.

"Is this Lieutenant Leander?" It was a woman's voice. Ginger to be exact. She was calling from a field hospital.

"Maybe we could get together?" she asked, "There's a couple other kids here who're sick of army chow, too." Women asking men for a date, an aspect of war that was not unwelcome. I invited her to the PT base for dinner, and any other nurses she could bring would be especially welcome. I hung up feeling better than good. Elated.

The U.S.S. *Canopus* was designed as submarine tender, but her repair shops could handle any job the remaining vessels in the Philippines required.

She'd suffered quite a few air attacks. Right after the navy base at Cavite was bombed she steamed over here to Mariveles and covered up with jungle camouflage. This didn't save her from an armor-piercing bomb which went through every deck and exploded on top of the propeller shaft. By all rights she should've gone down then and there, but sharp damage control saved her.

Her skipper, Commander Sackett, had some ballast tanks flooded and purposely set a severe list to starboard. He had his cargo booms angled in crazy directions. When the next wave of Jap bombers came by he had fires set from oily rags in smudge pots, and, from the air, the *Canopus* looked like a derelict. The ruse worked.

Two boats cruised from the PT base at first light. It's a short run from the base to Mariveles, less than half an hour, including cast-off and tie-up. I rode along in the 22, and the other boat, the 31, was the one which had its centerline engine out for overhaul.

Strip and I clambered up the *Canopus*' Jacob's ladder and went to the engine shop. Strip examined the overhauled Packard carefully; no quick look-see for him. When he pulled a hand-held tachometer from his back pocket and demanded a bench test I decided to go topside for a smoke.

I ran into Lieutenant Robinson, skipper of one of the two remaining minesweepers. His ship was alongside for a complicated repair job.

"Main condenser's salting up," he said sourly. We were leaning on the railing facing Bataan. Robinson and I were classmates; he'd been an upperclassman while I was still a plebe, back in those miserable days. But he'd been one of the merciful ones.

"You heard the latest?" Robinson asked. I shook my head.

He smiled. "There's been an air raid on Tokyo."

"You're kidding!"

"Nope. B-25s launched from a carrier."

"That's incredible. That's fantastic!"

He shrugged, as if unimpressed, but he was still smiling. "I don't think the Japs are going to roll over, but it's sure going to shake things up."

I slapped my hand against the rail. "The Japs are stretched way too thin; otherwise a flight of B-25s would've never gotten through to damn Tokyo. They're going to have to pull back and consolidate what they've got." I rubbed my jaw, feeling the blond stubble. "Maybe they were already doing that — think that's why General Homma slowed down? Second thoughts from on high?"

Robinson spat over the side. "Why should they stop? A lull is a lull — these things always happen in drawn-out battles. The ball could start rolling again anytime."

"Think so?"

He knitted his brows, looking at me as if I weren't catching on. "Didn't they teach you to expect the worst at the Academy? Goddamn, the biggest shock I have is when things go right."

And Robinson showed me just how prudent he was. He outlined his plans. If Bataan fell, he was going to take his minesweeper and make a run for it. Australia's nearest port was Darwin, eleven hundred miles to the south. He felt sure he could make it.

"It's either that or hiding in the hills here." He patted his holstered .45., a weapon which had some sort of engraving on the grip. "See this? No prison camps for this boy. No way."

"Naval Academy was enough for you, then?"

Robinson laughed. "Bet your life, Buck. Life may be sweet, but it ain't sweet enough for what the Japs have in store for their captives."

A sailor came walking toward us. "Mr. Leander? Boat's ready."

"Great. Be along in a minute." I turned to Robinson. "Care to come along for a ride? We're patrolling up the coast a little way."

"What do you think I am? Crazy?" And yet he followed as I made my way to the PTs. "I'd rather go in a rowboat against a battleship."

We came to where the PTs were nested. "Suit yourself," I said. I swung over the side, grabbed the first rungs on the Jacob's ladder.

"I heard about that weinie roast you had up in Binanga," he said, "You going after cans again?"

"Naw." I gave him a big grin. "We cleaned 'em out."

He rubbed his jaw. Then he smiled and slapped his worn leather holster. "Why not? Watching some Japs die might hit the spot. Let's go."

I descended awkwardly, the ladder swaying wildly as I climbed down. Robinson's shoes were on the rung just above my head. The PTs below coughed to life.

"You seem fond of that Colt," I called up.

"Stole it in San Diego. Knew it'd come in handy some day."

I dropped to the deck. I held the ladder taut as Robinson eased himself down.

"Got a name for it?" I asked.

"Betsy." He stepped on deck and unholstered the pistol. "Look at this. Had a jeweler in Singapore fix it up." Not only was the butt engraved, a scene had been worked into the slide. It was highly pornographic. Robingson smiled at it fondly. "In commemoration of my first lay."

"First one, eh? I see you were already into the fancy

stuff."

"Yep." He reholstered it and looked around the boat. "So this is it, huh?"

I smiled proudly. "This is it."

Second thoughts were starting to work across his face. "Seems kind of small."

I chuckled at his discomfiture as we cast off. The deck lurched forward as speed was put on, and we grabbed the railing on top of the day cabin to hold ourselves upright. The PT quickly drew away from the *Canopus*.

I turned my face to the sun and felt the heat press against my face. It was a fine day. I knew that I'd awakened early this morning, sweating from some horrible nightmare. What was it?

The main reason I wanted to go up the coast was for closer examination of possible landing sites. Yesterday's attempt worried me. If it was just a raiding party, like Major Southworth said, that would've been okay. But if the Japs were gearing up for a major waterborne sidestep of the front line, that meant big trouble. I was glad of Robinson's presence, for he'd actually studied amphibious warfare at the Academy. Not that there was much to study; amphibious assaults, in modern times, were rare and difficult to pull off. The Japs' successes in this area were unexpected, like so many of their other triumphs.

We cruised north, keeping two miles off the coast. The boats kept within two hundred yards of one another. Robinson and I parked our cans on the fo'c'sle, scanning the coast with binoculars. The western coast of Bataan slid by, an uninviting vista of thick jungle, mud beaches, stubby cliffs. But my binoculars kept slipping up to the clouds, and in their puffy folds I saw violet eyes looking into mine, full lips parting in slow invitation, a warm, voluptuous body ready to press against mine.

So it was Robinson who first spotted the Jap. I swung my binoculars to where he pointed. It bobbed on a swell and was gone. Then it appeared again. Very low silhouette. A landing craft.

I went to the cockpit and told the helmsman to jack it up to thirty. I pulled the radio handset from its clips and told the other boat to stick to small arms; no torpedoes.

The PT pounded and lurched through the chop as we picked up speed. Salt water fanned over the bow, drenching everyone topside. The gunners charged their fifties. Helmets were strapped on tight. There was an alarm button for general quarters, but I didn't press it. The men had gone on alert silently and quickly. We were all getting to be old hands at this, even the young guys. I was pleased.

We bore down on the landing craft like jaguars after an old man. The Japs didn't know what was up until we were on top of them and booming the fifties into their surprised faces. The clumsy vessel began a slow turn back to the beach.

We screamed along the windward side of the Jap, the combined power of eight .50-caliber barrels laying it square into the bucket. That should've done it right there, but the bullets ricocheted straight up and off the craft. Armored sides again. Well, we had something else up our sleeves. Two guys went aft to arm the depth charges.

We came about and were boring in for our next run. The return fire from the landing craft was light, very light. Just seemed like her two .25s were on the line, a snarling *tat-tat-tat* against our throaty *bub-bub-bub*.

We were three hundred yards away when I saw tracers from PT 30 march right into the landing craft's fuel tanks. There was a brief but loud explosion, and black smoke billowed upward. She was still afloat.

I got on the radio and told the 30 to lay off while PT 22 went in to investigate. The depth charge run was off. Robinson and I stood side by side, .45s drawn, slowly nearing the Jap.

Then, suddenly, I began to wonder what the hell I was doing here, acting like some kine of damn cowboy. The details of my nightmare came back, full force. My heart began to hammer; I took in deep gulps of air, hissed it out through clenched teeth.

Back off, I thought. Tell the helmsman to back off and we'll finish this barge with a torpedo. I looked back at the cockpit, licking my lips. I couldn't. Not now. Not in front of the guys. I turned back to the Jap, gripping the .45 so tight my knuckles turned white.

She was coasting along, trailing an enormous cloud of black smoke. I couldn't see anyone in her. I motioned for the helmsman to pull alongside.

We drew to within ten feet. Then I saw a shape at the landing craft's wheel, and the vessel began to nose right into us. The helmsman backed down hard, and we had inches to spare from the Jap's suicide-ram. Fiesty devils!

There were some grenades handy. I grabbed some and shared them with Robinson. The helmsman put her in forward, and the PT glided to within fifteen yards. Don't think about anything, I told myself, just do what has to be done. I convinced myself that my heart was racing with excitement, not fear. Robinson and I lofted the pineapples. Three landed in the craft's well. There were short, huffing explosions, bam, bam, bam, and the smell of burnt powder filled the air. I told the helmsman to bring us back alongside.

My guest and I went to the fo'c'sle and made ourselves ready. When we were close enough to jump aboard we did. We landed in a foot-deep muck of oil and blood. The water was coming in fast; there was a crack along her starboard side. There were four Japs at the far end of the well. Two were dead. One was severely wounded. The other, an officer, seemed unscathed. When he saw us hop aboard his mouth went slack. Robinson aimed his pistol. The officer threw up his hands and came crawling through the water on his knees. *"Me surrender!"* he screamed, *"Me surrender!"*

Robinson's trigger finger whitened with pressure. "Don't!" I said. The word came out before I knew it. Robinson eased off and looked at me. "He's an officer," I said hurriedly, "They'll want him for interrogation."

"Aw, I wasn't going to shoot him. I just liked the way he begged." He waded to the Jap, grabbed him by the shoulder and jammed Betsy in his ear. "Come along, handsome. This is your lucky day."

Two sailors jumped aboard and I showed them the Jap that was barely alive. They tied a line under his arms and roughly hauled him aboard the PT. I continued to wade through the mess, looking for papers, maps, anything of importance. I found two sheets of gummy paper, each bearing a list of delicately-written

Japanese characters. A muster list?

The water was to my waist by the time I decided to leave. I sloshed to the side and grabbed the hands of sailors leaning over the side.

We pulled away slowly. When the craft finally sank I told the helmsman to head back for the barn.

I told the radioman to get on the air and tell the army where we'd gotten the landing craft. Since the craft was empty, that meant it had already discharged its troops behind our lines. Then I went to the fantail, there to examine my prisoners.

The Jap captain was on his knees. His eyes were tightly closed, as if in the midst of some ritual meditation.

"He's waiting for us to finish him off," Robinson said disgustedly, "And here I stand with a .45, ready to go. A dream come true, eh?" He holstered the pistol. " 'Course, I guess you're right, Buck. He's more use to us a prisoner. I know the guys on the Rock would like to ask him a few questions."

The other Jap had his back against the little bit of armor plating built into this part of the boat. I counted five holes in him . . . He wasn't long for this world. I knelt and offered him a cigarette. He smiled, but seemed too weak to take it. I stuck it in his mouth and lit it.

One by one the sailors came by to give the Japs a once-over. Time and again I saw the same expression. The sailors were incredulous. Could these be the guys who were kicking our butts? Neither of them were as big as the smallest boy in the sqadron.

The officer finally realized we weren't going to execute him. He sat back on his haunches, keeping his eyes down, looking away whenever some sailor bent close. He looked miserable and embarrassed, as if he'd committed some terrible gaff at a cocktail party and now had to endure the stares until he could silently slip away.

The other Jap took his new surroundings for granted. He was beyond caring. His eyes lost focus and grew narrower and narrower. His arms hung limp, thumping against the armor plating as the PT pounded through the chop. A faint smile worked across his lips, and his eyes glistened. Maybe he was thinking about his rice paddy back home. Or his kids. A single tear rolled down his cheek. The last bit of the cigarette slipped from his mouth and landed on his light green tunic. I went over and brushed it away. I thumbed his eyelids down and eased his back to the deck.

I closed my eyes tight, swallowing hard to suppress the sob which was trying to get out. I did not feel as sorry for the Jap as I did for myself, for now I truly knew I had no more stomach for this war. And no way, no way at all, of getting out. I was sick of seeing men die, and scared that one day soon it would be me lying on the deck with bullet holes in my hide, my last sight some scared bastard watching me slip over into the bottomless void of nothingness.

I opened my eyes and saw a sailor standing next to me. He was staring at the dead Jap, eyes blank, a cigarette dangling from slack lips.

"Get a blanket and cover him up," I said roughly, "This guy's gone to Jap Heaven."

Chapter Ten

We came back to the PT base in the late afternoon. This was later than expected, but we had to make a trip to the Rock to drop off the prisoner and then over to the *Canopus* to offload Lieutenant Robinson.

Even as we tied up I could sense confusion in the air. Then I remembered why. The nurses were coming to sup with our hardy squadron. All of a sudden the war took a back seat.

Ginger was coming . . .

I got under the shower bag and pulled the cord to the jerry-rigged nozzle. I brushed my teeth vigorously. I longed for a shave, but contented myself with running a comb through my beard. I rummaged about my shack for my last pair of long khaki trousers. I even found a halfway decent shirt, and after I hastily sewed on a couple of buttons it looked good as new, almost. I whistled as I pinned on the salt-spotted lieutenant bars.

PT 38 served as host boat, and I had never seen any PT so thoroughly clean and inspection ready.

Would've made an outstanding advertisement for Elco—if the cameraman could keep the gash on the bow out of view.

Smartly dressed sailors—could these be my swab-bos?—bustled with last-minute preparations. Lieutenant j.g. Hokulani welcomed me aboard as if it were a soiree at his father's plantation. He offered me a drink, and this I readily took.

The drink was one of the things I, as commanding officer, wasn't supposed to know about. It is made from 190-proof torpedo fluid. There is, of course, "pink lady" in the juice, a chemical which makes the alcohol nonpotable. What you have to do is put the raw fluid in a canteen, fit some copper tubing on top, place the canteen on a hotplate, and run the coils through cold water. You place a cup at the end of the coils to catch the alcohol thus distilled. Add orange juice or whatever's handy.

Palm fronds framed the western sky, now blazing red. The early evening air was so balmy I couldn't tell where my skin left off and dusk began. I took a sip of the drink. I felt almost human.

The ladies came bouncing out of the jungle in a mud-caked jeep. I could hear worn-away brake pads press against metal as the vehicle skidded to a halt. Four gals piled out and thirty pairs of eyeballs watched them walk up the pier.

"Hello, Ginger," I took her hand and helped her aboard.

"Lieutenant, how nice to see you again." She looked a little cockeyed, like she'd already had a few. But what a gorgeous sight anyway! "These are my friends . . ."

Something made me take off my cap as I clasped

Lori's hand, then Mary's and Monica's. They were so pretty and fresh I wanted to get on my knees and weep. They smiled and giggled — darling girls fresh from their debutante cotillion, and surely entirely unacquainted with things like stinking field hospitals and the way a man screams as a doctor saws off his leg. This was a night for forgetting, for everybody.

I began introducing them around. They had come bearing gifts — coffee and a large can of diced mixed fruit. Carlos, the Filipino mess boy, took these to the small galley belowdecks.

The girls lit up the place like a light bulb. It had been a long, long time since most of the men had seen a stateside girl, and the courtliness and self-consciousness with which they were treated was touching.

Dinner was served buffet style, set atop the roof of the low day cabin. It was a no-holds-barred effort to show the nurses what navy hospitality could be like, and it was amazing what had fallen from the woodwork. A big canned turkey. A pile of baked potatoes. Pancakes. A serving dish full of scrambled eggs. Rice aplenty, though this pile didn't completely disappear. A couple of old gin bottles filled with the pungent torpedo fluid. Mixers in the form of canned juices.

Someone brought an old portable victrola and set it atop the charthouse. Muted swing music accompanied our dinner, and when it was done and coffee was served the music got lively and of course the girls were asked to dance.

So they cut the rug on the fo'c'sle. I'd planned on being alone with Ginger but this was almost as good. Those girls were wonderful dancers, their skirts hiking ever higher as they gyrated backwards, one hand in a grinning sailor's paw, the other held high and rocking to the beat. I got my turn with Ginger and Lori both, and when I closed my eyes it seemed I was back in the States, rocking to the solid base of a dozen saxophones, sweat popping out as I kept up with the frantic trumpets. All around sailors laughed and clapped in time to the beat, their lean and hairy faces avid.

Somewhere along the line I had to go sit by myself to catch some wind. I began walking aft and noticed something on the PT on the other side of the pier. It was Nash, sitting by himself on top of the day cabin, arms wrapped around his ankles and head resting on his knees. I almost went over there to talk. Decided against it. He needed to sort out things on his own. Give him a couple more days and, if he was still down, then we would talk.

I went all the way aft and sat down, dangling my legs over the transom. The music was muted here, and the waves lapped against the hull gently. And, as always, there was the distant boom and crack of the fighting a few miles away. I wished with all my soul that I was really in the States, passing time at a dance joint without a care in the world.

"Got a light, sailor?" It was Ginger, and I got up and fished out my Zippo.

"Thanks." She blew out a plume of smoke. "You don't look so hot tonight. Something eating you, Buck?"

I hefted my shoulders. "Nerves."

She nodded slowly. "Me, too." She was standing close to me, so near I could feel the warmth of her body. She had a dreamy look to her eyes.

"How's your . . . problem?"

154

She chuckled softly. "The morphine? Okay. Tell the truth, when you work around the clock it gets hard to tell the difference between high or not." Her eyes lost the dreamy look. "I thought I'd be scared—of watching men die, of getting killed myself."

"And you're not?"

"Sometimes. I don't know. I wake up feeling dead inside, like it wouldn't make any difference if a bullet did get me. Other times I feel so alive I . . ." she put her hand on my shoulder, ran her fingers down the length of my arm, "I get crazy ideas. Wild ideas."

Her eyes were half closed. The message wafted over me like wisps of smoke.

"My shack's over there," I said.

She sent her cig cartwheeling into the water. "Let's go, big fella. I'm so horny I could scream."

We went to the side, stepped onto the pier, and started walking. Some of the guys noticed our leave-taking—how could they not?—but proprieties seemed like something we had left on another planet. We found our way to the shack, found our way into each others' arms. Her body was more ripe and luscious than her tight clothes had suggested. At first we were like two machines, going at it like it was the oldest and greatest show on earth. We followed the steps right down the line, like it was out of a book, and yet it was endlessly, tirelessly fascinating. I wanted to turn off my mind and throw myself into the animal joy of it, this little bit of the best in life in the middle of all the killing. But a voice whispered have your half-hour of fun Bucky, because this is your last. Soon your rotting carcass will be floating in dark waters, the fish nipping away at your bullet-ridden hide. And I clutched at

Ginger desperately, saying her name, and she gathered me into her wonderful sweetness, sighing, her skin smooth and warm. And for a moment I wasn't alone in the world.

We wound it down slowly. Lying there all I could think of was that only last night, on this very rack, I had clawed myself awake from a nightmare of death. I pulled Ginger close, hoping that by doing so I could recapture that feeling that all would be forever well. But I couldn't block out the distant snaring of machine gun fire, or the record player blaring out brassy, frantic swing.

I woke up suddenly, wondering how long I'd been asleep. Ginger was sitting by the window, nude, looking out. The sounds of the party outside were still loud. I rolled out of the rack and padded over to Ginger. Smiling. I was ready for another session . . .

I put my hands on her shoulders and a syringe fell from her hands and clattered to the floor. She looked at me dreamily. "Hello, there." The words were slurred.

I pulled her up by the arms. "What the fuck are you doing!"

She was like a sleepy child. "Fuck." She wobbled those knockers against my chest. "Yeah, les' fuck some more."

I pulled her roughly over to where the clothes lay in a heap. "C'mon, Ginger. Get dressed."

"Aw, no," she said petulantly. She wrapped her arms around me, pressed her warm belly against my flaccid organ. "How 'bout a blowjob, big guy? Give you one you won't believe."

Then the noise outside abruptly changed. The

record stopped and there was shouting. I went to the window and saw the partygoers looking and pointing out at Manila Bay.

A red flare hung in the sky.

Now that the music was off I could hear the machine gun fire was not as distant as I'd thought. Goddamn close, in fact. And there was artillery fire.

I quickly gathered up my clothes. I shouted at Ginger to get dressed and she slowly started putting on her underwear. No complaints. She knew, however dimly, that something was wrong. I left her in the shack, buttoning my shirt as I ran down to the pier.

The boat on the other side of the pier was ready-boat. Thick exhaust billowed from her mufflers as the Packards kicked over.

"Party's over," I shouted as I stepped onto the pier. I had an uneasy feeling. "All boats underway! C'mon! *All* boats!"

There was no whining or bitching. The party broke up in less time than it takes to tell. The men ran to their boats hurriedly, glancing over their shoulders at the explosions erupting on the eastern coast of Bataan. It was close—looked like it might be just on the other side of Mariveles Bay. Jesus!

I felt a hand on my shoulder.

"Buck . . ." It was Ginger. She looked like she was in this world only halfway. "Something's wrong, isn't it?"

"Listen, you and your girls get back to your hospital. Something's up."

She looked at the boat as if she didn't know what it was. "Are you getting underway? Are you going out to fight?"

"Just get going, Ginger."

She stopped looking like a zombie as fear worked across her face. "Hey, I'm scared, Buck. Something's not right."

I laughed shortly. "I'll say. Now would you please—"

Suddenly there were velvety lips on mine, her hand pulling my head down, her other arm wrapped around my waist as she pressed against me. Then it was over. Exhaust fumes wisped around her skirt as she unsteadily trotted away.

I jumped aboard the PT. "What's holding us up? Cast off, goddamnit!"

Chapter Eleven

I was on the radio as soon as the lines were thrown from the dock. Thirty seconds later I had all PT skippers on the circuit.

The lead boat, PT 22, would go straight for the flare, which had popped up from somewhere in South Channel, a six-mile wide pass between Corregidor and the southern mouth of Manila Bay. PT 22 would hook around the eastern side of Corregidor—the side facing Manila—and head for the center of South Channel. PT 38 would follow. Lieutenant Nash would have tactical command of both boats.

I, meanwhile, would take PTs 30 and 25 through North Channel to investigate the nearby fighting, which looked to be somewhere along Bataan's southern tip. The Japanese army couldn't have broken through this far—it had to be an amphibious assault, and that meant we could be of use. But why hadn't the Army called for our assistance?

I got rogers from each PT—Ensign Cassidy, standing beside me at the 30's controls, nodded—and cradled the handset. Cassidy had already cleared the pier.

We headed toward Cochinos Point, carefully threading our way through the minefield. It seemed to take forever. I had a hand over the lens of my flashlight, pointing its weak light at the harbor chart spread on the console. All the action seemed to be concentrated on the other side of the Point. Bursts of light rose from behind it—explosions from artillery shells. But were they ours or the Japs? Small arms fire was close enough for it to sound like an endless stream of firecrackers.

What a night! Half an hour ago I was in my rack with a beautiful woman, thinking about how scared I—

I crammed that back into a cubbyhole and slammed the door.

Cochinos Point finally drew up to our beam. PT 25 was one hundred yards astern. Cassidy slowly pushed the throttles forward and the boat arched gently upwards, gaining speed.

Cassidy looked at me, breathing deeply. Sweat covered his face. Now that we had cleared the minefield I found that I too suddenly required lots of fresh air.

"Where to, skipper?"

"Head around the point," I said, and the ensign eased the wheel to starboard. "Let's keep well off the beach until we can get the size of it."

"Aye." It came out like a grunt.

It was a wide turn, bringing us around the Cochinos Point. Once we cleared we would have a view—in daytime, anyway—of the seven-mile length of the southern coast of Bataan. Cassidy stopped pressing the throttles forward when he had revs for thirty knots. PT

25, whose bottom hadn't been cleaned for a long time, would have a hard time keeping up.

We cleared the point and saw that two fights were in progress; both, widely-spaced, were beachheads of amphibious landings. The nearest fight was three thousand yards away, right off the starboard bow. The other ruckus was all the way down the southern coast, seven miles distant.

I pointed toward the nearer fight and told Cassidy, "Let's go in and mix it." I pulled the radio handset from its clips and got hold of the 25 boat.

"Proceed independently to the nearest landing. Take anything and everything under fire."

"Roger."

I called Nash and, after a moment, he answered up.

"Detach yourself and proceed to our posit."

"We, uh, we still haven't made our destination."

"Tell the 38 to proceed as planned. You've got bigger fish to fry up here."

"Ah . . . roger out."

I snapped the handset in its place. Nash's tone conveyed no confidence, and that worried me. By all rights he should be on thirty days' leave, sorting things out. But it was tough-titty time for everyone. Did he think *I* was having a grand old time? Did he think—

The starboard fifties opened abruptly, and I almost jumped out of my socks. Port turret followed by a gnat's breath.

We were four hundred yards from the beach, coming in at an angle. There were three, maybe four, landing craft on the beach, bow ramps down, dim outlines of soldiers running into the jungle. Tracers streamed from our fifties into the landing craft and along the beach. One of the craft erupted in a jagged explosion, and the gunners took advantage of the brief illumination to bring their weapons to bear with more telling accuracy.

I kept my eyes on the coastline, searching for the breakers which demarked the surfline. I caught one glimpse and that was enough. I told Cassidy to ease back out to sea.

He put the boat in a very wide turn. The closest we came to the beach was two hundred yards — our armament pumping out the lead like there was no tomorrow — as we circled back out.

The landing area was on our starboard quarter when bullets kicked and snapped and whined off our seaward side. The port gunner immediately swung his mount in that direction. I looked, saw nothing . . . then the brief muzzle flash from a low-lying silhouette. Another landing craft, one which hadn't yet beached. The aft gunner swung his 20mm and the antiaircraft shells started marching to the murky outline.

We pounded and slammed through the waves, Cassidy altering the turn so that we would end up heading toward the near-invisible landing craft. An explosion erupted three hundred yards away — the craft's fuel tanks. The rising ball of flame solved all mysteries as to its exact location, and our tracers fed the flames. There was another explosion and I could see the vessel's stern flip up. The port gunner took his hand off the firing bar long enough to clench it in a fist and let out a hearty "*Gotcha!*"

Cassidy spun the wheel in the opposite direction; time to head back to the beach. "Wish I hadn't drunk so much at the party," he said rapidly.

"Wish I'd had more! Okay, straight for the beach again, watch for the 25 boat."

"Aye."

We came pounding in with all guns ablaze, the tracers streaking into what little we could see of the Jap line. The landing barge we'd hit on the first run provided scant illumination. I searched the shoreline with my binoculars, looking for the defenders, saw some muzzle flashes coming from the jungle. These were dishearteningly few and far between.

Off to starbaord I could see PT 25—more correctly, I could see the point where her .50-cal tracers originated. They were turning toward the beach, preparing to run parallel as we had done before. They were coming into our field of fire.

"*Cease fire!*" I called. I caught a brief glimpse of the 25 boat as its silhouette blurred past the burning landing craft. All its mounts were sending stuttering streams of orange into the beach. Then the 25 started its turn back to sea, well off to our stern. We commenced fire.

It was a replay of our first run, this time coming in from the opposite direction. Aside from the burning vessel on the beach, our only reference point was the white foam etching the shoreline. The gunners concentrated their fire a little above that. I could see a ragged line of muzzle flashes—the defenders firing at the Japs? The Japs firing at us? The boat banked to starboard and we headed back out to sea.

"Let's stay out here for a while," I told Cassidy, "I want to make sure there's no more landing craft coming in."

"Right." He called to the gunners and told them

what to be on the lookout for. I began sweeping the waters with my binoculars. I latched onto the craft we'd half-sunk earlier. It was one-thousand yards distant, burning oil showing the last floating bits. Only the squat stern stuck up, and it was going down. I could see heads outlined against the flames, thrashing arms . . . I looked away.

An amphibious landing at night. You really had to hand it to the Japs. It was an audacious gamble. But where were their escorts? Could they have come all the way down from Subic alone? Cassidy and I talked it over. At night, the navigational problems would be too complex for the landing craft. There had to be an escort of some kind, if only to show them the way. But if there were an escort, why wasn't she providing supporting fire? Perhaps the escort was merely a captured yacht without guns . . . or it might be a destroyer, lying off in the darkness, letting the Army take care of its own while she waited for the PTs that would surely come.

We continued pounding out to sea. The presence of an enemy ship was a big if. The other firefight, the one seven miles down the beach, that was something we should be doing something about now. I told Cassidy to forget the search and start heading for the other party.

I pulled the radio handset from its clips and called PT 22. But Nash didn't answer. I recognized the voice of Lumanski, a Quartermaster First, who was evidently at the wheel. I wondered where the hell was Nash. Back aft taking a leak? Jesus! I pressed the transmit button and, careful not to use precise locations, asked Lumanski where his PT was. He reported that he hadn't yet rounded Cochinos Point.

"When you clear," I told him, "assist PT 25."

"Ah, where are they?"

"It'll be obvious."

"Roger."

Then I called the 25 boat, which I could see coming in for another run along the beach.

"Copy my last to the 22?"

"Affirmative."

"I am proceeding to the next party down the line. Remain in this area, continue assistance to the beach."

"Firm-titty, skipper."

By the time I recradled the handset Cassidy had nosed the boat toward the firefight seven miles away.

"We far enough out for you?" he asked. I looked toward the coastline, saw that it was one mile distant. I nodded.

Cassidy eased the throttles all the way forward for max rpms. Forty knots would get us there in ten minutes.

As we neared the beachhead I could see it was a bigger shindig than the first. There were bursts of white light on the beach—mortar fire from our guys. Had to be. I could see no flashes from sea which would indicate supporting fire from a naval vessel. Maybe that minesweeper we'd sunk was the last one they had handy. Maybe.

I went below to the charthouse, where the radio set was fixed to the bulkhead. I put the headphones on and began turning the dial. Maybe I could find out what was going on. In two frequencies I caught the high, excited jabbering of Japanese. I continued turning the dial. I heard, incredibly, the sound of Benny

Goodman's wailing clarinet. Then I hit the Army's frequency loud and clear. But they were as wary of Japanese intercept as I, and better at it: Icebox Easy Six, proceed to Apple Baker; Lampshade Charlie Five, hold at Point Oscar; and so on.

I turned the dial again. I had all the information I could get, but didn't want to go back topside. Now that I was alone, with nothing to look at but the radio, the fear came creeping back, sure as a Philadelphia loan shark. I wanted to roll up in a little ball and spend the rest of the night praying that no lead would come ripping through little old me. I took the headphones off and set the dial back to the PT frequency. I closed my eyes and took a deep breath, then another. Topside, I told myself. Get yourself topside. When you're in the thick of it you haven't got time to be scared. Down here you've got nothing to do but think about the way a bunch of sailors look at you while the flesh melts away from their skulls . . .

I pushed myself from the chair and rushed out the hatch, back into the night and the noise.

We were a thousand yards from our destination. I searched the area just to seaward of the landing. No evidence of a ship of any kind.

"Maybe they *did* find their way on their own," Cassidy said, "Maybe there wasn't any escort. Look how far apart these landings are. Maybe they were supposed to land together. Maybe they came alone, screwing up all the way, and screwed up their landings when they got here."

I grunted. It was a point to consider, but not right at this moment. I braced myself as the guys on the fifties went into lock and load, the sharp metallic snaps clearly audible even over the roar of the Packards.

We came pounding in at forty knots, the fifties opening at five hundred yards. I watched the action through my binoculars. The Japs were black shapes scattering across the ghostly white beach, some of them aiming their peashooters at us. I counted four landing craft, and saw the bright tracers careen off their armored sides. One's fuel tanks went up and the boat came apart like a balsa model. Cassidy spun the wheel to port, and our circle came within one hundred yards of the surfline. There was an explosion on the beach; mortar round, probably a 60mm. We angled back to sea and I saw the aft gunner swiveling his 20mm to the right and left, the firing lever pulled back to full auto.

Then the air split apart with a terrible, low-pitched howl. The sea exploded fifty yards to starboard, the huge geyser rising to an impossible height, and the PT wallowed fearfully.

"God damn!" Cassidy shouted. He was looking right and left, his hands spinning the wheel as he brought the PT under control. "What the hell was that? Where did it come from?"

The sound of whatever cannon fired the shot came a moment later, to port it seemed, out to sea. I raised my binoculars and looked.

Nothing. Nothing. Where was it? Then I saw fire blossom far away in the darkness, like little daubs of yellow paint on a black canvas. There was a ship out there all right, with four angry gun batteries. My hands tightened on the binoculars as that same whistling howl grew louder and louder. It streaked in low, just over our heads. blowing up the sea well to starboard.

"Try some evasive maneuvers, goddamnit!" I was shouting at the top of my lungs. "We're silhouetted against the fire on the beach!"

The boat banked sharply as Cassidy spun the wheel. I saw another burst of fire from the ship, a salvo from all four batteries. She was nearer than when she had fired the last salvo. Much nearer.

The howling grew louder and louder as the rounds screamed at us with incredible speed. I felt as scared and naked as a rabbit in a snake pit.

Mahogany and metal and water slammed through air and I suddenly found myself smashed flat against the charthouse door. The after port torpedo's tube unhinged from its moorings and bounced and clanged around like a loosened steel beam. The boat yawed uncontrollably, pitching to starboard steep, steep, ever steeper. I could feel the boat's center of buoyancy slip from below, to my side, then up and over my head. The boat rolled completely and we smacked the water with a wood-splintering crash.

Capsized and holed . . .

The water was dark and cold and black as pitch. I was wedged in so tight my butt was still glued to the deck. I loosened my hands and kicked hard, pushing down into the water. I began swimming and pumping frog-style.

I broke surface and felt heat as close and smothering as a scalding washcloth. The air was rich with the smell of 100 octane gas. I caught a brief impression of a burning hull, saw flames quickly spreading to the surface of the surrounding water.

I ducked back under and worked frantically at the

kapok, tearing it off. I let it float to the surface and then began swimming underwater, away from the flames on the surface. I went as far as my breath would allow, then put my fingertips above water to feel if there were a burning oil slick. There wasn't. I broke to the surface and gulped air.

The PT was only fifteen yards away. She was belly-up, the stern a mass of jagged planks and twisted propeller shafts. Hideous screams filled the air, and I saw a blackened torso thrashing in the water.

And there was another sound, something which I could even feel in my chest. I turned, looking for the Jap. Water fanned wide on either side of her bow, and black smoke poured from her stacks. The steady vibration of her screws carried right through the water.

She was coming at us, and fast as a goddamn locomotive. Her captain had decided on a brutal and straightforward way to finish the job.

She was going to ram.

I began swimming as hard as I could, slapping my arms against the water and kicking for all I was worth. The inside of my chest felt like a block of ice. If I were anywhere near when she hit the boat, her huge screws would suck me in like—

I suddenly found myself in a spin, caught by the force of the water pressed aside by the ship's bow. I caught a glimpse of the ship as I whirled—and saw it smash into the remains of the PT like an indifferent giant stepping on a hummingbird. Someone's screams were cut in mid-shriek.

I was yanked underwater abruptly, as if I'd been grabbed by a monster's tentacles. My ears filled with the sound of the huge propellers, a loud, hammering,

Whup, Whup, Whup! Violent currents closed over me with strong hands, pulling me down ever deeper. I was astonished at its massive strength. I brought my knees to my chest and wrapped my arms around them, making myself a little ball . . . and wondered if the propellers would take me instantly or leave me to suffer a few moments of unendurable pain.

The sound of the chopping lessened. The turbulence rapidly eased. Suddenly I was pressing against soft and silky mud. *Mud!* Jesus Christ! I was on the *bottom!* I kicked and shot straight up, grabbing water hand over hand.

It was an endless climb, a task that could never be completed. I knew I was going up fast, but the weight of the water above was awesome, like there was an endless distance to go. My lungs burned and screamed. Water began to seep past the gasket of my lips. Part of my mind wanted to go ahead and suck in the cold brine, and my chest began to heave in involuntary spasms.

I broke into the world of sweet, plentiful air. The first gulp whistled in so fast it felt like a knife. I thrashed helplessly, my mouth wide as I gasped and coughed. It took long seconds to get myself under control.

The water was flat and calm, here where the ship had passed. The Jap was far in the distance, churning away, making a wide turn to port and heading back out to sea. I looked for what was left of the 30 and saw nothing. The fires had been completely put out.

"Hello!" I called, "Anybody! Hey!"

I treaded water, holding position. I listened. Small arms fire from the beach. Mortar explosions. Then:

"Over here!"

"Where?" I bellowed.

"Here, goddamnit!" Not so far away.

I began swimming. A piece of wood bumped against my head and I stopped. It was mahogany planking, freshly snapped. I swam on, then saw the waving arm.

"Skipper it's you!" Strip Cunningham grabbed me by the shoulder. I put my arm over the piece of wood he was holding.

"Strip, what the hell were you doing on the 30?"

"The supercharger on centerline was acting up, so I came aboard to—" He coughed, spat out some water. "Guess it sure the fuck don't matter now."

We asked each other if we were okay. No wounds, no broken bones . . . none that we knew of yet. We began calling for other survivors.

Now and then we saw something bobbing the water and we treaded over to investigate. Always turned out to lifeless flotsam, of which there was a lot. Bits of wood, mostly. Some papers. Lifejackets. We abandoned the plank and grabbed the kapoks.

Then we came upon a wad of floating rubber. It was the PT's little inflatable life-raft, the spare that's carried in the day cabin. I popped the CO_2 cartridge and the inflation cells ballooned. We heaved ourselves aboard.

Up on our knees we had a better view. We cupped our hands and kept calling until our voices were hoarse. Strip gave up first. I tried a few more calls, but there was no response.

We were it.

* * *

171

We staggered from the water directly into a thick growth of mangroves. We collapsed in the mud and lay there, saying nothing, heads resting against the raft's flotation cells.

It had been a long haul, even with the life-raft. We angled away from the fight at the beachhead, which even now was still underway, making for a point down the coast. Strip sat up front and I was in back, both of us bent over as we used our hands for paddles.

I caught my breath enough to sit up and look around. Mangrove roots were everywhere. Strip was out like a light, already gently snoring. I got up and walked back toward the water. I should be sleeping too, but there were things to think about now. I got to the water and looked around.

The beach assault was two miles or so up the coast. I couldn't see what was going on at the first amphibious landing area, back toward Mariveles; a small promontory was in the way, blocking the view. Out to sea there was absolutely no trace of the PT.

I wondered how long it'd be before our guys figured out PT 30 had gone down. I wondered if any of them would meet with a similar fate this night. I wondered how the hell we would get back to the PT base.

I went back to where Strip was sleeping and sat down. I took my .45 from its holster and examined it, wondering how much damage had been done. I began brushing off the dirt.

When that Jap blew us out of the water we were finished. Ramming us had been totally unnecessary. He had done it just because . . . just because . . .

Every detail of that incident was branded deep inside my brain. I could recall each facet with extreme clarity. Even when I was spinning in the water, just before I was sucked down, I could call it back and look at it as if it were a photograph. Like how the flames of the PT lit up the bow of the DD, showing the distinctive lines of a *Kamikaze* Class destroyer. Or even the brief glimpse of a hull number, which was seventeen.

Had Ohiro smiled as he ordered his helmsman to steer for the flaming wreckage? Had he been on his bridge wing to listen to the sweet sound of plywood crushed asunder?

I yanked the slide back on the .45; particles of salt and sand grated inside the mechanism. I thumbed the release and the slide snapped forward. When next we meet, Ohiro, I'll be the last thing you'll ever see. Oh, yes. The very last.

Chapter Twelve

Exhaustion began coming at me in greasy waves. The image of the pistol and the things I was thinking about started to mix and blur. The hard, wet ground mattered not one iota as I lay my head against the moist lifejacket. There was a ticklish feeling on my legs as insects began their cursory inspection of my white and tender meat. Sleep came at me with a blackjack.

I awoke chilled, stiff, and unrefreshed. Strip was breathing heavily, and I could see his eyes rolling behind closed lids.

The early morning light showed the surrounding mangrove roots to be caked with stinking mud. The dark green leaves completely blotted out the sky, forming a sort of cave whose mouth gave to the sea. I could see water lapping against the two inches of black muck that was the beach. I got on my hands and knees and crawled to it. My mouth felt like it was covered with dry, rotting moss. I cupped some salt water, drank it in, gargled, and spat it out. I covered a finger with mud and rubbed it against my teeth, using the grit to clean them. I rinsed my mouth out again, then splashed water on my face. My toilette complete, I stood and looked around.

The sun had risen one handspan above the horizon, its heat drying my face in seconds. To my right was the beachhead. There was nothing there, other than the remains of the single landing craft we'd shot up and the black holes where mortar rounds had hit. This was bad. If the good guys had prevailed there'd still be Jap bodies on the beach.

To my left the promontory was a mile distant. It blocked out my view of Corregidor.

I hunkered back down and crawled into the leafy cave. I roused Strip and he woke slowly, bleary-eyed, smacking his lips. He stretched his tattooed arms luxuriously, as if it were noon and he'd passed the night in a starlet's heart-shaped bed. Then he took notice of his surroundings, and his brow wrinkled as he recalled the events of last night.

I sat on the mud and watched him splash water on his face. He crawled back in and we inventoried our supplies.

We had one .45, salt-encrusted but probably still working. Two kapok life-jackets, and the dark gray inflatable life-raft. Strip had a four-inch Buck knife which folded into a little case strapped to his belt, Boatswain's mate-style. And there was my trusty Zippo, working in apple-pie order.

We talked over the situation. Strip agreed it was likely the Japs had won at that nearby beach, and any patrols we'd encounter in this area wouldn't be friendly. I therefore decided not go inland in search of rescue, but proceed coastwise back to Mariveles.

I uncorked the life-raft's filler valve and it quickly deflated. We rolled it up as tight as we could, using the string which was attached to the valve's cap to tie it in a neat bundle. Strip slung it through the back of his web belt.

There was not much sense in walking along the beach. It was more mud than sand, and we would be in plain view. Nor was it possible to negotiate the mangroves. So we tromped into the jungle until the vegetation cleared somewhat, about thirty yards from the beach. From here we could get the occasional glimpse of the ocean; enough of a view, anyway, that should a PT cruise by we could rush down to the water.

We set a good pace after a while, walking along at a Boy-Scout clip. There was, surprisingly, little growth on the jungle floor—just fallen branches and twigs covered with moss, and a fine blanket of leaves. Mostly there were trees, their trunks soaring into a leafy canopy one hundred feet overhead. The canopy itself was so dense and complete no sunlight came down at all. It was gloomy and humid, the only sounds the occasional shriek of a far-off monkey or birds that let go with human screams. We'd occasionally come across a clearing where one of the huge trees had died and fallen, and here, where the sunlight streamed down, would be a dense mass of broad-leaved ferns and other sun-loving plants.

This was going to be a long hike. From the tip of Cochinos Point to where PT 30 had gone down was a distance of seven nautical miles, give or take. But that was a straight shot, and this was the sort of coast that twisted and turned upon itself so many times we'd easily end up walking many times that. So whenever the coast jutted out into a miniature peninsula we'd walk straight across its base, trying to keep on a more or less direct path.

We walked through the jungle gloom, saying nothing. But, at least on my part, thinking much. I wondered at the change in me, brought about by last night's ramming. I no longer wanted out of the war. I wanted more than anything to get back to the PTs. I entertained myself with images of stalking the *Matsukaze* and slipping a couple of Mark Eights up her ass. And hanging around to make sure there were no survivors.

The more I thought about it the angrier I became. Here, in this goddamn jungle, I was a brain without a nervous system, an artist with paralyzed hands.

It was while I was absorbed in these reflections that Strip grabbed my belt and hauled me to the dirt. Before I could utter a word of surprise his face was close to mine, his forefinger across his lips in an urgent gesture for silence.

I could take a hint.

We were about to crest a small ridge when this happened. We lay in silence, dead still. Presently the sound of snapping twigs and heavy footfalls reached my ears. We both slowly and carefully inched up far enough to look over the ridge.

Jap patrol. Twelve of them. They were forty yards away, crossing a sun-drenched clearing. They wore light green uniforms, a tropical dress of some kind with sleeves cut off below the elbow, pants cut below the knees. They carried rifles and some field gear, but not full packs.

Strip and I exchanged glances. The Japs had indeed triumphed last night. And at the southern tip of Bataan, well behind the American/Filipino line.

I knew little of army affairs, but this couldn't be all the Japs within the immediate vicinity. There should've been a guy well forward of the platoon, the point man, and another trailing well behind. And there'd be a couple guys walking on either side of the line—flankers—staying well to either side of the tiny column.

So I wasn't totally surprised by the sound of a soldier in back of us. I very carefully turned my head and saw him, less than a dozen yards away, clomping through the huge leafy ferns. He hadn't seen us. Yet. He was marching parallel to the main body, looking to the right and left alertly.

We held our breaths. We were lying prone and there was little shrubbery around us. Our outfits didn't blend in at all with the greens and browns of our surroundings. So we just lay there, rock-still.

The Jap was looking all around but his eyesight wasn't sharp enough. He was soon out of our view.

We looked back at the patrol in time to see the column depart the clearing. We waited and, sure enough, their trailing man came into view, walked across our field of fire, and was gone. I heaved a sigh of relief.

We gave it another few minutes. The only sound which reached our ears was their noisy progress, which gradually faded into nothing. We got up and continued. Our new pace was slower but more quiet.

It was getting on midafternoon when we found the

stream. It trickled by in front of us and coursed down a hundred yards before it emptied into the sea. It wasn't much bigger than a brook but the water was fresh and sweet. Most of it was in the shade, but harsh sunlight dappled the smooth above-water rocks. We stripped and waded in.

After preliminary refreshment we got down to housekeeping. First, still standing in the water, I broke down the .45 and cleaned each piece in the fresh water, getting rid of the salt. I laid the unassembled pieces on a sunny rock. Next were our clothes, which were likewise cleansed of salt and the larger hunks of mud. Last came the epidermis, which we cleaned by rubbing the soft sand of the stream's bottom against our skin. Then came secondary refreshment; a couple strokes upstream, continuous drinking of water, putting one's head under a midget waterfall.

We lay in a dry, sunny spot, the stream gurgling near our feet. When the clothes were dry we got dressed and continued the trek. When it got too dark to see we lay down and parked our heads on the kapoks.

Sleep finally came, and this time I caught up on the dreams I'd missed the night before. Lieutenant Ohiro Kagemaru had center stage, and I had my hands around his throat. I squeezed hard enough to crush his windpipe and make his eyes bulge from their sockets. I felt drool on my hand from his bloated and gasping tongue. Oh, this wasn't any nightmare, brother. It was downright enjoyable when I mashed his head against a rock so many times it felt like I was holding on to a bag of wet sand. And I was enraged when he finally croaked, for it was over too soon. I shook him back and forth like a rag doll, bellowing for him to come back to life so that I could have the pleasure of killing him again.

Explosions sent me into instant wakefullness.

It was night, but I could see Strip sitting bolt upright in the darkness. The explosions were distant, but close enough for us to feel faint tremors in the ground. It sounded like the Fourth of July.

It took us a while to figure out what was going on. We slowly crawled from our resting place, stopping when the jungle ceased and the stars shone above. We were on a low bluff, one which had a thirty-foot drop to the sea. We looked to the east; on the other side of a hill—three or four miles away—we could see the sudden and frequent muzzle flashing of many, many artillery pieces. And we could see Corregidor too; the shells from the barrage were landing all over the Rock, exploding in white blossoms, occasionally sending up fireworks whenever one of the small ammo dumps was hit.

The Rock's own howitzers were returning fire, but the tiny licks of flame from her batteries were few and far between.

"I don't believe it," Strip whispered. I didn't want to either, but you can't deny what's staring you in the face. The Jap field pieces were at Bataan's southern tip, and these batteries couldn't operate so far behind our lines unless . . . there was no more line at all.

This brought on a whole new range of problems. We could not continue our walk back to base; to get around those artillery pieces would entail a wide, wide circle into the jungle. And once we got past them what would we find? Those pieces were next door to Mariveles; surely the town had fallen. And, of course, the PT base was but a pistol shot away.

Talk about being orphans. This took the cake.

We watched the barrage, saying nothing, timid boys studying the adults at play. The Japs were excellent marksmen; I didn't see a single shot land in the water, and judging by the number of ammo dumps going up they were firing with deadly accuracy.

The good guys weren't doing so hot. Only rarely did I see one of our rounds explode in the approximate area where the Japs were firing.

The bombardment continued for hours. It wasn't until the eastern sky started to lighten that the American howitzers finally got their range. Shots began landing where the Jap batteries seemed to be, and presently their guns fell silent. Withdrawing, I imagine, to find another place from which to direct their next barrage.

Once the guns had silenced on both sides Strip and I discussed our options.

"No sense in trying to get back to the PT base," I said. "If Mariveles has fallen you can bet the base is gone, too."

"What can we do? Try for the Rock?" He was sarcastic.

"You got any better ideas?"

"You got any paddles?"

So that was it. I lay there, thinking, watching the coast turn lighter and lighter. I turned the problem over and over, like an old dame fingering cheap tomatoes.

"We've got to make some, that's all." My brilliant solution.

Strip nodded, too polite to call me an idiot. He got up. "Well, we might as well go down to the beach and start looking for a good place to get underway."

"Fine."

"Guess you wanna wait until it's dark before we cast off."

"Right."

We got up, went back into the covering jungle, and proceeded downslope until we were in the mangroves. The beach was dark and muddy, and it looked as good a place as any from which to launch the life-raft.

We spent the rest of the morning making paddles. We went back in the jungle and scavenged a couple of sticks, straight as we could find, and whittled them even straighter with Strip's knife. The finished product was good and strong, big around as a broom handle. Then we took the motormac's big shoes and cut them so that the heel and sole were intact but the upper leather flayed apart like the petals of a flower, nearly flat but still cup-like. Then, by cutting one hole through the toe and one through the base, we ran each stick through each shoe so the stick rested flat against the sole. We took one of the web belts and cut it into several long, tough strands. We used this string to secure the shoes at the end of the sticks, employing a series of unseamanlike and amateurish knots.

Strip laughed at the result, resembling, as it were, two grotesque leather pinwheels.

It was midday by the time we finished. We set about the job of reinflating the raft, taking turns blowing it up. Then we lay down to doze, to wait until dark.

I anticipated another evening barrage. There'd been little action that day; a high-flying formation of bombers had worked the Rock before lunch, but that was all. The night darkened and the stars came out but no artillery fire.

I dozed fitfully, each jungle sound making me wonder if Japs were lurking about. Strip slept sound as a rock, the deep breaths passing through his lips with maddening regularity. I wondered what the trick was to sleeping wherever you wanted.

Then it was time to go. I touched Strip and he woke instantly. We slipped on the kapoks and cinched them tight. We picked up the raft and carried it through mangrove-land and waded into the sea. We put it in the water and waded out until the water was waist-high. Then we rolled aboard, took our positions, and began paddling like mad against the breaking waves. By the time we cleared the breakers we had our rhythm. The paddles worked much better than I'd expected.

We went straight out, keeping Corregidor on our port bow. I planned to keep to this course until the Rock was square on our port beam, then turn and head straight for her. The tide was coming in, which meant the current would be running to the east. This would carry us toward Corregidor even as we kept the raft pointing south.

Strip set the pace. He had fooled around with canoes in his boyhood. He told me to sit in back as that position exerted more power. I watched his back, dipping my paddle on the side opposite from his. After an interminable number of strokes he'd deftly change to the other side and so would I.

Dip. Pull. Bring it up. Dip. I was woefully out of shape, at least for this sort of thing. The muscles in my back began to ache. Then burn. Then quiver in spasms.

"Whoa," I called, "Gotta stop a sec."

"Sure thing, skipper. I was just about to pop anyway."

I put my paddle across the inflation cells and laid my heaving face on top. I took in deep gulps of air. The pain throbbed down. I moaned softly as I sat back up. The Rock seemed to have changed its relative position not at all. I looked astern and saw that we had put but two miles between us and the coast. " 'Kay. Let's go."

My conscious mind kind of took a back seat as I settled into the brute, repetitive labor. I let myself think about Ginger, about that night we had shared in my nipa shack. The erotic memories were pleasurable but not all-encompassing. I kept thinking of that syringe clattering to the floor. Of her confusion and fear as she realized that an attack was underway.

Strip called me twice before I snapped from the trance.

The Rock was dead abeam. Joyfully I dipped my paddle and pulled for the turn. Other things came to my attention. The current had indeed angled us toward Corregidor; it was but three miles distant. And the seas had kicked up. They were at two to three feet, and blessedly pushing us toward our destination.

An hour passed and we came upon the La Monja Light, a lonely navigational beacon set atop shoals. It was extinguished. I knew it was a little over two miles from Corregidor's western coast. We continued.

My back didn't bother me so much now. Just felt like salt water taffy, hot and stretched.

Strip sat upright, resting his paddle across his knees. He looked as suddenly alert as a watchdog.

"Hey," I called, "What's the big—"

"Sssh!"

I pricked up my ears. Then, softly at first, the wavering sound drifted across the waves. It was an engine of some kind.

I straightened up and looked around. The swells lifted us up and set us down, giving me alternate views of chest-high waves and then a distant horizon. After we bobbed up a few more times I had it. Landing craft to port. Four of them. Half mile distant and heading for the Rock's western coast.

"Japanese?" Strip whispered.

"It's a cinch it ain't the relief force from the States."

"Japs invading Corregidor? Already?"

"Testing defenses, anyway. I don't want any part of this. Let's get clear."

So we turned away from the Rock's western coast, angling for South Pass and, hopefully, an unnoticed landfall on some other part of the island. I kept my eyes on the landing craft whenever we crested a swell. They looked to be chugging along at something under ten knots.

The current kept pushing us toward the western coast. Strip and I nosed the boat further and further to the south until we were almost broadside to the incoming tide, and still we were uncomfortably near the Japs. I began to wonder if there was anything we could do to alert the defenders. Fire the .45?

But the boys on the Rock must've been waiting for

it. When the landing craft were a half-mile from the beach a big antiaircraft searchlight swung across the water and caught them cold. Strip and I stopped paddling. The show was taking place on our port beam, two miles away.

The Rock's shore batteries opened up, turning the eastern coast into a string of orange and yellow explosions. Tracers fanned from machine gun nests, raking to the right and left, some of the rounds kicking up water near us. One bullet fluttered just over our heads, and we promptly got down and made ourselves as small as we could in the raft. Strip softly cursed. We lay there, unable to see, listening to the tremendous explosions of ten-ton mortars—big sons of bitches designed to take on battleships—pound and hammer away.

I watched the stars in the sky slowly fade. The blackness of the sky turned to violet. The howitzers stopped their barrage reluctantly, but the racketing of machine guns continued unabated.

I got up on an elbow. When a swell lifted us I saw there was nothing left of the Japs but pieces of wood and bodies floating face-down. The spray of machine guns was concentrated on these bodies, ripping them up.

We were near the beach. Strip got up and we began paddling, nosing the raft so it rode with the waves.

We beached just as the eastern sky was turning light. Our landfall was one mile down from where the Japs would've landed. We drew the raft halfway up the beach and threw our sodden paddles inside. We walked a few steps uphill, Strip hopping and cursing in his bare feet. The machine gun nests up the coast were still going full-bore, spraying lead into the remains of the Japs.

A high, nervous voice called for us to halt.

Strip and I immediately threw up our hands. *"Americans!"* we shouted together, *"Friends!"*

"Password?" The word drifted down on the morning breeze.

Strip looked at me with bulging eyes, his thoughts written all over his face. Is this how we're going to die? At the hands of some high-strung dogface?

I licked my lips and yelled at the top of my lungs: *"Hirohito sucks donkey dicks!"*

Chapter Thirteen

That we had been so alertly challenged implied a functioning chain of command. Strip and I soon found otherwise.

After the guard bought my watchword I anticipated being rushed to a cozy bunker, there to be fed while everyone marveled at our tale of jungle trek and treacherous voyage. But our captor merely waved us on, uninterested in how two Navy men had come up from the recently-attacked coast. We saw soldiers milling about in confusion, as if the Japanese had landed in force and the Rock was about to capitulate. We began walking toward the main buildings, and more than once several troopers stopped when they spied the bars on my collar and asked which positions I wanted them to take up. I pointed them toward the beach.

We went inside the large command tunnel and found similar disinterest — not apathy, but the impression that everyone had bigger fish to fry. Everywhere it was take a number and have a seat, bub.

I finally got sick of everyone's bad manners. I

backed a fat and bespectacled sergeant up against a wall.

"This is your last chance to talk nice, sarge."

He went goggle-eyed and dropped his file folders to the floor. "Hey! Take it easy, Captain!"

"I'm a lieutenant. A Navy lieutenant."

"Jesus, whatever you say, sir. No need to get so hot under the collar." Over his shoulder I could see Strip going through his file cabinet. The motormac held up a bag of donuts and grinned.

"Tell me where I can find Rear Admiral Whitefield."

"He's gone."

"Gone!"

"Ow! He's gone, sir. Went out on a submarine last night, along with some of the wounded and the rest of the nurses."

"Yeah? All the nurses make it okay?"

"All the ones that were here. The nurses that were over in Bataan got captured along with everyone else."

"What?"

"Where've you been, sir? Bataan's fallen. Everyone surrendered."

"C'mon. That's better than eighty thousand men."

"That's eighty thousand prisoners of war, sir."

Long ago they killed the messenger of bad news. I balled up my fist and heaved back, then was brought to reality by a crisp: "What the hell's going on here?"

I let him go and turned. Standing behind me was another sergeant, this one considerably bigger and with more stripes.

"Who's this?" he asked of the four-eyes.

"Some Navy officer, Bill. He just came storming in here and—"

189

"Ah! The *Navy* guy." His tone dripped with contempt. "Your name Leander?"

I nodded.

"Wait here a sec." The big sergeant walked to a desk, pulled open a drawer, and came back with a sealed envelope. "Before that admiral guy bugged out he wrote this for you."

I tore it open, began reading it as I walked away. Strip followed two steps behind, munching on a donut. *Secret* was stamped across the top. It said, in official language, that I was now the senior Navy officer in the Philippines. That took one long paragraph. Then: "Recommend you evacuate remaining USN personnel to Mindanao and locate guerilla forces under command of General Sharp." And the final kissoff: "Rest assured that my formal report to Admiral Hart, Commander-in-Chief Asiatic Fleet, shall favorably mention the gallantry of your crews, but due to the limited firepower and tonnage of the Motor Torpedo Boat, was unable to effect a significant delaying action against enemy naval forces."

The letter crumpled in my fist and I tossed it aside. As we walked into the sunlight I gave Strip the hot flash about Bataan. He grunted.

We found a faucet and took turns at the spigot. We stepped from the main entrance and into the sunshine. There were a lot more blast craters than on my last visit, but I was comforted to see most of the big guns had escaped damage. We came across a lonely concrete bunker which overlooked Corregidor's northern coast. We went inside.

No one was there, although there was evidence of recent habitation. A half-eaten can of salmon lay atop a battered desk. This Strip and I shared. A big pair of field glasses, attached to a swivel mount, faced Bataan. I took a good, long look.

Mariveles was but four miles away. I could clearly see Japanese flags flying from the town's flagpoles. I moved the glasses back and forth, scanning the harbor. One of the two U.S. minesweepers was on the bottom of the shallows, her blackened superstructure still above water. The other minesweeper was gone — I wondered if Lieutenant Robinson had made his run to Australia. The *Canopus* was still there, but now her damage wasn't fake. The U.S. landing craft, four of them, were snugged to a pier, captured. Japanese landing craft were also present, but there were no big ships of any kind.

Next door, separated by Gorda Point, was the site of the PT base. Or I should say the *former* site. All I could see was the chow hall we'd built, and at that only its blackened frame. All that was left of my little nipa shack was four charred stilts. No sign of the PTs at all.

I stood aside and Strip put his eyes to the glasses. I went over to the far side of the bunker while he drank it in. Bataan was as gone as gone could get. Eighty thousand men captured. Surely the greatest loss in the history of American arms. And the PTs . . . how many had gone down that night? There wasn't any sign of them at either of Corregidor's docks.

The motormac straightened up from the glasses. "Sure was fast, wasn't it? I didn't think the Japs were set up for something like this."

"Yeah." Fast. The Jap steamroller was on the move, grinding through the Philippines as if there weren't any resistance at all. And we had fooled ourselves into thinking we were giving them a good fight. God!

"Wonder if that nurse made it," Strip said.

"Ginger?"

"Yeah. Her and her buddies. Sure were nice girls."

I sighed. If Ginger was still alive her ordeal was just beginning. That poor, fucked-up broad. She had more problems than she could handle without benefit of . . .

"Hey, skipper. You looked kinda funny. Maybe you should sit down."

"No, no . . . that's okay. I'm all right."

"What should we do now?"

"Let me think."

The bunker seemed as good a place as any to sit it out. It was cool and shady. I thought about what had happened and where we stood. I turned the equation over and over.

Maybe one time I would've tried slamming my fist against the concrete wall. Now I felt like an old man. The starch had purely gone out of me.

It was getting on midafternoon when Strip excitedly called me to the binoculars. Steaming from the northeast was a PT. Strip and I didn't exchange words. We left the bunker and ran down to the docks.

It was PT 38. Hokulani was at the wheel, bringing her in dead slow for a portside tie-up. He had one arm over the cockpit's armor plating, looking like Casey Jones at the throttle, concentrating on the ever-narrowing space between the boat and the pier. The sailors standing on the bow weren't so occupied they couldn't notice me and Strip. A shout went up.

Hokulani nearly slammed the boat into the pier

when he saw what the commotion was about. He regained himself in time to back down, and when the first line was over—Strip caught it—he came bounding out of the cockpit and onto the dock. He ran to me grinning, then clapped both hands on my arms. He looked like a kid who'd gotten exactly what he wanted for Christmas.

"Jumpin' Jesus!" he shouted, "Back from the dead!"

"Good to see you, Hokulani. I thought you guys had had it. How many other PTs went down besides the 30 boat?"

"None. I mean . . . well, the 30 *did* go down?"

His face fell when I told him Strip and I were the sole survivors.

"So where've you guys been?" I asked.

Hokulani shook himself like a wet dog. "Uh . . . we've found an inlet at the southern mouth of Manila Bay that seems okay."

"Why didn't you park here at the Rock?"

"Air raids."

"Oh, yeah. Where's Nash?"

Hokulani took a deep breath. "He's dead, skipper."

It hit me in the chest like a fist, but I kept my face a mask. "How'd . . . it happen?"

Hokulani glanced at the sailors clustered around Strip, who were laughing and slapping him on the back. Hokulani motioned me to follow, and we walked to the bow, where there was relative privacy.

"I don't know how to tell you this, skipper."

"Just spill it, will you?"

"He, well . . . he shot himself."

I worked my lips but no sound came out. "Say again?" I whispered.

Hokulani's eyes flickered over to the sailors and he lowered his voice. "Nash turned the wheel over to Lumanski and went down to his cabin. Ski says he heard the shot a few minutes later. He went down there and found him with the .45 still clutched in his hand."

I passed a hand over my face, looked around at the clouds floating by, the deceptive peacefulness of Corregidor, the sparkling blue water of North Pass.

Hokulani cleared his throat. "Lumanski's been passing the word that it was an accident."

I nodded. Lumanski was a good man. Same size and build as Strip Cunningham, but a much more serious and thoughtful sort. I coughed, looked stern and thoughtful. "So, ah, what brought you guys to the Rock today?"

Hokulani shrugged. "Odds and ends. Want to make sure Oakey made it on that last submarine."

"What do you mean?"

"When I heard there was going to be one last run, I had a little visit with the head nurse. Told her Oakey was Roosevelt's son."

"She buy it?"

"Yeah. They never had his service record to begin with, and I fixed that little clipboard hanging from his bed. Wish I could've thought of something for Chief Turner. Hell, wish I could've thought of something for *me*. Anyway, I want to try and find some more chow for our guys, but mostly I'd like to coordinate with an Army observer who can call us in whenever the Japs try putting landing craft ashore."

I nodded. "Yeah, that sounds good. Why don't you go tend to that."

"Sure thing, skipper. There's some hot chow below if you want it. Coffee, too."

"Yeah, yeah."

He smiled briefly. "You don't know how glad I am to see you. For awhile there I thought I had the whole shooting match, and I didn't like it one bit. I had no idea what we were supposed to do next."

He gave me a slap on the shoulder and went away. I watched Hokulani hop off the boat and start heading down the pier.

Hokulani, old boy, do you think *I* know what we're supposed to do next?

Two hours later we were underway. I stood next to Hokulani in the cockpit, and he filled me in on the details of what the other PTs did the night the 30 went down.

One boat went looking for us after awhile, but a Japanese destroyer gave chase. The PT made it back to our minefield, which shook the destroyer loose. By that time it was obvious that Bataan was starting to fall all the way—the Army had dropped all pretense of radio security and was babbling in the clear. The PTs rushed back to base and quickly salvaged what they could. One of the LCMs was loaded up with as many spare drums of gasoline as it could carry. The boats left just as the first Japanese tanks started to roll in.

"And then I found this garden spot," Hokulani said.

We nosed into the inlet just as the eastern sky was beginning to redden. Being away from the boats a couple of days gave me a chance to see them with fresh eyes, and it seemed like they'd been used harder than I recollected. Paint flaking here and there, the mast on one completely shot off, bullet holes stitched across the wood, dents in the armor plating . . . lounging about the boats were sailors, if you still could call them that. These guys had reverted back to an earlier species of seafarers, the kind that ended their careers dangling from an Admiralty gibbet. Some of the guys had scrounged army fatigues and hacked them into something that resembled shorts. Those dungarees still existent had faded into a blue that was almost white. Nobody had had a shave in months. Deep circles framed suspicious eyes, but I was surprised to see them perk up when I waved hello. Some even grinned.

PTs 22 and 38 were in halfway decent shape. All bullet and shrapnel holes were above the waterline. PT 25 looked like a horse with a broken leg—and I decided to put her out of her misery. I designated PT 25 as repair boat. Pistons, carburetors, steering cables, gaskets . . . everything that could be pulled from her would be given over to keeping the other PTs healthy.

Hokulani asked me what exactly we were going to do. I shrugged inwardly, but kept my face as impassive as a rock.

"We just keep on doing whatever we can, Hokulani."

Chapter Fourteen

"Anyone receiving this message please transmit it to the Commander-in-Chief of the Imperial Japanese Forces on Luzon."

It was a broadcast from Corregidor's main radio station. Hokulani, a radioman, and myself were cramped inside the PT's charthouse, hunched over the radio's speaker, holding on as the boat pounded and rattled through the chop. The message repeated itself several times; finally the prologue was done and the announcer got down to it.

"For military reasons which General Wainwright considers sufficient, and to put a stop to further sacrifice of human life, the commanding general will surrender to Your Excellency today the fortified island at the entrance to Manila Bay together with all military and naval personnel and all existing stores and equipment."

So this was it. The surrender. Hokulani and I exchanged tired glances. What was coming over the loudspeaker was hardly a shocker. It was kind of like when my great-aunt Lilah died. She was a big, robust woman, and much loved by us all, but after a year of fighting the cancer it was kind of a relief when the misery was over.

I opened the narrow door and went out into the brilliant sunshine. "Okay," I said to the helmsman, "Slow it down. Cut port and starboard, make five knots with centerline."

He nodded and pulled the throttles back. The bow eased down smoothly and quickly, then our stern briefly lifted as our wake surged by. I rested my elbows on top of the console and lifted my binoculars.

The southern side of the Rock was four miles away. Puffs of smoke rose from where Jap shells kicked up dirt. The eastern half of the island was entirely Japanese now. Yesterday they'd finally fought their way onto the Rock and established a firm beachhead. The first wave consisted of two dozen landing craft; we did what we could with our two PTs, nipping in and out of the formation, sinking three of the crowded vessels. Then the second wave came, this one weighed down with small tanks and artillery pieces. We stormed into the thick of this one too, but had to break off when a formation of Zeroes came screaming in out of no-where.

The beachhead blossomed from a contained circle to a front which ate up the eastern tip of the island. The Jap line steadily advanced, the squat tanks and field pieces pushing the Americans further and further back. I got on the radio and called the Army officer who'd lately been directing us against the Jap landings. No answer. Night fell and we headed back to our little inlet.

There was nothing to do that night but sit it out. All the action was taking place on land. There were now three destroyers thrashing around, but they were too scared to run into Manila Bay and get us — not as long as that minefield was in the way, or as long as Corregidor's shore batteries were still in working order. One of those cans, of course, belonged to Ohiro. And whenever I spotted one through my binoculars I tried to summon up that terrible rage that had consumed me, that all-consuming thirst for revenge. But couldn't. My insides seemed as dry and empty as a cornhusk.

This morning we came out to see what we could do. Then Hokulani had excitedly called me below, gesturing at the radio's loudspeaker . . .

I pulled the radio handset from its clips and pressed it against my ear. The surrender message was still going.

"If all of your firing and aerial bombardment has ceased at twelve noon local time the commanding general will send two staff officers by boat, flying a white flag, to the Cabcaben dock to meet a Japanese staff officer, whom the commanding general requests that Your Excellency have there, empowered to name the time and place for the commanding general to meet Your Excellency in order that he may make the formal surrender and arrange all details."

I jammed the handset back in its clips. "Turn around," I told the man at the wheel, "Back to the barn. Party's over."

It was an hour before noon. I rested my forehead on my clenched fists and sighed. It was done. It was all over. The Japs had licked us. It would only be a matter of time before they mopped up whatever resistance was left in these islands. The Philippines were theirs.

Defeat. Surrender. Capitulation. I whispered these words quietly, letting the strange consonants roll off my tongue and drop to the deck. The words sounded odd, like Beelzebub, or Quetzalcoatl. I opened the charthouse door and went back inside.

The English part of the surrender broadcast was over. The voice spoke in Japanese, probably a direct translation.

Out of the corner of my eye I could see the radioman's face flush red and the veins start to stand out on his neck. He suddenly got up and gave the bulkhead three short, savage punches. Then rushed through the companionway to the berthing compartment. Hokulani watched the little scene impassively, then turned to me.

"So what do we do now, skipper?"

By the time we slid into the inlet I had made up my mind. The sailors on the other boats watched us nose into the bank, and their faces were quiet and grim and . . . accusing, somehow? As if *I* had something to do with it? I shook the thought off.

I had Hokulani muster all hands. It took him twenty seconds to make sure everyone was present, and then I went to the tip of the 22's bow and stood there as if it were a pulpit. Some guys were standing on the bank below. Others sat on the PTs flanking the 22. Seventeen guys altogether. Seventeen. God, when I first assumed command there were . . . I cleared my throat.

"I'm sure y'all heard the broadcast on the 25's radio, so you guys know the score. General Wainwright is going to surrender." I paused to let that sink in, but the guys kept staring at me silently and impassively. "Well, that doesn't necessarily have to include us. Not while we've got these boats. We can make it to Australia, men, and that's what we're going to do. There's enough islands along the way so we can tie up by day and cruise at night. Fuel's gong to be a big problem, but some of those islands contain secret fuel dumps. We'll hit those and—"

"But what about the troops on Mindanao?" one sailor shouted. "How about we tie up with them, Mr. Leander?"

I was taken aback enough to let my trap hang open. I hadn't planned on this being some kind of classroom discussion. I was giving these guys their *orders*, for Christ's sake. I let anger add an edge to my voice.

"How long do you think they're going to hold out? A week? A month? They're going to slide down the tube with everyone else. Face it, guys. We've been beaten. All this territory belongs to Japan now."

"Then we should surrender!" It was Webster, a skinny quartermaster about nineteen years old. "Those Japs find us trying to get away and they'll kill us! They'll kill us for sure!"

I went bug-eyed. On the one hand for Webster's extreme stupidity. On the other for the lack of anyone trying to shut him up. What the hell had happened to these guys?

"Nobody here's surrendering!" I roared.

Webster turned to his shipmates. "He's a crazy man! He's going to get us all killed! All we have to do is go

201

back to Manila and turn ourselves in and the Japs will—"

Bungo Callahan, a bandy-legged little boatswain's mate, stepped forward and drove his fist into Webster's gut. The quartermaster doubled over and collapsed in the thick grass.

Finally!

I put my hands on my hips and glared at my troops. Most of them still had that impassive look, but a few glared right back.

"All right," I said crisply, "We're only taking the 22 boat. Underway at sundown tonight. Spend the rest of the day taking everything off the other boats and putting them on her. That's all."

I turned my back and strode away. I kicked open the charthouse door and walked through the tiny compartment in two steps. Went down the companionway to the berthing compartment, hooked around to the officer's cabin, slammed the door behind.

I glared at the bulkhead. I grabbed the pillow off the rack and began tearing at it, getting angrier by the second. I could feel my face flush and teeth grind together.

My arms suddenly went apart and a thousand chicken feathers filled the air. I looked at them, stupidly astonished.

I sat in the chair, dazed. Watched the feathers seesaw through the air. Then remembered this was where Nash had done it. Maybe sitting in this very chair. I closed my eyes tight and tried to summon up the image I wanted to maintain of Nash, of him crouched behind the 44's wheel as he followed the destroyers that were after me, calculating the torpedo shot that ended up saving my life.

Instead all I got was a picture of Corregidor, of the men hiding in the tunnels and waiting for the word to come out with their hands up.

I felt tears rolling down my cheeks, leaving tracks that stung like acid.

It took an hour to collect myself, then I went back on deck and started supervising the preparations for getting underway.

The 22's gas tanks were topped off, using the final reserves of PTs 38 and 25. Surplus amounted to three fifty-gallon drums, and these were lashed down on the fantail. This gave us a grand total of 3,150 gallons, which was not enough to get us to Australia, but more than plenty so far as making one of the secret fuel dumps.

We slid the forward torpedoes from their tubes and let them splash. This was to save weight. Hokulani wanted to discard the other two, but I insisted we let them be, without really knowing why. It was a surety we weren't going hunting for trouble anymore. Maybe it was just because I felt the 22 was like an old bum in the soup line, and the Mark Eights were his last shreds of dignity.

All 50.-cal ammo belts were moved aboard, a tally of five hundred measly rounds. There was no 20mm ammo at all. Then we gathered up the .45s, the Springfields, the lone BAR.

Food came on next; the berthing compartment became knee-deep with coconuts. A few bunches of green bananas were laid on the fo'c'sle, there to hopefully ripen. Then the strings of sun-dried fish, a total of two-dozen chewy fillets. Fresh water was laboriously carried from a nearby stream, using steel helmets for buckets, and poured into the two-hundred-gallon freshwater tank. Canteens were filled and stowed.

The two other boats were carefully checked for spare parts. The carburetors were detached, along with gaskets, hoses, plugs, belts . . . anything that looked remotely useful.

Swifty took care of the disabled PTs' remaining armament. He swung a ball peen hammer against the delicate mechanisms of the fifties and 20mm. The fish we let stay in their tubes, disarmed.

Everything was ready to go. It was dusk, the skies red as blood. I asked Hokulani if there were any loose ends.

"It's Webster . . ."

"What about him?"

"Nobody's seen him for the last couple of hours."

I sighed. "He took off, eh?"

"Want me to get up a search party and go after him?"

I shook my head. "If he's so hot to turn himself over to the Japs, let him. Anything else?"

"Nope."

"Then let's get going."

A couple of guys lit off the LCM and backed her up the inlet. Cut the engine and opened the seacocks. They jumped off and swam back to the PTs.

I kicked over the 22's centerline engine and backed away from the bank, held the boat steady while lines were thrown to men stationed on the fantails of the stripped PTs. They caught them and made them fast.

I backed down, pulling the PTs to the middle of the inlet, then the sailors threw off the lines and dropped anchors over the side. They dived overboard and swam to the 22.

I carefully maneuvered near the anchored and empty PTs. Each had its engine-room hatch open — a hatch large enough to facilitate the removal and installation of the big Packards. Sailors lofted one grenade after another into the engine-rooms, their faces grim as they performed this sorry task. It was a sad little spectacle, like shooting a crippled thoroughbred. The grenades went off. The clean lines of the hulls kicked and warped outward, and finally the boats started to sink. The two portholes on the forward part of the Elco's charthouse looked like mournful, human eyes. I hung around long enough to watch them slip to the bottom. Maybe at low tide you might see a bit of the mast sticking up; now there wasn't a trace.

I nudged the centerline throttle and the PT slid from the inlet, cruising at the same speed rowboats use in the Tunnel of Love. Indeed, 'twas a night made for love, the air balmy and soft as silk, the early evening stars crystal clear against a purpling canopy. We slid into Manila Bay and I turned left, hugging the coast, following it out of the Bay to hook south.

Our last sight of Corregidor was that of a black, lonely-looking lump. One of the sailors studied it through binoculars and announced he could see a Jap flag flying from the parade ground's tall flagpole. He offered the glasses to anyone who wanted a look, but there were no takers.

My heading was due south, 180° by the magnetic compass — variation in this part of the world was zero.

Hokulani asked if he could drive. I moved aside and he took the wheel. "Keep her at five knots," I told him, "There's no hurry. Nice and slow." He nodded.

The only sound was the humming of the single engine. Nobody was talking. It wasn't exactly a festive night. I busied myself in going over the chart one more time. This present course was good for twenty-eight miles. Then, as the coast snaked eastward, we would turn to the southwest, to 220°, and make a twenty-one mile leg across Verde Island Passage. Our destination was the northeastern tip of the big island of Mindoro, where we would spend the daylight hours of tomorrow tied up somewhere in the bushes. Total trip time at this speed would be ten hours.

I killed time preparing a coconut. I stripped the husk, a tedious chore. Then I made a hole in the top of the nut and sucked the milk. I broke the nut and ate the chewy white meat. Then I lit up one of my last Luckies.

I hoisted myself over the cockpit and lay across the top of the charthouse, the back of my head resting against the tiny windscreen. It was warm enough to go naked. There were ten billion stars dangling from the sky, the Milky Way a heavy scattering of dust.

I thought about the way the guys had acted this morning, of all the backchat and surly looks I'd gotten when I was giving them the score. It had angered me more than I thought possible. Perhaps because it was so unexpected—up until then morale had been good. Excellent really, considering the circumstances. But the news that Wainwright had decided to throw in the towel had hit them where they lived.

Maybe they were just coming to grips with defeat.

Trying it on for size, and not liking it a bit. They wanted to give it back, like an ill-fitting suit, but pretty soon they'd realize it was on for keeps. America had been defeated. It was like coming home to find your mother lathering up her face, or your father using makeup. It was grotesque and nonsensical.

My anger softened.

I blew out a long, lazy plume of smoke. I thought about the guys—sixteen of us now—and what I knew about them. Most were from the Midwest. A few were from the Northeast, and a couple guys from the West Coast. I was the only Southern boy, except for Strip, but then I'd never counted Texas as a "real" Southern state.

Maybe that was why I was having an easier time of it. I already knew all about defeat. My childhood had been full of reminders of the Confederacy's surrender. Every little town had at least one sad monument to the Glorious Dead, erected in the middle of the town square for all to see and ponder. And ponder it I did, all through my boyhood. My heroes had been those proud men in gray, and I devoured their stories hungrily, thrilling to their great feats of courage and daring . . . but always, as I read, shuddering in the awful knowledge that these were actors in some Greek tragedy, that their great deeds would avail them nothing of the ultimate catastrophe. And wherever I traveled, visiting my many cousins, there was this common ground, this consciousness of defeat, as if the entire Southern nation had grown up knowing their house had once been beautiful and proud, but was now a run-down shack. Defeat. Its taste is sour with might-have-beens and only-ifs, its inheritance a bitter and bottomless cup.

I looked to port and saw the land curving away to the east. Time to turn. I got up on an elbow and told Hokulani which course to come to. He spun the wheel and we began our transit of Verde Island Passage. Here we'd have no nearby coast to mask our silhouette. Nor would we have anywhere to run and hide should a destroyer chance upon us. I told Hokulani to pass the word to all hands that now was the time for an extra-sharp lookout.

The current was more insistent here. It came against our starboard beam, making the boat sway up the three-foot swell and roll down the other side. I had to climb off my perch.

It was along 0300 when we caught sight of the destroyer. She was well astern of us, five to six thousand yards, crossing Verde Passage from south to north. There were no running lights, but her silhouette was sharp and unmistakable. Her bow lifted and fell as she ran head-on into the seas. Her speed looked to be moderate; fifteen knots, perhaps. I walked aft and looked at our wake. There was little foam and some phosphorescence, nothing at all to give us away.

She passed out of view, leaving us unmolested.

Golo Island loomed to starboard, and we passed her with a half-mile to spare. It was ten miles from this point to our destination. I looked at the eastern sky and thought I discerned streaks of gray. I told Hokulani to bump it up to ten knots.

Within an hour we were at our destination, the northeastern tip of Mindoro Island. We scouted the coast until we found a likely inlet, then cruised in. A sailor stood on the bow, throwing the lead line as we slowly nosed toward a shoreline overhung with thick vines and leaves. The bow mushed into soft mud, the overhanging leaves swallowing up the fo'c'sle. We tied lines to tree trunks, worked the stern nearer the bank, and heaved the anchor overboard. Big trees shaded us completely, hiding us from aerial view. The PT's paint was but one shade lighter than the surrounding vegetation. We cut the engine and settled down for the day's rest.

I didn't sleep at all. At midmorning a high-flying Zero drifted overhead. Men lay around the boat, shifting and dozing. Restless, I went inside the sweltering charthouse, put on the earphones, and spun the radio's dial.

I caught an English-language broadcast on KZRH out of Manila, a follow-up speech on yesterday's surrender. Startled, I recognized the voice as that of General Wainwright himself. I felt sorry for the old bastard. The way he talked sounded like he'd been worked over with blackjacks. He repeated the surrender speech, then ordered all American forces throughout the Philippines to give up and turn themselves in. He repeated the message several times. *All* American forces.

I turned off the radio and went topside. The green bananas looked strangely inviting. I yanked one off and began to peel it. Some sailors lay nearby, and I almost mentioned what I'd heard on the radio, just to make conversation. But stopped.

Was Webster the only likely deserter? Would someone else start getting itchy if I told them about Wainwright's order?

Whatever, I decided to keep my own counsel. And

walked away, feeling sad. My relationship with the crew had changed.

As soon as night fell we were underway for Busuanga Island, some eighty-two miles distant. This leg would take us across Mindoro Strait, and at ten knots it was going to be an all-night transit. Eighty-two miles across open ocean is a damn long hop, but Busuanga Island, at thirty-five miles across, was just too big to miss. Also, there was a beacon at Apo Reef, which we'd pass close by during the journey's midpoint, and this gave me further navigational comfort.

That night we had following seas, and no enemy warships were sighted. The Apo Light came up just as expected, a faint white light five miles to port. We made Busuanga just as the sky was beginning to lighten. Easy as a cheerleader.

Next night we hugged the Palawan Islands, making a ragged southwesterly course, navigation no problem as long as there was land to starboard. We tied up shortly before dawn at Dumaran Island.

I would've liked to continue down Palawan, a big island 240 miles long, and then make the sixty-mile hop to Borneo. But this would take us out of Philippine waters without having visited one of the fuel dumps.

The nearest was Calusa Island, eighty-three miles away. But this was an entirely different proposition than finding something as big as Busuanga. Calusa was a mere flyspeck, barely more than a mile wide. There were no navigational reference points along the way. We could miss it very easily.

I spent the day looking at the chart. It was a big one, showing the whole southern half of the Philippines, so it wasn't terribly precise when it came down to fine detail. I laid the course down very carefully, coming up with 132°. So be it. No fooling around on the helm tonight!

We got underway at dusk with Lumanski at the wheel. I felt bad as soon as Dumaran slipped below the horizon astern. We were now entirely dependent upon the PT's magnetic compass, a simple piece of commercial yachting gear for which there wasn't even a correction card—deviation was *assumed* to be zero.

The wind came in off our starboard bow, brisk at fifteen knots. There was a squall line well off to starboard. Stars winked out as the cloud cover increased. Would've been nice to have had a barometer, I thought sourly.

The squall hit near midnight, our journey half-done. The seas become more insistent, giving Lumanski serious trouble in keeping to course. Rain came suddenly, stinging as it whipped across the deck.

Lumanski increased speed in order to hold course. I prayed for this to be one of those quick squalls that come and go in a matter of minutes. But no dice. The wind kicked up to twenty hard knots and shifted to our starboard beam. The PT wallowed like an overstuffed oiler, rolling so often and so steeply that the antenna swayed to and fro like a deadly whip. Wind increased to thirty knots. I was next to Lumanski and saw the compass points spinning back and forth—he couldn't keep course within twenty degrees! One particularly bad swell set the port gunwale completely awash, taking the bananas on the fo'c'sle over the side. The seas were up to six feet and getting bigger. Next decent wave would roll us completely over.

"That's it," I yelled, "Head into the sea."

Lumanski eagerly spun the wheel but the PT did not respond. He immediately pressed the starter buttons for the port and starboard engines, then worked the boat into the seas using throttles alone. A wave smashed the bow and forced us to port, the bow quickly nosing away from the seas. But before we were broadside-to Lumanski had the starboard engine back full, port full ahead, and the bow moved sluggishly back into the waves. He kept on enough power to keep the bow pointing into the oncoming swells, constantly alternating the combinations of port-centerline-starboard. The bow lifted and slammed, over and over, and Lumanski fought hard to maintain control.

The charthouse door swung open and a sailor crawled out on hands and knees. Unless you had something to hold onto, this was the best way to get around topside. He looked at the storm, disbelief written on his face, then turned around and crawled back inside. It was a toss-up as to whether it was more comfortable to ride out the storm topside or below-decks. It was dry in the berthing compartment, but you had to keep to your rack and hold on tight as the compartment whipsawed through the seas. Up here there was fresh air, but a constant danger of being washed overboard.

Lumanski's tongue started hanging out after an hour, so I relieved him. I soon found it was bone-wearying work indeed, the muscles in my back aching with the strain and effort of the constant jockeying, my mind burning with the concentration of the expert shiphandling required.

The cabin door swung open again and another sailor crawled out. It was Lehr, a big cornhusker from Kansas. He moved slowly aft, pressing his arms and legs against the armor plating on either side. He got about four feet from the door—almost to the day cabin—then suddenly let go with a stream of yellow vomit. The deck was so wet the chow immediately washed away. Business complete, he crawled backwards and pulled the door shut.

Hokulani relieved me a thousand years later, and it was all I could do to hold myself upright and let the storm rage against my face. I wedged myself tight against the starboard gun tub, letting my head loll as the PT surged over the swells and crashed down the other side. It began to seem there was no other life than this storm, and that it was my fate to drag myself to the cockpit and relieve the mass of jelly at the controls.

The morning dawned beautifully calm and lovely. The boat gently lifted over one foot waves. I went all the way forward and stood on the bow, the relative steadiness of the boat feeling strange after the night's pitching and rolling. Hokulani was there too, sitting with his legs dangling over the side, big head slumped in exhaustion, eyes looking blankly at the water. The boat was drifting; Strip asked that all engines be shut down for a quick inspection, so we were coasting silently.

I looked around, the horizon utterly still and featureless for 360 degrees. Big puffy line of cumulus astern. Other than that, nothing.

Where the hell were we? How far had the storm pushed us off course?

"There it is," Hokulani announced.

"What?"

He pointed at the water. "There."

"What?" Impatience crept into my voice. Last night had pounded everybody's marbles loose.

Hokulani got up and came to my side. He hooked his arm through mine and drew me close, pointing into the sea. "Don't you see?"

I didn't.

"The wave patterns," he said, as if it were the most obvious thing in the world. "Can't you read them?"

Read them. Hokulani had something to say but he was going in the back door. Now I could do the traditional thing—jump up and down and scream—or I could mask my impatience and listen closely.

"Keep talking."

He pointed at the foot-high seas. "That's the ground swell, okay? The pattern is the same all the way to the horizon. But there's another pattern. See it?"

I did. It seemed but a few inches high, but a definite and steady pattern of tiny wavelets which marched over the larger waves of the ground swell, angling in from another direction. "So?"

"So the lesser swell is actually the force of the ground swell bouncing off the island."

"Say again?"

Hokulani knelt and put one meaty fist on the deck. "This is the island, right?" I nodded. He used his other hand to make sweeping motions toward the fist. "This is the ground swell." I nodded again. He made sweeping motions in the opposite direction, away from his fist. "When the ground swell hits the island, part of it bounces back. All you have to do is read the wave patterns and you know where to find the island."

He pointed to a direction off our port quarter. "So the island's there. Right over there."

I looked at the waves carefully. I had read many books on navigation but had never heard of this technique. And yet it made sense. "Where did you learn this?"

"My great-uncle taught me. He was a *kahuna*, a navigator." He stood, looking to where he thought the island lay, the lines of concentration wrinkling his brow. Then his eyes widened and his lips parted in a white grin. "And there's the icing on the cake."

I turned, saw nothing but the clouds on the horizon. "What?"

"Right there. On the underside of that cloud. See it?"

"See what?"

"That speck of green. It's real tiny, Mr. Leander, real hard to see. But it's there."

"So?"

"It's the reflection of the island, reflected right on the underside of the cloud."

I squinted hard. The undersides of the clouds were dark gray, it seemed. A speck of green?

"It's there, Mr. Leander. Honest."

I got the binoculars and looked. Still nothing.

"C'mon, Mr. Leander. What've we got to lose?"

Chapter Fifteen

I told Lumanski to kick over centerline. There was one grind on the starter and the engine coughed to life. Shouting above the rumbling, I told Lumanski to haul around to port.

I watched the Hawaiian carefully. He was pointing where he thought the island lay, his arm inching to the right as the bow slowly swung around. When he pointed straight ahead I gave Lumanski a steady-as-she-goes.

We chugged along at ten knots. Hokulani kept his hands in his pockets, his eyes flickering from the seas to the skies, the gentle breeze pushing his black hair off his forehead. Now and then he'd point a little to the right or left — course corrections.

I took a look through my binoculars every few minutes. I scanned the horizon, then the clouds. Then, quite suddenly, a thin line of green appeared on the horizon — tops of palm trees.

"Settle down, skipper!" Hokulani shouted. I was jumping up and down, laughing. "Don't tell me you didn't think I'd hit it right on the nose!"

I told Lumanski to increase speed. I laid my elbows on the forward cabin and watched Calusa increase in size. Finally it was entire—a long, low strip of white sand, a stand of palm trees and shrubbery clustered on the right quarter of the island.

We came to the island and made a long, slow circumnavigation. It was shaped like an "I," a mile long, one hundred yards in width, its axis north-south. Three quarters of the island was perfectly flat, consisting of nothing but white, hard sand. The northern quarter was palm trees and thick, waist-high shrubbery.

The fuel dump had to be amongst the palms. Every man on the boat was topside, looking at the island intently. I was beginning to wonder if this was Calusa at all when one of the sailors started shouting and pointing at the middle of the palms. I swung my binoculars in that direction and saw it. It was well concealed, the camouflage net clinging to the sharp outlines of neatly stacked drums.

Hokulani and I had a quick conference. How far could we bring in the boat? There was no dock of any kind. The bottom—the water was clear and we could see it—sloped up gradually, meaning there was no way to nose the PT up to the beach. We decided to drop the hook and swim ashore. The anchor was heaved overboard and I watched it hit bottom two fathoms below.

I took off my shirt. There didn't seem to be any coral, but I tied my shoelaces together and dangled the boondockers around my neck. I jumped overboard cannonball-style. It felt like a warm bathtub. I broke surface in time to hear the splashing of the other guys diving in.

The PT was anchored thirty yards from the beach, an easy swim. As soon as I felt bottom I stood upright and waded ashore. The wide beach was as perfect as any you'd find in the Caribbean, white and sugary soft. The palms were tall and gracefully curved, their long trunks gently bobbing against the breeze, their fronds trailing with a pleasant flutter. All a man needed was a hammock and a rum-and-coke.

We walked to the shade and quickly found the fuel dump. We took off the netting and saw the stack was arranged forty across, three-high, three-deep. They were fifty-gallon drums, and the first one I examined was marked: "If you are reading this you are shit out of luck." I looked further, found the magic stencil *100 OCTANE* and felt like the king of the world.

Strip Cunningham let go with a shout and we walked over to see what it was. Hoses with an in-line fuel pump. We watched Strip attach the hand crank and give the pump a few turns, then he told one of the junior motormacs to swim back to the PT and fetch some oil.

Hokulani and I went for a little walk, discussing the problem of how to get the fuel to the PT. Presently we were out of the palms' shade and the southern three-quarters of the island stretched before us, a natural landing strip. Here the ground was hardpacked beige dirt. There were some grooves where an unlucky airedale or two had touched down.

"There're four links of hose," Hokulani said, "We couple them together we've got maybe forty feet."

I scratched my beard. "Think we can work the PT

in close enough to link up?"

"Bottom's sand. I could nose the bow in gently, hold her steady . . . "

"You put the stern against those waves and you're going to have a hard time keeping her from going broadside-to."

"So how 'about a Med moor, stern to the beach?"

Sounded all right. "Let's go see where the best place is to do it."

We walked back to the shade. All eyes were on Strip, who grunted and cursed as he slowly moved the crank on the fuel pump. "Screw it," he hissed, dropping it down. He reached in his back pocket, withdrew a screwdriver, and began taking the pump apart. "Bet the goddamn thing's cockeyed. Piece of crap."

"It gonna work?" I asked.

"If it ain't I'll just get some of these guys to suck up the gas in their bellies and puke it into the tanks." He paused to look at the sailors. The young ones had expressions of disbelief. Strip roared with harsh laughter.

Hokulani and I collected two sailors and we went to the beach. We waded in the water, heading toward the PT. The bottom eased down smoothly; soon it was up to my neck. I began swimming. A PT's draft is six feet, so the depth I needed was that plus a little gravy. I held my breath and maneuvered underwater, finally got so that my feet were on the bottom and I was standing more or less upright. I extended my arms straight up and felt air on my fingertips. I broke surface swam a little further out, treaded water and looked around. We were thirty feet from the beach. Perfect.

"Okay," I called to Hokulani, "This is the drop-dead point. I stay right here and guide you in."

Hokulani spat out some water. "Right." He and the two sailors began swimming toward the PT while I maintained station. They clambered aboard, started the engines, and heaved in the anchor. Hokulani worked the boat in cautiously, finally turning so that he was parallel to the beach. He glided along slowly and I saw the first anchor thrown overboard. He continued on the same course, dead slow, and the second anchor splashed. Then he swung the stern to the beach and let the waves start pushing him toward me. I watched his progress intently. I swam sideways, getting out of the way and keeping Hokulani in view. Finally the boat was where I wanted it; I raised a clenched fist—the signal for "hold steady." Hokulani immediately relayed the hand signal to the guys on the bow, and I saw their arms working as they made their anchor lines fast to the forward cleats. The PT gently bobbed in the easy swell, nose to the sea, the taut anchor lines forming a "V" on the bow.

I swam backwards until sand brushed my feet, then stood. The PT's centerline engine was still burbling; Hokulani would cut the Packard once he was convinced the anchors were holding. I waded back toward the fuel dump.

Strip had the pump working. He'd also figured out what I was doing—two sailors were already rolling a drum toward the beach. I watched them roll it to the waves, then strongback it upright when the depth was two feet. One end of the hose was slipped through the cap on top of the drum, the other was held high as two sailors slowly sloshed toward the PT. The nozzle was heaved aboard, connected to the fuel tank, and a man at the drum began turning the crank. It was going to be a slow job, but it was going to work.

I walked to the shade and parked my butt in the dirt. I felt good. We were really going to do it. We were really going to make it to Australia. The trip was no longer a pipedream.

Suddenly I felt very tired. Sleep began coming at me in greasy, dirty waves, and I leaned my face against my knees.

"Skipper! Skipper! C'mon! Wake the hell up!"

It was Hokulani shaking my shoulder, his big face close to mine and tight with worry and concern.

"Why — what —"

Hokulani thrust out his arm, pointing to the north. "Over there!"

I turned and . . .

Ice. Yes, it felt exactly like a lump of ice. It formed in my crotch and spread up to my belly.

Jap destroyer.

Hokulani handed me a pair of binoculars as I scrambled to my feet. When I put them to my eyes I had to hold on tight in order to keep them from shaking.

She was five miles away and heading in our direction. Looked like her track was southeasterly, a course which would take her right by the island's southern tip.

"Well, Hoku, what do you think?" I was surprised at the calm in my voice.

"I don't think she's seen us. Otherwise she'd have on full speed."

"Think she's just on patrol?"

"Yeah. And it's our bad luck we happen to be here." He licked his lips. "What're we going to do, skipper?"

I looked around. No way she wasn't going to notice the PT. No way at all.

"Back to the boat," I said, "We're getting the hell out of here."

"But —"

"But what? You want to take her on toe-to-toe in broad daylight?"

Hokulani looked pained. "But we haven't finished taking on fuel!"

I grabbed his arm as I started to run. "C'mon! Get everyone back on board now!"

We ran back to where the working party was clustered around the fuel drums, shouting as we approached. The whys and wherefores consisted of our pointing at the Jap can on the other side of the island.

Guys ran to the water and began swimming. It seemed an incredibly long thirty yards.

I clambered up the cargo netting we'd slung over the side, and ran to the cockpit. I shouted for Hokulani to give me a thumbs-up when everyone was aboard. The Jap was now four miles away, but still plowing along at a leisurely clip.

Hokulani gave me the signal. I punched the starters for all three Packards. While they rumbled and smoothed out I shouted for the little Danforth anchors to be hauled on deck.

I pushed the throttles forward slowly and evenly, and the languid silence of the tropical isle was shattered. The bow lifted from the water and the wind whipped and pulled at my sodden trousers. My heading was due south.

Hokulani was suddenly at my side, his face still covered with droplets of salt water. "So now what?" He had to shout above the roar of the Packards.

I looked over my shoulder. Calusa was rapidly falling astern, and in between the widely-spaced trunks of the palms I could see the silhouette of the destroyer. She still hadn't put on more speed or altered her course.

"Get down to the charthouse," I yelled, "Break out the chart and the navigational kit."

I saw Lumanski and beckoned him. By the time he was moving to the cockpit I'd moved away from the wheel and — still holding on to it with one hand — shouted into Lumanski's ear that he was to keep the southernly heading and the forty-knot speed. I ducked into the charthouse.

Hokulani already had the big chart spread across the table. The navigation kit was open and I scooped out a mechanical pencil, parallel rulers, and a divider. I bent over the chart and started to work, and for some reason was reminded of a navigation exam back at the Academy . . . as soon as the instructor wrote the problem on the board he pressed the button on a stopwatch and told us to hop to it.

If he could only see me now!

To the southeast was the big island of Mindanao. I laid the course and measured its length with the dividers, laid the pinpoints against the latitude marks on the margin.

"One hundred and sixty miles," I announced.

Hokulani spun the overlay on the nautical slide rule. "At this speed we can make it there in four hours. But

Christ, the fuel . . ."

"We're just going to have to eat it. Forty knots is the only thing that'll lose that can."

"Shall I give Lumanski the course?"

"No, wait . . ." I studied the chart. "Now's the time to fake 'em out. Tell Lumanski to steer to the south-west. That way they'll think we're making a try for Borneo. When we lose the can over the horizon we'll turn back toward Mindanao."

"Aye." He tossed the slide rule on the table and ran back above. I went back to work, laying a dead-reckoning course from Calusa to the southwest. I took the compass and set it for ten miles—the distance we would travel in fifteen minutes at this speed, according to the slide rule—and began making ticks along the course. I noted the time, wrote it down at beginning of the course, then wrote it alongside each tick, adding fifteen minutes as I progressed.

There was a roar from above. *"Hey, skipper! She's opening fire!"*

I dropped my tools and ran back above. Just as I put my shoulders through the hatch I heard the distant rumble of her gunfire, the sound waves finally reaching our ears. A moment later two big geysers erupted one hundred yards off our port quarter.

"Jee-suz!" Hokulani shouted. "Those guys are mad!"

I took the binoculars off the console. Black smoke poured from the destroyer's stacks, indicating a sudden increase in speed, and white water fanned high on either side of her bow. She was seven thousand yards away and still on her original heading—and would have to remain so until she cleared Calusa. An orange ball of flame suddenly erupted from her forward

224

battery.

"Turn!" I yelled, *"Hard to starboard!"*

Lumanski spun the wheel and the boat pitched steeply. When the rounds landed—well to port, and so far off as to make the turn unnecessary—I had Lumanski come back to the southwest heading.

The next salvo was a double-blast from both forward and after batteries. I had Lumanski haul out to port this time, and only twenty degrees off our heading.

This time four geysers erupted very near where we would have been, had we not altered course.

We zigged every time she fired, veering off to port or starboard in ways that I hoped confused the Japs. Occasionally I had Lumanski keep a steady heading in order to add to the confusion factor.

By the time the DD had cleared Calusa we had opened the range to nine thousand yards. It was working. We were going to outrun her. Assuming the worst—that she could make an honest thirty-five knots—we would gain 2,500 yards every fifteen minutes.

I studied the outline of the ship intently. I had long ago pegged her as a *Kamikaze*—now I was trying to read the hull numbers off the bow. The ship was pointing directly at us, making this difficult. All I could see were two digits—might've been seventeen. Or just as easily nineteen.

Could Ohiro be on that can's bridge, staring into his binoculars and trying to pick me out?

The forward battery erupted and we went into our evasive maneuver. The shot landed wild. We were reaching the extreme range of the 4.7-inchers.

Things settled down—relatively speaking.

The destroyer no longer fired any shots, but she kept up a full head of steam. I wondered how quickly Japanese aircraft could be scrambled, if they would be overhead before sundown. We outdistanced the destroyer a little faster than I planned, and I recalculated her speed at thirty-two knots. Her bow was the first thing to slip below the horizon, then her pilothouse, and finally her mast.

It was two hours since the chase had begun.

I went below to the charthouse to see where the dead-reckoning position put us. I drew a line from that spot to Mindanao, went back above and gave the new course to Lumanski. He asked if I wanted to slow it down some.

Reluctantly, I shook my head no.

Chapter Sixteen

There were only two lines holding us fast, and they came aboard as soon as I gave the nod. The helmsman applied speed and we pulled away from the ramshackle pier.

Everyone was so eager to leave the isle of Maju they didn't bother giving it a second look. But Hokulani and I stood there on the fantail, watching the island recede.

It wasn't big—only five miles across—but by far the largest island we'd touched since we gave that destroyer the slip, eight days ago. And of all the islands we'd visited this past week, it had been the worst. *More* than the worst, really. The island had the same flavor of being on the wrong end of a drop-kick.

Hokulani shook his head. "I only hope we can come back at the Japs some day. I only hope—"

"Yeah, sure."

"Something eating you, skipper?"

I gave him a tired look. "Naw. Let's get on up to the charthouse and start figuring out what we're going to do next. Tell the helmsman to keep to the southeast until we can come up with an exact course."

"Aye, skipper."

The big Hawaiian went forward, but I didn't immediately follow. I couldn't stop looking at the island.

Even while we were making our approach this morning, while Maju was still some miles distant, the place had given me the creeps. The harsh morning light made it look alien and forbidding. A tall, barren mountain dominated its interior, and the vegetation on the surrounding coastal plain was dry and sparse. I spotted a little village through my binoculars, but no people moving about.

It was during the approach to the village that we spotted the remains of what turned out to be a U.S. minesweeper. She was resting in the shallows, and from a distance it looked like a bunch of burnt sticks poking up from the surface. It hadn't been there long, either — some of the brightwork glinted in the light.

We tied up at the village pier, and I led the landing party ashore. All twelve of the thatched huts were completely empty. In the village square we found three poles, each topped with a fly-encrusted ball.

These turned out to be human heads.

Two of them were Indonesian, but one was someone I recognized, despite the decomposition and horrible rictus of agony. I had met him a long time ago, when I was a plebe and he an upperclassman. Then later, as he leaned on the lifeline of the *Canopus* and told me of the plan to take his minesweeper and make a run for Australia.

We searched the village thoroughly, but we only found another human head. It was in the lone freshwater well, floating around like an overripe grapefruit. We buried it along with the others.

To say the crew was shocked would be putting it mildly. It was more like someone had taken a twelve-pound skillet and whanged them upside the skull. The minesweep guys had, after all, been trying to do the same thing we were doing now . . .

There was nothing left to do but wait out the day at the village pier, counting the hours until the safety of nightfall. The oppressive heat made the minutes tick by slowly. Eventually some guys started working their jaws, and wondered exactly what in hell had happened to the minesweep boys. And to the villagers. Some speculated that the villagers themselves had somehow done it, and were now in hiding until we left.

I found that ridiculous. The minesweep's hull was visible in the clear water, and it was shot through with cannon fire. It had been Japs all right. A Jap warship of some kind, come to call on Maju only to find an American minesweeper nestled in its cove, its crew succored by the villagers.

And the Japs hadn't fooled around. No, sir. Americans had been ordered to give up, hadn't they? Surely those who disobeyed this order realized the protection of any treaty was forfeit . . .

I watched the wake trailing aft. The western sky was painted with soft tones of orange, making Maju a dark silhouette. I turned and went forward, past the day cabin, and stopped at the cockpit. I glanced at the helmsman, Petty Officer 3/c Lehr, and saw that the big cornhusker's face was grim. I watched him keep heading by steering to the right, a compensation for the fact that tonight we were running on starboard engine alone. These past days we stuck to one engine at a time, in order to cut down on gas consumption. The thought of fuel made my stomach clench unpleasantly. I went on down into the charthouse.

Hokulani already had the chart spread out, a small-scale layout of the middle part of the Dutch East Indies. The easternmost peninsula of the Sulawesi was the chart's northern boundary, and the chain of islands which spread easterly from Java our southern mark. This covered such a big area it was imprecise in the details which interested me most: soundings, location of shoals, exact contours of possible landfalls. The chart was only a hair better than what you'd find in a medium-sized library's atlas.

"These islands here," I said, pointing to the right side of the chart, "The Halmahera. We could follow its coastline, heading south, for 140 miles."

"Plenty of good cover," Hokulani agreed. "But we have to make another sixty-mile cruise tonight in order to get there. I don't think five knots is gonna do it."

I fooled with the nautical slide rule, calculating a new speed. "So we'll . . . bump it from five and go eight knots. What do you think?"

Hokulani took the dividers and began measuring distances from Maju to other places we could go. I moved aside, letting him get closer. Hokulani could take all the time he wanted — I had great respect for his navigational savvy, especially after that trick with the waves.

The two rectangular portholes above the chart table were wide open, letting in a breeze that was so sluggish and humid I felt like I could grab a hunk of it with my hands. I thought about the past eight days.

We made the jungly shoreline of Mindanao after giving that destroyer the slip, and stayed hidden that night and throughout the next day. All we saw of the Japs were two low-flying Zeroes, skirting the treetops and hugging the coast. We got underway that night, crossed the Basilan Strait and holed up at Basilan Island next day. Underway again for a ninety-five mile run across the Moro Gulf for a point just south of the village of Lebok. Next night we continued working our way down to the southernmost tip of the big island of Mindanao, staying near the coast. Hid in the bushes for the day, and that night left Philippine waters for good.

There was a chain of atolls and small islands leading south, down to the Dutch East Indies. We island-hopped, traveling about sixty miles each night. Three days later we were hidden at the tip of the eastern peninsula of Sulawesi.

A lot of traveling for a PT, but it wasn't all just a travel story. Things had changed on the boat. The men became different, somehow, reacting to things in a way I hadn't seen in Bataan. It made me think of that psychology course I had at Annapolis, where they told us how Dr. Pavlov worried these dogs into salivating whenever they heard a bell. The same principle was at work on the boat. Only instead of a bell, the far-off drone of a reconnaisance plane would be the thing that'd make you feel all edgy inside. You'd prick up your ears and maybe even your eyes might bug out as you wondered if this was going to be the time the Japs would luck out. This same principle was at work in other areas as well. Nighttime had become the time of comfort and safety. Daytime was the time of hiding and watching and waiting.

And that wasn't all.

There didn't seem to be much talking anymore. Not about Japs, not about the war, not even about ball games or women or any damn thing at all. Everyone stood their watch silently, and spent their off-time sprawled somewhere on the boat, staring at nothing. And this wasn't the result of some kind of tropical lassitude. This was more the look some slow-witted but intent kid might have as he wound the key on a toy car tighter and tighter and still even tighter, until you just knew the next turn would bring the little metallic *snap*.

Hokulani turned on the little red lamp above the chart. It was starting to get dark. He tossed the dividers on the chart and sighed. I raised an eyebrow in an 'anything to say?' gesture. He shook his head.

"Okay," I said, "Give me a course."

He laid the parallel rulers against the chart and drew a line, then walked the parallels over to the compass rose. "One-two-zero, magnetic."

"Fine. Let's get on up and give the word to the helmsman. Set up the same watches as last night."

"Aye, skipper."

We went above. Stars were beginning to bloom in the sky, and the western horizon contained only a faint hint of rose. Hokulani went over to Lehr and started talking.

I heard a noise from up forward.

It was something I couldn't quite put my finger on, something I knew and didn't know at the same time. I went around the charthouse, the sound becoming familiar.

There was a guy sitting by himself up by the life-raft. He had his arms wrapped around his knees, and his back shuddered as he let go with another muffled sob.

I went over and hunkered down, putting a hand on his shoulder. "Hey . . ."

Seaman Calwell turned his anguished face to me, his cheeks wet with the tracks of greasy tears. "Oh, skipper . . . oh, Great God Almighty . . ." He began sobbing in earnest. He was only eighteen, but now he looked even younger, like he was in kindergarten.

But the sight didn't make me feel sad. Quite the opposite—it made me so mad it surprised me. Where was the sympathy? part of me wondered. The compassion? I gripped hard on Calwell's shoulder, forcing myself to contain my anger. "Take an even strain, boy. Things are going to be all right."

"Oh, no they're not!" The sudden outburst startled us both. He regained first. "We're going to get *killed*! We're going to wind up with our *heads* stuck on some goddamn *poles*! We've got to turn ourselves in to the Japs, don't you see! We've got to—"

"Shut up!" I rose from the deck, pulling Calwell up by his shirt. "Nobody's turning themselves in! You hear me! *Nobody's* turning themselves in!"

Hokulani was suddenly between us, breaking us up. "Hey now, skipper! What the hell!"

I backed off, and Calwell dropped to the deck. I was stunned at the speed with which the anger had taken total control. And baffled. Calwell was pushing himself up on his elbow, coughing.

"Come on, skipper." Hokulani's tone was subdued. "Let's go somewhere and talk, eh?"

But I resisted him. There were some other sailors

further up the bow, and their silhouettes were upright and attentive. That they had been witness to this little scene made me realize my anger was not entirely spent.

"You guys hear that?" I glared at the black outlines on the bow. *"Nobody's* turning themselves in. We going to make it to Australia, don't anybody doubt that for a minute. Understood?"

The dark shapes said nothing. Well, what did I expect? A thunderous *aye, aye, sir*, like they were a bunch of braced-up recruits at boot camp? I turned and walked back aft, Hokulani following. We found a relatively private spot on the port side of the day cabin.

Hokulani dropped his voice low. "You laid hands on that man, Mr. Leander. You know that's a court-martial offense."

"I didn't strike him."

"But you sure as hell lost it, didn't you, skipper? You really tripped off the line. You think the guys like to see that in the C.O.?"

He was right, and that made me angrier. "He rated it."

Hokulani sighed in exasperation. He put his hands on his hips and faced me squarely. "You're riding these guys too hard."

Anger changed to astonishment. *"Me? I'm* the one who's riding them hard? I haven't been doing anything to these guys. The problem here is that half the Jap Navy is breathing down our necks."

"Yeah. Right. But why aren't you cutting them some slack on account of it?"

"Why?" I forced a laugh, but it came out harsh and short. I searched for a snappy reply, and found one soon enough. "Because these guys have let me down."

"Yeah?"

"Yeah!" My mind took the let-me-down ball and ran with it. "Back when we were operating out of Mariveles they were doing great. There wasn't one yellow guy in the whole bunch. Now things are different. Now things are *tough*. These guys are acting like, like —"

"Like they're not sailors anymore?"

I don't know why that silenced me, but it did. Hokulani had put his finger on something which I hadn't wanted to think about.

But now it was out in the open.

The Hawaiian's tone softened. "Look, try and see it from their point of view. First the Pacific Fleet gets nailed in Pearl. Then the Asiatic Fleet runs from Manila. The reinforcements the brass hats promised never show up. Then Wainwright surrenders. And now here we are, in the middle of several thousand square miles of Japanese-controlled territory. Can you blame them for . . . well, not acting like they're fighting a war anymore?"

I sighed as I looked at the deck. "Why don't you go and check the course — I want to be alone for a while."

"Aye, skipper." He started walking off.

"Hey, Hokulani . . ."

"Aye?"

"Thanks."

He nodded and went toward the cockpit.

I walked back aft and stood at the fantail, looking at the foamy, sluggish wake. I undid my fly and began relieving myself. Hokulani was right. We weren't fighting a war anymore. We were nothing more than a pesky rodent running loose in the Japanese cabbage patch, frantically burrowing around as the ground was chopped with a sharpened hoe.

I buttoned my fly and sat by the antiaircraft gun. All it was good for was leaning against, there being no more 20mm ammo.

I guess it does something to your typical American boy when the U.S.A. turns out to be a total dishrag against small guys with slanty eyes. Makes them not so hi-ho hearty anymore. Makes them start to wonder about all the other things they've been told, from the Constitution right on down to the lieutenant's bars on my collar.

Ah, that might be how the kids act, but what about the old salts? Don't they get to think about things too, Hokulani? Don't they get to wonder if they're going to live through to the end of the month?

I leaned my head against the twenty's elevating wheel and let my mind drift. I thought about the last summer I had as a civilian, before I went off to the Academy. I spent it with my cousins, people who lived in the wild, hilly country of upstate Georgia. There was a terrible incident while I was there — an old couple had been robbed and killed by a drifter. I was hastily deputized, along with the other men of the county, and we went through those hills on foot, on horseback, with a pack of baying hounds. We caught up with the drifter two days later, and his long legs pumped furiously as he tried to escape across an open field. An old coot dropped him at one hundred yards with a pistol shot. We dug in the stirrups and rode across the field, coming to where the skinny down-on-his-luck cracker lay gasping in a ditch. The men looked down at him, contempt in their eyes, noses curled up as if the cracker were garbage. The witness kept yelling *that's him, boys, that's the one who done it*. The murdered couple had been well-liked. Blood was running hot. Two more shots finished the drifter, the high-velocity slugs kicking him deeper into the shallow, brackish water.

Now the shoe was on the other foot. *I* was the one running through the unfamiliar woods, out of breath, looking over my shoulder. And knowing that when they caught up with me I'd look into eyes that were cold and unfriendly, and the bullets would come too quick for even a prayer.

Chapter Seventeen

"Hey, skipper! Wake up!"

I clawed my way to wakefulness. Seaman Weffert was looking down at me, leaning forward with his hands on his knees.

"Mr. Hokulani's looking for you! What the hell you doing back here by the twenty?"

I got to my feet quickly, rubbing my face as if I could wipe away the sleep. "What's up?"

"Mr. Hokulani's spotted some kind of ship."

We went forward. The sea was still black but the sky had perceptibly lightened. Dawn was almost at hand. I made it to the cockpit, where Hokulani was standing next to the helmsman. Hokulani pointed out a tiny red light one mile off the starboard bow — a navigational light. I picked up a pair of binoculars.

I couldn't make out any details, but seeing the red light alone meant I was looking at the boat's port side. I couldn't see her sternlight, so that meant she was broadside-to. The boat's course would probably be across our bow. Hokulani was studying the contact with his own binoculars.

The guy who relieved Lehr on the helm was a lanky young seaman deuce named Milton. He didn't like that light one bit. "Should I turn, Mr. Leander?" he asked, voice a little high. "Slow down, maybe?"

"No. Hold steady." I quickly checked the button for our own navigational lights, making sure they were off. "But stand by to light off those other engines."

"Aye, sir."

Hokulani had his elbows propped on the console. "Got a mast," he said slowly, "Could be a lugger."

"They got a sail up?"

"Nope. Must be underway on an engine." He put the binoculars down. "What do you think?"

"Japs don't have any patrol boats with sails."

He shrugged. "That's true, but what do you want to do about this? Go dead in the water or turn around?"

I took another look at the light, thinking about it.

"We're going to follow her." The words were out before I'd really made up my mind. "We're going to follow her and take her."

Hokulani looked like he hadn't heard right. "What for?"

"Maybe she's a small cargo vessel. How would you like to have something to eat besides coconuts and bananas? Maybe she's got some gas, too." But that was window dressing. It just seemed that going after this boat might be the tonic we needed. Yeah. The more I thought about it the better I liked it. Turn on all engines and have at it . . .

Hokulani glanced at Milton, lowered his voice. "I recommend against it."

"Aye." I put the binoculars against my eyes. In a

way, Hokulani was right. This didn't make much sense. But he overlooked the larger issue. Here was the opportunity to become the hunter again, to live and feel as if we were the pursuer instead of the pursued. A warm feeling uncoiled in my belly, familiar and comforting.

The boat crossed our bow, three-quarters of a mile distant. We continued on our course, letting the unknown slip to our port bow. Her white sternlight came into view, and I told Milton to heave on around and steady on the light. As we wallowed over the unknown's red light winked out and only her white sternlight showed. Now we were following her from dead astern, and although this meant we'd stray from our original course, it was no big deal. Our landfall was 180 miles of coastline, so there was no way we could miss it.

There were few stars left in the sky, and more details were becoming visible on the boat. It was a cargo vessel all right, a distant relative of the most dilapidated of tramp steamers. And a small one at that. There was a tiny pilothouse situated all the way aft—two decks tall, the upper part being the wheelhouse, the lower level windowless and streaked with rust. There was a carelessly-dogged hatch on the starboard side of the wheelhouse. The rest of the weather deck was bare save for a cargo boom up forward—what Hokulani had mistaken for a mast. Poking out over the stern was a little pole from which a flag hung listlessly. A red ball was in the center of the dirty white field. Jap—but Jap merchant marine, not military.

My insides tingled. "Okay, Hokulani. Let's get the troops at general quarters. Nice and quiet."

Hokulani went below wordlessly. I turned my binoculars to the east, saw the Halmahera Islands. We could do our business with the Jap and be amongst the islands before it was fully bright, easy.

Men began filing out of the charthouse, Springfields in hand. One look at the small cargo ship and they knew what was going on. Gunners hoisted themselves into the two gun tubs, slid the canvas covers off the twin fifties. Hokulani came out and handed me my holster, and we discussed our plans as I buckled it on. Then I went forward and stood on the bow.

The other two Packards coughed to life and Milton eased the throttles forward. The PT gained speed rapidly, the bow canting up as the screws dug in. Milton brought it up to twenty knots, a speed which was reached with reassuring swiftness. The sudden breeze was refreshing.

This was going to be fun.

The PT pounded through the easy chop, water spraying to the sides each time the bow smacked down. I felt great. It'd been a long time since we'd done something like this. I held onto the lifeline and looked aft. Everyone was ready, their Springfields at port arms, each bearded face slashed with a grin. Two guys leaned together and said something, their eyes still on the vessel, then laughed merrily.

Like old times.

I turned back to the vessel. We were coming in fast, roaring in on her port quarter. I could see a lone silhouette in the pilothouse, his head turning as he observed our approach. There was no one else about.

Milton cut the speed to six knots and we immediately slowed. The PT wallowed as our own wake surged by, then we slid forward to exactly where I wanted to be — beam to beam, thirty yards of water separating us.

The crew of the little vessel started coming out on deck. Though oriental, I could see right off they weren't even close cousins to the Japanese. They wore cheap sarongs, the skirt-like affair men wear in this part of the world, and torn skivvy shirts. Malaysian, perhaps. I pointed my Colt straight up and squeezed the trigger — Black Bart's in town! — and the Malays immediately scattered. One of them waved at their little pilothouse, yelling something at the top of his lungs. The guy behind their wheel pulled back on a lever, and I heard their lone engine burble down and off.

Milton slowed the PT. Finally we were both dead in the water, bobbing over the chop, the distance between us still thirty yards. Now, in accordance with the plan Hokulani and I had worked out, Milton would carefully work the PT alongside, using various engine combinations . . .

But the vessel's crew wasn't making ready to receive us, as I had anticipated. Three of them came to the side closest to me, pushing and shoving a short, fat guy. And this one was a Jap, no doubt about it. He wore sandals, grease-stained khaki pants, and an undershirt. Their captain.

They pushed him to the side, holding his arms tight. The Malays grinned at us and jabbered — I couldn't understand but the import seemed to be *this is what you want, right?* There were catcalls from the PT, the sailors razzing and hurling insults at the helpless Jap.

The Malays' grins grew bigger, pleased at our reaction. Then, in less time than it takes to tell, a rusty machete was produced and whacked across the Jap's belly. There was a piercing scream, silencing us. The Malays let the Jap drop to the deck. His executioner lifted the machete on high, and, two-handed, slammed down mightily. There was another scream, this one making the hairs on the back of my neck stand on end. The Malay raised the machete again and cleaved him once more. The Jap's screams ceased abruptly, but his limbs jerked and spasmed in the most horrible way. His undershirt was now completely red. One of the Malays put his foot against the Jap's butt and pushed him overboard. There was a splash, and it looked like the Jap went straight down.

I was stunned. The swiftness of it had taken the breath out of me. A couple of the sailors laughed, and I heard a languid "Sayonara, Mr. Jap." More titters.

The Malays' message had been clear and quite convincing. No need to kill us, we're on the same side.

The Malays looked at us expectantly. One of them nodded his head and said something.

I raised my voice, speaking with great and friendly heartiness, hoping that my tone alone would reassure them. I kept my eyes on the Malays, but the message was for my crew. "Okay. These people want to know we're not going to hurt them. I'm going to put my pistol away, but I want you guys to have your guns ready for anything funny. Don't aim at them, just have your weapons ready and keep me covered."

Then, with exaggerated movements, I very deliberately holstered my .45, the Malays watching me with intense interest. I held both my arms out, palms flat, grinning. Peace, brothers. Why should you be afraid of us? We've only come roaring out of nowhere, in a boat which is obviously made to do nothing but sink the likes of you, a bearded bunch of men with no recognizable uniform of any country. The Malays grinned back. At least we were white, and the Malays knew the Japs were at war with the whites. "Bring her alongside," I yelled merrily. The Malays called back an equally cheerful message.

As the PT drew near I made up my mind about something else, and this I called out to my guys. "We're not here to rob these people. Everything we get from these guys we're going to trade for fair and square."

There was a loud, theatrical snort, and one of the sailors grumbled something about us taking what we wanted, nice guys be damned. Another sailor silenced him with a "anyone who kills a Jap is a friend of mine." There was more grumbling, but the execution of the Jap captain had made a favorable impression on the majority.

We slowly drew near. The coastal tramp was bigger than the PT, perhaps a 120-footer. Three Malays were on deck, making ready to receive. Another man appeared from behind the pilothouse, and I saw blood on his forehead. This guy wore trousers, like the Jap, and . . . he extended his arm, leveling a small pistol, and fired into the small group of Malays.

I dropped to the PT's deck immediately, reaching for my pistol at the same time. Milton put on power, knowing enough to get the hell away if things didn't go according to plan. Two of the Malays were hit, one of them rolling over the side to join his late captain. Swifty, the most senior gunner's mate aboard, squeezed off one quick burst of his twin fifties, the rounds splintering the side of the tramp's pilothouse. Two Springfields fired together.

"Cease fire!" I screamed, scrambling to my feet. "Get us out of here, Milton!" I trotted back aft, toward the cockpit. A seaman deuce, Dryden, too young to have more than a spray of peach fuzz, squeezed off another round. Hokulani began yelling at him to cease fire.

Another guy further aft calmly aimed his Springfield and squeezed off another round. Hokulani went wild, roaring "What are you? Fucking *deaf?*" The sailor slowly snapped the bolt, looking at Hokulani innocently. " 'Scuse me, sir," he said, undisturbed.

"Let's see what the hell's going on," I told Hokulani. "Hand me those binoculars. Milton, this looks good enough. Hold us right here." Here being a good three hundred yards from the tramp. Milton pulled the throttles back slowly and evenly. I lifted the binocs to my eyes.

Of the three original Malays, one was in the water, another sprawled lifelessly on deck, and the third was slowly walking toward the pilothouse, doubled over, obviously wounded. That other Jap—must have been the first mate—was nowhere to be seen. I thought about the blood on his forehead and worked out a scenario: American PT boat comes out of nowhere, crew hastily decides to overthrow their Jap masters. One quick machete chop to the first mate, then drag the captain topside, there to demonstrate to the Americans the sincerity of their affections. Whoever'd taken care of the first mate had done too quick a job.

Hokulani came up to my side. "Looks like one of our guys got hit by a stray bullet."

"What? Who?"

Hokulani jerked his thumb back aft, where two sailors were attending the prostrate form of Bungo Callahan.

"How bad off is he?"

"Don't know . . . it was a head shot, skipper."

I looked back at the ship, cursing myself. One minute ago I'd been having a good time. *Damn!*

There was a flat, muffled explosion on the tramp. The Malay struggling back aft dropped to his knees as his boat shivered. Black smoke began to pour from the pilothouse hatch.

"What the . . ." Hokulani whispered, puzzled.

"First mate must've gone below," I said. "Sabotaged his own ship. A last little banzai."

"Christ."

And, as if in confirmation, the Jap first mate struggled out of the pilothouse hatch, coughing from the oily smoke. He still had the pistol in his hand, and Lord knew what he intended to do with it. Fire at us until we did him in, probably.

"Don't fire the fifties," I said crisply, aiming my voice at the gun crews. "One of you marksmen take that guy."

Three Springfields cracked in quick succession. One slug took the Jap in the shoulder and spun him in a complete circle. He dropped to the deck like a loose puppet.

"That's it," Hokulani said. "It's all done, skipper. Let's get the hell out of here. Please."

"Not without at least one look. You take charge of the boarding party and see if there's anyone else below. I want to check on something in the wheelhouse."

I told Milton to hump it over there and this he did. We approached the tramp quickly. In times of leisure it is always a matter of interest how a man brings an eighty-foot PT alongside a pier or whatever, the ideal being a smooth approach which kisses the pier gently. But we were in a hurry, and Milton made no bones about smacking the PT against the tramp's side.

I went to the side and leapt over to the tramp's deck, several other men close behind. Lines were secured fore and aft, a man standing by each cleat and ready to let go instantly. The PT rocked and bumped against the tramp's hull.

Hokulani led a couple men below, coughing against the smoke. I, meanwhile, scampered up the rusted ladder and into the tiny pilothouse. There was a miniature chart table, a wheel, and a compass. I opened the lower cabinets of the chart table, found nothing but a bunch of old wires and electrical tape. What I wanted was a sextant and a nautical almanac. That way I could've determined our latitude. If there'd been a chronometer I could've found longitude as well. But no dice. This boat was so broke there wasn't even a radio.

I took a look at their chart. It was greasy, folded many times top accommodate the table's small dimensions. According to the original stamp the survey was Dutch, but it had been reissued by the Imperial Navy. All the lettering was chop-chop. The vessel's origin was a large island three hundred miles to the south. Destination seemed to be the northernmost island of the Halmahera group, some 140 miles to the north. There were no marks on the penciled track which indicated they'd taken a fix — the crew probably made this run so many times they navigated by seaman's eye alone. There were neatly-written times on the track, laid out as anyone would when preparing a dead-reckoning track. I compared the present time with the mark on the track, discovered their DR position put us eighty-five miles to the north of where we actually were. Or where I *thought* we were . . . I put the chart down and looked out the dirty windshields.

Hokulani was standing directly below, shouting to the men. He had one hand around the arm of a boy, holding him upright. The boy spasmed with coughs.

I quit the small pilothouse, slid down the ladder, and went over to Hokulani. "Two small Malays below," he shouted. "Dead. Shot by that pecker." He nodded at the first mate's body, which lay sprawled at our feet. I leaned down and yanked the pistol from his hand. It was a Nambu, crudely made and ugly, evidently a 7mm variation of the Imperial Army's 9mm issue. I tossed it overboard.

"How's the damage below?"

"Jap set fire to the engine room. Looks like he's opened the sea cocks full bore. This old whore's going down."

"Then let's get going."

The boy was helped aboard the PT, then the wounded Malay was eased over. The rest of the boarding party went over, and Hokulani and I jumped aboard as the lines were loosened.

We pulled from the tramp with hardly a scrape to the PT's hull. I told the helmsman to make ten knots and head for land. I went back aft to examine the wounded.

Doc was tending them, the "doctor" being a nineteen-year-old seaman by the name of de Neuman. He had, in prewar days, been studying to make rate as a medical corpsman, and one day probably would. He'd once confided that when his hitch was up he wanted to become a veterinarian.

Doc was putting a compress against the left side of Bungo's face. One look at that mess made me wonder why Bungo wasn't screaming his head off. The Malays were nearby. The older one, thin but graying, was on his back, his face tight with the strain of coping with a couple pieces of lead in his gut. The boy was kneeling with the old one's head in his lap, holding his hand, speaking softly.

I shook my head wondrously, marveling at my stupidity. The morning had turned out to be an utter fiasco. Four Malays were dead, people who would've still been alive had I not gotten ants in the pants. The only Japs that were dead were a couple of merchant marine officers, veritable noncombatants. And, of course, Bungo was nursing a slug somewhere inside his brain. Jesus!

"There she goes," one of the sailors remarked. I turned and saw that the tramp's main deck was awash. Black smoke poured from the wheelhouse, the only thing beside the cargo boom still above water.

"Come on, Milton," I called, "Hurry it up! It's almost full light."

Chapter Eighteen

"Skipper?" I turned to the voice. It was Strip Cunningham, chewing on the stub of an unlit cigar. He looked weary. "Bungo's ready."

"Muster all hands not on watch on the bow."

He nodded and went forward. I put my hands in my pockets and followed.

It was just past sunset, the sky bathed in tones of orange and purple. The last of the Halmahera Islands were slipping astern. It had been two days since the cargo vessel had gone down. Two days of such an unrelenting grimness it seemed as if a weighted blanket had been thrown over the boat.

And how many more days like this, I wondered. How many more?

The old Malay had died yesterday. The boy — in broken English he told us his name was Sevu — persuaded me to make a stop at an uninhabited islet. There he had built a pyre and cremated the remains. We were underway before the smoke rose very high.

Bungo went this afternoon. Once that slug entered

his head he was a goner, but . . . he had lingered. For two days he had lingered. Talking nonsense, calling out to a brother who died long ago, taking up most of our ampules of morphine.

No cremation for Bungo; he was going the sailor's way. His shroud was a dirty piece of canvas, sewn tight. Secured between his feet was a spare anchor, a little Danforth.

Suddenly I realized I was going to have to say words, and the service for burial at sea was not among the speeches I'd memorized. Buck's motto: Never Prepared. I was going to have to make up something which would lend dignity to a death which was in large part my doing.

Sailors began appearing, and I stopped Donnythorn, a twenty-year-old seaman first. He might be of some help — not only was he the son of a Methodist preacher, he had been a chaplain's assistant on a cruiser before coming to our unit.

"Hey," I whispered. "You been in on any burials at sea?"

He looked nervous for some reason, and kept his eyes away from mine. "No, sir."

"C'mon, you were the chaplain's assistant on the *Indianapolis,* weren't you?"

He looked at me briefly, and his eyes had a funny glint. "I was for a while, sure. But the chaplain kicked me out and put me down with the deck apes. Didn't you read that in my service record?"

"Yeah . . ." I did remember looking at his record, and getting the feeling as I read between the lines that there had been some kind of trouble that was hushed up. "But you can still give me a hand with this."

He looked back down. "I don't know nothing about burials," he said stubbornly. "All that religious crap is just mumbo-jumbo to me."

"Okay." I let him go.

Finally everyone was topside, save for Lumanski, who was driving, and La Salle down below standing watch over the Packards.

"Mr. Hokulani," I called formally. He turned, eyebrows raised. "Have the men fall into quarters." He looked at me as if it were a nonsense order. Well, it *had* been a long time since our last formation . . . and I realized the last one was before the war started.

"All right!" Hokulani barked. "Let's form up. Let's go. Fall into quarters."

Slowly the crowd coalesced into a line running from the charthouse to the tip of the bow, all facing west, the canvas shroud before them. I'd seen bums in a soup line looking better than this.

My command.

"You two," I said, pointing at Cochrin and Frum. "Stand on either side of Bungo and . . . heave him over on my signal." They took their positions stiffly.

I took off my cap. Those who had hats did likewise. I bowed my head, trying to think of what to say, but the only thing which filled my mind was the cap in my hands. The khaki part was splotched with grease and dirt, the chinstrap faded to a tired yellow, the officer's insignia tarnished. I raised my head, cleared my throat. Damn. What was Bungo's real name? All his dogtag read was "T.R. Callahan."

"We are here to commit the body of Petty Officer Callahan to the deep. All of us knew him pretty well, knew him well enough to depend on him when he gave his word. He was always ready with a good joke, always ready to pitch in. He was a good shipmate and a good boatswain's mate, and that's all anyone can ask of a sailor. I was looking forward to bending a few with him in Australia, but when your times comes . . . well, your time comes. He had a bad time toward the end of his life, but that's not the part I'm going to remember. When I think about him it's going to be about the old days in Manila, and about the way he proved right handy when we went on that raid up in Binanga. I'm going to remember that until I'm an old man, and as long as he's not forgotten he'll not be truly dead. So now we commit his body to the deep in the hope that he may rest in peace. Amen."

There were mumbled Amens. I put on my cap, nodded at Cochrin and Frum, and raised my hand in salute. They grabbed the shroud, grunted as they heaved it overboard.

Splash.

All eyes followed it as it trailed aft, sinking.

The formation started breaking up, even though there'd been no order for dismissal. I should've said something about that, but I was thinking about something more important. Like that Bungo might still be alive if it wasn't for me.

Then I remembered a part of service I'd forgotten to mention—the bit about the sea giving up its dead.

I chewed on that a while, thinking about Bungo coming to me at night, ribbons of seaweed dangling from his outstretched arms.

I was hunched over my log, noting the details of

Bungo's demise, the approximate location of his committal. I wrote under the dim light of the red-lensed DC lamp, working on the chart table. The boat rolled slowly as we worked our way through the glassy seas.

I capped the pen and put the log on the shelf. The chart was still spread out, and I examined it again, refreshing my memory as to the particulars of the course.

The track was laid across the Ceram Sea. Our destination was the big island of Buru, almost 128 miles due south, and in order to get there before sunrise we would have to go twelve knots.

"You busy?" It was Hokulani. Standing next to him, dwarfed by the Hawaiian's bulk, was Sevu.

"No, just finishing up. What do you want?"

"Want to talk with you about this kid here. What do you think we should do with him?"

"Put him ashore when we get to Buru."

"No!" His vehemence startled me. "I want to go with you!"

"Listen, kid. Half the Jap Navy's after us. This PT is where you don't want to be."

He stepped closer. "I do not want to go back. Take me with you to Australia."

"I'm sorry."

He was close enough now for the red light to show his features. Young kid, wiry build, with eyes that were too big for his face. Looked to be sixteen or seventeen. "I can be of use to you."

"Yeah? How?"

He looked down at the chart and pointed to where my track made landfall on the northern coast of Buru. "You should not go there. Many Japanese. This little

254

village even has a military governor." He indicated a cove on the island's western side. "No one ever goes there. It is plenty safe, you bet."

Hokulani and I exchanged glances. This little bit of news just might have saved our lives.

"Please take me with you," Sevu repeated. "I want to go to Australia. I know there are people like me there, training to fight the Japanese. Take me."

I sighed. The information he'd given us *was* useful . . . "Okay, kid. If that's what you want, you can tag along. You may be of some use after all."

He grabbed my arm. "Oh, you not be sorry, Captain. I serve you good, you bet."

"Uh, listen," Hokulani interrupted, "It's time for my trick on the wheel, so—"

"Yeah, okay. I want to have a little chat with Sevu here, but I'll be up later. I want to talk with you about something."

"Aye, skipper. See you." Hokulani shouldered his way out of the cabin. I snapped off the light, pulled out a pack of cigarettes and offered one to Sevu. He took it, his grin so broad I could see it even in the dark. I leaned against the chart table and studied his black silhouette.

"Sevu, how come you know so much about Buru?"

"That is where the *Santri* came from."

"Was that the name of your ship?"

"Yes."

It was a sad tribute to my curiosity that I had only now gotten down to asking him about that ship. I turned the light back on and started writing details in the log.

He told me about the setup—it was as I surmised.

The *Santri* had been requisitioned by the Japanese shortly after the Dutch East Indies had fallen. The crew often spoke of deposing their new masters, but there seemed no safe way to do it. Until, that is, we came on the scene.

Sevu spoke rapidly and eagerly, like any smart young boy giving the right answers to his teacher. But I soon found it wearying. I would've felt more comfortable had he been sullen and uncommunicative, as if holding me responsible for the death of his friends. As was indeed the case. But he jabbered on, and I finally cut the light and told him to go find someplace and rack out. I was anxious to talk with Hokulani.

Chapter Nineteen

There were so many stars Hokulani's silhouette was sharply defined. The sparkling canopy was huge and vast, and it worked its old trick on me again, making me wonder if there really were a God. The Packard rumbled evenly, and now and then there was the slap and spray of wavelets pushed aside by the hull.

"Evening, skipper."

"How's it going?"

"No problems. What was it you wanted to talk about?"

I looked around. There were a couple guys sprawled on top of the day cabin, and a few more up on the bow. I dropped my voice. "How do you think these guys are taking Bungo's loss?"

It was long seconds before Hokulani said anything. Finally he shrugged. "They've seen a lot of their shipmates go down. It isn't fun, but there's not much that can be done about it."

That had a false ring to it. And it made me want to stop beating around the bush and ask him what was really on my mind. *Do they blame me for it, Hokulani? Do they talk about what a fuckup I am? Do you?*

I wanted to grab his arm and turn him from the wheel to face me. I wanted to spill it all out in a torrent — Am I handling things right? Are we going to make it? Are the Japs going to get us?

But I couldn't do it. I couldn't break down and start babbling my darkest fears like I was . . . like I was any other guy on the boat. I was C.O. I was the one who was supposed to see things in black and white, and choose accordingly. I was the one who was supposed to allay doubts by my very bearing and strength of resolve.

So would say a textbook on leadership. But I didn't step out of any book. I was just as full of doubts about this trip as any man on the boat. I spent plenty of time wondering if we could make it. But there was no one to whom I could turn for succor. Not even Hokulani.

The Hawaiian drove on, silent with his own thoughts. I looked up at the stars, and . . .

"Hey, Hokulani."

"What, skipper?"

"You hear something?"

The Hawaiian cocked his head and listened. "Yeah," he said finally. "Something with the starboard Packard, maybe?"

I listened harder, trying to sort it out. It was a faint, mechanical whine, very high-pitched. Like something wrong in the supercharger? Something in the noise made me think of compressed air . . . and my stomach did a slow flip-flop when I thought of the worst possibility.

I picked up a pair of binoculars and began scanning

all sectors. It didn't take long to latch on something, and when I did it made my throat feel dry and cottony. "It's a destroyer."

"What!"

I gave him the binoculars, held the wheel steady while he looked. I knew he spotted it when I heard his quick intake of breath.

It was two miles off the starboard bow, its outline jet black against the starry velvet. A *whee-ee-ee* drifted across the night—the sound of her forced draft blowers sucking air down into the boilers. The pitch of the whine grew higher and higher, which meant she was taking in more air, which meant the boilers had an increased demand, which meant she was putting on speed.

Our course was due south, but the destroyer looked to be heading southwest. I judged her speed to be fifteen knots and rapidly increasing. Like us, there were no running lights. She was going to cross our bow at a distance of perhaps three miles.

"Think she knows about us?" Hokulani asked.

"No. Not yet."

"Want me to stop? Slow down? Speed up?"

"Hold everything as is."

He let out a long breath of air. "Aye, aye, skipper."

A red light flashed on from the destroyer's bridge, then began blinking rapidly. It was a signal lamp, and pointing directly at us. The flashing stopped. Had she spotted us and was asking for identification, or . . .

I turned around, using the binoculars in a fast sweep of the horizon astern.

There was another destroyer.

She was two miles off our port quarter, and heading

directly for us. A red signal lamp flashed from her bridge, blinking rapidly in code. I turned and looked at the first destroyer, saw that she was answering these blinks.

"They got us?" Hokulani asked.

"I think we're in their line of sight," I said slowly, speaking my thoughts as they came. "They're just passing messages to each other. If they knew we were here they'd already be firing."

"Yeah, that's what it is." A note of desperate hope crept into his voice. "Maybe they're out here on some sort of exercise. We're just caught in the middle."

"Go ahead and start the other engines anyway."

He hit the starters and the port and centerline Packards sputtered and caught.

The destroyer astern was picking up speed. The other destroyer was almost directly ahead, signal lamp stuttering. *Take station one thousand yards astern* I imagined the dots and dashes to be. Yeah. A little night-time maneuvering to while away the long watch.

But what a place for us to be!

"Bump it up to twenty, Hokulani. Let's get the hell out of the way."

His hands were already on the throttles. The bow canted upwards as the roar of the Packards increased. Enough for the Japs to hear? Enough of a wake to be seen?

The charthouse door opened halfway and Lumanski poked out his head. "What the hell's going on?"

"Japs," I said. "We're right in the middle of some kind of goddamn formation."

"Sweet humpin' Christ. You want the guys at general quarters, skipper?"

I hesitated. "Yeah. But pass the word to keep the noise down."

Lumanski went back below, pulling the door shut.

We were now on the same course as the first destroyer, heading southwest. Distance to both destroyers was the same, two miles each way. I watched the other can intently, wondering if she would turn as we had, correcting her course for an intercept. But she stayed on her original heading, cruising, as near as I could figure, for some station off the first destroyer. They were still blinking their signal lamps at each other.

"I think we're gonna be all right," Hokulani said, "I don't think they know about us at all."

I mumbled assent, eyes still locked to the binoculars. They might just be playing around, but that didn't mean they weren't ready to go to battle stations instantly. We weren't out of the woods, not by a long shot.

Guys began piling out, Springfields in hand, ready to take up battle stations. This consisted of finding a good spot to hunker down and lay your rifle across something steady. Swifty and Boeke clambered into the gun tubs, eased off the fifties' canvas covers. I raised my voice just enough to carry around the boat. "If the Japs find us, it'll be with the searchlights. Aim for those. You guys on the fifties, fire only on my direct order."

There were answering grunts. There was little hope of hitting a searchlight with a single-shot weapon, but we were just too low on .50-cal for promiscuity. I would save those for . . . what? If a destroyer came right alongside?

"Look at that," Hokulani said urgently. It was the can we'd first spotted. She was heaving over in a sharp turn, but without running lights it was impossible to tell if she was heading directly for us or directly away. The other can was still on her course, slicing through water we'd occupied moments before.

"What's happening now?" Hokulani asked. "What the hell are those guys doing?"

"Shit, practicing intercepts for all I know."

It was very hard to figure out what was going on. They could be trying some high-speed maneuvers, or maybe something was indeed up. No searchlights on, just those flashing red blinkers going like mad. I still couldn't tell which way the first DD was going.

"All stop," I told Hokulani. "Let's go dead in the water for awhile." He used one big hand to bring the throttles back, then we were bobbing in the three-foot seas.

The nearer destroyer suddenly snapped on her running lights—from our vantage all we could see was one green light and the white sternlight—then just as abruptly snapped them off. The other can put hers on momentarily—port and starboard lights, white masthead and range lights. Now I knew which way they were going—directly for each other.

The two black silhouettes turned, avoiding collision.

Hokulani laughed aloud. "Things must be getting a little hot on those bridges. They almost hit each other! That's why they turned on their running lights. They don't know what's going on either."

I smiled at some memories of my own, back when I was an Officer of the Deck on a destroyer. "They definitely don't know we're out here; they're just using this stretch of water for practice."

"That's it, skipper. Probably got their junior officers up on the bridge for a little practice in night maneuvers."

"Jesus. That one's heading this way again. Let's get out of here."

Hokulani brought the engines up carefully, this time holding it to ten knots. One destroyer was so close any greater speed on our part would kick up enough wake for them to see.

We got out of the way and stopped again. The destroyers' sleek outlines cut through the night, coming close to each other and then turning away. It was extremely confusing. Once I saw they had formed a column—one directly astern of the other—then they executed a simultaneous turn, winding up on each others' beam. They executed another maneuver and I again lost the sense of it. I could picture the junior officers on those bridges, sweating over maneuvering boards, eyes so intent on the other ship there'd be little chance of seeing us.

We jockeyed around, trying to get clear. But as luck would have it the DDs kept dogging us, conducting their maneuvers in our immediate vicinity even as we slowly headed south.

"I'm getting tired of this," Hokulani said after a half-hour of it. "I'm just about ready to open up this baby full bore and get the hell out of here once and for all."

"They spot our wake, they have us. Just keep your shirt on a little while longer."

"Yeah. Here comes one again."

Hokulani spun the wheel to starboard, bringing us to a course perpendicular to the destroyer's. The can turned immediately, steadying on us for a perfect intercept. Hokulani and I exchanged tense glances. He spun the wheel in the opposite direction, bringing us completely about. My hands tightened on the binoculars as I saw the destroyer turn again. Something was up.

"Full speed, *now!*"

Hokulani didn't have to be told twice. He slammed the throttles to the console and the deck canted up so sharply and so suddenly I had to grab the windscreen to hold myself upright. The roar of the Packards was deafening. We began pounding through the waves with stiff, bone-jarring smacks. A spray of warm salt water fanned up and over the bow.

The white beam of a searchlight suddenly cut through the night and fell on our churning wake. It swung quickly along the path of white foam, and I closed my eyes against the brightness that would surely come. Through slitted lashes I saw the world explode with a brilliance more intense than any sunlight. It was so strong it washed out all colors, making everything look like an overexposed photograph.

Christ!

Hokulani commenced zigzags, desperate to throw off the beam, spinning the wheel in erratic patterns. I held on tight to the armor plating behind Hokulani's back. The white cone of light slipped, found us, wavered, then locked on tight. The Springfields began to crack intermittently, guys holding onto the boat with one hand as they squinted into the bright light and squeezed off.

"*Get the smoke screen generator going!*" I yelled. "*C'mon! C'mon!*"

264

There was the high snarl of a Jap machine gun and the water around us began to pop with tiny white geysers. Suddenly and unexpectedly there was the throaty boom of twin fifties, a single roaring *buda-buda-buda* that sounded like a small rapid-fire cannon.

The searchlight went out, throwing us into blessed darkness. Cheers rose from all around. Swifty, in the after gun tub, had done it. Disobeyed my orders in firing without command, but . . . my own cheer was loudest.

There was the bark of the Jap's forward battery, illuminating her fo'c'sle. The round screamed over our heads like a rocket, and a column of water and spray exploded two hundred yards ahead. We roared through as the geyser fell back onto itself.

"Steady up," I told Hokulani. "Let's get distance while we can."

The Japs no longer knew exactly where we were, but they were going to take their best shot while we were still in the neighborhood. The nearer DD, the one whose searchlight Swifty'd taken out, was eight hundred yards on our port quarter. The other was three thousand yards on the starboard quarter, its searchlight fanning back and forth as it tried to pick us up. Black smoke poured from both ship's stacks as they continued the process of coming up to full power, which would be . . . what? Thirty? Certainly not thirty-five — what I'd seen of their silhouettes indicated they weren't anything new.

Our smoke screen generator finally got going and oily smoke fanned upward and billowed astern. Rifles were lowered; the outlines of the cans had become obscured. The searchlight beam sliced into the screen, sharply defined in the expanding haze. The beam swung right to us, its light weak and diffuse, then swung away. I heard a bullet whine off the armor plating near the 20mm.

I squeezed myself next to the cockpit and took a look at the compass. Hokulani had steadied due south, our original heading.

I looked back aft and only caught the occasional glimpse of a Jap destroyer. Both were falling rapidly astern. I called for the smoke screen generator to be cut.

"We got it dicked," I said to Hokulani, clapping him on the shoulder. "We've got 'em outrun." Something fluttered over my head, sounding like a hornet. Stray bullet.

"Think we can make it to Buru in time to find a good hiding place? It's a cinch there's going to be some hard looking for us tomorrow."

"Just keep the engines opened up and we should get there in plenty of time. I'm going below to check the chart."

"We're really burning up the gas, skipper."

"Yeah. But first things first, right?"

Chapter Twenty

Hokulani and I were in the charthouse, leaning over the table and trying to work out a course. It was steaming hot, and I found it difficult to keep my mind on the job. My brain seemed ragged and loose, and my eyes kept drifting to the little rectangular portholes just above the table.

All I could see out there was jungle. If I were to go out on deck, I'd find myself inside a leafy cave.

We were snugged in close to a riverbank. Thick leaves and vines had been drawn over the PT, and the limbs of some trees had been pulled down and tied to the cleats.

We had beat the Japs by three hours, losing them over the horizon well before dawn. The eastern sky was just starting to lighten as we pulled into this inlet — Sevu was up on the bow, acting as pilot — and the camouflage job got underway immediately. A long-range recon plane roared directly overhead shortly thereafter.

Like a police dispatcher calling all cars, the Jap cans

had radioed all points to be on the lookout for one Yankee PT. There had been at least one overflight every hour, sometimes more. Once there were even two Zeroes, flying just above the treetops.

But they wouldn't find us, not in one day. Buru is a fairly sizable island, being ninety miles from east to west and fifty north to south. One hell of a lot of bushes for the Japs to beat.

"Hey, you listening?"

I snapped back from my reverie. "What was that, Hokulani?"

"I was saying it might be a good idea to lay low here for a couple of days."

I shook my head. "If we stay here a day we'll end up staying a week. We've got to keep moving."

He nodded slowly, one hand rubbing his chin as he studied the chart. "All right, skipper. Then how about heading east? There might be a better place to hide over in Seram Island. It's only twenty miles away."

"No. We're heading south. I don't want to fuck around these islands forever."

"Then we've got an awful long stretch tonight," Hokulani said, tapping the chart.

Indeed. From Buru to the next chain of islands down south was 226 miles of the Banda Sea.

A long haul, but . . . even so, it looked mighty tempting. For those islands on the other side of the Banda Sea were the southernmost of the entire Dutch East Indies. From there it would be only 280 miles to Australia.

Two-hundred-and-eighty measly miles!

We discussed the upcoming cruise. There was a tiny island in the middle of the Banda Sea, Lucipara according to the chart. It was almost midway between Buru and the southern chain of islands. We would therefore take the Banda Sea in two whacks—sail 98 miles tonight, hide in Lucipara the following day, then cruise the remaining 127 miles tomorrow night.

"Once we get there we're almost home free," I said, trying not to let optimism creep into my voice, as if that would jinx it.

"Yeah, only now we don't have enough fuel to get to Australia, not after that forty-knot run last night. Where are we going to find the extra?"

Anger rose in me, hot and bright, and it was directed at Hokulani. "Think we're going to find some here? Distill it from bellyaches?"

The Hawaiian tossed the dividers on the chart and narrowed his eyes. "I asked you a civil question, Mr. Leander. If you'd rather have a screaming match I'm ready to go to the mat."

I looked away, and already the anger was simmering down. Emotions seemed to be on a yo-yo string these days. "I'm sorry, Hokulani. It's just that . . . everyone seems to have a lot of complaints, but no one's got any bright ideas."

I looked back at Hokulani, expecting to see the soft lines of forgiveness. But didn't. He was still angry, breathing hard, hands on hips.

"Skipper!" An urgent voice from above. "Get up here quick!"

Hokulani and I bounded from the tiny cabin and clambered out into a leafy green world. Seaman Weffert, at seventeen the youngest guy on the boat, held aside a limb and pointed out at the view.

I looked at the inlet's mouth and saw the ocean, or

rather the body of water which separated Buru from the island of Seram. Cruising therein was a Jap destroyer.

She was only a couple of miles away, heading due south. From the way her bow split the water I judged her speed at twenty knots.

She was an ugly, businesslike piece of machinery, painted a light, sunbeaten gray. Her sides were streaked with rust, which meant she'd been at sea a long time. Every horizontal surface held up an antiaircraft gun or a heavy machine gun. There were four 4.7-inch mounts, one forward, one between the stacks, and two atop the after deckhouse. Two torpedo launchers, boxy-looking things with four fish per. From her mainmast the Jap flag snapped straight out, its ends tattered from so much use, the meatball's bright rays covering the white field like blood splattered across snow.

The lines of the destroyer were quite distinctive. *Kamikaze* Class lines. And even at this distance I could make out the hull number.

Seventeen.

Ohiro, I whispered. Whispered so softly that Hokulani and Weffert did not hear. So we meet again. And, as usual, I've nothing more than a pair of deuces against your inside straight.

Weffert, goggle-eyed at the sight, licked his dry lips. "Think she's seen us, sir?" It was a whisper.

I shook my head. We were as well hidden as a mouse behind a baseboard. But brother, was I ever scared. If Ohiro had the slightest inkling of our whereabouts I could count on dying. There was just no question about it. It was a cold, hard fact.

270

The destroyer slid out of view, churning south. Weffert let the branches snap back in place.

"Still want to get underway tonight?" Hokulani asked. "The waters hereabouts are going to be choked with patrols. This may be a good spot to wait it out until things blow over."

"We've got to keep moving or we're dead. The Japs aren't going to let this rest until our heads are stuck on some goddamn poles."

I heard Weffert swallow hard, sweat running down his narrow face. I clapped him on the shoulder. "Don't you worry about a thing, Weffert. They'll behead only Mr. Hokulani and myself, since we're officers. The rest of you guys'll probably luck out with a firing squad."

He was bug-eyed. Hokulani and I laughed at Weffert's discomfiture. But the laughter was a little too high-pitched, a little too strained.

The overhanging limbs were untied from our cleats, and leaves were brushed from the deck. High tide came at sunset, lifting the PT off the soft mud. I put the starboard engine ahead and the port engine back, and the PT's stern pushed away from the bank. Then I put both engines in reverse and we backed into the middle of the inlet. The place was so narrow I couldn't turn around, so I backed all the way out into the channel, then nosed the PT south.

Lumanski was standing next to me, watching my actions carefully. Boatdriving is a thing which fascinated him to no end. "Where to tonight, skipper?"

"Lucipara Island, about ninety-eight miles south."

"So to get us there before dawn we're going to need . . . what? Twelve knots?"

I nodded. "Lucipara's right in the middle of the Banda Sea — no navigational reference points at all. So it's especially important there be no doping off at the wheel tonight. Have you got the first watch?"

"Yes, sir." I sidled out of the cockpit and Lumanski eased in. He pushed the throttles for the port and starboard engines, bringing the tach needles to the rpms for twelve knots. Centerline engine was down for the night.

"Course?" he asked.

"Steer one-seven-zero."

"One-seven-zero, aye. No sweat."

"How did things go with the foraging party today?"

"Fairly well. You saw those jerry cans we brought back, all of 'em filled with good, sweet water."

I suppressed an urge to ask if he hadn't come upon a pool of 100-octane gas and filled the cans with *that*.

I stepped around the charthouse and went forward, found Sevu sitting by himself. He started to get up, but I motioned him to keep sitting. I hunkered down.

"You did good this morning, Sevu. You led us to the river like you were a born pilot."

He smiled broadly. "I am pleased that you are happy, Captain."

"Listen, tomorrow we're going to be on a little island called Lucipara. Know anything about it?"

His brow wrinkled. "No . . ."

"But you can translate for us if there're any natives."

"Oh, you bet. I am very good with languages."

"Where did you learn to speak English so well?"

He smiled broadly. "I lived with a planter in Singapore, after my family sold me. I was with him many years, and he not only taught me English, but also some Chinese and Japanese."

"Wait, wait, wait a minute. Did you say *sold?*"

His tone reflected sincere puzzlement. "Why, yes. And at five sacks of rice it was a very good price. Enough to feed my family for six months."

"Let's back up a bit. Start from the beginning."

Sevu Kartasasmita was his full name, born in Semarang on the island of Java. He was another mouth to feed in a large, dirt-poor family. At eleven his father sold him to a planter in Djakarta, where he became an apprentice house-servant. He balked at his new station in life, and was frequently beaten. But at twelve an English planter, visiting Sevu's master, was much taken with the boy. Sevu was promptly resold, and taken to live in Singapore.

"These were good times," Sevu said glowingly, "He treat me like a . . . friend. He like to teach me things."

The years passed, and Sevu's instruction began to include the plantation's management. But the more he became familiar with these arts, the uneasier he felt about the rank exploitation of brown-skinned people by the Europeans.

It was on a business trip to Djakarta with his English master that Sevu's unease, previously unvoiced, came to full bloom. He met a hot-blooded young man who was an Indonesian Nationalist, and was introduced to a group of revolutionaries. Sevu was inflamed with their slogans, and the group was incensed at his detailed report on the exact workings of a colonial plantation. A pact was made that night, and Sevu given his assignment.

273

He went back to the hotel, intent upon killing his master. But by the time he entered the bedroom the revolutionary fervor was gone. All he could think of were the many kindnesses his master had shown him.

But Sevu had been followed. It was the young nationalist he had first met, come to ensure Sevu would complete his errand. A fight ensued. The Englishman was killed.

"I try to stop him, but he was so strong, so big. And when it was done all I could do was flee."

Sevu eluded the police, although the revolutionary was captured. He made it back to his home island of Java, but the long arm of colonial law reached for him even there. He fled to the island of Flores, one half-step ahead of the authorities.

Then the world turned upside down. The Japanese launched their multi-pronged conquest of the Pacific, deposing the Dutch easily. "The Japanese say they come as liberators, but I knew their oppression would be worse than even the stinking Dutch. I know I have to find my way out of Indonesia. That is why I sign on as deckhand with the *Santri*. And now here I am."

"That's . . . some story, Sevu."

He put his hand on my arm. "I am so happy I am with you, Captain. I want so much to help you Americans fight the Japanese."

"Yeah, well . . ." There was something about his story which just didn't jive, somehow. How could he be so eager to fight the Japanese after they had done him and his nationalist buddies the favor of giving the Dutch the boot? Surely he knew we and the Dutch were allies . . . but then, maybe I was reading too much into it. After all, Sevu was just a kid.

"Why don't you find a place to rack out," I said. "I want you to be all ready for your translating duties tomorrow."

"Oh, you bet."

But before we could get up there was a far-off whizzing noise, then a faint *pop*. The world was suddenly bathed in horrible green light.

I was on my feet instantly. A flare hung in the eastern sky like a bright green star.

"All stop!" I called to Lumanski. "Shut the engines down!"

Another flare rocketed upwards, revealing its source on the eastern horizon — the sleek, black silhouette of a destroyer. Another *pop,* and we were all sketched in shades of green and black.

The deck gently rolled as we bobbed in the sea, engines completely off. The first flare kissed the water.

The destroyer was five miles distant, right on the starboard beam. No running lights, but her own flares clearly revealed the lines of a *Kamikaze* Class DD. Ohiro was hard at work indeed. Another flare shot up, fired from just aft of her pilothouse.

Her big searchlight snapped on, and my gut turned into a cold lump of ice. Brother, this was going to be it.

But the beam swung away from us, toward something further to the east, over our horizon. The faint popping of heavy machine gun fire reached my ears, and the destroyer's aspect changed as she hauled around and began her hot pursuit of . . . what? A local fisherman out for some midnight trolling? Talk about being in the wrong place at the wrong time.

I waited until the destroyer was over the horizon before I told Lumanski to start the engines back up. My hands shook so hard it was near impossible to fish the Lucky out of my crumpled pack.

Chapter Twenty-one

No matter how good a navigator you are, no matter how long and successfully you practice it, you can't help but feel a twinge of pleased astonishment when you're right on the button.

Lucipara was a black smudge on the horizon, its outline faint in the just-lightening sky. It took shape and definition as we approached, and in the back of my mind the old magic was at work, telling me this unexplored landfall bore a promise of new wonders, of a fresh start.

A palm-fringed beach formed a "U" around a clear lagoon. There was a tiny village amongst the palms, and small boats littered the beach. No pier. Several figures were bent over the slender boats, readying them for the morning's work. We were half a mile away when they finally noticed us.

Some started running back and forth while others gathered in little groups. There seemed to be much consternation and confusion. Finally several men pushed one of the boats into the surf and began paddling toward us.

"Hold the boat steady," I told Lehr, who was driving. He nodded as he clicked the port and starboard throttles to the neutral slot. The tide was running out, and Lehr maneuvered with little bursts of either engine in order to keep us on station.

"Swifty," I called.

"Aye." He was standing next to me, watching the approach of the native boat.

"Go below and get Sevu up here, would you please? And get me a forty-five while you're at it."

"Want me to break out a few Springfields, too?"

"Yeah, but I don't want anyone waving them around. Just keep 'em handy in case something comes up."

"Got it."

It didn't look like the little boat would give us any problems, but who knew? I lifted the binoculars to my eyes. The narrow, canoe-like boat was an outrigger, and the seven men aboard seemed to be its absolute capacity. Three men on each side dipped their paddles while the boss back aft worked the tiller. The sun was not yet fully up, and at this distance I couldn't tell if they were Negro or Malaysian-type people.

Sevu came out of the charthouse, the only person I've ever known who didn't have to stoop as he went through that narrow door.

"Morning, Sevu."

He bobbed his head eagerly. "Good morning, Captain."

"Ready for your translating duties?"

"Oh yes, you bet."

We stepped around the charthouse, heading toward

the bow. The native boat was two hundred yards away, the paddles dipping and rising in perfect synchronization.

"Recognize anything about those people, Sevu?"

He studied them, his back straightening. *"Wong tjiliq,"* he announced.

"What's that? A tribe or what?"

"No. Peasants." There was a note of disapproval in his voice. "What do you wish me to tell them?"

"Well, first I'd like to know if there're any Japs around. Then I want to trade for water and food."

He nodded.

The boat closed rapidly. I could see the crew more clearly now, and they were the same type Malaysian as Sevu. The paddles dipped at lessening intervals, and finally the boat was orbiting just off our starboard bow. The man at the tiller stood and began shouting at us, the language a mixture of harsh vowels and discordant highs. He was an elderly guy in a faded sarong, thin as a rail, black hair peppered with gray. Wore some kind of black cap with no brim, like a fez.

Sevu's eyebrows knitted together and his mouth set into lines of displeasure. He barked a message back. The headman jabbered with manic intensity, his arm pointing in one direction and then another. Sevu gave a long, angry reply, pointing at me and then at the sailors standing back aft. The headman nodded, said something to his men, and the outrigger began coming alongside.

"There are no Japanese here," Sevu reported. "But this lagoon is not safe. There is a cove nearby where we can go. The chief will come aboard and guide us there."

279

"Okay."

Boeke and Frum helped the chief aboard, who was very spry for such an old gent. The chief barely had his feet on deck before he was bowing to me, his hands together in prayer-like fashion.

My mother brought up a polite boy. I instinctively put my hands together in a likewise fashion and began bowing, but Sevu put his hand on my arm and hissed an urgent *"no!"*

I shot him a quick look; he was shaking his head vigorously. Guess he knew more about this than me, so I just stood there while the old man continued his . . . obeisance?

He muttered something, head still bowed, and Sevu answered with that same angry, impatient tone. The chief bowed lower.

"Start engines again, Captain. He is ready to guide us to the stream." A little of that imperious tone had crept over to Sevu's English, I noticed.

I called back aft for Lehr to follow the old man's pilotage instructions, which consisted of his pointing to where he wanted us to go. We backed out of the lagoon and cruised to the island's western side. The outrigger followed us one hundred yards astern. The village slipped to our port quarter and finally disappeared behind a stand of palms. The old man guided us to a cove, this one split by a stream. From here the village was half a mile to the east, completely obscured by palms and waist-high shrubbery. I called Milton forward, instructed him to throw the lead line as we cruised up the tiny inlet.

Lehr kept on bare steerageway as we cautiously entered. Milton swung the lead line in a complete

280

circle, then let it fly forward and plunk into the water ten feet ahead. He hauled in the slack briskly, called out the depth when the line was vertical. Even though the tide was running out, there seemed to be plenty of gravy.

There were palms on either side, and the further we went the better hiding place it seemed to be. I finally called a halt when we were two hundred yards up the inlet, even though there was still plenty of water beneath the keel. Lehr worked the boat to the left-hand bank, and we made the PT fast broadside-to, securing lines from the bow and stern to the trunks of palms.

"Thank the chief," I told Sevu. "Tell him we appreciate his guiding us to a safe spot."

Sevu let out three harsh syllables and the old man bowed to me deeply.

I gave the chief a brief nod in return. "Okay. Tell him we want to do some trading. I'll turn over some medical supplies in exchange for water and food."

Sevu's reply was immediate. "There is no need for trade. We are here as honored guests."

"That's mighty nice," I told the chief, grinning. He averted his eyes. "But go ahead and tell him we'll make him some presents."

Sevu talked rapidly, his tone like a mother chastising a naughty child. The old man bowed and bowed.

There were twenty houses in the village, all the same — stilts, steep roofs, thatched walls with big open windows. Sevu and I were in the chief's house, the biggest. The chief conferred with his wife in a corner, jabbering in excited tones.

Now that the sun had fully risen I could see that their beach was a perfect, sugary white, the lagoon a deep, incredible blue. Hokulani was leading the landing party out of my view, following a native.

"Hope this doesn't take long," I told Sevu, "I want to be underway by sundown."

"Maybe we stay one day here, Captain. It plenty safe. We be better ready for the next trip across the ocean."

"Listen, Sevu—"

He placed his forefinger across his lips as the chief and his wife approached. The chief bowed and grinned and bade us sit. The three of us arranged ourselves on mats, and the chief's gray-haired little wife set a large wooden plate before us, bowed, and left.

"First the sirih," Sevu announced. He reached into the dish, gathered up a few green leaves, and put it in his mouth. He chewed it, indicating I should do the same.

Sirih? One thing was for sure—in all the places I've been and all the peoples I've met, it seems to be a universal rule of thumb that the host must always offer his guests the equivalent of a martini.

I took a small handful. "What is it?"

"The betel nut and betel leaves smashed together and covered with lime juice. Chew it."

I did. It was sharply bitter, but I managed to keep my face from screwing up. The chief, who'd been working on a wad for some time, leaned toward the window and spat it out. He looked at Sevu and uttered a few hopeful syllables.

"He wants to know if the sirih is to your liking,

Captain."

I nodded. "Oh, it's delish all right."

Sevu laughed. "What you expecting? Whiskey? These people are Moslems, very devout."

"This is fine, Sevu." I went to the window, spat out the wad, sat back down.

"Have more," he indicated. I did, and this batch didn't seem so awful.

"Tell the old man we appreciate his hospitality."

Sevu and the old man had a rapid-fire conversation.

"There is to be a feast tonight," Sevu reported. "To honor you and your men."

"Tell him thanks but no thanks. I want to be out of here by dark."

Sevu narrowed his eyes. "I think it is best your men have one day rest, Captain. We stay here tonight."

My jaws locked in mid-chew. "Excuse me, but who the hell are *you?*"

Sevu bowed low immediately. "Please excuse me for speaking out of place." He addressed a few words at the chief. The chief stood and, smiling, backed out of his hut, bowing all the while, muttering and grinning like an egg-suck dog.

"My home is yours," Sevu translated. "Everything I have is for your use."

"Mighty friendly guy."

"More sirih?"

"Sure." I stood to spit out the present wad, felt a little dizzy as I walked to the window. This sirih stuff, whatever it was, was indeed working. I felt a little buzzy inside, and a little excited. I hawked out the wad, sat back down. Sevu and I chewed in silence.

There was a woman's call from outside. Sevu took

my elbow and stood. "Come," he said. "That was the headman's wife. The mandi is prepared."

"The what?"

"The tub . . . the bath."

"Bath? You're kidding." I stood and was led outside. I hadn't had a bath in . . . hell, I couldn't even remember.

It was at the rear of the house, a round wooden tub underneath its own little thatched roof. Even though it wasn't indoors there was plenty of privacy. I began pulling my shirt apart, yanking so hard a button snapped off. I laughed, and Sevu tittered at this hilarious incident.

Sevu went back to the house and I continued stripping, letting my soiled khakis fall in a heap. My regular Navy shoes had long since given way to Army boots, and when I unlaced these I was greeted with a nauseating stench. I took everything off hurriedly, even my dog tags, then eased my carcass into the mandi. It was exactly what I wanted—deliciously cool, exactly perfect. I leaned my head back, letting out a long sigh.

The chief's little wife appeared and gathered up my soiled clothes. She looked at me and grinned. I grinned back and gave a little wave. The old woman's smile broadened. She went back to the house to deposit my clothes, then came back with the bowl of sirih and placed it within reach. She took this opportunity to unabashedly peer over the side of the mandi and take a look at my privates. Sophisticated joe that I am, I did nothing to cover them up. She went away, giggling delightedly.

Man, this was nice. I took another mouthful of the

sirih and laid back, chewing idly. Now that I thought about it, it *had* been a long goddamn time since I'd relaxed. *Really* relaxed. Springs I didn't know about were unwinding.

I heard someone coming, and when I turned I saw that it was a young woman. I stopped my sirih-chewing in mid-stroke. At first I thought it might be some sort of mirage. The girl was fantastically lovely. She smiled shyly even as she . . . undid her garment . . . and let it fall away . . . She slid into the tub as if it were the most natural thing in the world. Well, hell. Wasn't it? Her black hair was down, floating around her shoulders.

Nice custom, this. Every country should make it a point for their guests to have appropriate bathing-companions.

She indicated I should turn around. I did.

Soap was coconut oil. She lathered it into my back, then worked her fingers into my shoulders expertly, like a masseuse. The muscles in my back started coming undone, like metal snaps being pulled apart.

She lathered me up good, combining the soaping-down with restful massage. It wasn't long before an old friend in my crotch began uncoiling its warm length.

"Your turn now, lady." I took up the gourd of coconut oil, pouring some in my hand. "Let old Buck return the favor."

She laughed, a sound that tinkled in the cool air like windchimes. She quickly sloshed from the tub, giggling as she neatly twisted from my grasps. Her tiny butt wiggled enticingly as she walked back toward the house.

I called after her, only to be answered by her

laughter. I debated heaving myself over the side and going after her. But the crunching of boots reached my ears, and I turned to see the Hokulani approaching, .45 holster canted over his hips like a gunslinger.

"Well!" he laughed. "Well, well, well! Having a good time, skipper?"

I sighed as I leaned back. "What's the word, lieutenant?"

He put one hand against the lip of the mandi. "Nothing but good news. We've already got enough dried fish fillets for a week, and these people even stowed them for us. A working party of natives are taking care of filling our fresh water tanks."

"Great. Why don't you get yourself a bath?"

"Sure, in a while. Some of the other guys are already in some of these tubs."

"Yeah?"

"Yeah. These people have really rolled out the red carpet." He looked around. "I've been thinking, skipper. Maybe it wouldn't be such a bad idea to lay here overnight. Give everyone a little chance to rest up."

"And a little boost to morale, too? Sure, why not?"

Hokulani seemed surprised by my ready acceptance. But pleased. "Sure it's okay, skipper?"

"If anyone needs to recharge batteries, it's us. One night's layover won't hurt anything. Here, try some of this sirih stuff."

Chapter Twenty-two

Decision made, I knew it was a wise one. I surrendered myself to the pleasures of the bath, and to the slow waves of sirih-induced euphoria. Somewhere along the line I found myself being led from the mandi and helped into a clean, cool sarong. The chief led me to the center of the village, where the feast — or *gotong-rojong* as Sevu called it — had been prepared. The backdrop was a lurid technicolor sunset. Palm fronds whispered in the gentle breeze, and the temperature was comfortably balmy.

The entire village was sitting in a big circle — maybe two hundred people, give or take — and in the sea of brown strangers was the occasional face of a sailor, freshly scrubbed and grinning. The chief sat to my left, Sevu to my right. Next to Sevu was was the girl who helped me with my bath, and whenever I glanced her way I found those dark eyes on mine, sparkling and merry.

Food consisted of baskets of fruit and rice, eggs fried in the multipurpose coconut oil, and tiny silvery fish.

These were eaten whole, popped in the mouth like french fries. It was a leisurely sort of eating, with plenty of time out for laughing and back-slapping. I kept dipping into a handy bowl of sirih — which by now I was finding to be agreeable stuff indeed.

Suddenly, without my noticing, it was full dark. Torches ringed the assembly, and its flickering orange light played tricks with my eyes. It seemed that every quick movement left an after-image which was slow to catch up, and the laughing and gesticulating of the people began to look like some kind of weird double-exposed film. The gathering took on the aspect of a flowing sea of happy faces.

The chowdown portion of the feast wound away slowly, mixing into the dancing part. A group of local girls began a delicate little performance to the accompaniment of drums and cymbals, moving their arms with the precision of a Marine drill team. The head dancer was the girl who helped me with my bath. After prodding Sevu who in turned prodded the chief, I discovered her name was Sabana.

It was an interesting dance, made more so by Sabana's continually looking at me. The wavering light enhanced her strange movements, and once I found myself doing a double-take during an especially neat little trick — the other girls formed up behind Sabana so that I could only see her . . . and a hundred snaking arms. It was nice, but . . . something about it was strangely disquieting. It reminded me of those statues I'd seen of one of those Hindu gods. Siva, I think it was. The Creator and the Destroyer. And I was dismayed that a bunch of dancing girls could make me feel so uneasy.

But it was only for a moment, and it passed, it passed. A trick of the funny light.

The dance was slow at first, then the tempo built and quickened until it had us all excited and clapping, and Strip Cunningham was the first to get to his feet and join in. He too wore a sarong, and he shook his bare gut at the natives until everyone roared with approval. Then some of the other guys grabbed local girls and joined in, improvising with a few stateside-swing twists. Some of the girls didn't seem too eager at first, but they soon got the hang of it.

I tried my hand at a few dances, the tiny native girls laughing as they tried to show me what to do. My steps were loose and clumsy, but I didn't care. I was having a great time, even though I couldn't locate Sabana, who had somehow managed to fade into the woodwork.

The party wore on and on, but I was far from bored or tired. I hoped it would never end. And if anyone was up for all-night partying, it was these natives. The old chief grinned and grinned, constantly chewing on the sirih. I talked with him and slapped him on the back, and even though I knew he couldn't understand he just kept beaming and nodding. I decided what the old gent needed was a really nice present. Right now, in fact. Yeah. I could see myself making a formal presentation before the present assembly, sealing our nations' undying friendship.

Back in his shack, where my drying clothes were, there was an expensive folding knife in my pants pocket. It would be perfect.

I slipped from the party and went to his place, already rehearsing the little speech I'd make. I went in the shack, which had no lights of its own. Scant illumination was provided by the distant torches of the village party. I started rummaging around for my khakis.

Then I heard the tread of a foot. I turned and looked at a black silhouette in the doorway.

I told myself that sometimes dreams *do* come true, that now and then you step up the table and the dealer can't help but throwing you tens and aces, over and over.

Sabana came across the thatched floor slowly, orange light flickering across her oval face. Her eyes were dark and serious, and her hand moved up to caress my cheek. She was a tiny thing, barely coming up to my chest, and so delicate-looking it seemed she might break if handled too roughly.

But when I took her in my arms it was as if somebody tossed a match on a lake of high-octane gas. She clung and pressed against me mightily, grinding and rolling her hips in a way that was far beyond mere suggestion. I felt the long, smooth muscles of her back, felt the width of her lovely little hips. She dug her nails in the back of my neck, wormed her other hand between us and tore at my sarong.

We began sinking to the thatched floor even as Sabana fondled my privates. She finally released my neck and began breathing in quick little gasps, as if the air was suddenly too thick to breathe. She pushed my sarong down to my knees, and I felt no need to kick it all the way off—there was no time now for anything but the bare essentials. I pushed up her sarong and discovered she wore nothing underneath. She grabbed me and without preamble pulled me up into her. She cried aloud and began clawing at me and bucking her hips, and it felt for all the world as if I were on a wild horse at a rodeo. I pummeled her without mercy, surprised at my own savagery, and all she did was spread her legs wider, pulling and straining to draw me more deeply inside.

I moaned and gasped at the strength of my orgasm, like it was some kind of high-explosive phosphorous shell erupting into a thousand brilliant streamers. I collapsed to my elbows, and dimly, from faraway, felt her arms tighten around my back and her hips pump and work against mine, the tempo rapidly increasing. Then she cried, legs tightening around my butt like a pair of strong scissors. Sharpened nails dug into my back with such brutality I had to clench my teeth against the pain. Then she went slack, and I rolled off and onto my back.

I lay there for a while, gasping, spent. Sabana got up on an elbow, brushed her hair away and looked down at me. In the darkness I saw that her mouth was slack and open, her breathing heavy. She said something quietly, then laughed. I shook my head and smiled. I let my arm flop her way, intending to give her an affectionate pat . . . but when I touched it seemed her cue to get up off the floor.

She walked away slowly, her arms working at the knot in her sarong. The garment fell away and she stepped out, continued walking toward the low-slung bed. Her figure from behind was every bit as alluring as I remembered from the bath. Her shoulders were broad but delicate, the back tapering down smoothly and gracefully to the wide flare of a Valentine ass. Her legs were long but not skinny, the thighs and calves muscled into entirely perfect proportions. She stepped gracefully into bed, rolling so that she came to rest turned halfway toward me, one leg propped up like an A.

Something in my crotch stirred. Reinforcements already . . . and no wonder. I sat up and kicked my sarong away from my ankles. I got up and walked toward the bed naked, thinking that now would come the time of studied carnal knowing, the savoring full and unhurried, the exploration slow and sweet.

But I hesitated. I just stood there, drinking her in, shaking my head in reverent awe. Her figure was not voluptuous, but its invitation had a power that weakened my knees. She had one arm behind her head, absently running her fingers through hair that was thick and glossy in the darkness. Her lips were slightly parted, her eyes glazed and faraway. Her breasts were the size of teacups, round and lovely, rolling in slow, sweet geometry atop the definition of ribs.

Thoughts of tender lovemaking vanished. I climbed into bed eagerly, taking her into my arms like I was tackling a running back. I wanted it as savage and frenzied as before . . . no, ten times more savage . . . and for a hundred nights . . .

We did it plain and we did it fancy, lying down, sitting up, bent this way and that, halfway off the bed, once even back on the floor. We did it every way imaginable, except maybe hanging from a trapeze. I surrendered to a kaleidoscope of delicate sensations, each one fair driving me to madness. Skillfully she drew me to new brinks, maneuvering me into ever-changing, endlessly fascinating variations. There were moans and cries, tempos slow and fast, a lovely oriental face thrown back, eyes closed and mouth forming a tiny "o."

I awoke with a start, and for a moment thought I was back in the Philippines, secure in my nipa shack.

Then I felt the warmth of the girl next to me, and knew where I was.

Dawn was but an hour away. Sabana was sketched in tones of blue; a peaceful sight, and . . . the memory of our lovemaking washed over me, memories which my body recollected far more vividly than my brain, a montage of sweaty flesh, bizarre positions, and honeyed sensations. I reached down to touch her hair.

There was a far-off scream, slicing through the night like a whirling hatchet. I sat upright, eyes wide, ears straining. Sabana sat up too, her face contorted with puzzlement and fear. The sound came again, and it was a woman's scream.

I bolted from the bed, grabbed my pants and ran outside. I hopped forward, putting one leg on at a time, going toward the noise. It seemed to be coming from the middle of the village. Other figures began spilling from the huts, Americans and natives, everyone shaded in the hard blue of pre-dawn.

Pants on, I sprinted toward the screams. I rounded a hut and what I saw stopped me cold.

It was the body of a girl. Her sarong was torn, and her torso was splattered with dark blood. An old woman stood in the doorway of her hut, looking at the dead girl and screaming.

I went to see if the girl might still be alive. But . . . no way. No way at all. She was dead as dead could get.

I looked at the woman in the doorway.

She pointed at me and began screaming even louder.

Word spread through the village quickly, and it was clear who they thought were responsible.

Us, obviously. The visitors.

Most of the villagers were scared—and they ran from us as if in fear for their lives, taking off into the jungly interior of the island. But I saw a few of the native men fetching machetes and knives and talking urgently to each other in angry groups. Things were going to get ugly, and very soon.

I found Hokulani and told him to hustle our guys back to the PT. I went looking for the chief, to try and explain the unexplainable. But the village had suddenly become a ghost town, and the chief was nowhere to be found.

I returned to the boat, and at first glance everyone seemed to be on board. They were at battle stations, Springfields broken out, gun tubs manned, helmets on. The Packards were already rumbling. Hokulani grabbed my hand and helped me aboard. "All hands accounted for?"

"No, sir. Donnythorn's still out there."

"Who you got looking for him?"

"Wh—why, nobody."

My eyes bulged. *Nobody's looking for him?*

Hokulani looked shocked, but it wasn't long before the expression changed to a fierce scowl. *"I only just now got a muster!"* he roared, *"I was just getting ready to send a couple guys after him!"*

And right then I was mad enough to want to jump down his throat and start hammering away, but I became aware that all eyes were upon us, and wouldn't a slugfest between the C.O. and exec be just a dandy example of how the world *had* turned upside down? I looked at them individually, feeling something very much akin to loathing.

And now, I thought, *and now one of them's a goddamn murderer, too.*

"Looky there," Swifty said in a conversational tone, and to no one in particular. He looked comfortable in his gun-tub perch. "Here comes old Donnythorn now."

And so it was. He was running flat-out for the boat, a group of native men not too many yards behind. Donnythorn weaved between the palms as neatly as any top-prospect running back, arms and legs pumping furiously. Some of the native men had their machetes drawn.

"All right, Swifty." My tone was crisp and clear. "Fire one burst over those natives' heads."

"Over their heads, shit." He spat over the side and brought the twin barrels to bear. "Just watch me grease these fucks."

I could not believe my ears, just as I could not believe that I had somehow drawn my pistol and was ready to take a hip-shot as Swifty if he gave me a wrong answer to my next order. "Fire over their heads, god damn you."

He sighed, elevated the barrels, and thumbed the firing bar. There was a five-round burst, sounding like a string of cherry bombs.

Some of the natives dropped, but it wasn't from being hit. They were looking for cover. Those still standing looked like they were wondering whether they should drop, too. No one was chasing Donnythorn anymore, who continued his pell-mell dash for the boat.

I looked at the cockpit and saw Lumanski was at the helm. I told him to stand by to get underway, and called for the linehandlers to cast off. When Donnythorn clambered aboard I gave Lumanski the nod and we began backing down.

Donnythorn lay on the deck, his dark hair matted with sweat, breathing as if the act were a source of pain. The PT went down the little river backwards, Lumanski driving with his head constantly over his shoulder. We moved at about five knots, and the men who chased Donnythorn got up and followed us, careful to keep an exact distance.

We pulled into the cove, and Lumanski put on a twist and the boat began turning around. Some of the natives started appearing on the beach. I told Lumanski to hurry things up, and he put more power, and we drew away from Lucipara, heading to the south. It was now the full light of day, and the day was only just beginning. We were naked, and there was nowhere to go. Unless, of course, we went back to Lucipara and shot the place up. Which, no doubt, would be just what some of these guys wanted.

I faced the crew. I still had my .45 in hand, though its muzzle was pointing at the deck. I looked at them skeptically, with contempt. And was met with same.

Chapter Twenty-three

"All right. Which one of you guys did it?"

Some looked away, but most continued to stare at me stonily.

"Which one?" My voice became louder. "Which one of you bastards killed that girl?"

Sevu stepped forward, a pleased smile on his face. He pointed at Donnythorn, who still lay prone on the deck, though no longer gasping.

"He is the one," Sevu said. "He did it, Captain."

"*He's a liar!*" Donnythorn scrambled to his feet. "*He's a goddamn liar!*"

He began rushing toward Sevu, but I stepped between. "Hold it."

"You ain't gonna believe him, are you, skipper? You ain't gonna believe that little brown bastard!"

I looked at Sevu. "Did you see him do it?"

"He is the one who did it."

"*Did you see him do it?*"

Sevu looked away. "No, Captain, but . . ."

"There, you see!" Donnythorn shrieked, "he doesn't

297

know that the hell he's talking about!"

"Shut up, Donnythorn!" I turned back to Sevu. "Why do you say he did it?"

Sevu looked at me, then at Donnythorn. "I saw him dancing with that girl. I saw the way he held her, the way she tried to get away from him."

Donnythorn shook his head. "Why you little shit."

"It was an ugly dance," Sevu continued, "I could see what was going to happen from the way they moved. She trying to get away. He trying to kiss her and feel her with his hands. And when she finally broke away and went into the night I saw him follow."

Donnythorn stepped around me and with a cry of rage threw himself upon Sevu. The two tumbled to the deck, Donnythorn's hands locked to Sevu's throat.

It took some doing to get them disentangled.

It was a long day.

I took Donnythorn down to my cabin and had a talk with him, and he was steadfast in his denials. I let him go, and had another talk with Sevu. He was convinced that Donnythorn was the one, but had no firm evidence.

Hokulani and I spent a long time talking it over, running it around and around. Suppose Donnythorn was the one? Suppose he *wasn't*? How to go about finding out? Interview the crew one at a time? Maybe with some hotlamps and a blackjack to hurry things along?

Some state things had come to!

All we could decide was to let things sit for a while. Maybe the murderer would act peculiar or strange.

Then Hokulani and I could cut him loose from the herd and break him down.

But as the day wore on it didn't look like anyone was going to 'fess up. Everyone lay in their usual positions around the boat, eyes blank and empty. Maybe they were chewing over recent events. Or couldn't get accustomed to the oddity of cruising in broad daylight. Our destination was Romang, 127 miles due south.

I kept sweeping the horizon with my binoculars, looking for trouble. Thinking things over.

When the sun kissed the horizon it seemed like the longest sunset in history. When it began to get dark I went down into my stuffy little cabin and took out the log, and began recording the events of the past two days.

It was hard writing. I had to drag out every word and coax it onto the page. After a couple of lines I put down my pen and began flipping restlessly through the other pages. It made for some sorry reading indeed. And at the core of it was the C.O.'s failure to act like a C.O.

The door to my cabin quietly opened. It was Sevu.

"Am I disturb you, Captain?"

"What do you want?"

He shut the door behind him. "I have been watching Donnythorn. I *know* he is the one."

"Yeah? How?"

Sevu's eyes were bright even in the weak light of the desk lamp. "He sat by himself all day, and no one talk to him. His eyes were always wide, and he kept wiping his mouth with the back of his hand, all day long. He is troubled, Captain. Troubled because he is guilty."

"This is the same kind of crap you were talking about

this morning, about that dancing. You aren't giving me any facts."

"Fool!" he hissed. "You must do something *now*. Do nothing and you lose *control*."

I got up from my chair and looked down at Sevu. "So you're going to tell me how to run things, eh? You know all about it."

He looked at me fiercely, completely unintimidated by my size. "Yes, I know! I know how to oversee workers, and I know you need their *fear*!"

This boy was starting to get on my nerves. "Listen, pipsqueak. You don't know what the hell you're talking about."

"No? How come you think those island people give us food? Respect?" He laughed harshly. "It was fear! They plenty scared of you Americans, you bet!"

"What are you talking about?"

"I tell headman you kill everybody if they not give tribute."

"*What!*"

"You think they give you food and bath and woman because your skin so white? Hah!"

I got him by the shoulder and hurled him against the door. It banged open and Sevu sprawled to the deck of the crew's berthing compartment. I came right after him and stood over him. "You did what?"

The starch had completely gone out of him. He was scared. "I am sorry, Captain! I was only try to please!"

I felt like kicking him. "Get out of here. Keep your face away from mine."

He scrabbled away on all fours, then got up and dashed up the companionway into the charthouse.

I looked at the guys in the berthing compartment.

There were only two, and both were sitting up in their racks, staring without shock but not without interest, either.

I turned my back and went into my cabin, slammed the door behind me. I sat in my chair, looking at the overhead.

Was there ever to be an end to this? Was there ever any way to get off this goddamn hotseat, even for a goddamn moment!

Let's face it. I was a lousy C.O., reeling from one crisis to another like a blind drunk. I wasn't in control of shit. I was behind a gigantic eight ball, running scared, wishing I was anywhere but here . . .

An angry voice reached my ears and I sat erect, listening. There was an outraged scream, then feet pounding across the main deck just above my head. My chair flipped over as I shot from the desk and threw the door wide.

I bounded up the short ladder to the charthouse; as I passed through I grabbed a pistol belt, buckled it on as I stepped through the narrow door which opened to the main deck.

There were several men gathered on the fantail, black shapes churning against the billions of stars hanging in the sky. I ran aft into the confusion, shouldering guys aside until I got to the heart of it.

"Let him go, Donnythorn!"

Sevu was on his knees, screaming. Donnythorn had him by the hair, his free hand pulled back for the punch that would rearrange his face. I got in between, pushing Donnythorn backwards. He stumbled to the day cabin, cursing.

"What the hell's gotten into you, Donnythorn?"

"He keeps watching me! All day long that little bas-

301

tard's been watching me! And now I'm gonna fix his ass!"

"Shut up. You aren't going to fix shit."

He pushed himself off the day cabin and faced me. "Oh, yeah?"

"Donnythorn, how would you like a court-martial when we get to Australia?"

"Australia!" he shrieked. I could see the black silhouettes of the gathered men turning to Donnythorn, listening. "That's a fucking laugh! We ain't never going to get to Australia!"

"What the hell are you talking about!" I yelled angrily. The black silhouettes swung to me, as if Donnythorn and I were engaged in debate. "We're going to make it to Australia if we have to goddamn *swim!*"

Donnythorn pointed at me, his whole figure shaking with rage. "We ain't got enough gas to make it! We should be finding a good place to hide from the Japs instead of wasting it on a trip we can't finish!"

I laughed, but a lot of it was forced. "You think we can hide out for the rest of the war? Is that what you want? Stay on some goddamn pesthole for ten years?"

Donnythorn turned to the assembled men, his arms outstretched. "You see! You see! The man's crazy! He's going to kill us all!" He pointed aft. "I say let's go back to that island! They gave us all the food we wanted, and all the women we wanted! I say that island's a safer bet than goddamn Australia!"

Then, unbelievably, I heard the mumbled voices of assent, saw the nodding of bearded faces. I thought back to the chronicle in my log, saw all the incidents finally and inevitably coming down to this. The skin drew so tight on my neck the hairs came to rigid attention. "You've lost your marbles," I said evenly. "Those people will kill any one of us who shows up."

Donnythorn's reply was immediate. "Not if we show 'em who's boss! We got enough guns on this boat to set ourselves up like kings!" There were more noises of assent, and they were louder. "If only we'd put a few holes in them natives when they came after us on the boat we'd still be there sittin' pretty!"

There were hearty "yeahs." Things were getting out of control and all I could do was stand there, aghast, too shocked to believe what was happening. Donnythorn turned to me and crouched low, and in the darkness I saw a long knife in his hand. It was a Springfield's bayonet. Where had he gotten it? Had someone slipped it to him? My belly turned to ice.

"Like that goddamn prick-teasing broad!" Donnythorn shouted. "She thought she could shove me around, but I showed her! I showed her who was boss!"

I was shocked enough to forget the bayonet. So he really was the one.

"You'll hang, Donnythorn," I said. "By Christ you'll hang. When we get to Australia I'll—"

"We ain't going to Australia!" he screamed *"We're going back to that island!"*

"You're talking mutiny."

I let the awful word hang in the heavy air, and for a moment even Donnythorn was slapped into silence. I slipped my hand to my holster, then froze. The holster was canvas, not the leather of a government-issue .45. In my haste I had grabbed a *flare* pistol. Christ! When it rains it pours!

"Mutiny," Donnythorn whispered. He was working the word over, trying it on for size. He raised his voice. "You see! He won't be satisfied until we're all dead! Are you

303

with me or against me?"

"Seize him!" I ordered. "Take him down below!"

Donnythorn swung his blade at the assembled men, though I saw none make a move to grab. "Stay back! Back off!" He crouched down and slowly began coming at me. "Come and get me yourself, Lieutenant." He swung the blade back and forth. "Come on and get it."

I didn't want any of this, not this crazy guy, not the knife. I whipped out the flare pistol, leveled its squat barrel. "Drop it, Donnythorn. Right now."

Donnythorn hunkered lower. He came at me, waving the blade.

The pistol kicked against my hand and the world exploded into blinding, hissling light. The sound was like a rupture in a high-pressure steam line.

The white light suddenly faded into green, then telescoped down into a foot-square patch of bright, burning chemicals—centered in Donnythorn's gut. He looked down at it, mouth wide but no sound coming out, the green light throwing long shadows across his forehead and cheeks.

He dropped to his knee, one hand resting atop the after torpedo tube, bits of sizzling potassium chlorate falling to the deck. The air as heavy with the stench of burning flesh. Donnythorn suddenly threw back his head as if to scream, but still no sound came out, and that seemed even more horrible. He arched back further and further, and finally went backwards over the torpedo tube, hitting the black water head first.

Chapter Twenty-four

I sat at the forwardmost part of the boat, right at the tip of the bow, legs dangling over the side. When dawn began to streak the horizon I became conscious of the flare pistol still in my hand. I relaxed my grip without thinking, and the pistol dropped in the water.

The isle of Romang should have been on the horizon, but I didn't look for it. It would be better, I thought, to be entering the waters of the Dutch East Indies again, magically given another chance to sail these areas and sail them right. And if I screwed up again — bang, back to square one, over and over, until I *did* do it right. Or kept at it until the end of time. Buck Leander, the Navy's Sisyphus, condemned to eternity to sail a PT Boat to Australia, never quite making it.

And could anyplace else be a more fitting hell?

I was hunched over, my raggedy khaki shirt stretched tight across my shoulders. A good target, if anyone wanted to try shooting me. I wondered if that was what some of the guys back aft were thinking about. I could hear hushed voices, quiet whisperings. Finally, soft footfalls as someone warily approached. Maybe this was going to be it.

"Skipper?" It was Strip Cunningham. He squatted next to me, an unlit stub of cigar jammed in his mouth. "Is it okay if I talk?"

I gave him a sidelong glance. "Sure."

"You been sitting out here a long time. You wouldn't be all racked up about that thing with Donnythorn, would you?"

I just looked at him.

He took the cigar from his mouth. "Everybody thinks Donnythorn rated it."

"Is that so?"

"Yeah. They think you did right. Hell, you *did* do right. I could see that Donnythorn was a bad actor from way back."

"But I didn't notice anyone trying to subdue him last night. Matter of fact, when Donnythorn talked about going back to that island, there seemed to be some voices of assent."

Swifty dropped his gaze. "Yeah, there was some. And maybe . . . us senior p.o.'s shoulda jacked some guys up." He sighed. "But things haven't been right lately. Not since Bataan fell. You know." His eyes flickered back to mine. "But now all of a sudden they do. Now things seem like they're gonna be all right. It seems like we're honest to God gonna make it."

I thought about it. Wondered if it might be true. Sometimes the slate *does* get wiped clean . . . but now? No, I told myself. I had screwed up too much.

"Hey, now." Strip smiled, pointing down at the water. "Would you take a look at that."

It was a porpoise. About six feet long, and a strange-looking one at that. Same color scheme as a panda bear — its head and forward fins were jet black, the main trunk white, and the tail and dorsal fin black again. He was slicing along, just underneath the water, not more than a yard off the bow. He kept his station effortlessly, the streamlined body canting to the right so he could aim an eye up at us. And it wasn't the least unsettling to see a man's eye in this creature. It was warm and intelligent, merry and friendly.

I smiled. Porpoises were a sign of good luck.

Another porpoise eased alongside, sliding into station like a fighter plane forming up on his leader. This one had larger sworls of black. Then another floated up from the depths until his dorsal fin split the surface. Twenty yards away another black-and-white leapt from the water and splashed. Further off another made a perfect little arc out of the sea.

We were in a school of them.

There were shouts and laughter from back aft. Sailors were pointing at the porpoises and talking excitedly. I got up and Strip and I walked back to the cockpit. There were dozens of porpoises now, all leaping, racing ahead of the boat, surprising us with their ever-changing locations.

Now and then I caught some of the guys giving me a quick look. And it was a look I hadn't seen in a long time, like it was something that bordered on respect. Could it be so?

Hokulani was standing by the cockpit, a pair of heavy binoculars dangling from his neck. "Morning, skipper."

I nodded, smiled. "Morning."

307

We looked at each other for a moment, and it made me think of the time Hokulani had first come to the unit with a shiny gold bar on his collar, all friendly smiles and eagerness.

He took the binoculars off and handed them to me. "Romang's on the horizon."

I took a quick look, saw twin peaks on the horizon, corresponding with the notations on the chart.

I smiled. Strange how a festive mood had descended on the boat, considering the events of not too many hours ago. Maybe I *had* done the right thing for a change. I was by no means a master of what is called the art of handling men. I had, ever since I'd first been on ships, been constantly surprised at what makes men content or not.

Like when I was an ensign, fresh from the Academy, a spanking new division officer on an elderly destroyer. There was one guy in my division who seemed to be in a perpetual state of high piss-off, the kind of guy who has a personal grudge against everything. Finally he got written up for being late for watch. First guy I ever took to Captain's Mast. The captain threw him in the brig for three days of bread and water. I was flabbergasted. It was harsh punishment for the offense, far more severe than the captain usually handed out for similar incidents. Not only that, three days on bread and water was going to cook this guy's juices just right; I was sure he'd be homicidal when he got out. But much to my surprise the brig did the trick. He became one of the best guys in the division, cooperative, hard working, eventually meritoriously advanced to petty officer.

Like his slate had been wiped clean . . .

"Small boats," Hokulani called. He pointed just to the right of the Romang peaks. "Looks like two of 'em."

I swung my binoculars in that direction, spotted them right away. Fishermen? Japs? The silhouette became familiar.

"Japs," I said. "Landing craft."

"Yeah . . ." Hokulani took the binoculars and had a quick look. "Same type as in the Philippines. Think they've spotted us?"

I shrugged. "Doesn't make any difference. We're going after them."

"Say again?"

I smiled. "These guys could be our ticket home."

"How so?"

"Could be they've got something onboard we could use. Could be we end up driving one of those goddamn things to Australia. You got any better ideas?"

Lumanski was at the helm. I told him what I wanted, and he hit the button which set the battle stations alarm clanging. Then he kicked over the starter for the one engine which had been down for the night, getting all three on the line. Guys started scrambling over the boat, breaking out the rifles, strapping on helmets, feeding the belts of ammo into the fifties. The men worked together like the gears of a well-oiled clock, quickly and with no wasted motion

I was astonished to find there was a stinging in my eyes. It was a beautiful sight, each man doing his job with the practiced economy of a seasoned veteran. There was no other unit in the Navy like this, not anywhere. And it was mine.

Lumanski watched the tachometers for the Packards, and when he had an even reading across the board he slowly brought the throttles up. The eighty-foot boat picked up speed easily, the deck canting upwards as the three screws dug in.

I took a look aft and saw both sets of fifties were ready. Swifty was on the starboard set, Boeke was back aft in the port gun tub. I raised my voice so both could hear. "This is it as far as ammo goes. Use whatever's necessary to rake these boats clean, but I want 'em to stay afloat." Nod from Swifty, thumbs up from Boeke.

Lumanski brought the throttles all the way up and I could hear the superchargers' high-pitched scream. We were doing forty knots, easy. The boat lifted and bumped as she made quick smacks against the glassy sea.

Hokulani was next to me, putting on his pistol belt. His legs were wide apart as he balanced himself against the quick up-and-down motion of the deck. I gave him a sudden pat on the back. "Maybe those porpoises did bring us good luck," I shouted above the noise. I spread my hand to the Japs, offering Hokulani the view. "Behold the provender of our mighty father Neptune!"

He roared with laughter. It was like old times, when the boats were new and we looked like human beings. With a full load of ammo and torpedoes we could knock off a few of these landing craft before lunch. Now it would be a little more difficult—Swifty and Boeke had to make every round count—but I had no doubt who'd end up dying this day. This was as preordained as the practiced moves of classical ballet.

The range closed to one mile; the two landing craft lumbered along, oblivious. Surely they had seen us. But then, an American PT boat would be the last thing they'd expect on such a fine, fine morn. By the time they convinced themselves, the impossible had happened, it'd be too late.

We were almost upon them and there was still not a peep. Lumanski kept the bow pointed between the two Japs, intending to drive between them. One craft finally opened fire at a range of one hundred yards, giving us a spray of his 25mm. The familiar sound of its high-pitched chatter made me crouch lower, but the bullets stitched only our wake. We tore between them, taking one on each side with twenty yards to spare. I saw that both had empty holds—just a three-man crew aboard each. Swifty took the one to starboard while Boeke aimed his twin barrels into the bucket to port. The four .50-cal barrels boomed like cannonfire, erasing the 25mm chatter with quick authority. Swifty and Boeke swung their barrels rapidly, keeping a steady stream of lead pouring at their targets. Then we were through, leaving both landing craft wobbling in our expanding wake, and the guys let their thumbs off the firing bars. Lumanski spun the wheel, banking the PT into a wide turn to starboard. The guys with the Springfields took over, trying to hold themselves steady while the PT canted, the rifle fire sounding like a ragged string of firecrackers.

Boeke had done a good job. His target's machine guns swiveled on their mounts unmanned. The other was still firing at us, however, both twenty-fives snapping with wild bursts. Slugs whipped over our heads, hit the plywood with hollow thunks, pinged off the odd bit of steel plate.

Lumanski went down.

He writhed on the flats of the cockpit, one hand pressed against the red oozing from his shoulder. I grabbed his belt and yanked him out, stepped over, grabbed the wheel. I hauled around to port and eased back the port throttle to tighten up the turn. The port gunwales hit the water and there was spray over the torpedo tubes. I jammed the rudder in the opposite direction and the boat snapped to an even keel. I steadied up with the Japs dead ahead, and brought the port engine back to full revs.

I was going to make the same play, running between them, but the surviving Jap skipper decided to cut me off. The squat boat swung around rapidly, closing the distance between itself and the other landing craft. Security in numbers, he was probably thinking, perhaps unaware the other crew was dead. I swung my bow to starboard intending to take them both along my port side.

Too late the Jap skipper understood the fate of the other crew. Pilotless, the other landing craft did not stop when the two boats were at a comfortable distance. The pilotless craft smacked into the other broadside, knocking it sideways so that two of its crew cartwheeled into the water. Then the boat slapped back down and both landing craft started grinding at each other, spinning in the water in a big crazy circle. We roared by the mess at a range of fifty yards, and Swifty let fly with two judicious bursts. These tore into the lone surviving gunner, knocking him backwards into the other boat's well.

I made another circle to see what was left. Only one Jap was still kicking, and he was in the water, holding onto a life-ring. He fired his pistol at us, his

312

face a mask of fearless rage.

Three Springfields took their bead and sent him
under.

Chapter Twenty-five

Romang was a big island. A wide river cut through the heart of it, and this we followed for some miles. The vegetation was thick and green and there were occasional stands of palms, but mostly it was a relentless mass of tall trees to either side. Astern the two Japanese landing craft were under tow, one undamaged and the other half-full of water. The river's depth was such we could've followed it indefinitely, but when we seemed safely out of reach of any prying eyes, I decided to go ahead and park.

We nosed the PT into the bank bow first, worked the two landing craft so that one was lashed broadside to port, the other to starboard. Strip Cunningham began a careful inspection of the prizes.

I went down below to my little cabin and visited Lumanski. Sevu was kneeling next to him, wiping his forehead with a damp cloth. Lumanski was out like a light. The slug had gone clean through the right upper shoulder, the kind of Hollywood wound you see in a movie. De Neuman had carefully read the instructions on the medical packages before he fixed Lumansku up.

Sevu looked at me in an odd sort of way. He started to say something, but I left and went back above.

I poked my head from the charthouse just as Strip leapt from the starboard landing craft to the PT. I invited him into the shade of the charthouse, and called over to Hokulani. It was time for a little command conference. Three was a crowd in the tiny compartment, and we were already sweating copiously. "Well?"

"Both diesel," Strip reported. "One engine each. Six cylinders per, look in pretty good shape."

"How about the hulls?"

Hokulani took that one. "The one with the water in the well is shot. The other is sound."

"Strip, how much fuel do we have left?"

"Eighty gallons."

"Not enough, then."

Strip took the unlit cigar from his mouth. "Well, how much would be enough? How far exactly do we have to go?"

I unrolled the chart and the two men bent close. "Here's Romang," I began. "Almost but not quite out of Indonesian waters. I figured on our next stop as being Moa, forty-six miles to the southeast. From there it's twenty-four miles to this little atoll, Morau." I tapped this spot. "You'll notice the chart lists a beacon on this island, the only one in this area. I'm sure its light is extinguished, but I want to hit this island and find the structure."

"Why?"

"Because it'll give us a definite reference point, the kind we're going to need for the big hop to Australia.

Savvy?" Both men nodded. I rolled up the chart, grabbed the next one and spread it out. At the top was the Morau atoll with its light, and I put my finger on it. "Okay. We pull alongside this beacon and get our fix. That's our jump-off point."

I slid my finger down the chart to the huge mass of Australia. "We set our course for 155°. Two hundred and thirty-one miles across the Timor Sea. Then, when we're abeam Bathurst Island, we alter course and it's forty-nine miles to Darwin." I felt butterflies in my chest when I said it; by Jesus, we really were almost there.

"Well," Strip said. "We sure as shit don't have enough gas for that."

"Then how do you guys feel about taking one of these Jap barges and trying it?"

Hokulani, eyes on the chart, shook his head. "Those boats are't ocean-goers. First squall would take us."

Strip chimed in. "It *would* be a kinda rough ride . . ."

"Just wanted to know how you guys felt. So try this on for size — we take one of the diesels off the Jap and rig her onboard here."

Strip's eyebrows knitted together. "What? Rig her how?"

"Take out the centerline Packard, bolt the Jap diesel in its place, couple the centerline shaft back up and we're ready to go."

Strip grinned like I was making a horrible joke. "Just like that, huh?"

"Yeah. Then we transfer all the remaining gas to the starboard tank, fill the port with all the diesel fuel we can get aboard."

No reply. They were chewing it over, working the idea for any flaws.

"I figure one diesel rigged like that might give us five or six knots," I continued, "We can make it on that. Of course, if we get into trouble we can light off the remaining Packards; that eighty gallons should give us enough of a burst of speed to get out a jam."

Strip rubbed his jaw. "I *do* have a chainfall down below . . . and one of them big wrenches that can take on those foundation bolts . . ."

It was going to be a big job of work, an all-hands evolution. But everyone threw themselves into it gladly, for the light at the end of the tunnel was shining bright. Wisecracks bounced around as the men bent to their labors, and it was an atmosphere not unlike those which prevailed at the Cavite Naval Station just before Saturday night liberty. It was a dream come true, this new cohesiveness, this eagerness to shunt aside their personal bellyaches and participate in something meaningful. Come to think of it, this was *better* than the old days, back when the war was new and no friends were dead. I had never seen morale so high. But even as I beamed and smiled I also wondered. What exactly had done it? The successful attack on the Jap landing craft? The nearness of Australia? The shooting of Donnythorn? I did not know. But the crew's morale had definitely changed.

I felt suddenly faint, like my brain was doing somersaults, and I sat atop the day cabin heavily. I closed my eyes and put my head in my hands. An image burned brightly in my brain, sharp and crisp as a photograph.

Was this what they called having a vision?

Whatever, it was of me and my crew riding the PT into Darwin. It was a spectacularly beautiful morning, the old workhorse of a PT slicing through the harbor at top speed, bow raised proudly, a pristine wake trailing aft.

The image faded. It was really going to happen, I felt. Really and truly.

Hokulani sat next to me. "Talk a minute, skipper?"

"Yeah, sure." I grinned at him.

"About these landing craft . . ."

"Yeah?"

He wiped the sweat off his brow. "Well, uh, don't you kind of wonder where they come from?"

I continued grinning, but the heartiness had gone out of it. "How so?"

"These guys just didn't sail down here from Japan, you know. There's got to be a base around here, or a ship."

I knew it was childish, but I felt angry at Hokulani. He was throwing a wet blanket over my good times. "Don't worry about it," I said crisply. "We'll be out of this neighborhood tonight."

"But—"

I got up. "Let's get back to work, Hokulani. Don't be such a goddamn pessimist."

It wasn't an easy job.

Rigging something to attach the chainfall to turned out to be a Rube Goldberg arrangement of cut-and-lashed palm trunks. And once the diesel was finally in,

318

the big problem turned out to be aligning it with the shaft coupling. And the coupling itself was little sonofabitch in its own right, but Strip managed to jam three big bolts through holes which more or less lined up, and that was it. Connecting the saltwater cooling lines turned out to be no sweat, and likewise the transfer of diesel fuel to an empty gas tank.

By sunset we were ready.

I used port and starboard engines to haul us away from the bank, and swung the bow downriver. I got us cruising along at five knots, then gave Strip the pre-arranged signal: two longs on the engine-room buzzer. Presently there was the unfamiliar cough of the little diesel, and when it settled out it was completely drowned out by the rumbling V-12s.

There were two sharp buzzes on the console's bell. That was Strip's "ready" signal. I pressed my thumbs against the cutouts, and the big Packards rumbled down and off.

We continued cruising along at five knots. The diesel sound was faint and faraway, like a dragonfly on a hot day. Everyone was silent and watchful, waiting for the diesel sound to give out, or for the boat to go dead in the water.

Hokulani walked up to me. "I think it's working."

I nodded doubtfully. "I think so, too. Why don't you go below and tell Strip to wind it all the way out."

Hokulani ducked into the charthouse. The leafy banks slid by slowly but steadily. Presently the diesel sound grew louder, but not by much. I watched the riverbanks intently. It seemed they were beginning to slip by a little faster. Like for six knots' worth?

Someone up forward laughed and slapped a guy on

the shoulder. A conversation started up back aft. Tension began to unwind on the boat. It was working. Working for maybe even *seven* knots' worth . . .

Hokulani stuck his head out of the charthouse door. "Is it doing it, skipper?"

"Yeah, she's pushing us right along. Has Strip got it maxed out?"

Hokulani nodded. "Yeah, but he doesn't like the looks of it. Is it okay if I tell him to bring it back down?"

"Sure, yeah, go ahead."

Hokulani went back below.

The light overhead was rosy, and slowly purpling toward the east. The details of the foliage on the riverbanks were becoming less distinct, and more of an unbroken cutout that looked like the background drop in a Tarzan movie. Small, slender waves fanned away from the bow, trailing behind in a expanding cone. I rolled the wheel to starboard and we came around a bend to the next stretch of the river.

One mile further and two bends downriver was the sea.

It was like a dream, setting out for the last portion of our trip to Darwin. We had really done it. Hell, *I* had really done it. Brought these guys all the way from Manila to the very doorstep of Australia. Somehow. Someway. Despite all the setbacks.

I began to look on the past week in a different light. So I had screwed up a few times. So what? I had gotten us through, hadn't I? These men were alive, weren't they?

The guys had gotten rid of their first nervous laughter and were beginning to settle down for the voyage. Some were sitting up forward on the bow, while a couple were sprawled on the day cabin's overhead. I turned the wheel slowly, nosing the bow around the bend.

Yes, it had been a perilous trip, all right. But old Buck had brought them through. All the way until the end. I began whistling through my teeth.

Hokulani came out on deck and took in a deep gulp of the balmy air. "Looks good, skipper."

"Yeah," I said, "Real good."

He wiped his hands with an oily rag. "How do you think that little diesel will handle on the sea?"

"We'll soon find out, won't we?"

I began turning the wheel in the opposite direction. The PT eased its way around the bend, and the sea lay before us, the waves running at easy two-to-three feet from south to north. The dark shape of Maopora Island lay on the horizon. The sky had completely lost any hint of a rose color. It was a soft velvety purple where the sun had gone down; a much darker color everywhere else. Stars were beginning to show.

As soon as we quit the river the effects of the sea were immediate. The PT lifted and fell, and I saw one guy up forward put a hand on the lifeline to steady himself. The bow slapped down abruptly, making water spray to the side with a loud smack.

If only we could get some more speed. The ride would be a lot smoother. Not to mention faster. But . . . this was the ticket home. This was going to do it. What a story we'd tell when we pulled into Darwin! The inside of my chest tingled with pleased excitement.

We continued cruising. It seemed we were hardly moving at all, but whenever I looked astern Romang was further and further away. Were we making five knots? Four?

"Jap! Jap! Port beam!"

321

I froze. *No*, I thought. *No! No! NO!* I couldn't tear my eyes from the gauges on the console. I dreaded more than anything looking over there.

But somehow I did.

It was a destroyer all right. She was coming our way, and at that angle it was difficult to discern her class. Three, maybe three-and-a-half thousand yards.

Hokulani put his hand on my shoulder. "Think she's seen us?"

I shook my head in negation, although I didn't know for sure either way.

Damn! Damn! Damn! My mind ran in helpless circles. *Damn!*

"What do you think we should do, skipper?" Hokulani's face was grimly intent. "Turn back? What?"

Turn on the other engines, I thought. Get 'em rumbling. But my hands wouldn't move from the wheel. I felt like a man made of straw, all loose nothing inside. I looked around the boat. It was a strange scene. Everyone was rock-steady, staring at the Jap as if the sight didn't make any sense, like it was one of those weird paintings which shows a rock floating in the sky or maybe a locomotive coming right through your living room fireplace.

But we had our bucket of cold water soon enough.

Her forward battery let go with a flash of light that was surprisingly brilliant in the gathering dusk. Seconds later there was the sharp report, then that low-pitched howl of a round coming in fast and coming in low.

I ducked.

It went over our heads and landed well to starboard, sending up a column of water that sprayed the PT. There were shouts from the men. I punched the starter buttons for the Packards, meanwhile screaming at Hokulani to get the guys at GQ.

There was another rumbling *crack-boom* as I brought the throttles up, and I didn't bother to look the Jap's way. The bow pushed up and surged ahead and I spun the wheel to port. There was a watery explosion to starboard and shortly thereafter another *crack-boom*. As the bow swung around I got another glimpse of the Jap, and part of my mind registered that she was a *Kamikaze* Class destroyer, that Ohiro had finally caught up with me, but most of my mind was occupied with getting the boat around and heading back toward Romang, back into safety of the river where the destroyer could not follow, and there was another eruption of water which drenched us afresh and another crack-boom and I pushed the throttles all the way to the console and we began smacking our way back to the island.

And all I could think of was that sun-baked day in Georgia, of a desperate cracker running across an open field, his pursuers so close he dared not look over his shoulder. He heard only the sound of galloping horses, the thunder of their hooves growing loud, coming at him as relentlessly as a harvesting machine. There would be a sudden hammerblow between the shoulders. Life would spill out in the mosquito-breeding brackishness of a ditch. A circle of faces would loom from far above, twisted with hatred, unmerciful and cold.

Chapter Twenty-six

We went upriver at thirty knots, and I didn't pull back on the throttles until we had two bends behind us. And the only reason I slowed was because it was getting too dark to navigate at that speed. I shut down the Packards and had the little diesel put back on the line.

We cruised way the hell upriver. By the time we came upon the spot where we had made our engine-change it was already fully dark. I sailed on by.

Hokulani came up, folded chart in hand. He put it on the console and snapped on a flashlight, covering most of the lens with his fingers.

"As you can see," he said quietly, "This river only goes so far as this valley here. It looks like we're pretty well boxed in."

"Yeah."

"So . . . where do you want to stop?"

I shook my head and sighed.

He clicked the flashlight off. "The way I see it, we can take enough food with us for two-three days."

"Take food with us where?"

"Well, into the jungle, of course. You know that can is going to send some small boats after us as soon as it's light."

"Yeah."

"I figure maybe we can hide this boat pretty well, and if by some chance they don't find it, then we're okay. But the only thing we can do now is get the hell off the boat and go into the jungle."

"How long do you think we could survive here?"

"A hell of a lot longer than if we stick with the boat."

I shook my head slowly. "There's got to be a better way."

Hokulani sighed as he refolded the chart. "Okay, skipper. I'll be standing by." He started to go.

"Hey, Hokulani."

"Aye, skipper?"

"Go ahead and start getting things ready for that jungle trek, just in case."

"Aye, skipper."

I don't how much longer I drove. I became lost in my mind, looking for some way to get out of this jam. It was like I was looking at a pool table, picking up one ball and feeling its weight, putting back it on the green felt and giving it a little shove to see what would happen when it clicked off another ball.

The river started to narrow to the extent that I had to devote myself fully to the driving. I looked at my watch and saw it was midnight. Enough of this. I called Hokulani, and got the process going of getting ready to go against the bank and tie up.

I walked around the boat while the lines were being fixed. I had the glimmering of some idea, and I did all I could to make the wavering flame grow bigger and burn bright. Finally Hokulani was at my elbow, telling me that everyone was below getting ready for the hike. He asked if now might be a good time to leave the boat. I told him I wanted to go below and talk to everybody.

Hokulani preceded me through the charthouse, and I followed him down the companionway to the berthing compartment. Everyone was going through their tiny lockers, picking up items that might be of use in the jungle trek. A couple stopped when they saw me, and soon everyone was looking at me, waiting for the score. I had expected looks of grim despair, but that wasn't what I saw now. They were merely expectant, trusting, and . . . respectful.

And then the plan crystallized. It could work. And with these guys behind me, why shouldn't it? I started grinning. Some started grinning back, easily and readily.

"All right, guys," I said, "Here's the game plan."

By the time we got where I wanted the sky was starting to lighten. I told Hokulani to go below and tell Strip to cut the diesel.

Hokulani was reluctant. "You really want to go ahead with this?"

"Sure. Don't you think it'll work?"

He looked pained. "Name one time something like this has *ever* worked."

"C'mon. Don't tell me you've never heard of the

Trojan Horse."

He was silent for a moment; stunned, I supposed. "But that's just a *legend*!"

"Maybe. But the idea still seems pretty good to me."

He shook his head slowly. "What if the Japs decide not to accept this kind gift? What if they just decide to blow your ass sky-high?"

"You think they'd pass up the opportunity to capture a PT? Once they see this thing's adrift and unmanned they'll take it for sure."

"You're banking one hell of a load on that supposition."

"Yeah, I am."

he bowed his head and sighed. "At least let me go with you guys."

"No. I want you and your people on the beach, ready to take the PT as soon as you see it being cast off from the can. I . . . may not be aboard. But you can be sure when you see the boat's adrift the can won't be able to get underway. Reboard the PT and get the hell away."

"But—"

"We're going with it, Hokulani. Get on below and get that diesel engine cut."

He looked at me and . . . was there a slight little grin, pearly white in the darkness? "Okay, skipper. Let's get this show on the road."

The tide had almost finished going out, and we drifted along with the slow current, engine off. I took one last look at the chart, and as best as I could determine we were two miles upriver from the sea. All three of the inflatable life-rafts were already blown up, and men milled about on deck with last-minute preparations. In the distance I heard the fitfull cawing of a bird.

"Captain?"

I turned to the voice. "Is that you, Sevu?"

He stepped very near. "Please take me with you, Captain."

"I thought I told you I didn't want to see your face any more."

He put his hand on my arm. "I must do something to make you happy with me. I cannot live without your forgiveness."

I shook his hand off. "You can make me happy by beating it." I gave him a shove which sent him tottering backwards toward the day cabin. The guy gave me a pain.

Hokulani came up to the cockpit. "My people are ready, skipper. How about you?"

"Yep. Any last questions?"

"No. All I'm supposed to do is make that riverbank and hide. Observe you, paddle along after you when the Japs take the PT in tow, hide again when I see you tied up to the can."

"And stand ready to paddle back out to the PT when you see it cast adrift."

"Right. Okay, Mr. Leander. Let's get you below and tucked in."

We went down below, and though the engines were off it was still uncomfortably hot in the space. Strip was already there, and he gave me a brief nod. He was the only other guy going. I was glad he volunteered, for I would've volunteered him otherwise. He was a

328

handy enough individual, but it was his engineering knowledge that'd be essential to the mission's success.

We lifted up selected deckplates and looked at the bilge. There was two feet of vertical space between the deckplates and the keel. A little bit of oily water sloshed around.

"Well . . . here goes."

I stepped down and started the process of lying myself flat. It was harder work than I imagined. My spot was near the starboard engine, and there was a maze of thick pipes and hoses, and even some kind of electrical cable run. Eventually I was on my back, more or less stretched out, looking up at Hokulani's grinning face. He handed down a canteen, then a small bunch of ripe bananas. The oily water was warm.

"Comfy, skipper?"

"Oh, just fine and dandy, fuck you very much."

He winked. "So long, Ulysses."

The steel deckplate slid into place, clanking as it settled in. Some light filtered down through the chinks.

I listened to the bangs and grunts associated with getting Strip settled in. His spot was up near the engine-room's forward hatch. Then the lights were snapped off.

I listened to the other guys walking around the main deck, then, very faintly, the far-off splash of water as the inflatables were put over the side. More steps and splashes as the guys got themselves situated.

Then nothing, except for the pitty-pat of wavelets against the hull.

It was uncomfortably quiet, and Strip spoke up just as I decided I was going to break the silence. He told a joke, something about a Polish actress trying to get a job in Hollywood. I didn't really listen, but dutifully laughed when I heard his rumbling chuckle. He told three more, and I reached down into my bag of tricks and told him the one about the nun and the lumber-jacks.

Things began to wind down after what seemed an eternity, the silences between jokes growing longer. I checked the luminous dial of my wristwatch and saw only two hours had passed. Finally there were no jokes at all, and there was nothing much to think about but the way the boat gently bobbed and drifted.

We hit something, very gently, and the seesawing motion stopped.

"What's going on,?" Strip asked.

"We're aground."

"Where?"

"We could be against a riverbank. We could be on a sandbar. We're okay. Just sit tight."

"Aye aye, skipper."

I heard him sigh and move around a little. I took a sip from my canteen, then tried to make myself more comfortable. There was nothing to listen to but the wavelets slapping against the hull.

Maybe I dozed. It was hard to tell in the pitch dark, whether my eyes had been closed or open, whether I'd been turning over memories or merely watching dreams.

My watch, however, said it was 0800 — time had

330

suddenly whipped by. I took a drink from the canteen, then yanked off a couple bananas.

The texture of the waves slapping the hull had changed. Seemed stronger. Maybe the tide was turning. Maybe there was some wind. I listened hard to gather more clues, and that was when I caught the faint, far-off buzz . . .

It came and went, then held steady. Definitely the screws of some busy little engine. I wondered how far they were. And how many. And how soon the ball'd start rolling.

Bullets punched through plywood abruptly, as if a hundred guys had taken to smacking the boat with crowbars.

"Jee-suzz!"

"Keep it down, Strip! They'll stop when they see no one's aboard!"

There was another sustained burst, and I heard one of the bullets whine as it ricocheted off a Packard.

Then silence . . .

The sound of the approaching engine — engines? — grew louder. I settled myself in, trying to make myself smaller in the slimy goo of the bilge. My heart was beginning to beat very fast, and I concentrated on slowing it down.

There was a loud bump and a tearing crunch and the PT rocked and shifted. A boat was alongside, and the coxswain did not seem to be the sort to drive with tender loving care. We were still rocking when the first pair of boots hit the main deck, and this was immediately followed by the sound of dozens of running feet. I could hear their shouts and cries, and soon several pairs of boots began clambering down the ladders and then there was the clunkety-clunk of shoes against the steel deckplates of the engine-room.

They found the switch and the light which shot through the chinks was so surprisingly bright and unexpected my heart leapt into my throat.

There was a little slit just above my eyes, and more than once it was blocked by the bottom side of a boot. There was a lot of back-and-forth gabbling, and the urgency of the running slowed down to a more leisurely walk. One by one I heard a pair of boots leave the compartment, until only one pair was left.

This guy took his time in looking at the engines, walking a little and then stopping, muttering to himself all the while. I heard him lift a deckplate, and my pores came alive with prickling sweat. The Jap grunted, then let it slap down with a bang. He left the compartment briskly — his boot covering my slit for a moment — and then there was nobody in the engine-room . . .

Nobody, that is, but us chickens.

I allowed myself the luxury of letting out a long gasp of pent-up air.

It took them an hour to finally get us rigged for tow, and I could hear the engines of the Jap boats straining mightily as the PT slowly slid from the mud. Then we were free, the PT wallowing and rocking in the Japs' wake.

Finally — an hour later by my watch — there were some more rude clunks and jolts as we were . . . made fast alongside the *Matsukaze*.

This was followed by a fresh round of heavy footfalls

as we were once again examined. There wasn't any frantic running around this time, although the inspection did not seem particularly thorough. The voices above were more measured and conversational, and once I even heard some harsh laughter. This was cut short by a quick bark and a communal click of heels. Then the purposeful stride of one man coming into the engine-room — Ohiro himself, perhaps. He walked around a little, asked some questions to which there were fervent replies, then left. This was followed by a general exodus, and then there seemed to be no one in the engine-room. The lights had been cut.

I could hear footsteps around the boat for hours, but gradually it subsided until there was no sound at all, except the creak and pull of lines as we rode alongside the *Matsukaze*. I became so used to it I actually dozed.

I looked at my watch. A bit after 0200. I'd been here twenty hours.

"Strip?" I whispered.

"Yeah?"

"This is it."

Chapter Twenty-seven

I gently pushed up on the deckplate and slowly eased it back. The grating seemed as loud as a bunch of New York garbagemen picking up a tenement's trash. I pulled myself upright and looked around, eyes wide in the darkness, ears pricked to full intensity.

Strip began pushing back on his deckplate, and I made toward the sound. I felt where the deckplate was moving and tried to help it along but in the darkness things got confused and the deckplate slipped free and slapped down backwards with a resounding *clang*!

I froze for a moment, then grabbed onto Strip's shoulder.

"Out!" I hissed, "Let's get up against the bulkhead. When the watch comes down, we'll take him."

We quickly scrambled forward and arranged ourselves near the hatch, where the sentry would come through. I heard the click of Strip's Buck knife as he made himself ready. We waited, breathing shallowly.

And waited . . .

"I don't think there's no watch aboard," Strip

whispered.

"Yeah, could be . . ."

Then there was the sound of another deckplate being moved.

At first I thought maybe there *was* a watch onboard, that he'd been asleep, and was now walking toward us, rifle leveled. But it wasn't the sound a loose deckplate makes when you walk on it. It was being slid aside, as Strip and I had done.

I was next to the bulkhead, and there was a battle lantern fixed to its mount. I thumbed down on the big rubber button and a beam of light sliced through the compartment.

Standing square in the beam's light, blinking his eyes, was Sevu.

"*What're you doing here?*" I hissed.

He came walking forward rapidly, whispering urgently. "I could not stay behind, Captain. I had to come with you."

I grabbed him by the shoulder. "You *idiot!*"

"I can help you, you bet! I can read the Japanese signs, I can—"

"You guys better pipe down," Strip said in a low voice. "There might be somebody up on deck, you know."

I took my thumb off the lantern's button and the light went out.

"All right," I said, "Sevu, you just stick with us and keep quiet. Understand?"

"Yes, Captain."

"Let's go."

We filed out of the engine-room, climbed up a short ladder, and went forward into the main berthing compartment. It was pitch black, and no one was there. We climbed the small ladder up into the charthouse. Faint, watery light came through the cabin's open ports, and we kept ourselves crouched down below the chart table.

I got up slowly and cautiously, stopped when my shoulders were level with the chart table. The open ports gave me a view of the PT's fo'c'sle, and I saw we were alongside the destroyer's starboard side, our bows pointing in the same direction.

The *Matsukaze* seemed enormous, the clean lines of its hull stretching forward into the darkness. No lights were on anywhere, but I could make out the dim, boxy outline of the aft torpedo launcher just off our port bow . . . which meant we were tied up pretty far aft. Her two big smokestacks blocked out the stars, and a thin trail of steam wisped slowly upwards.

Strip and Sevu raised their heads and drank it in. There was no sound except for the low turbine hum of a forced draft blower.

"Well, guys," I whispered, "What do you think?"

"At anchor like this," Strip said, "There's probably only two of the four boilers on the line. That'll probably be the forward engine room, so there'll be a steaming watch there."

"And back aft?"

"Just a couple guys to watch gauges."

"And the main electrical switchboard is in the after pit, right?"

Strip nodded. "That's the setup on every ship I've been on. There'll probably be a guy on watch at the board, so let's call it three guys in the after pit."

"And the emergency generator?"

"It'll probably be a big diesel in a space on the port side, almost all the way back aft, just below that after deckhouse there."

"Okay, let's go over it once again. Priority one is to knock out their electrical power. That way she won't be able to get her 4.7-inchers or searchlights working. Priority two is to knock out one of their shafts."

"What about the other shaft?" Strip asked.

"I've changed my mind. Once we disable the main electrical switchboard all hell's going to break loose. We'll barely have enough time to get back to the PT and cast off, much less get down into the forward pit."

"Maybe I could go down there now—"

I shook my head vigorously. "It'll be enough. Without any electrical power and only one shaft, we'll get out away easy."

"Okay, skipper."

"So—to the emergency generator first. Then on down to the after pit. Disable the watch, throw some junk in the reduction gear to disable the shaft, then do our tap dance on the main switchboard. Once the lights go out we beat on back here and cast—"

My lecture was interrupted by the sight of a hatch opening on the *Matsukaze*. It was directly underneath the amidships 4.7-inch battery, between the two stacks. It let out weak, yellowish light, and a Japanese marine stepped out, rifle slung over his shoulder. He banged the hatch closed and began walking toward us, puffing on a cigarette.

We watched his progress intently. The sentry seemed to be swaggering a little, as if he'd taken too much sake with din-din. He stopped a little way forward of us and went to the lifeline. He tossed his cig into the drink and unbuttoned his fly. We watched him urinate for what seemed an eternity, then he rebuttoned his fly and continued his patrol. We heard his steps as he passed alongside the PT, and he did not come aboard to check anything over. His footsteps receded into the background.

"All right, guys," I said, "Let's go."

I opened the little door which led to the cockpit and stepped out. The main deck of the *Matsukaze*—low-slung like most destroyers—was within hand-grabbing distance. Strip boosted me up and I scrabbled aboard. I grabbed his hand and helped him up, then we both leaned down and hoisted Sevu on up.

The after deckhouse loomed before us. On top of it were two of the 4.7-inch batteries, barrels trained to centerline. The deckhouse hatch we wanted was on the other side.

We went to the fantail, at the rear of the deckhouse. We moved quickly but silently, crouched in whatever shadows presented themselves. We came to the destroyer's port side and once again approached the deckhouse. All three of us worked at undogging the hatch, making it as silent as we could, and the steel door finally pulled open. We stepped into a small vestibule and took a ladder down. We found ourselves in a long, dimly-lit passageway. A hatch was near the bottom of the ladder, and Sevu pointed at the lettering just above it.

"This is it, he whispered. "These are the characters for 'generator' and this is the character for 'emergency.' "

I gave Strip a quick glance, and his eyes had the same look as mine—maybe this kid would be useful after all.

We undogged the hatch and stepped inside the space. Turned a huge barrel switch and the space was illuminated. The diesel was big, maybe a sixteen-cylinder job. The switchboard was against the aft bulkhead. All its gauges were on zero; no juice flowing here.

There was a box of tools handy and we went to work. We unscrewed the panels and began ripping and pulling at anything that looked likely. We made the work as quiet as possible, not smashing anything. Some cables I pulled came loose from three-pronged male connections, and once I had a few disconnected I reconnected them back up—but not in the right order.

The job looked done ten minutes later, and we made ready to leave the compartment. Sevu had his hand on the first dog when I heard something and quickly grabbed his hand. Footsteps, clicking down the outside passageway, coming this way. I turned off the lights and we waited, listening to the click-clock growing louder. I hoped this guy's job wasn't to check on the emergency diesel. His steps came nearer and . . . clicked on up the ladder.

We gave it a couple minutes and opened the hatch. No one in the passageway. We went out, closed the hatch, and gently climbed the ladder. Then we opened the hatch which led to the main deck and peeked out. No one seemed to be about. We stepped outside and crept along, ever alert for any sound. All we could hear was the distant splash of an overboard discharge. We made it to the forward deckhouse, and Sevu indicated which hatch we should try.

Each of us worked at undogging it, as we had done

before, casting quick glances over our shoulders as we worked at it. We pulled it wide, and—

A Jap came along with it, one of his hands on the hatch's inside handhold, yanked into our midst. He was in his skivvy shorts, eyes wide with disbelief.

Strip drove his fist into the Jap's gut. The air went out in a quick whoof and he doubled over. When Strip drew his fist away I saw there'd been a knife in his hand. The short, broad blade was shiny in the darkness, and part of it was slick with blood.

I worked my jaws once, but no sound came out. I tried it again. "Over the side with this guy. Make it quiet."

We lifted him up and walked to the lifelines, eased him on down to the water. When we just had him by his hands we let go and he dropped a couple feet, the splash fairly loud but quickly over.

We went back to the hatch and went inside. No lights were on in the passageway, but there was some illumination from a big open hatch on the deck. It was propped up with two steel poles, and there was a broad ladder leading below decks.

"That's it," Sevu whispered, looking at a little brass plate just above it, "It leads down to the . . . number two main machinery room."

We started to go below. Warm air pushed up at us, and . . . the sound of laughter and talking. We froze. There was some more jabbering back and forth, then more titters.

"There are more than three men down there," Sevu said.

"Sounds like a baker's dozen," Strip said, shaking his head. "I don't get it." He looked up and down the passageway, alert. "Now what, skipper? We can't take that many guys."

I looked down the ladder. It led to a vestibule one deck below, then underneath that, a long, narrow ladder leading two decks further down and into the engineering space proper. More laughter floated up. Maybe Ohiro had *both* pits fully manned, all four boilers up and ready to go at a moment's notice.

I stared hard at the ladder, trying to think of what to do, marveling at the strangeness of the situation. Here I was, inside a Japanese destroyer, my cockamamie plan to disable her going awry. And yet where was the panic? The fear? I felt alive and alert, and never so sure of my powers.

What to do? An alternative slipped into my consciousness smoothly and quickly, and it wasn't the result of any frantic rummaging around. Like I'd just asked the dealer to hit me again, and he sent a six skittering across the felt to make it a perfect twenty-one.

"Outside," I said, "We're heading to the pilothouse."

Strip furrowed his brow. "What?"

"C'mon, let's go."

Chapter Twenty-eight

We went back out and dogged the hatch tight. There was a ladder nearby, and we climbed it until we were on top of the forward deckhouse. The after stack was here, and the turbine sound of the forced draft blower was loud. We scampered forward, past the amidships 4.7-inch battery, and felt our way around the forward stack. Steam wisped out of a relief valve at the top. We paused at the foot of the forward mast—it towered up into the darkness, signal halyards empty, antenna lines strung forward. Before us was the boxy, multi-decked structure containing the gun directors, signal bridge, and pilothouse. I huddled with my guys.

"We're going to capture the ship's captain."

"What!" Strip's voice was getting away from the whisper-level. Sevu's eyes were wide and easy to read in the darkness.

"I know the captain's stateroom is belowdecks," I said, "But destroyer C.O.'s only use that inport. There's a small sea cabin for his use whenever the ship's underway or at anchor. It should be just aft of the pilothouse. Sevu, I hope you can translate as good as you say."

He bobbed his head quickly.

"Okay. Let's go."

We went up one short ladder to the boat deck, then up another ladder to the signal bridge. Here the halyards were attached to small running blocks, and two flag bags stood nearby, canvas covers neatly drawn. Forward there was a hatch which led to the pilothouse. We opened it, and a short corridor stretched before us — at the far end was another hatch, the entrance to the pilothouse itself. On either side of the passageway was a door — the starboard one was a plain hatch, probably leading to the charthouse, but the one on the port side was of polished mahogany.

It didn't take too much figuring to guess which one was the captain's.

We tiptoed down the passageway. I put my hand on the fancy brass knob and pulled out my .45. I looked at Sevu and Strip briefly. "You guys don't know how many times I wanted to do this back when I was on a can."

Strip smiled. I turned the knob and we quickly filed in, shut the door and hit the lights.

Ohiro was halfway out of his rack, eyes wide but glossily sodden with sleep. He wore baggy khaki shorts and a skivvy shirt. I leveled the .45.

"No noise, Ohiro." I thumbed back the hammer. "Just take it easy."

He looked at me, then Sevu, then Strip, then back at me again. He was fighting mightily to disbelieve what was before his eyes. "Buck . . . ?"

"Long time no see."

Out of the corner of my eye I could see Sevu and Strip having their turn with a few startled glances. "It's all right, guys," I said, "Mr. Kagemaru and I have met before, socially."

Ohiro was staring so hard veins stood out on his forehead. "How did you . . . ?"

"We hid on the PT."

He nodded jerkily, as if it were difficult to delegate muscles from the staring job to the nodding function. "I knew it. I knew you were here, Buck. Somewhere on this island. I felt it."

"Okay, Ohiro, here's the deal. You're going to get the *Matsukaze* underway, and you're going to do it from this cabin, giving all your orders through that voice tube."

"But—"

"It's an emergency, see? Underway as quickly as possible. I want you to order that PT set adrift, you're in such an all-fired hurry to get underway."

The sleep that had fogged his brain was gone. His eyes were sharp, alert, gleaming.

I nodded toward Sevu. "This guy here speaks Japanese fluently, so don't try anything funny."

Ohiro glanced at him briefly, then back at me. He started to talk, but something caught in his mind. He looked at Sevu again, closely. "You are Javanese!"

Sevu looked startled.

"Why do you help these Americans?" Ohiro demanded. "They are fighting for the *Dutch!*"

"But . . ."

"He's with us," I said. "Why don't you get busy calling your watch up in the—"

"We came to *liberate* you!" Ohiro persisted. "You

344

betray your own people!"

I moved in on Ohiro, ready to jam the .45 against his skull if that was the kind of persuasion he needed. "Let's knock this off, Ohiro. Tell your boys on watch to get the ball rolling."

There were two voice tubes set right next to the bunk. Ohiro pushed himself back onto the bed, looking from me to Sevu with equal contempt. He leaned toward one of the highly-polished brass funnels and withdrew some kind of stopper—there was a whistle built into the stopper and this Ohiro blew in order to get attention on the other end.

Ohiro began speaking rapidly. There were quick replies. Sevu leaned next to me, softly translating the gist of it: set the sea and anchor detail, make all preparations to get underway immediately.

I looked around the tiny cabin. The big porthole was open, letting in a heavy, sluggish breeze. Next to the voice tubes was a gyrocompass repeater. Bolted to the forward bulkhead was a steel drop-leaf desk, clean and bare save for a pair of heavy binoculars. The binocular's body was painted with the two-and-a-half stripes of a lieutenant commander . . . my, my, my. Leaning against the bulkhead was Ohiro's naval officer's sword, a big samurai-looking thing which I recognized. He'd worn it with his dress uniform at my wedding.

Ohiro finished talking and replugged the tube. He leaned back against the headboard as speakers throughout the ship came alive with the piercing trill of a boatswain's pipe, followed by a guttural announcement.

"That is it," Sevu said, "The call for the sea and

anchor detail."

The ship came alive with the sound of men running up ladders and down passageways. I could hear bells going off in the pilothouse as the engine-order telegraph was tested.

Ohiro began reaching into the pockets of his baggy shorts.

"Hold it," Strip said, pulling back the hammer on his .45.

Ohiro froze, eyebrows raised. "You do not mind if I smoke?"

"Good idea," I said, "Pass 'em around."

He took out a crumpled pack of military-issue cigarettes — brown paper wrapping with Japanese characters stamped on it. The butts were passed around and we lit up. It tasted as smooth and mild as donkey shit wrapped in cardboard. Sevu turned on the little fan which was bolted to the bulkhead.

There was a piercing little whistle in the cabin — someone was trying to reach Ohiro over the voice tube. He uncorked it and began listening.

Sevu leaned close. "It is the executive officer, and he is asking . . . when the captain is coming to the bridge . . . the captain is saying that he does not feel well . . . the captain is reasserting that they are to get underway without delay . . . the executive officer is asking whether they should take the PT boat in tow . . ."

"No," I broke in, leaning toward Ohiro, "Tell him just to cast it off."

Ohiro spoke into the tube accordingly, then plugged it back up.

Strip went over to the porthole and leaned his arms out, looking at the night and smoking his cig. Sevu moved back by the door, giving the knob a little turn to make sure it was locked. I went over and took the desk's chair, sat it down near Ohiro. We had a few minutes. I felt a strange urge to visit.

"So you're a lieutenant commander now. Congratulations."

Ohiro looked at me like I was a repulsive but interesting bug in a display case.

"You are not going to get away with this, Buck Leander."

That made me angry. I narrowed my eyes, thinking that if he didn't want a nice little visit, so be it. "I was on that boat you rammed, Ohiro."

His smile broadened. "I thought you might be."

"Why you son of a bitch. Never would've guessed you'd end up like this from the way you were in Califor—"

He sat up suddenly, eyes blazing. "That part of me is no more! I hate America now, and all things American! America is my enemy!" He narrowed his eyes. "I hate you especially, Buck Leander, for you are the typical American. Your swaggering vanity and shallow soul make me sick unto death."

Strip and Sevu stared at Ohiro open-mouthed, as if witnessing a messy scene at a cocktail party.

Ohiro turned his eyes to Sevu. "You, how can you betray your people for the country of . . ." Ohiro screwed his mouth into lines of bitter contempt. "Billboards and cowboys and hypocrisy about justice and a fair shake for everyone? You surely know that all the Americans will do here is restore the Dutch to power. Is that what you want?"

"All right, Ohiro," I said, standing up. "Let's shut

the fuck up and stick to business."

He turned his black eyes to me, and they shone so brightly they seemed to be giving off sparks.

The whistle on the voice tube trilled. Ohiro uncapped it and listened to some rapid-fire Japanese.

"What's being said, Sevu?" I looked over at him, saw that his head was hanging down, face blushed crimson. "Sevu!" I shook him and he looked up. "Uh . . . it is the executive officer again," Sevu said, "He is reporting that all departments are ready to get underway."

I turned to Ohiro. "Tell him to heave in the anchor and get underway. Tell him to con the ship away from Romang and report when he's five miles southeast of here."

Ohiro leaned toward the tube and spoke rapidly, then put the stopper back in. I noticed his eyes kept flickering toward Sevu.

Presently there was the sound of the anchor being heaved in, a loud, clacking noise that reverberated throughout the ship. There were muted dings from the pilothouse as the executive officer ordered various engine combinations.

"Hey," Strip said, "We're moving."

I went to the porthole and looked out. The dense foliage along the bank began to slip by as the *Matsukaze* slowly maneuvered. After riding a PT, the destroyer felt as steady and smooth as the *Queen Mary*. I prayed that Hokulani would figure out what was going on.

I had an idea which might help him some.

"Ohiro, order your running lights turned on."

He gave me a five-second stare, then uncorked the voice tube and barked his command. I poked my head through the porthole and looked forward, saw the red

348

glow of the port running light. Now there would be no question in Hokulani's mind that we were leaving. I hoped to God he was already paddling for the drifting PT. I looked aft, caught a brief glimpse of the PT adrift, a couple hundred yards astern. Looked forward again, saw we were steaming to the southeast. There was another set of dings from the pilothouse, and presently I could feel the deck humming and vibrating—more speed had been ordered.

I went back to the chair and sat, sighing heavily. I wanted a cigarette, but didn't feel like asking Ohiro the favor. Ohiro, I saw, had regained his composure, and was supine on his rack. No overt hostility in his eyes now—just the hooded stare of a cobra contemplating its lunch.

"So now we are underway," Ohiro said, "What do you plan to do? Have me order a course for San Diego?"

I allowed myself a little grin, but did not reply. Strip, however, was looking at me with keen interest, no doubt wondering what in hell I *did* have in mind. I'd give him the score in a few minutes: order a small boat over the side, then walk on down with Ohiro leading the way, my .45 tight against the back of his head.

The deck gently rolled to starboard, then steadied. It rolled again. We were getting away from Romang; the ocean current had us.

I looked at Sevu, saw that his head was still hanging down. Christ, Ohiro had really gotten to him.

"Hey, Sevu. Perk up. Things are going to turn out okay."

He looked up and . . . I was astonished at the sight

of a tear rolling down his cheek.

"Hey . . ." I started to get out of my chair. "Don't tell me you're worried about that garbage Ohiro fed you."

"You see?" Ohiro spat, "You see how Americans are? Do you really want to keep white men in this part of the world? Their day is over!" And Ohiro switched to Japanese, firing off a prolonged burst of atonal barks.

"Shut up, Ohiro." I raised my hand. "Shut up, or by God I'll shut it for you."

Ohiro ignored me completely, his rapid-fire chop-chop growing louder.

I let him have it right across the side of his head, open-palmed, and the talking stopped as if I'd pulled a switch. Ohiro looked up, startled. There was a drop of blood at the corner of his mouth.

I looked at Strip, who was shaking his head in exasperation. I sat back down, a tired feeling washing over me. There was another set of dings from the pilothouse and the deck vibrated again. The exec was pouring on more coals.

I decided to give in on one thing. "Ohiro, toss me another cig, would you?"

He reached in his pocket and produced the crumpled pack. He tossed it over and it landed at my feet. I scooped them up and managed to get a match going.

I blew out a plume of the shitty-tasting smoke. "You know, this little reunion isn't quite like I imagined."

"Oh, no?" Ohiro's tone dripped with false solicitude. "Perhaps I could get my steward to bring us some sake."

I smiled. "A drink would be nice, but I'll take a raincheck." I took a drag off the butt. "Remember that last drink we had? At the Top o' the Mark in San Fran?"

He kept his eyes impassive, but I was pleased to note

350

that his cheeks colored. "That was a long time ago."

"Indeed it was."

"And things are different now."

I took another drag. I'd half-expected Ohiro to be a little more friendly than this, even under the present circumstances. But he'd truly changed. I didn't know this guy at all.

The voice tube whistled. Ohiro uncorked it and a stream of urgent Japanese flooded out.

I looked over at Sevu, eyebrows raised. Sevu was looking off into the distance, but he had evidently regained his composure. "It is . . . it is the executive officer reporting the present course and speed."

I turned to Ohiro. "Tell your boy he's doing fine. Just keep on steaming southeast, and to add some more knots."

Ohiro leaned toward the funnel and spoke rapidly, then recorked the tube. He sat back in his bunk and folded his arms. He sighed, as if I were a dinner guest that would never leave.

I tilted the chair back on its legs. Pretty soon it'd be time to go into Phase Two. Give it another ten or fifteen minutes. That way, with the speed we had on, we'd be at least . . .

Speed.

Where were the dings from the engine order telegraph? Why hadn't the exec ordered up more speed?

The front legs of the chair snapped down and I got up. I went to Sevu hurriedly, intending to grab his arm and shake him and demand to know if—

Chapter Twenty-nine

The mahogany around the doorknob splintered and the door was flung wide and the world became a kaleidoscope of khaki uniforms and rifle butts and shouting men and I found myself engulfed by a human tidal wave. Strip's .45 exploded, sounding like a battleship's main battery in the tiny cabin, and one of the marines went down. Then I was on the deck with five guys holding me down and I heard Strip scream as a bayonet backed him up against the bulkhead.

It was over as suddenly as it had begun. I was roughly hauled up and slammed against a bulkhead, then held steady by two men.

Ohiro's face swarmed before me, the muscles contorted into a horrible rictus of fury. "Yes," he hissed, "Things have indeed changed, Buck Leander. I am no longer the weakling you knew in California. I will show you who I really am, and with the greatest pleasure."

He grabbed his officer's sword by the scabbard. He put his hand on the elaborate grip and quickly pulled it out, the sharpened steel making a metallic, snickering noise. He tossed the blue scabbard aside, and it clattered near where Strip lay moaning.

He barked something to his men.

I was pressed down to my knees, one guy taking a hunk of my hair and thrusting my head forward so that the back of my neck was nicely exposed.

The deck was steel, painted a shade of gray that was the same as any American ship. I could feel the faint vibrations of the main engines through my knees.

How long does the brain live after it's severed from the body? One second? One minute? Will it still receive sensory data from the eyes, so that I might look at my now severed torso? Or will the pain be so great that it blocks out all else?

They say that when the executioners of revolutionary France held up the heads of the guillotined for the crowd's acclaim, some could see that the lips still moved . . .

The deck was gray and hard. The main engines hummed and vibrated. The ship gently rolled.

When was it going to come?

I turned my head slowly, looking up.

Ohiro stood with his feet squarely planted, the sword raised on high and firmly gripped with both hands.

But his face. It was a face I'd seen before, one that I recognized, full of anguish.

"Maybe," he had said, at that farewell drink in San Francisco, "Maybe it was the happiest day of my life."

There was a monstrous, ear-splitting explosion. The compartment whipsawed violently, turning everything into a reeling blur.

Another thunderclap, and the deck heeled over suddenly. The lights went out, and the mass of us tumbled in the darkness. I rolled against some skinny guy whose air went out of his lungs in a sharp grunt. Then someone collapsed on top of me. There were cries and shouts, and I scrambled frantically, pushing guys off me, trying to get some purchase with my feet. The deck was canted at a steep angle, and the destroyer was not righting itself.

I was pushing to where I thought the door was when the next series of explosions hit — two of them, the detonations so close together they were almost one and the same. The shocks hit the compartment as violently as if we were in a huge garbage can being whanged by a giant's sledgehammer. There was a brief sensation of weightlessness. My calves smacked against something, then my whole backside slapped up against a bulkhead, sending the air out of my lungs. I slid to the deck and banged my head, and I lay there gasping, trying to suck in some air. Urgent messages of pain came rocketing from various parts of my body.

There was a strange, complete silence throughout the ship . . . a moment of stasis, the lull between being shot and letting out a bloodcurdling scream. I looked around, seeing nothing but a black veil, wondering where the hell I was. Then the floodgates of pandemonium opened wide, sending out a torrent of alarm bells and shouting men, running feet and distant machine gun fire. I tried to get up, but the deck was so steep I slipped backwards against a bulkhead. Someone shouldered by, his sweat sharp and pungent. One of the emergency lights flickered on, a small battery-powered lantern attached to an overhead ten feet away.

Its weak beam illuminated some of the passageway, and I saw that I was just outside Ohiro's sea cabin.

Silhouettes flickered by the battle lantern's beam, some shouting, some holding wounded comrades upright. Then the light began to haze as the passageway filled with smoke.

I went back into Ohiro's sea cabin grabbing anything that would make a handhold, my feet constantly slipping on the angled deck. I wanted to find Strip. I had no worry about anyone fooling with me — not now, not with things like this.

I skidded the last few feet and whomped up against the bulkhead near the porthole. I knelt down and began feeling along the deck, suddenly grabbed an ankle.

"Strip?"

"Yo?" Weak, almost inaudible.

I moved to where I thought his face was and looked close. The light was so dim all I could make out were the barest hints of his profile. "That you, skipper?"

"Yeah. How you doing?"

He grimaced. "In the gut. They stuck me right in the gut."

"Listen, we gotta get out of here. This ship's going down, and fast."

"I ain't arguing with you, skipper."

I tore off my oil-soaked shirt and wadded it up. I fumbled it into his hands, which were clasped around some slimy gunk near his navel. He took the shirt and pressed it against the wound. I whipped out my webbed belt and wrapped it around his middle, then cinched it tight against the wadded shirt. I took one of his arms and hooked it around my neck. "C'mon,

Strip. Let's get going."

I heard his sharp intake of breath as we hoisted ourselves upright. I considered the possibility of going out through the porthole, then quickly discarded it. The *Matsukaze* was listing well to port, and if we dropped into the water from this side there was a good possibility of her rolling over on top of us. We began making our way up the steep incline toward the door.

It was slow work, like climbing up a goddamn mountain. Strip did what he could, grabbing and pulling himself along with his free arm. Once he grabbed something that tumbled against us loosely, almost making us fall down.

"What the hell was that?"

"A body," Strip grunted, "And I hope to fuck it was that goddamn Sevu bastard."

We made it to the door and shouldered our way into the passageway. It was choked with smoke and the battle lantern had gone out, but there was a good source of light now. Back aft, where the signal bridge was, a nice bright fire was going.

"To the pilothouse," I said, "That's the nearest compartment with open access to the sea."

We stumbled our way forward. We stepped over two bodies, rolled up against the port bulkhead. We coughed out as much smoke as we could. The pilothouse hatch hung loose and wide, and the sound of confused shouts and stern orders grew louder as we neared.

Chapter Thirty

"We've got to make this fast, Strip. As soon as we're in the compartment we've got to make our way to the starboard bridge wing, then over the side we go."

"Right."

We pushed our way into the pilothouse. It was small and cramped, like any pilothouse on any destroyer, and its close quarters seemed to add to the confusion factor a hundredfold. There was a dozen men inside, black cutouts against the row of windshields . . . through which I could see a good-sized fire going full blast on the fo'c'sle. The pilothouse crew was shouting and gesticulating, barking into voice tubes and screaming into handsets.

I felt the corner of a small chart table and grabbed on. I pulled us along, keeping to the compartment's after bulkhead. There were plenty of cable runs and switch boxes back here, and Strip used his good arm to help pull us along.

We made it to the starboard bulkhead, pulled ourselves along a couple feet, then found ourselves at the narrow hatch which led to the bridge wing. We pulled ourselves through and out.

There was a racketing series of sharp explosions—I looked over the wing's forward shield and saw the *Matsukaze*'s forward 4.7-inch battery, located up on the fo'c'sle, going up in a confusion of deadly fireworks. We made our way up the incline to the starboardmost part of the wing—a narrow area where the lookout is normally posted.

There was a steel box attached to the deck, and I opened it and found some life-jackets. I picked up as many as I could and flung them over the side. I helped Strip climb the shield, held him steady when he had both legs dangling over the side. I hiked my leg over and took a moment to get my bearings.

A billion stars hung in the sky, shining down on the scene with an awesome indifference. I made the black outline of Romang, judging it to be three miles distant. I looked down and saw that the *Matsukaze* was dead in the water. And, if she heeled over any more, we would be dropping down on her hull instead of the sea. The starboard running light, still on a standby battery of its own, glowed a bright green.

I took one last look at the pilothouse. There was enough light from the conflagration on the fo'c'sle to give form and definition to the man who was looking at me.

It was Ohiro.

He was near the windshields, holding onto a voice tube with one hand and the engine order telegraph with another. His men shouted and rushed about him, but he was frozen rock-solid, staring at me with an expression of . . .

It only lasted a moment, but it was a moment that stretched out like a piece of taffy. At one end was a sunny day in California, the wind snapping the signal flags of the ships in the harbor, a young Japanese naval officer staring at the view and then turning as I came walking up, his face wary and skeptical and then suddenly friendly . . . and then now, superimposed over the snapshot, the rugged face of a full-grown man, a warrior of ancient heritage.

He nodded.

I nodded.

He turned to his men and began shouting orders, his back lost in a growing cloud of smoke.

I lifted my other leg over the side, and Strip and I went plummeting down through the soft, velvety air.

By the time we made it to Romang it was almost dawn. It was all I could do to hold Strip halfway upright as we staggered into the jungle.

All during the swim I thought nothing could be sweeter than to be on old terra firma and slide down the rathole of sleep. But, as we sat amongst the mangroves, I found that all I wanted to do was stare at the *Matsukaze*.

Or what was left of her.

There had been a final, monstrous explosion after we'd swum a mile away. The shock wave was sudden and sharp, like the kick of a mule. Strip went under that time, and I almost lost him. I got him back to the surface and did my best to get one of the crummy little life-jackets fitted so that his head would remain upright. I turned and looked back at the *Matsukaze*, and all I could see was her fantail sticking up in the air, her screws and rudder clearly visible.

Now there was nothing . . . except for some drifting crud. The world was brightening rapidly, enough so I could make out any men in life-jackets.

Had there been any.

Strip moaned and started to get up, and I eased him back to the bed of sodden life-jackets. He asked for water, but there was none to give. Not that it's a good idea to give water to a man with a belly wound anyway. He finally passed into a fitful sleep, and I watched him for a while.

Exhaustion washed over me heavily and I began to have bits and parts of dreams even though my eyes were open. For some reason I began to think about a man — some king or something — who trained himself to sleep with his eyes open . . . and maybe that's what happened to me, because all of a sudden it seemed a hell of a lot brighter and I got up and looked around and saw the sun had risen to mid-morning height.

The sea was blue and calm, and there were still bits of crap floating around where the the *Matsukaze* had gone down. I heard a faint, droning sound, and I saw the PT, chugging up the coast at a sedate five knots.

I sloshed into the water, waving my arms, shouting. The PT put on a little speed as it came my way, and I saw that both after torpedo tubes were empty.

Chapter Thirty-one

It was like a dream, a wispy, cottony haze clinging to the horizon, the early morning light all silvery and flat. To the north were the green hills of Bathurst Island, floating eerily atop a low bank of clouds. And dead ahead, to the southeast, the heavily-forested hills of the Australian mainland.

"I think I see a buoy." Hokulani said. He was at the wheel, shirt half-unbuttoned to catch the slow breeze.

His eyesight amazed me. All I saw was the tiniest black speck, half-shrouded in the dissipating mist. I leaned in the cockpit, took the binoculars, put them to my eyes.

"That's it," I said. "The sea buoy for Darwin."

Hokulani gave me a broad smile. "You did it, skipper. You honest to Christ did it."

I smiled back. "*We* did it."

He shook his head and laughed. "Don't count me in on that."

"No, I didn't mean just you and me, Hokulani. I mean everyone. We all did our part."

But Hokulani continued to shake his head and smile. I looked at the guys sitting and standing around the boat. They were all strangely quiet, but far from somber. I don't think a one of us had been asleep for the past twenty-four hours—not since we'd caught the earthen aroma of land.

"Hokulani, how much gas do we have left?"

"Just checked the tanks this morning, skipper. Sixty gallons."

"Well, then."

His grin showed he didn't need further instructions. He clicked the engine-room buzzer, and La Salle down below cut the little diesel. Hokulani thumbed the start buttons for the Packards and the big V-12s turned over and caught. Some of the men were startled at the coughing rumble, then their faces broke with easy grins. We were going in Darwin proud and sassy.

Hokulani let the engines idle until the temperature gauges began to rise, then put one big hand on the port and starboard throttles and began pushing them forward.

The roar grew louder and louder, and the bow pushed from the water. The gentle breeze was gone in a hard wind that snapped Hokulani's half-open shirt. Up on the bow I saw Boeke take Swifty's arm and give him a fun-punch, and Swifty returned the charley horse. Both men laughed, their feet braced against the upward cant of the deck, but the Packards drowned out their merriment.

"I'm going below," I shouted to Hokulani. "And get the chart for Darwin."

I ducked inside the charthouse and found it— would've been nice to have had a harbor chart, but this would have to do — but instead of going back above I decided to take another look at Strip. I went down the companionway into the berthing compartment, and over to his rack. His eyes were half-closed, and dull looking.

"We're almost there, Strip."

"Thought that's why you lit off them Packards."

"There's one ampule of morphine left. Want it?"

He closed his eyes and shook his head. "If I need it, I'll just give you a little yell."

I smiled. Strip was as tough as I'd ever come upon. He'd been nursing that wound for five days now, and only cried out once. A truly remarkable man. I turned to go.

"Hey, skipper," he called.

"Yeah?"

"Now that we've made it, I . . ." And he searched for words. Finally he just extended his hand. I took it.

"Thanks, skipper."

I smiled and gripped his hand harder.

I turned to go up the companionway, but stopped. I went instead to my tiny cabin and picked up something and jammed it in my pocket. Then I went up on deck.

We were coming up on the sea buoy fast. Lumanski was standing next to Hokulani, his arm in a sling, and I handed him the chart. He took it and smiled and said something, and even though I couldn't hear I nodded as if I could.

I went walking back aft, to be by myself for a moment, to think things over. I was happy, but there was a touch of sadness mixed in with it, and I couldn't figure out why. I got to the fantail and stood there, looking at the clean, geometrical lines of the deep wake.

Hokulani took the sea buoy down the starboard side, and it whipped by in a blur. He spun the wheel to starboard, making the final course alteration for Darwin, and the PT banked into the turn like the smooth thoroughbred that she was. From here it was only eleven miles to go. I watched the buoy bob and swing in our wake, rapidly decreasing in size.

I had once read something about the Duke of Wellington that puzzled me. When he toured the field of Waterloo after the battle, he supposedly remarked to an aide that the only thing more sad and poignant than defeat was victory. I hadn't understood it when I read it, but when I stood on the bow of the PT as we cruised through the remains of the *Matsukaze*, I began to have the first glimmering of comprehension.

I remembered how a piece of manila line was pushed aside by the bow. A shard of deck planking thumped against the hull. Sodden charts and Japanese banknotes lay all about. One of the guys worked a long boathook into the water and snared a leather binoculars case.

There wasn't much talking. Everyone was somber, working out their thoughts. It was a strange scene, like I'd stepped into an alien church full of mysterious symbols, interrupting a ceremony so arcane and preternatural as to be obscure even to the participants themselves.

I saw something and told the guy with the boathook to get it. He worked the pole in the water and caught it, levered it up on deck. I picked it up.

It was a khaki field cap. The small, oval insignia

showed a cherry blossom superimposed over an embroidered anchor. The hatband had two blue stripes, denoting an officer.

I wondered if it were Ohiro's.

I took it from my pocket now, and examined it again. I had intended to keep it, but now I wondered why. I was no longer interested in the momentos and trappings of victory. War was not some game for big kids with real guns. War was more like life itself, full of its own intensities and mysteries, with an outcome that only sometimes favored the swift and the strong.

I let the cap drop over the side, and it was immediately gobbled up by the churning wake.

TRIVIA MANIA: TV GREATS

TRIVIA MANIA: I LOVE LUCY   (1730, $2.50)

TRIVIA MANIA: THE HONEYMOONERS   (1731, $2.50)

TRIVIA MANIA: STAR TREK   (1732, $2.50)

TRIVIA MANIA: THE DICK VAN
DYKE SHOW   (1733, $2.50)

TRIVIA MANIA: MARY TYLER MOORE   (1734, $2.50)

TRIVIA MANIA: THE ODD COUPLE   (1735, $2.50)

Available wherever paperbacks are sold, or order direct from the Publisher. Send cover price plus 50¢ per copy for mailing and handling to Zebra Books, Dept. 1664, 475 Park Avenue South, New York, N.Y. 10016. DO NOT SEND CASH.

NEW ADVENTURES FROM ZEBRA

DEPTH FORCE   (1355, $2.95)
by Irving A. Greenfield

Built in secrecy and manned by a phantom crew, the *Shark* is America's unique high technology submarine whose mission is to stop the Russians from dominating the seas. If in danger of capture the *Shark* must self-destruct — meaning there's only victory or death!

DEPTH FORCE #2: DEATH DIVE   (1472, $2.50)
by Irving A. Greenfield

The *Shark*, racing toward an incalculable fortune in gold from an ancient wreck, has a bloody confrontation with a Soviet killer sub. Just when victory seems assured, a traitor threatens the survival of every man aboard — and endangers national security!

THE WARLORD   (1189, $3.50)
by Jason Frost

The world's gone mad with disruption. Isolated from help, the survivors face a state in which law is a memory and violence is the rule. Only one man is fit to lead the people, a man raised among the Indians and trained by the Marines. He is Erik Ravensmith, THE WARLORD — a deadly adversary and a hero of our times.

THE WARLORD #2: THE CUTTHROAT   (1308, $2.50)
by Jason Frost

Though death sails the Sea of Los Angeles, there is only one man who will fight to save what is left of California's ravaged paradise. His name is THE WARLORD — and he won't stop until the job is done!

THE WARLORD #3: BADLAND   (1437, $2.50)
by Jason Frost

His son has been kidnapped by his worst enemy and THE WARLORD must fight a pack of killers to free him. Getting close enough to grab the boy will be nearly impossible — but then so is living in this tortured world!

Available wherever paperbacks are sold, or order direct from the Publisher. Send cover price plus 50¢ per copy for mailing and handling to Zebra Books, Dept. 1664, 475 Park Avenue South, New York, N.Y. 10016. DO NOT SEND CASH.

FAVORITE GROSS SELECTIONS
by Julius Alvin

GROSS JOKES (1244, $2.50)
You haven't read it all—until you read GROSS JOKES! This complete compilation is guaranteed to deliver the sickest, sassiest laughs!

TOTALLY GROSS JOKES (1333, $2.50)
From the tasteless ridiculous to the taboo sublime, TOTALLY GROSS JOKES has enough laughs in store for even *the most* particular humor fanatics.

UTTERLY GROSS JOKES (1350, $2.50)
The best of tasteless, tacky, revolting, insulting, appalling, foul, lewd, and mortifying jokes—jokes so sick they're UTTERLY GROSS!

EXTREMELY GROSS JOKES (1600, $2.50)
Beyond the humor of gross, totally gross, and utterly gross jokes there is only the laughter of EXTREMELY GROSS JOKES!

GROSS LIMERICKS (1375, $2.50)
This masterpiece collection offers the funniest of rhythmical rhymes, from all your favorite categories of humor. And they're true-to-form, honest-to-goodness, GROSS LIMERICKS!

GROSS LIMERICKS VOLUME II (1616, $2.50)
Rhyming limericks so bold, sassy, and savvy they'll leave you laughing right through the night with delight!

GROSS GIFTS (1111, $2.50)
It's the Encyclopedia Grossitanica, with everything from gross books to gross cosmetics, and from gross movies to gross vacations. It's all here in the thoroughly and completely tasteless and tacky catalogue we call . . . GROSS GIFTS!